THE
FORT SHOWALTER
BLUES

A novel by Harold L. Johnson

IRVING COURTS PRESS
Portland 2015

Cover image by Anne Johnson
Interior design by Vinnie Kinsella

ISBN: 978-0-692-22884-5

This book is for my relatives, known and unknown.

Sole judge of truth, in endless error hurled,
The glory, jest, and riddle of the world.

ALEXANDER POPE, *Essay on Man*

Act like you got some sense, boy.

WILLIE JOHNSON

Acknowledgments

I must not fail to take note of the inspiration and guidance from Tom Spanbauer and his Dangerous Writing group that were crucial to the beginning of *The Fort Showalter Blues.* Without them, the book would have remained one of those hazy eternally deferred projects languishing in a far corner of the mind. Also helpful have been readings of the manuscript by Carolyn Altman, Anne Johnson, Miles Johnson, Ken Pallack, Joanna Rose, Stevan Allred, and Stephanie Van Horn. To the extent that the final organization of the text succeeds, much credit must go to Sarah Cypher of The Three Penny Editor. Shortcomings in the work result from my own limitations as an artist.

I should also like to thank The Ragdale Foundation of Lake Forest Illinois for providing time and space to work on this project and others.

Part One:
Anthropology

The Thirty-eighth Parallel

1)

Game over, my teammates danced in front of home plate because we were Valley champions and headed for the playoffs in Spokane, which was mucho cool, but I broke away and beat it to the locker room to be alone with something bigger. On the bench in front of my locker, I closed my eyes, breathed in, and there she was, her blue eyes and her warm scent, filling up everything, all up against the walls and ceiling. My trumpet was in the locker. I opened my eyes just enough so I could pull out the case. The mouthpiece was cool, dependable comfort on my lip. She was still there when I closed my eyes again and blew a soft concert A until my breath was gone. Voices and cleats on concrete approached in the hall. I put away the horn and grabbed the bottom of my sweaty jersey, pulled it over my head and held it there, breathing in the warm, damp entrapment with her image, before pulling it all the way off.

Feet, hands, shoulders hit the door, and voices of the victorious Kayakaw High Pirates blasted in and ate up the silence. Two Jay's big blocky brown feet walked up on me. He hung over me, a baseball shoe with a sock stuffed in it in each hand, watching me rub the skin of my instep. He said, "What are you doing after we shower, Joe?"

Absorbine Jr and foot sweat fumed out of Two Jay's cleats. He wore out shoes in a hurry with his hard running and heavy feet. A big gap-toothed grin stretched his face—he'd doubled off the rightfield wall and driven in two important runs for us. I went hitless.

"Got to meet somebody," I said. His shoes fumed close to my face, and I slapped at the nearer one. "Man, put those things on the floor, will you?"

He swung the shoes past my nose. I covered and ducked away. He dropped the shoes. "Meet somebody. Do I know who it is?"

Nobody needed to tell us to do it, but sometime in junior high we stopped mentioning names or used code names like The Meadowlark or The Mustang when talking about white girls around our white teammates that we'd been playing with or against since grade school. And we kept our voices down.

"Yeah. You know who it is."

He studied me for a minute, bobbed his head. "Oh yeah."

Two Jay fought to get his jersey pulled over his big football shoulders, more like a college player than a high school player. He was a long ball hitter. Outweighed me by thirty pounds and could outrun me too. Central wanted to give him a baseball and football scholarship for next year. I wasn't going to play college ball of any kind. Five-nine, a hundred and fifty-five, and not all that fast. Have to stick to music or something else. I didn't grow like Two Jay or my big fast brother who could have played college ball if he hadn't signed the pro baseball contract, could keep playing and get paid for it, could maybe make it to the major leagues. But no war was going on when the Dodgers signed Zeke. War started the summer of his first season, and by the middle of his next season Zeke's going on patrols and getting shot at in Korea.

"Did Luke pick her up for you?" Two Jay's voice, low.

Luke had been able to get his folks' car for the game and he did pick her up for me. She and Carola were in the stands with him. He'd given me the okay sign when I looked into the stands, and she waved to me, little quiet flutter of her fingers.

"Yeah. He picked her up."

Two Jay propped his foot on the bench, pulled his little toe away from the others and studied the skin between, put his foot back down. "Shoot, you got you a good deal, man. Got old Luke to pick the girl up for you."

She was my girl, mine, not Luke's, the way people assumed, seeing them together, just because they were both white. Two Jay and I stepped out of our pants and jockstraps at the same time. "Well, it's not a good enough deal," I said.

"Joe! Jimmy! Catch!" The student manager tossed us each a towel.

We were the first ones into the shower with its bumpy layers of off-white paint and high row of chickenwired, frosted windows. Water in the old pipes didn't warm fast, so Two Jay went around and turned on all the taps. That was Two Jay, taking care of things. Since the stroke killed Daddy in October, and Zeke was eating dirt and dodging bullets in Korea, Two Jay and I spent more time together than ever. Two Jay and Luke, my substitute brothers since grade school. Two Jay's family were some of the new colored that arrived in town toward the end of the war against Germany and Japan. Luke's folks arrived from North Dakota late in The Depression. Two Jay's dad was a laborer at Hanford where Negroes had a hard time getting housing.

Walter Lynn, captain of the team, stuck his hand into the shower next to me, testing. "Nice game, Jimmy. You too, Joe."

"Thanks, Walt."

"Yeah, thanks, Walt." Walter was six-two, the smooth looks of a movie boy, a pretty good first-baseman. Our team captain.

Pretty soon the whole team was in the shower, yakking and laughing, loose because we *thumped* Ellensburg as the *Daily Republic* would say. The part of me racing to meet Sylvia got slowed down by the part of me that loved the steam and the hot water hitting the base of my neck. A school pleasure, no hot running water at home.

I breathed in satisfaction from the game, from the love music inside me, from the water-shiny bodies of my teammates. Everybody naked under a shower, the room clouded with steam. Naked pricks and balls hanging loose, loosened up in the warm shower after being cramped in a jock-strap for two, three hours. About half the guys circumcised and half not.

I massaged soap into my groin. Everybody said prick, guys called each other pricks. Everybody in Kayakaw, except for Southerners, used pretty much the same vocabulary, but when they were talking business, white guys said *cock* and colored guys said *dick*. One time, I overheard this sexy woman say to a guy, "I've got cock that's real cock, buddy." Man, I almost fainted.

Talking with Luke all my life and living down on Eleventh Street, I never learned to say *dick*. Early on, I had been taken by Luke's way of talking. He was never interested in sports but could he ever sling the words around. It was one day in second grade, we stopped to play in a vacant lot on our way to school. A couple other boys joined us, kicking dirt clods and whacking the ground with twigs. After a while Luke yelled, "Hey! We'd better get out of here or we'll be late. And then we'll be in a fine kettle of fish." That kid's words were silvery and flipping, and we ran for school. From then through high school, Luke and I talked and grew together in vocabulary and nuance. We said *penis* on Eleventh. Sometimes we said *prick*. Two Jay lived up on Sixth and said *dick* easily.

Saying *dick* almost as hard as saying *nigger*.

Everybody feeling studly this night because we beat Ellensburg under the lights in front of a big crowd and were going to the playoffs.

"Hey, Walter," Aker said, "my girlfriend said she was going to give me some tonight."

Water splashed off Aker's head, and his face shone from the run-off, his lips and nose red above the ripple of his stomach muscles. Aker owned a snappy yellow Model B coupe. "Yep, gonna get me some tonight," he said.

"You wouldn't shit me now, Aker, would you?" Walter Lynn said.

Aker, our shortstop, was small but as fast as Two Jay. He didn't know anything, though, didn't study, couldn't find Ireland on a map or identify Mao Tse-Tung, didn't know if Paris was a country or a city, couldn't do quadratic equations. Aker thought "Ninety-nine Bottles of Beer on the Wall" was music.

"Hell no, man, I wouldn't shit you," Aker said. "Would I shit my team captain?"

Walter Lynn turned the castiron handle on the hot pipe and said, "Yeah, you sure as hell would shit your team captain."

"Hey, I'll give you a whiff of my love finger in the morning."

Jesus! His love finger.

Everybody laughed. Two Jay whooped. I kept my face straight and turned the hot water halfway down, turned up the cold, and faced the wall. Cold water beat on my head.

Old Aker, in his yellow Model B, cruising out to Terrace Heights or someplace with Geri. A hot, backflipping cheerleader. White girl.

I turned up the hot water, let it hit me between the shoulder blades, and closed my eyes. Sylvia's silky pageboy flowed back and forth with the movement of her head. I turned off the water.

"Hey, Two Jay, I've got to go. See you tomorrow."

"Okay, man, see you."

He clapped me on the shoulder and his lips stretched wide in the grin that was him, the grin that said to me *You ought to make some progress tonight.* Two Jay believed in "making progress" with girls, always talking about getting him some, always telling me, "You don't know what you're missing, boy."

Sylvia's face in the back window of the car became clearer as the distance in the chillier-than-usual air closed, and I could see her eyes. She moved to open the rear door, put out her hand and said, "Let me take your bag."

My bag. She wanted it, to help me. "Oh, thank you."

She closed her fingers around the handles and set the bag between herself and the far door. I got in beside her and set the trumpet between myself and the door. "Hi, Carola. Hi, Luke. Go, Pirates."

They said, "Go, Pirates."

Luke twisted halfway around, shadowy, raised his fuzzy darkbrown eyebrows at me, and sighted down his nose. "What in heaven's name took you so long?"

"Calm down, pal, I'm sure you wanted me to shower. I thought I got out of there pretty fast."

Sylvia's eyes fingered my face. Her just-parted lips rode my words. "Is your shoulder all right," she said.

"Yes, it feels all right." Running out a slow roller to the pitcher, my last at-bat, I collided with the first-baseman and hit the ground.

"You played a really good game."

One of my running catches wasn't bad. "Thanks. Did you miss me?"

"Yes." She put her hand on my head, ran her fingers into my hair and got a worry frown on her face. "Your hair is still wet. Your scalp is freezing." Her fingers in my bad hair, on my scalp, sent five kinds of warm waves down my body. She said, "Do you have a towel in your bag?"

She put her hand on the bag, but I reached across her and put my hand on her hand. Couldn't have her opening that thing and whiffing my sweaty shoes and socks, seeing my jockstrap. "No. There's no towel in there."

She put both her hands on my head, rubbed her fingers in fast circles all over my scalp, dried her hands on the front of her coat and did it again. Jesus, man, the tingle. "There," she said, "that's better."

And it was. She dragged her fingers across the front of my coat. Talk about better. She took my hand onto her lap and held it between her hands. My hand, as if it were precious to her. She moved closer to me. She had on her long dark red coat with the black collar, but her weight and warmth and curve and softness came through the coat. I slipped my hand from between hers and put my arm around her and kissed her on the cheek, breathed in the smell of her hair and skin. My inhale caught a few strands across my nostrils, and I sneezed.

"God bless you," she said. And I felt a blessing.

Carola piped up, "Sounds like somebody's allergic to you, Syl."

"Very funny, Crayola," Sylvia said. She laid her head against my chest. Carola swung her freckled face around to see how she scored with her little remark. With her freckles and her cheerleader body, only she wasn't a cheerleader, Carola was cute. She and Luke looked good there together in the front seat, both of them dark-haired and blue-eyed. Not even boyfriend and girlfriend, Luke and Carola, just aiding and abetting their chums. They could go anyplace in town together, anyplace they wanted. Be seen on the street. Go to each other's houses. Hang out together as long as they wanted, till curfew. Nobody too interested in their business.

Sylvia and me, though, the whole barking dog world too interested in us. The shaky jelly feeling came in my stomach. In the *Pittsburg Courier* that showed up at the barber shop on Saturdays, I'd read about the recent lynching of a young Negro down in Alabama who was accused of having something to do with a white woman. They even cut off the guy's private parts. Nobody got in trouble for the crime, which was what the article mostly talked about.

Cold, but I could have gone home right then, for sure, and thought all night about Sylvia's fingers through my bad moss, against my scalp, her fingers that played flute and piano, sending heat down my spine.

Her hand, that inside my jacket now patted my ribs. "Are you all right, Joe," she said.

"Sure, I'm fine." Her body rested against my ribs, her arm and hand across my stomach and side. Her body against me, a painless blow that knocked me halfway out. Knocked me open too, open so I was ready to tell her everything I could think of to bring that liquid look into her eyes.

"Did I tell you I wrote to Portland State this week?"

"Do they have a good music department?"

"No, not much in the way of music, but they do have ROTC, and that's what I'm looking for. So I don't get drafted. I'm not in a hurry to go fight in Korea. I got a letter from my brother this week, and he says it gets really scary." I couldn't tell her what he wrote: that he'd seen his platoon sergeant splattered by a burst of machinegun fire.

Her bones, flesh, clothing, sank into my hug. "Oh no. I don't want you to go to war."

I squeezed her and then squared my shoulders against the seatback. "Luke's going to WSC," I said. "Aren't you, Luke?"

"That's the plan," he said.

Luke didn't have to worry. His folks could pay his way through college, besides which old Luke was a money saver, the tightest kid I ever saw. Years and years when we caddied and picked fruit, he saved his money like an old man.

Carola said, "I guess I'll be the only one left in town." She rolled and unrolled what looked like a three by five card into a tube the size of a tootsie roll.

"And next year will be the first time in history Luke and I don't start school together," I said. "Breaking up the old team."

Carola's eyes stayed on her tootsie paper roll. "I guess so."

I said, "Hard to imagine you two girls apart."

"Well, we're not exactly married," Carola said.

"Now there's an idea for you," Luke piped up. "Remember Miss Cromwell and Miss Wilde?"

"Oh yeah," I said, "Mr and Mrs Cromwilde."

Carola pushed Luke in the chest. "You two are awful. Just stop it, right now."

"Okay, okay, I'm sorry."

We caught ourselves. This wasn't the way to start the evening, nothing like the peaceful inhaling of Sylvia I'd been imagining all day. No time to goof around. Sylvia's long fingers that I was holding onto would be someplace else too damn soon.

Against her ear I said, "I sure hope you go to Central next year. It would be pretty easy to see each other if you went to Central."

"I know, but I told you Mom still wants to send me to Nebraska."

I cranked the window down and put out my free hand. The air was sharp but not unbearable, and Walnut Street was quiet as far ahead as I could see. Friday night's cruisers were busy on Ka-myakin Avenue, a block north that we dared not step onto. "I've got an idea," I said.

Sylvia lifted her head off my chest, leaving a warm print, her eyes into my eyes, head tilted so her hair floated along her shoulder in a blonde curtain. "Yes?"

"Why don't we walk home—I mean why don't we walk to your house, to the corner of your block?"

She sat up straight beside me for a minute, pressed against the seatback. Both of us as if absorbing some G forces. She drew her shoulders up toward her ears, clasped her hands in her lap, eyes on the back of Carola's head in the passenger seat, and lightly bit her lower lip. I saw the pictures going through her head. Late enough. Dark enough in the shadows of the trees on Lincoln Avenue. House far enough from the corner, no neighbor to worry about seeing her. Her in her red coat, with a colored boy about the same height, sometime before eleven on Friday night. Her shoulders loosened so her arm touched mine again. "Okay," she said, "if you want to."

"Let's do it. Hey, Luke, Sylvia and I are going to walk to her house. To the corner by her house, that is. You only have to deliver Carola. I'll walk home."

"Are you sure that's going to be okay?" He half-turned in the seat, the way Daddy used to do before wheeling all the way around to come down with his final word.

"Sure I'm sure."

The straight line where Carola's lips met didn't look exactly like it was okay when she twisted around. Sylvia put a hand on her shoulder. "It'll be okay. I've got until eleven o'clock and it's just now ten-twenty."

Man. Thirty blooming minutes of walking with her. Alone. But Luke could act like a corny old adult sometimes, and now he gave us his crewcut profile, looking at Carola. He said, "Shall we allow these children to do it?"

"Hey, boy, the Proclamation was issued in 1863. How many times I got to tell you, you ain't my master?"

"You'll excuse me if I'm just trying to protect you from yourself, buddy."

He rocked me with that one, but I said, "B.S., we're walking."

Carola didn't say anything, closed her eyes.

I got out of the car, took Sylvia's hand, the sleek-boned fingers that she played Bach inventions with, that she rubbed my head with, that rubbed this idea into my head, maybe. I helped her onto the sidewalk. She stood in front of me, nose to nose. Almost an Eskimo kiss. I stepped back. Empty both ways, the sidewalk, and as still as a painting of a street at night. Sylvia patted Carola on the shoulder again. "Call you in the morning," she said.

On the driver's side, my words to Luke came out chattery. "Say, I left my gym bag and my horn in your back seat. Put them on your porch, will you, and I'll grab them when I walk by later. Don't forget—there's some sweaty stuff in the bag."

He started the car, looked out at me with the wrinkled-nose look that lifted his upper lip off his two front teeth that in grade school made me tease him with the name Rabbit. "Yeah, sure, on the porch."

"Thanks, buddy. Bye, Cray."

The car's metallic purr in first gear carried to the corner where the Plymouth became two tail lights, exhaust marbling the red. Sylvia stood on the other shore of the space the car left, buttoning her coat. After the last button, she put her hands in her pockets and studied me. Our first time trying this with streetlights all over the place. We needed to walk up Walnut or cut through the middle of downtown to get her home on time. We couldn't cut through the middle of town though. I shuffled away some grit under my leather soles, missed my sneakers that I should have worn.

Sylvia tilted her head to the west. "Well?"

I stepped onto the sidewalk. Walnut was empty but had a streetlight on every corner of the mile ahead of us. Hands in my coat pockets, I moved as close to her as I could without touching, there on the street, in all that light. "There'll probably be a lot of people parked at Rolfe's," I said to her. "When we get up there we'd better take a detour over to Spruce."

"All right," she said.

Kids with cars did their cruising on the main drag, just north, but I kept my eyes moving because you never could tell when the wrong party might swing up Walnut Street. Close enough to her face to feel its warmth, I said, "I love the way you look in that coat."

"Thank you," she said. Her lips parted but her teeth remained together, sweet pearls. Her face played me Artie Shaw's "Frenesi", Mr B singing "My Foolish Heart", Johnny Ray doing "Walking My Baby Back Home." I heard *Fur Elise.* Trumpet fanfares. All jumbled together, pulling this way and that way inside my chest. We walked in step with all the music between us from three years together in orchestra. I put each foot down with care so my walk was smooth, not bouncing, and I didn't swing my shoulders, and walking along like that with Sylvia was almost as good as holding hands. Our breath created clouds that we walked through. My ears were on alert for sounds behind us, and my eyes stayed peeled for anything in front of us.

Walnut Street dipped under the concrete viaduct ahead. In the underpass I took her hand, and we walked a few feet holding hands on the street for the first time, the flesh of our palms locked together. We stopped and hugged. I put out feelers to both ends of the passage, into the street. Nothing. I put my arms around her again. Her fingers cradled the back of my head. Fingers into my scalp, the softness and pressure of her lips, way beyond any sweet berries I ever tasted. I undid the top four buttons of her coat fast and ran my hand around her waist, the lining of her coat warm and slick against the back of my hand, her back and ribs warm and solid against my gliding palm. The brassiere strap under her sweater was electric but not shocking to my palm. She kissed back as hard as I kissed her, reached down and unbuttoned her coat all the way so that she was along the whole length of my body, breasts printing my chest, thighs rubbing against mine, hips pushed against me. Against my mind-of-its-own hardness that she didn't seem to mind. I hadn't known Sylvia was that strong. She let out a quiet, "O-o-o-h."

Moisture collected in my eyelashes. The shaky feeling in my gut turned into balloons of laughter that pushed against my throat, stretched it, trying to get out to make tunes nobody ever heard before. I slid my arms from around her, memorizing her shoulders, back, ribs, with my hands. Her thighs against mine. I held her coat closed for her, and she moved her hand up the buttons and studied me studying her in the bad light. Her nose, not small but not exactly large—I didn't know I could love a nose like that. And her eyes, a warmer blue than Luke's, her lips and skin full of something I couldn't get my mind around. Like a painting that grabs a moment out of existence, catches something that makes people stare at it for five hundred years.

In no way was I ready to leave the viaduct, that gentle descent below groundlevel with Sylvia. A distant horn blared, however, told us our time-out was over. We let go of each other and walked the slope onto the lighted sidewalk.

At the corner ahead, two blocks after the viaduct, was Rolfe's Drive-in and its big neon sign with the red off-on arrow that showed cars the way into the jaws of the parking lot. There would be a bunch of people from the game, people we both knew.

"Hold it." Of course, the first car we spotted up ahead, squatting in one of the parking slots, was Bob Aker's shiny yellow Model B roadster.

All we needed was to be seen by Aker and his girlfriend, the busiest mouth in the whole school. Sylvia's mother had already received a phone call from the psychology teacher, informing her that Sylvia was being "indiscreet," meaning she was seen talking to me at my hall locker or walking half a hall with me. "Let's double back to the corner and over to Spruce."

Trying to walk separate and together at the same time, we bumped arms every few steps on our way back to the corner. Car lights came toward us. The outline of heads looked like teenagers, but nobody ever cruised up Walnut this time of night on Friday. An unfamiliar white boy was driving the car with a girl in the front seat. Another pair was visible in the back. Ellensburg license plate. Bulldogs. Sylvia and I waited at the corner. The gray Dodge came through the intersection. The boy driving looked left and right, trying to find someplace, probably Rolfe's. I saw the driver seeing me and Sylvia. I saw the back window of the Dodge go down and kept my eyes on it. The car slowed and the backseat boy stuck his head halfway out and shouted. "Hey, Sambo, what you doing with that white girl?"

The car sped up and turned the corner at Rolfe's. Jesus. Echo of the lynch mob. Cold sweat ran down my back and my stomach danced. Sylvia hawked in a big gulp of air. Her fingers massaged my forearm. Her forehead touched my temple, the cool tip of her nose against my cheek. I shrugged away from her. "It's okay, it's okay," I said. "Let's get across the street."

We hustled across. On the other side we continued into the shadow of the old creamery building where the doorway was set back a few feet from the sidewalk, and I pulled her into the space and put my arms around her. We stood there getting our breath and listened. Only normal night sounds. "I just wanted to make sure they weren't going to come around the block again," I said.

"So mean," she said. "How can people be so mean?"

"Easy. That was nothing." But I was lying. My stomach didn't think it was nothing. I took her hand and we walked toward Spruce Street.

She said, "Oh, Joe, I don't want you to feel terrible on account of me."

"I never feel terrible on account of you." I put my free hand on top of hers that held my arm, her cool knuckles against my palm. "And I don't want anything terrible to happen to you."

"Please don't worry, hon. I'm not afraid of anything that could happen to me."

Hon. What she said felt true and like what I felt. When I inhaled, the cool air rushed in and through me like the first breath of life to waken me. My cranium was porous and expanding. All the water in my body pressed on my eyes, ready to wash me out. Don't call me Sambo. Call me Liquid Boy.

Walking and talking, holding hands, I carried on to her about becoming a great musician and a man who would care and know things about the world. "You sound pretty sure that you're going to school in Portland this fall." she said.

"Yeah, it's my best bet. They like my grades, and I can find a job there and live at my aunt's house for free."

"That's nice," she said. "Wouldn't it be fun if we could go to the same college?" She pressed my forearm between hers and her side.

"That's a dream I can't even imagine."

"I know. It's just that I can't imagine us being apart." She said things like that and my head filled up with helium.

"If you went to Central, we could probably arrange a couple meetings during the year," I said.

"Yes, if I went to Central. But I've told you Mom can't get Nebraska out of her head." We let the subject die. We'd been over it too many times and knew we couldn't do anything about it. We walked past Lion's Park, cut back over to Walnut again and then west to Eighth Avenue among trees and houses, most of them dark. Past the high school, we turned north toward her neighborhood. Under the protection of night and tree shadows, we stopped often to print ourselves on each other.

At the corner of Eighth and Ka-myakin, headlights from our left. The black and white police car hummed across the intersection and stopped in front of us, blocking the crosswalk. Sylvia's fingers pressed into my arm. We stood at the curb, her hand still on my arm, the police car so close we were forced a step back when the cop in the passenger seat opened his door.

He stepped out in his heavy black boots and leather jacket, handcuffs, gun and bullets at his waist, in his right hand a long black flashlight that looked like a club—Big Ivan Booth. Nobody liked him. Six-feet three inches tall under his navy blue cap with the short black visor, pale face that never smiled, a cop everybody knew because he pitched semipro baseball in the summer. He'd also been a floorwalker at Montgomery-Ward. His eyes stayed on Sylvia. He reached back and opened the rear door of the police car. Flat, level as death, Big Ivan Booth's voice said, "Get in."

Sylvia's mouth hung half-open. She didn't look my way. She closed her mouth and her eyes, crossed her arms and brought her shoulders up. After a second or two, she opened her eyes, on big Booth standing there with the door open, flashlight pointing to the backseat. Still she didn't look at me. She dropped her arms and moved toward the car. My mouth dusty dry, I moved with her. The cop's flashlight slammed to a stop half an inch from my chest. "Not you," he said.

Booth's body sealed off my view of Sylvia getting into the backseat.

My voice struggled out thin and sick, a little chicken croak: "What did she do?"

I leaned so I could see past Booth. She sat, eyes on her hands, shaking. The cop didn't look at me or say anything, shut the door on her, and got back into the passenger seat. The black and white Ford moved off down Ka-myakin Avenue.

I put my head against the four by four that held the stop sign at Eighth and Ka-myakin, hugged the post while my empty stomach heaved and heaved as if it really had something to throw up.

City of Roses

1)

It's a Saturday. I take my trumpet and catch a noon trolley to downtown Portland so the day man at the parking lot can have the afternoon off, a way to earn a few extra dollars. The trolley crosses the Hawthorne Bridge. Four bridges over the Willamette River connect the east and west sides of the city. This one, the only one I've traveled on, feels like my bridge, a presence bigger than any people I've yet met in Portland. Hugging the trumpet against my chest, I close my eyes. The trolley wires hum and snick overhead, and the tires sing low when we come onto the metal grillwork of the bridge. I open my eyes. In the grey light, reds, blues, white of painted signs on building walls, various shades of brick, stand out. *Color, color, everywhere and not a spot of pink.* Once across the bridge, the trolley is a small boat among the buildings of downtown Portland, no skyscrapers, but bigger than anything I knew in Kayakaw.

It's a slack afternoon, and the six by six metal and glass shack grips the space around the counter, the stool, the cash register, and me like a warm jacket. I put in a couple hours on my French and reading assignments. Two or three times an hour, I go out to park a car or to collect from a returning parker. Using a mute so nobody hears me from the outside, I blow long tones and lip slurs into the space under the counter until it feels like my face is pouring into the horn and then like every cell of me, riding on my breath, is going through the horn. The close space presses the sound back onto me and there's only the bright or neutral or dark sound in the place, me at the center of it, kissing and breathing it into existence. I would close my eyes and disappear but I have to watch the parking lot. Sometimes I get a stretch between cars that lets me get far enough into sound that it starts to feel like light. I don't need to close my eyes. I don't need anything.

***

"You been here since first semester, huh, man?" The stocky brown kid, carrying a spiral notebook caught up with me outside the university library, grinning, relieved to make contact I can see. "I'm Booker Bain. What's your name, man?"

It's the first day of the second semester, middle of January, cold and damp out in the air next to the old brick building where Booker Bain is beaming. The sky hangs smeary grey. The line of small weatherbeaten evergreens alongside the building had me thinking of sad, dark-coated soldiers. Soldiers in winter. Booker Bain seems surrounded by a whole different weather.

"Joe Birdsong," I tell him. "Yes, I've been here all year."

"Pleased to meet you, man." He sticks out a thick-heeled hand. Bain is an inch or so shorter than I. His grin narrows his eyes to shiny slits and reveals that one of his two front teeth has a slight drift forward of the other.

I say, "You just enrolled?"

"Yeah, man, I just got here. I was down at Pasadena City College on a football scholarship you know but I decided to come back home."

Bain is short but muscular, could go one seventy-five or one-eighty, and is probably fast.

"How come you decided to come back to Portland?"

"Man, I didn't like the program down there you know and I was able to work me out a deal back here. I'm going to run track."

"You must be a sprinter."

"Yeah, I run the hundred and the two-twenty."

"What's your time like in the hundred?"

He bounces and rocks his shoulders. "I won city last year in ten flat."

Tin flat.

"Fast. I doubt if I could break eleven right now." The only time I run anymore is to catch the bus after work.

"Well, I expect I'll be breaking ten this spring," he says.

Then: "Say, man, where you from? I never seen you around Portland."

"No. I'm from Kayakaw."

"Oh yeah? Up there in Washington, a Washingtonian."

"That's right. You, you're from Portland, huh?"

"Sure am," he says. "You know many people in Portland?"

"No, man, I'm living with my cousins out in southeast, only been over to Williams Avenue three times to get a haircut."

"Oh yeah?"

"Just been working and keeping my nose to the grindstone here. I don't know anybody."

"Nose to the grindstone," he repeats and giggles. "Well look here, man, why don't we get together this weekend and let me show you around a little bit. You got to meet some people." He beats the air with his spiral notebook for emphasis.

I say, "I've got to work Saturday evening."

"What kind of work you doing?"

"Parking cars downtown."

"Oh yeah? Whereabouts?"

"Twelfth and Washington."

His eyebrows shoot upward. "Right next to the Coney Island?"

"Yes."

"Man, we wore that place out when I was in high school you know." He rubs his fingers back and forth on his chin, then says, "Well, Sunday is cool."

Booker Bain's house sits on a side street near a park at the edge of the main colored area. The houses on the street are a mix of two-story and one-story, solid and quiet in the light of winter Sunday. Bain lives in one of the taller houses with his mother, father, and grandmother. No brothers and sisters.

"Let's walk down to The Stem," he says.

"The Stem?"

"Yeah, man, Williams Avenue."

"Oh."

We walk sidewalks through streets of good-sized houses and large leaf-less trees and frequent evergreens, trees different and more various than Kayakaw trees. These city houses have plumbing and basements, like my cousin's house, not like the small, knocked-together or rundown houses most of Kayakaw's colored live in. My buddy Luke's house in Kayakaw didn't look as solid as many of these houses. Bain carries on like a field trip leader, telling me who lives in which houses and who used to live where. The names mean nothing to me, but it isn't exactly wasted breath because it tells me he knows a lot of people and about the neighborhood. Our breathing puts vapor in the air.

"Now most all of these Negroes that live in these houses used to live in Vanport before the flood."

"Is that right?"

"Oh yeah. We was living in Vanport. I saw my house floating in the water that day, you know. Houses was floating with people and their dogs on the roofs. Man, I'm telling you it was hard to believe, you know."

"I know it was. We heard a lot about it in Kayakaw, and I've seen newsreel pictures." In *The Daily Republic* at home there had been grainy photos from the Vanport Flood.

"Lucky it was Memorial Day you know and most of the people was over in Portland when that dike broke, else a whole lot of people wouldn't be here right now. And I'll tell you another thing," he says, "there was quite few white people that took in Negroes that didn't have no place to stay at first."

"Is that so?"

"Yeah, man, and you know Vanport was the second largest town in Oregon," Bain says. "If that thing had of broke at two o'clock in the morning, the whole town could have been gone."

"That would have been most of the colored people in Oregon, right?"

"Right, man."

"Kind of thing could give you bad dreams."

"I dream about Vanport all the time you know. Not about the flood, though."

We come to Williams Avenue, The Stem, as Bain called it, and I begin to notice that the people on the street are colored. I'm in another country. Some of the people in the cars moving up and down the street are white, but most are Negroes. Somebody yelled "Book-ah," bellowed it, from a passing car. Booker laughed and waved.

"Let's go in here," he says when we come to a corner place called Citizen's Lunch. I follow him in.

A row of booths lines each street side of the place and there's a counter with stools and a soda fountain fronting the kitchen. Nothing but colored people behind the counter and in the kitchen. No white people in the place. Colored people coming in, colored people going out. Colored people in the booths and at the tables. Behind the counter are the same shiny metal mixing bowls, stainless steel, and pea green plastic mixers, as those in the drugstore on Ka-myakin Avenue back home, but here in a colored soda fountain with brown women handling them. I take my hands out of my pockets and rub them together to erase the bite of the chilly meander from Booker's house.

A brownskinned girl in the first booth inside the door snags Booker's hand. "Hi, Booker." She draws out the words in a sticky singsong, making two slow syllables out of "Hi."

"Hey, Barbara, how you doing?" Two younger girls across from her fix their eyes on Booker and me. Barbara's full, lipsticked lips part wide at the sight of him. She waggles his hand.

"I'm fine," she says. "I thought you were supposed to be in California. What are you doing here?"

"Yeah, I was down in California. Down in Pasadena, you know, but I decided to come back. I'm down at PSU now. Say, this here is Joe. He's a student down there. Joe, this is Barbara."

She lets go of Booker's hand and offers me her limp fingers. "Pleased to meet you," she says.

It's the first time I can remember being introduced like that to a colored girl. In Kayakaw, just about everybody colored was acquainted from year zero.

"Nice to meet you too," I say to her. I can see she's not interested in an average-looking Negro, and my words evaporate fast in the heat of her focus on Bain.

"Oh, Booker, do you remember my little sister Alice?" She pushes her hand across the table to touch the arm of the girl to her right who might be a well-developed fifteen. "And this is her friend Eristine."

Booker lays his shiny narrow-eyed look on the girls. "How're y'all doing."

"Fine," they say.

"Hey, Booker." A voice from the other side of the place. "What's goin' on, man? Stop over here when you get through shuckin' them chicks. Hi, Barbara."

Barbara flutters her fingers at the speaker.

"Excuse us a minute, y'all," Booker says to the girls. "I got to go holler at Nate. Come on, man."

Booker introduces me to Nate and the other two guys in the booth. We push in beside them and Booker explains his reappearance in town so soon after leaving for school in Pasadena. "Yeah, man, Portland gave me a track scholarship and got me a little job, you know, at this cooperage place out by the river."

"What you doing there, Booker?"

"Making boxes, man."

"Oh."

"It ain't much," Booker says, "but it's part of the deal. Knocking together boxes a few hours a week. I got to find me some kind of car to get back and forth."

"This the first time you seen Barbara since you got back?" Nate says.

"Yeah, man. First time I been out since I got back. I ain't even called nobody on the phone."

The hefty, light-complexioned guy named Quenton says to me, "So you down at Portland State University too, huh? You run track too?"

The other four faces lock on me, three of them neutral, Booker's eye slits shiny with amusement and status in his old stomping ground.

"No, no track," I say. "I'm just a regular student."

"That's cool," Quenton says. "Old Booker thinks he bad because he won city last year."

"I *am* bad, Negro. You want to race me? Leave your ass so far behind..."

"Ain't no use gettin' into that. You know runnin' ain't my thing, boy."

"I got your thing, boy," Booker says. Everybody laughs.

A brown girl wearing a white apron comes over with pad and pencil, and I order a cherry coke, something I had once or twice in Kayakaw. Booker says to her, "Give me one of those too."

Nate taps my elbow with the back of his hand. "Say, man, you from California?"

All eyes on me again.

"Oh no, I'm from Washington. I'm from Kayakaw."

Heads go up and down as if agreeing that, yep, I am from Kayakaw.

We drink our cokes. Booker looks at the clock and says, "We got to move, man. I told my grandmama I was going to church with her this evening."

"How come you such a good boy, Bain?" somebody says.

Moving out, Booker gives the speaker the finger. I stand up and wave to the booth. "Nice meeting you guys."

They all say, "Nice meeting you too, man."

We pay for our cokes, and on the way out Booker stops to apologize to the girl for not getting back to her. "I'll call you," he says.

"You better," she says.

***

Saturday afternoons, if I don't go to work early, I can practice in my base-ment room without a mute if I want to. After the long tones, I do some lip slurs and trills. I should rig up a mirror down here so I can watch my embouchure up close, the way Mr Trudeau recommended—he's a brass player too, trombone, and pretty good with the baton. By the time I do my run through Herbert Clarke's chromatic exercises and a sixteenth-note study from the Arban book, I'm ready to get onto the Stravinsky pieces. The symphonic band is doing *A Soldier's Tale,* that's got some juicy trum-pet work in it along with the written script. It looks like I might get the job of reading the soldier part when we perform the piece.

Mr Trudeau is partners with a trumpet player in the The Horn Studio, two blocks down Washington Street from the parking lot, in fact, which specializes in teaching brass players, and he referred me to his partner for lessons after saying he thought I had a future as a horn player if I worked at it. My dream agreed with him. After my mother, the trum-pet was the first thing I knew I loved. Then came Sylvia.

And then went Sylvia. To Nebraska. We're still friends, but things never got to be the same after the night the cops took her away and gave her a talking to. Scared her. She acted sort of shellshocked. I don't know when I'll ever get over the depression from that night. Maybe never. Big Ivan Booth. Like I didn't exist.

I bring my lips over the mouthpiece, open the spit valve, and blow. A few drops of moisture hit the floor. It's getting to be time to catch the bus for work, time to put the horn away and pack my English lit anthology, my *Grammaire Francaise,* and a couple notebooks into my briefcase. For dinner I'll grab one of those hotdogs smothered with chili and chopped onions from the Coney Island.

Booker Bain has invited me to cruise with him and his friends tomorrow in the '37 Ford he just bought.

2)

Mr Trudeau comes over to me after symphonic band class with a folder full of music in his hand. I'm putting away my horn."Got a minute minute?" he says.

"Sure."

"Well let me ask you," he says, "are you doing anything Sunday afternoon?"

"Nothing in particular. Just be at home studying and practicing as usual."

Trudeau's eyes have a laugh in them behind his horn-rimmed glasses. He's a quiet guy from Boston, but he's energetic with the baton, gets a lot out of the players. "Good," he says. "I was wondering if you'd be interested in filling in on second trumpet with my quintet, Sunday afternoon. My regular guy has an out-of-town emergency. Jim will be playing first trumpet—he recommended you."

Jim, his partner in The Horn Studio is my teacher and a super player. Trudeau and his brass quintet play a lot of jobs around town that get mentioned in the newspaper.

"Well, sure I'd be interested."

"Good. This deal is going to happen at Trinity Episcopal from two to four o'clock. That works for you?"

"Yes. No problem."

He opens the folder and waves his hand over a score. "We'll be reading this stuff. It'll be a piece of cake for you," he says. "Now I want to get everybody together at the studio for an hour on Saturday. Can you make that?

"What time?

"Noon."

"That's good."

He gives me the folder and extends his hand for a shake. "It's a deal," he says. "This comes with a little cash, you know."

Money! Something I've hardly ever thought of in connection with making music, but being so broke these days the possibility of a little windfall raises my heart rate.

So Sunday afternoon I'm up front in a borrowed dark suit of my cousin's husband, inside a big grey stone church building in uptown Portland with the Rose City Brass Quintet. Long way from the house-sized wooden building down by the river with simple board benches and potbellied stove, woodbox sitting alongside. What we got here is heavy duty pews out of oak, carpet on the floor, stained glass windows. The place is almost full, a few noticeable girls out there, the audience all white and proper-looking like most of the audiences I ever played for in public. Mr Trudeau's group can really play and it's dream time hanging with them through arrangements of things like Handel's *Royal Fireworks Music*, a couple Bach preludes, *Jesu, Joy of Man's Desire*, a piece of music that knocks me completely out, and on top of this, Trudeau is going to slap some change on me. Pinch me.

***

"Man, I never seen nobody likes to study as much as you do," Bain says. We're getting ready to leave the library, where he has seen me reading and where I'm comfortable. He might be telling the truth. The night I went riding with him and his buddies, all they did was sing and play the dozens and argue. At first, it seemed too rough, even ruthless, but it was their game from way back, tied them together, I began to see, and all of them could handle it. A lot of their jive was funny and witty, but I ended up understanding that I was some degree of alien.

"Yeah, study," I say. "I guess it's kind of a habit." The job with Trudeau's quintet was a surprise break in my routine, and a boost, playing with those precision guys.

"Well, look here, you want to meet a girl, man?" Booker Bain has introduced me to a few colored girls, but it's always on the fly and none of them has felt all that appealing, so I haven't made any connections.

Old Bain is a busy, popular woodchuck and likes to talk about the girls he's trimmed. Besides his footspeed, the size of his penis and the number of girls he gets makes him feel good enough about himself so he doesn't worry about much else. He can see that he has way more experience with girls and that I have some interest in the subject, and that's what we talk about. That, and what he's doing, how he's feeling, or what he's fixing to do.

Bain isn't dumb at all, but I see that the *me* and the meat stuff in his head is more important than *Survey of English Literature* or *Introduction to Philosophy.* Him and his buddies. Looks like they studied each other and created each other in a way that shut out a lot of the world that started opening up when I began to read the Kesslers' books during my junior year in Kayakaw—Kesslers, Nat and Betty, Jews from Brooklyn who hired me to work in their little grocery store and gas station. I got more from listening to Betty carry on about the Holocaust and society, and from reading their books, than I ever got at school, except for music. With Bain and his buddies, except for my color, I feel like part of the shut-out world, an outsider. Old Luke and I used to look at subjects out there in the world and try to get into them so that we'd know what an acre was, or a stere, or a hypotenuse, or the order of the planets, or mitosis, or an adverb, or the system of checks and balances, or what the Soviet Union was up to, or where Madagascar was. These guys don't seem interested in such things. These guys don't read but talk sports and sing hard, and jump and sprint, talk about pussy. Some of them, like Bain, have expressed carnal knowledge to a degree that I can relate to only through pictures or stories. Luke and I competed to know more and more about the world outside our bodies. Might have been different, though, if I had been bigger and faster like Zeke and Two Jay. Like Two Jay and some other man-sized guys, I could have got a pick and shovel summer job on one of the dams they were building in the Columbia River. Could have made enough money to get into trouble.

The sex pictures: Nat Kessler, my employer, told me he'd once worked in a Manhattan camera shop and that whenever they got hot sex shots to develop he'd keep one for himself. One night while babysitting his children, I got to thinking that Nat's collection was probably close at hand. He'd only mentioned it once, but I couldn't see why he wouldn't still have it. Sure enough, it was right in front of me, in two stuffed brown bags, behind the sliding doors of the wall cabinet above Nat's desk. The swarm of naked female and male bodies, the array of penises, vaginas, breasts, asses, a few dogs, donkeys and one elephant, was the most massive satisfaction of curiosity in my life. Way beyond *What a Young Boy Ought to Know,* the secondhand book with the dark red cover that appeared in our house one day with no mention. No pictures in it, a lot of talk about the "secret sin." Many of Nat's photos were of mixed couples, colored and white, and mixed groups, getting all kinds of sexual exercise. A howling surprise, breathtaking, these images of themselves taken by ordinary-looking people, doing things I'd been given to believe would send my non-believing ass hurtling toward fire and brimstone. The few snapshots I eased from the collection into my wallet were secret gold. A few times in the weeks after that, a classmate would sidle up to me and whisper, "Hey, Birdsong, I hear you got some dirty pictures. Can I see 'em?"

Bain's question is still hanging:

"Meet a girl?" I say. "Sure. Who is she?"

"She looking for somebody to take her to her prom."

"High school girl?"

"Yeah."

"She must have asked you. How come you don't take her?"

"Man, I'm tied up right now you know." He does his back and forth shuffle and bounce.

"What does she look like?"

"She real cute and she got a fine body," he says. His hands carve hips in the air. "I think y'all might get along."

"How come she can't get a date?"

"She can get a date, man. She ain't looking for just anybody to go with. I'm trying to help the girl, you know. Trying to help you too."

My innards go icy at Bain's presumption. "I'm wondering why she needs help."

"Well, number one, there ain't but one or two colored guys in her class, man."

"Oh." Colored has to have a colored date. Got to get that straight. Sylvia and I never made it to any senior prom.

Booker is bouncing from ball to ball. "Yeah, man, she a real cute girl. She kind of quiet, but the girl will surprise you. Here, let me give you her telephone number. I'll tell her you're going to call her. She live just a few houses down from me."

The phone rings twice before someone picks it up. A woman's voice. "Hello."

I say, "Hello, may I speak to Maerene, please?"

"May I ask who's calling?" That's what the flat voice answers when I ask for the girl.

"Would you tell her it's Joseph Birdsong. I believe Maerene is expecting a call from me."

"Just a minute." Through the phone line I hear her call out the girl's name.

The next voice is soprano, not loud or full. "Hello. This is Maerene."

"Hi, Maerene. You don't know me, but Booker Bain said he was going to tell you to expect a call. I'm Joe Birdsong."

"Oh yes." Her voice gets a little more air in it. "Thanks for calling— and please call me Mae. Nobody that knows me calls me Maerene."

"Okay, thank you. Mae is easier to say. Booker told me we could maybe meet at his house, Sunday afternoon, and get acquainted."

"That's what he told me too."

"Is that all right with you?" No need to mention the possible prom date. She's not mentioning it, wants to see what kind of gorilla I look like first. Booker probably told her something. Told me she was cute, but he and I don't speak exactly the same language.

"Sure," she says. "That's fine with me."

"Say, your last name is Dupree, huh?"

"That's right."

"Are you French?"

She laughs. "You know I'm not," she says. "We're from Louisiana. Lots of people have French names down there."

"Oh, I see." From Louisiana just like Booker, but her speech sounds more standard than his. The first new colored people I saw in Kayakaw were a family from Louisiana, whose father worked at Hanford near the end of the war, down there doing pick and shovel work. They said "Y'all" and they called Pepsi and Coke "soda water."

"Booker said you were from somewhere in Washington. Is that right?"

"Yes, that's right, Kayakaw."

"Really."

"Have you ever been up that way?"

"No, I haven't."

"I'll have to tell you about it sometime." The words were out of my mouth before I could check them. She might think I'm trying to be fresh. Too early for that. And I have no idea what the girl looks like except that Bain says she's cute.

She says, "Maybe so."

"Well look, Mae, it's been good to talk to you. I'll be over to Booker's at two o'clock if that's okay with you."

"That'll be fine. He's only three doors down from here."

"Great. Bye now."

"Good-bye, and thanks for calling." Her receiver clicks and I hang up.

She didn't sound bad. I put my lips to the horn, blow a long low tone, letting the conversation play back through it, and try to think about what's going on, how to talk to this girl.

Booker Bain wasn't lying about the girl's fine legs and behind, and her smooth honey-colored complexion and feathery black hair. She had on light blue pedal pushers. Sunny Sunday afternoon, we sit side by side on Bain's front steps and talk about how nice the weather is. "Are you glad to be graduating," I ask her.

"I sure am," she says.

"What are you going to do next year?"

"I don't know yet." She sits relaxed forward, bare forearms against her thighs, palms together between her knees.

Bain, on the other side of her, stands up. "Y'all want a 7UP or something?"

"Nothing for me, thank you," she says.

"Sure, I'll have a 7UP," I say. Bain goes into the house.

Mae speaks to the space in front of me. "Booker told you I was going to invite you to my prom, didn't he?"

"Yes, he told me that."

"Well, would you like to go with me?"

"Sure I would." I take her hand and shake it. "Let's call it a deal."

"Okay," she says. Her cheeks dimple up as if she's going to spill over, laughing, and her eyes move to my face. I've still got hold of her hand when Bain comes out with two bottles of 7UP.

"Hey, lookee here. Y'all havin' fun."

"Yeah, man, why not? I just got me a prom date."

"That's good. That's good," he says. He hands me one of the green bottles and sits down again on the other side of Mae. "You two ought to have a real nice time."

I take a swig of 7UP. "Well, I'm looking forward to it."

Mae's eyes are on the sunny sidewalk and street in front of us, but I can tell that her ears are wide open. It's a good afternoon for lounging on a porch with a drink and soaking up some sunshine. "Why don't we walk down to my house when we finish here," she says. "I want my mother to meet you."

In the front hall at Mae's house I wait while she fetches her mother. To my right, behind French doors, is a dining room with an upright piano against one of the inside walls. On the left is a large living room whose furniture focuses on the television set at the back wall. I stand straight and put my hands behind my back in front of the full length mirror on the door of the closet that faces the front entrance. Mae comes back with her mother.

The woman is a larger, tougher-looking version of Mae, skin a couple shades lighter, with good hair. "Joe, this is my mother, Maude Esther Dupree. Mother, this is Joe Birdsong."

Mrs Dupree keeps a straight face and extends her hand. If I'd had the nerve, I would have taken her paw with a wide gesture and said, "*Enchanté, madam,*" to see what the woman would come up with. I give it a brief shake and say, "Pleased to meet you, Mrs Dupree."

"Joe is from Kayakaw," Mae says.

"How long did you live there," her mother asks me.

"All my life. I was born there."

"I see," she says. "We don't know any folks up that way."

"Well there aren't a lot of folks to know up that way." My words ring silly and loose the minute they pass my teeth, even though they respond clearly to Mrs Dupree's words. Hell, there are over thirty thousand people in Kayakaw, and it used to feel as if I knew most of them from reading the newspaper, from school, talking to people, playing sports and music, picking hops, cherries and apples, caddying at the country club. I could have said, "There aren't a lot of colored folks up that way," but I didn't have to say it. I'd feel funny, though, if some white person assumed that I didn't know a lot of white people in Kayakaw.

"What church do you belong to?"

Her question comes out of nowhere into the nowhere of my church affiliation. "I haven't really been to any of the churches around Portland."

"I see," she says. "We'll have to get you down to Greater Faith."

"That's our church," Mae says.

Mrs Dupree's eyes shine in her fair face, and one corner of her mouth curves upward. "You kids excuse me now," she says. "Have him sit down, Mae. I imagine you want to talk. It's nice to meet you, Joe. I'm glad Mae found herself somebody to go to her prom with."

From where we're standing, the sight of the small upright in the dining room gives me a throb. "Do you play the piano?" I ask her.

Her face dimples up and she shakes her head. "No, I never could stand practicing."

On my way back home, I stop at Booker Bain's place to give him a short report on the state of things. "Everything looks cool, man. She's all right. Nice house."

"You met Mrs Dupree?"

"Yeah."

"What did you think?"

"What do you mean?"

"I mean what did you think of Mae's old lady?"

"Well, to tell the truth," I said, "she didn't seem exactly unfriendly but she seemed a little chilly to me."

"That's what I'm talking about," Bain said. "Ain't nothing wrong with Mae, but her mama is color struck."

"Oh yeah?"

"She don't say much but she ain't particular about nobody too dark and with nappy hair hanging around Mae."

"Really?"

"Yeah, man. Mae told me a long time ago when we used to mess around together her mama told her to 'keep the coal out of the family'."

"Man, that's a wig. According to my mother, my grandmother said the same damn thing. Grandma had a lot of white blood and some Indian in her. My father was dark coffee-colored and wiry-haired, and after I became hip I remembered Grandma never had much to say to Daddy."

"Ain't that some shit?"

"Sure is."

"Mae is a sweet chick, though."

3)

She doesn't talk much, but at the prom I can tell she doesn't mind when my leg rubs against her thighs while we're dancing. After the prom, Maerene Dupree and I go out on more dates. Late on the first warm night, we walk to the park at the end of her block and lie under a shaggy camellia bush. We press lips together, play tongues inside each other's mouths. My inexperienced member pushes against my pants, and she churns her middle against it. On top of her, meeting her grinding motions with my own, I run my hands under her buttocks and take in the excitement through my palms and fingertips. Little cries come from her, and her breath and the motions of her hips are a rising threat. I seek safety in words. "Jeez, Mae, I'm sorry I don't have any protection with me and I don't want to do anything without it."

She eases from beneath me, unzips her pedal pushers, and guides my hand under the elastic and rayon across her abdomen to the hair of her crotch where I discover my fingers to be prodigies. From much reading about female anatomy since eighth grade, the simmering, juicy territory of her vagina feels like a familiar field of study heightened by actual contact. Her clitoris against my fingertip is like the small erect penis in the books, straining as I slide up and down it. Mae sucks in her breath, flaps her thighs around my hand and breathes a long tremble. Our lips stay together, tongues ying-yanging around each other, and she stirs against my hand several more times, deferring my desire to have a whiff of my fingers. My middle finger never felt such power even on the second piston of my trumpet. After the spasms and intertwining and sucking of tongues, she places her hand on my hard pants and says, "O-o-h, poor thing."

"I'm okay," I say.

"No," she says. My chest choked with curiosity, expectation and undefined hope, I ain't about to proffer nobody's phony protest as the girl unbuttons my corduroys, extracts my penis, and tethers it with the tender collar of her hand, squeezing and pumping. Something like a low whinny escapes my throat. She lays her fingers on my lips. "S-s-sh," she says. "Do you have a hankie?"

I gurgle, "Uh huh."

She pats my pockets, finds it and draws it out, her other hand keeping an up and down massage. Me, sprawled halfway under the camellia bush, a happy battlefield casualty, eyes bugged at the stars and the darkness beyond. On her knees beside me, hand working, she brings her face close to mine. Brushy notes from her voice, "Are you all right?"

"Uh huh."

She squeezes me, plugs my mouth with her tongue, and speeds up her hand until all the electricity of the night comes charging through my stem, and I'm choking on the biggest ball of glee in my life.

***

My brother says in a letter from Korea, "Joe Chinaman ain't talkin' no peace over here," but peace negotiations have started in Paris and, according to the papers, the war might end before long. He might get out of Korea alive with only two small flesh wounds. Over fifty-thousand guys have been killed over there. Supposedly to stop communism. I buzz into my mouthpiece. Sometimes I think he should have gone to college, taken one of the scholarship offers. When we were little boys, all kinds of information came to me through Zeke's curiosity about the world. He could read. I hurried to read. With his first money from caddying he bought *Wonders of Science* a book we lived in for months. Before he left elementary school, though, it was discovered the boy had great hands and nobody had seen a faster kid. He put down the trombone and Daddy took it back to the rental place. His mind sold out to sports the year round. He grew four inches taller than I'd ever be and left me in the dust as an athlete. He could have gone to college for free, studied something.

***

Mae finds a job as a page at the public library and closes the book on the subject of continuing her schooling. "I've had enough of going to school," she says. But we have our subject for the summer: screwing under the camellia bushes.

Into the boyfriend role with Mae like a windup toy, I keep the rubbers handy. Already Two Jay knocked up his whacky girlfriend and had to leave Central at mid-year to go back to Kayakaw, get married, and get a job on a city garbage truck.

Mae has had a couple boyfriends before me and doesn't make things complicated, so now that I've got the idea, it's knees against the ground, it's nose into the grass inhaling earth and leaf smells, pounding away on the dry summer grass, and rising light enough to fly. By September, on a blanket under the bushes, she's saying, "I love you," as we come together.

I'm saying it too.

A few lip slurs, some arpeggios from the bottom to the top of my range, concentrating on support for the column of air, trying for a shiny, liquid sound. No mouthpiece pressure on the lips. Louie picked up the horn in that orphanage down in New Orleans and started blowing like Gabriel, but he sure messed up his lip. Looks like a piece of twisted licorice. I'm not doing that. My teacher thinks I could improve and extend my upper range.

I ascend through G major, see Mae's legs pass the basement window, headed for the door I left unlocked for her. She's a little early. I continue blowing until she taps.

"Come on in."

She steps in smiling and rolling her eyes, shy about the interruption. "Hi," she says.

She's wearing a sleeveless summer dress with wide red and white stripes that emphasize the curve of her buttocks and calves. She sets her shoulder bag on the bed. I swing my arm around her waist and kiss her lips. "Hi, honey."

She hugs me with both arms and then lets go. "Practicing, huh?"

"Yes. Give me a couple more minutes?"

"Okay. Don't hurry." Out of her bag she takes a small bottle of lotion and shakes a couple drops into her hand. She slides her palms and fingers together and through each other and watches me continue pushing tones up through the arpeggios. Done with her hand massage, she walks over to the shelf above the drawers, takes the ashtray she keeps there to the bed and sits with her legs crossed. Since leaving school, she's decided to become a smoker like her parents. I told her I thought smoking was bad for her health, but she looked at me as if of course I was kidding, and she sits now with her smoke, anchored in family habit. When I put away my trumpet, she stubs out her cigarette and returns the ashtray to the shelf.

I stretch out on the bed, face up. She slips off her sandals, lets herself down on her stomach beside me, and rises onto her elbows. "How are you feeling today," she says.

The night before, I stayed late at her house, watching television with her family. Everybody—mother, father, three brothers—watches the Ed Sullivan show and Alfred Hitchcock on Sunday evenings. It's come to be an easy habit. In Mae's big house, we rolled around on the living room rug after everyone else was gone to bed.

"I feel fine," I say. It's her day off from work at the library. Light lotion scent enters my nose.

"You know, I was reading some things about sex the other day at work." The pitch of her voice goes up at the end so her statement has the sound of a question.

"Oh yeah? What about sex?"

"Well this book was telling how people in love put their mouths on each other sometimes when they make love."

"You mean kissing?"

Her dimples put commas in her cheeks, and she snuggles her head against my neck and the bedspread. She must have known that her meaning would explode in my head, as it did. Here I am almost nineteen, just getting things started that I've been reading about for years. Old stuff in the books and in talk and imagination. And pictures. All the laughing and joking about sucking cocks or dicks and eating pussy was big fun on the playground or in the lockerroom, like food-fighting with forbidden fruit. And just lately, listening to my new acquaintances play the dozens, I heard the theme wax large. And flush against me here is my curvy, demure, hungry girlfriend, who doesn't read much, talking about "put their mouths on each other" that she read about, her hand already sliding along my brainless member.

"You mean you want to try some of that?"

"We could try it if you want to."

"Well, okay."

We get up from the bed and she pulls her dress over her head and hangs it in my closet. Her pale pink panties and brassiere against her tawny skin, are delicious in the light from the window. I put my arms around her and lick her neck. She unhooks her brassiere and shrugs out of it, steps back from me and slips off her panties. I take off my clothes while she folds her undies and sets them aside. We fall across the bed, and after a couple long engagements of lips and tongues, she kisses her way down to my penis that she kisses and takes into her mouth. Holding it with both hands she moves her head up and down, warm mouth, tongue, lips. I lie back and massage her head and neck, a shaft of sugar clogging my throat. After a few minutes, I pull her up and kiss her.

"Did you like it," she says.

"Oh yes, it felt nice. Let me try it now."

My head between her legs, face against her inner thighs, the breast-softness of her flesh there surprises me. Old Two Jay never talked about any such wonders. Bain either. Flesh of unreal, mysterious soft-ness, that answers the hunger for *soft*. I rub my face against it, kiss it, lick it, and stick my tongue inside her, find her clitoris, feel and hear her tremors, feel her thighs close around my ears. She pulls me up and rolls a prophylactic onto me, brings her mouth around it, pressuring with her lips and tongue before guiding me between her legs.

4)

Mae's whole family dresses up on Sundays and goes to Greater Faith Baptist Church where the times I go with them I see more Negroes in one spot than I've ever seen before. Men and boys in suits and ties, shoes shined, matched by dressed-up women and girls. Two of Mae's brothers and her father and uncle sing in choirs, and so do her aunt and mother.

"How come you don't sing in one of the choirs?" I ask her.

She brings up her shoulders, drops them. "Oh I don't know, I guess I'm not much of a singer."

For these believers, mostly Southerners who came to Portland to work during the war, it looks to me as if God is something like the old white man on the ceiling of the Sistine Chapel, just like with the Pentecostal people back home in Kayakaw and the pictures in Sunday school quarterlies. The idea I had, once. And Heaven is a place where they're going to meet all their dead relatives that didn't go to Hell. Everybody's mama is going to Heaven. Mae's aunt heard me saying to her, "You actually believe there's an old man up in the sky, or somewhere, watching everything you do? I sure don't believe that stuff."

Her aunt patted my demented head and purred, "That's all right, honey, but I think you ought to keep those ideas to yourself."

And they seem to have it in their guts that white people are some-thing different and special because they own more stuff than colored people do. Hell, where she came from, Negroes were some of the stuff white people used to own, which screwed up everybody's view of reality. Mae thought she was giving me a compliment when she said, "You sound just like a white guy."

"No, honey, I sound like me. Do I look white to you?"

"Oh you know what I mean. The way you pronounce your words."

"White people don't own the language, honey. I'm just speaking plain old English, what I was born into, and I do whatever I want with it." First time I ever put the idea into words. Saying it hatches more words: "If I want me some more language, I'll go out and get it." Like I've been doing with French, which I'm seeing now as taking possession.

"Well," she says, "You talk better than most of these guys around here."

5)

A finger against my shoulder. My eyes open to students around me laughing or looking at their hands when I scan the row. The history professor says, "Are you with us, Mr Birdsong?"

My mouth is dry, but sweat pops out on my forehead. "Sorry, what was the question?"

"I hadn't asked it yet, Mr Birdsong. I was waiting while your neighbor roused you from the arms of Morpheus."

Titters, snickers, a guffaw from the back corner. It is a Monday. Last night I hung out late at Mae's house, waiting for everyone to go to bed so that we could make love on the floor behind the sofa. Before that, we'd been to a party where I had several drinks. By the time I caught a bus home it was early morning. Then there was this eight o'clock class. I pull myself to attention for the rest of the hour, eyes fast-ball wide to fight off the cap of dullness trying to settle on my head.

Can't trust myself right now, and I'm drowsy too much of the time. Running back and forth across town to screw with Mae has loosened my grip on study. Only two years of ROTC are required, but if I drop it after the second year, I'll need to keep up my grades to avoid getting drafted before I graduate. ROTC has started to be a pain in the ass, the most un-college kind of classes I can imagine. And I've had enough of the uniform every Friday, like I'm going to do a light opera singing gig. No more worry about the war in Korea, though, which ended during the summer. Hallelujah.

After putting in at San Francisco on his way home to Kayakaw, Ezekiel stops in Portland over a weekend to see me and the cousins. We have a family dinner for him. I introduce him to Mae. Everybody is happy to see him back from the battlefield whole and healthy. Zeke is the quiet, easygoing brother and doesn't have much to say about his experiences in Korea, just like he never had much to say about his athletic exploits, but I don't remember a time in our lives when he didn't seem to exist for competition. And I know he does love stardom. In his letters from Korea, he sometimes wrote as if he were in a match where trying to be a hero counted. He wrote me once how he almost won a medal for his participation in a skirmish with a North Korean platoon. Growing up in Kayakaw, he always won. In the newspaper year-round for sports during high school, the colored boy from down on Eleventh Street was the best-known person in town. Then his ascension into the Kayakaw-supposed heaven of pro baseball, ignoring a couple college scholarship offers. Drafted for the Korean War, he lost two good years, but that's over and I can see he's feeling blissful, headed for spring training in Florida and a season of Class B ball in the Piedmont League.

But things don't look like they used to look.

Since high school we haven't seen much of each other with him off playing baseball and then to Korea. During infantry training, he got three days leave to attend Daddy's funeral. Now, sitting down to relax at The Porters Club, the upstairs café and lounge on Williams Avenue, there's a wide gap of experience to deal with. We don't say much about Daddy. Zeke never had any trouble with him even after we stopped going to church. He looks bigger and stronger than ever, Zeke does. He must go a good one-ninety now, and I know he's fast. I tell him about my experience so far at college. He says, "You think I could have been a big man on campus?"

"Oh yeah, I think so." A sportswriter for *The Daily Republic* once called him "the dusky speedster" in a column about my brother.

Somehow I don't feel overshadowed today. I feel centered many books and concerts and dreams away from our life in Kayakaw. I've got carnal knowledge I didn't used to have.

"How's the music going?" he asks.

"Not bad. I've been playing a lot at school and I'm studying with a really cool guy."

"Your girlfriend is pretty cute."

Our conversation is fitful until a bell seems to go off, and we start talking sports. Then for a while we're back home.

Zeke's in good shape and ready to get back on the field with his great throwing arm, his good bat, speed, and his dream of a shot at the big leagues. And I'm happy for him, even with the long odds, and happy realizing I've been loosed from such dreams for a long time now.

***

"We ought to get married."

In my room, sitting on the edge of my bed, finishing a cigarette. She says that.

"What?" I shut my trumpet case and set it near the head of the bed.

"I said 'We ought to get married.'" She stubs out her cigarette in the ashtray cupped in her fingers.

Mae is eighteen, I'm nineteen. The idea of being married is not a notion I ever related to except in my dream of endless expansion with Sylvia. And with her, it was never anything I could see how to actually ink-paper-altar accomplish. I've got to get through college and find out things about life and become a great musical artist. Mae's idea increases the fatigue and dullness I feel from the weekend. She sets the ashtray on the shelf above my drawers.

"How could we ever get married," I say. "We don't have any money. We're not ready to have kids. I don't want any kids." After graduation it's a couple years of military life for me.

"Well you could get a full-time job," she says, "and I have a job. We could have enough money."

Quit school, work, and fuck full time. Have babies. Buy appliances.

Mae seems to listen whenever I talk about what I'm doing at the university, my reading and writing, or about my ambition to play in a symphony orchestra, but she never asks questions. Our wild good time grinding and sweating together tells her all she needs to know.

"Look, honey, if you mean I should quit school, I couldn't do that. I'm only halfway through."

"But I love you. You could always go back." She puts all her sweet weight into the four-lettter word.

"Yeah, go back when? No, baby. For me, it's get that degree now or never. And you're forgetting one big thing."

"What?"

"If I'm not in school, the army will snap me up in a minute. The war is over but they're still drafting people."

She sits with the ashtray in her lap, hugging her middle, eyes watery, lips pressed together.

Tne idea of quitting school, dropping out or getting drafted has the nightmare feel of sinking in quicksand. Some kind of death. I have never not been in school where there were warm rooms, plumbing, waxed hallways, crayons, pencils, paper, books, terminology, pianos, classmates, games, maps, the prospect of expansion. Some teachers have been great. Nothing in school stops me. When I get out of school, I intend to keep making music, and if I can't make music I'll make something else.

Mae's watery eyes let go some tears and her voice tightens into a wail. "You're just using me."

She jumps to her feet with the ashtray in her hand, and for a moment I'm ready to dodge, but she takes it to the shelf, comes back and sits on the edge of the bed.

"What are you talking about, Mae?"

"I love you and I've gave you everything."

The mangled cliche ambushes me, inside our playlet here, where my lines come so easy from the screwball warehouse of movies, love songs, and soap operas, triggers a spasm in my abdominal muscles. I fight to keep from laughing myself to pieces.

A long deep inhale that I hold for a couple beats helps me stay upright. I lower myself to the bedside. "Well I love you too, Mae, but so what?

We have not got what it takes to get married. We ain't got nothin', honey. We got plenty of nothin'."

"You don't really want me."

"What makes you say that?"

"If you did, you'd want to marry me right now."

"It's not that nobody wants you, honey, it's just that it's impossible for me to even think about getting married right now. It takes money, income, to get married."

"You don't love me."

"I told you I did."

"You don't mean it."

"Come here." I pull her down onto the bedspread, kiss her hot, soppy face, but she wrestles out of my arms and sits up, bawling into both hands. I pull her down again and kiss her moist lips, rub her breasts. A muted tingle meets my fingertips, riding over the light cotton between them and her erect nipples. She locks her legs around my thigh and moves against it. Reaching out to the drawer of my nightstand she brings out a prophylactic and tears away the paper band with her teeth. She rolls it onto my penis and brings her mouth down onto it, runs her tongue around it. The rubbery tang in her kiss charges the storm I seem to be stumbling along in front of.

"If you were a real man, you wouldn't treat me like this." She's buttoning her blouse.

"Treat you like what?"

"Using me for your pleasure and not even thinking about us getting married."

"You haven't been getting any pleasure?"

"I didn't say that. It's just I don't feel comfortable to keep doing what we've been doing if we're not thinking about getting married."

"You want to break things off, Mae?"

"I didn't say that, either."

"I think about us getting married, and I think it's impossible."

She puts her face in her hands, and pretty soon tears are leaking between her fingers. "You don't have any real feelings for me."

"Don't be ridiculous, honey."

"I just can't go on like this indefinitely."

"Like what?"

"Like somebody that's just a sexual pleasure object."

"Come on, Mae, you know you mean more than that to me."

Trying to think of something between us that rivals the routine pleasure of sex with her, I fail.

"You know we should get married," she says.

"Mae, this is not a good time for us to be rushing into anything. I've told you, we're not prepared."

***

It's close to ten o'clock, and three people haven't returned to the lot for their cars. I lock the cars, put the keys in envelopes, and leave a card on each windshield that directs them to the hotel across the street where they can pay and pick up their keys. It was a long evening. I was sleepy when I got to work after a long day on campus. Mondays have become like that since I started spending Sunday evenings at Mae's house and not getting home until after midnight. Foggy Monday. A fight to stay awake in the eight o'clock class which I've missed a couple times. Study at work this evening was more struggle to keep my eyes open and not keep reading the same sentence over and over. *Enumerez les diverses causes de la tristesse d'Edmond.* It's a sleepy nine-block walk to the stop where I catch the Eastmoreland trolley. On the trolley I wake up and find myself a mile past the house, jump off and walk home.

So here she comes today with her buzz saw. "My folks say they'd let us live at the house till you get out of school if we get married," she says. "We'd have the big room downstairs. Let's get married. Please. Please. Please." All over me, hugging, tongue in my ears, in my mouth, massaging my thigh. The big room downstairs with a cozy bathroom across the hall. No more running around, no strain, more study. A large comfortable house with mostly friendly, sober in-laws. Her mother didn't have a whole lot of smiles for me, but she was polite. Mae told me the woman had asked her, "What are you going to do about that hair," meaning my woollier than the Dupree hair. Mae laughed it off, and I pretended to. My travel distance to school would be cut in half if I went for the deal. All that time catching buses to get to Mae would evaporate. Luxurious mating without a break, a nice table and time for study. I could drop ROTC. We wouldn't have kids. After graduation, I would be subject to the draft but I would have my degree.

Greater Faith

1)

Just inside the chapel doorway, I'm waiting for Mae to finish talking to some people up front. One of the Sundays I dropped down to Greater Faith Baptist with the family. Someone in the foyer, just beyond the door, says, "How you doin', Dupree? Ain't seen you in a while."

"Ought to bring yourself to church more'n once a month," Mae's father answers.

Gravelly laughter. "Listen at you, boy. How that business goin'? Y'all got plenty work?"

"Oh yeah, we doin' all right."

"I reckon you ain't lyin'. I see you got you a new shiny black Pontiac. Nice-lookin' machine."

"Yep, thank you."

"Say, they tell me your oldest girl got married, had a big weddin' at y'all's house. Is that the fellah she in there with today?"

"That's him."

"They livin' with y'all?"

"Yep."

"Look like a nice young fellah. Where he come from?"

"He from up in Washington. Kayakaw. He down here goin' to school."

"Goin' to school? What kinda school?"

"College."

"College?"

"Yep. Boy don't know nothin' about no work. Got a little job parkin' cars."

"You say he from up in Kayakaw. He ain't got no Indian in him, do he?"

"What he look like?"

"Look like a genuine spook to me. What he gonna do when he get out of college?"

My straining ear gets no more. The two talkers stepped out the main church door before I could find out what spooky thing I'm going to do when I get out of college. Take my spooky butt to the army, that's what. Old Man Dupree, the most I ever heard him talk. Thickset hard-working Negro in his forties, walks like a farmer, he's all about work, a subject I avoid getting into with him. That's all Daddy thought about too, doing the job. Lif' dat barge. Tote dat bale. I can feel Old Man Dupree wondering why I don't do some real work, hook up with the family business and make some real money pushing around floor waxing machines. He works hard and buys whatever he wants. Man has cash. Forget that school business.

Jesus, I can't get over that if I had been a larger, faster, and stronger specimen, like Zeke with his burning speed, I probably wouldn't have taken up with Luke and music and reading so much, might have ended up with no schooling, working like a horse, like Two Jay now. What Mae would like, stuffing me with oats.

Might have ended up in Korea. And not as lucky as old Zeke.

On the horn I've got speed though. And more. I draw in a deep breath, feel the air in my nostrils, in my lungs, let it out, and rest against the back of an oak pew. The Amos and Andy duet I just heard in the foyer runs through my head until Mae shows up.

Mae complains that I never want to go out, as if I weren't working six nights a week and studying, or maybe should quit school and get a regular day job. "I want to have some fun while I'm young," she says. "We never go anywhere."

"I'm trying to get through school, Mae, and I have to keep my mind on it."

It's true that I've stopped socializing. Bouncing Booker Bain and his girlfriend were our main link to parties and other happenings, but Booker couldn't get his mind trained on study, had to leave school, and got drafted into the army. He's up in Alaska now, in the artillery, looking over at Russia.

"You act like an old man sometimes," she says.

Reading, studying English and French, and playing in the college concert ensemble works just fine right now and shows me more color than the smoky parties with endless rhythm and blues records, dancing, which is not my forte, and sitting around talking about plans or about whoever happens to be not present. And I watch myself easily drinking too much. Maybe Mae is right, but cooling it in the pad with Keats, or reading *Tom Jones,* or practicing my horn doesn't have the waiting-for-something-to-happen feel of the social scene. Feels the opposite. And then I've discovered that studying French lights up English. I mean I can see the bones of the lingo dancing. It's a gas.

2)

"It's really better than my reading makes it sound, but you certainly get the idea." Shakespeare class. The professor just read a few paragraphs from my paper on *Othello,* which we've been studying. I take in a quiet breath and keep my eyes on the front of the classroom. He was playing my music to the class. Word music. My paper was about Desdemona's moral consistency and purity even when she appears to fib to Othello about the handkerchief she lost. About her I said:

> Desdemona has, against convention, married the Moor
> and publicly affirmed the fact to the Duke and her
> unhappy father (l. iii.180—189). Her expression
> regarding the marriage is reasoned and articulate,
> silencing her father and satisfying the Duke that
> no breach of Venetian law has occurred. Those who
> know Desdemona uniformly praise her character,
> expressing open admiration for her talents as a human being.

Of course, Desdemona was Sylvia, though Sylvia and I had no hope for justice. I inhaled the play, lived in it, and my heart beat for Desdemona to the shattering mess at the end. I was nobody's Othello. He was a big guy, and a general, had power. No damn city police were going to screw with his personal business. That was the paper I didn't write. There was some justice possible in Shakespeare's play. Othello screwed himself, though. Rage once had me steaming with boxing practice and thoughts of weapons and murder, and I've still got pockets of anger, but I can see how dangerous and contradictory it is, just like Othello's jealousy. You can knock yourself out with that stuff.

"Very nice job, Mr Birdsong," the professor says, "a model paper." Class eyes on me like after a trumpet solo when he steps over and lays the essay on my desk.

When I come out of the classroom, Margaret Strom is standing across the hall, eyes watching the door. Margaret is a tall redhead with a longish face. Her glasses have lightblue frames. In class discussions she's alert and one of the quickest to come up with observations that move things forward. The sound and precision of her speech are easy to take in. My idea of her is that she might make a great English teacher someday, something like one of the women I had at Kayakaw High who got a big kick out of seeing that students understood what was in front of them. She walks up to me, holding her books against her chest, so close I don't feel the white barrier. Not grinning or smiling, her look still has some shine in it. She taps my sleeve with the back of her hand. "I was waiting here to tell you how much I enjoyed your paper," she says. "What Professor York read of it."

"Thank you."

"He seemed to be quite impressed with it."

"Yeah, I guess so."

"You guess so." She laughs and flicks me on the sleeve again. "You heard him say so, and I certainly agreed with him."

"Okay. It did make me feel pretty good to hear him say what he thought of it."

"Have you ever seen *Othello?*" she says. Her blue eyes are darker than the lightblue frames of her glasses.

"Nope. Have you?" I never heard of Othello being performed anywhere except for Paul Robeson doing it someplace that I couldn't imagine. But there must be such a place. Places. In a magazine I saw a picture, once, of Robeson with a white actress in a scene from the play, side by side, not quite touching. He must have had to touch her during the play. I knew of no colored actor who might play Othello other than Robeson, and right now Robeson's star was down because everybody seemed to think he was a communist. People wouldn't want to see a play about love between a nice white woman and a powerful Negro. Down South there would be killing.

"That's too bad, isn't it," she says. My thoughts drift down to a poisonous level, but the sharpness of her words and eyes bring me back up.

"Yes, it's too bad people aren't more interested in watching Shakespeare's plays."

"It is a shame." Margaret Strom says.

Getting Mae to a performance of Shakespeare would be thorny with challenges. I might be able to sell her on Othello by telling her the main character is a Negro, but I know she'd wonder why we bothered to spend the money—couldn't understand half what the people were saying.

"You really think it's a shame?"

"Yes I do."

We're standing close enough to feel each other's breath and getting a few looks from people passing in the hall. But this isn't high school. Margaret Strom has a way of focusing behind her glasses so that she appears conscious of only the zone she's addressing. Me, I keep my feelers out. In class, I've always heard Margaret well because of the familiar feel of her precise, intelligent-sounding delivery. Like Luke's, which he got from his mother.

"Could you possibly do me a favor," she says.

"A favor?"

"Yes. I wonder if you'd be kind enough to let me borrow your paper sometime that Professor York just read," she says. "I'd like to have a close look at it."

She's taller but not tall enough to tower over me. Willowy. The energy in the girl's face, limbs, and posture, though, puts beaucoup pressure on my sensorium. "Sure," I say. "Can I give it to you tomorrow or the next day, after I look it over?"

"Of course."

During the next class, her eyes are looking into mine every time I move my head in her direction. After class, I hand her my paper on *Othello*.

"Oh, thank you, Joe," she says. She holds it in both hands for a moment as if basking in the shine of the first page. "Do you do your own typing?"

"Yes."

"I'm impressed."

"Well, thank you. I had typing in high school."

"So did I—my dad made me take it," she says. She slips my essay into a folder. "I promise I'll return it to you in a couple of days."

"Don't worry about it. I don't need it for anything. But I would like to hear what you think after you read it."

"Good," she says. "We can meet over a cup of something in the commons."

Margaret's easy words set off a gong that starts up a flock of shady anticipations in my stomach. Everything becomes waiting and then imaginings of my next encounter with the good-talking girl who wants to talk about my paper.

***

A colored women's club that Mae's mother belongs to is having their annual fashion show in a hall just off Williams Avenue. It's Sunday of the weekend that Margaret Strom has my Othello essay. Mae thought we ought to go. The room is big and warm with a runway built out from the stage, and people at round tables in groups, everybody dressed up. Lots of people of all ages, eats, drinks, music.

In Kayakaw I never saw anything like this with so many colored people, not even the big A.M.E. church doings. More Negroes in the room than there are Negroes in Kayakaw. Girls and women strut across the stage onto the runway in their garments while a schoolmarmish woman in a white knit suit pronounces from a script. The models come in a variety of weight classes, shapes, and complexions. One of the big dark women, sashaying in a filmy blue low-cut frock gets the loudest applause. A couple girls parade with escorts. The featured entertainment besides the fashions is a quartet, piano, bass, drums, and alto saxophone that opened the show with some jazz numbers that didn't sound bad.

Several guys come in with white girls and occupy two tables across the room where they laugh, talk, and lean against each other while they watch the goings-on. This is the first time I've seen colored guys out with white girls in Portland. Or anywhere else. At my distance I can keep my eyes on them and not look like a gawker. I see a couple colored girls with their heads together, noticing the group, but nobody else seems to be staring or paying special attention. Two of the guys get up and walk off to bring back drinks for their dates, strut like they own the joint. Booker Bain would know these guys. One of the white girls is a slim blonde, hair in a pageboy cut, whose looks revive my own slim blonde experience back home, an aching for it. My face heats up and under my ribs feels gutless. Two of the girls smoke while their guys are up and down, walking around schmoozing and shaking hands. The room shines with talk and Sunday-go-to-meeting clothes. Here they are, shiny girls that look like the mostly untouchable ones I worked with on the high school newspaper, sang and played music with, classmates familiar as cousins at school, neighbors, some of them, from first grade on. In junior high and high school they became white girls, and the white fences went up, though we still spoke the same language. But I discovered that the most expressive one wanted to talk to me like I had never been talked to before.

These girls here are nibbling food with their colored dates, drinking, touching, laughing. Envy and shame prick me from all directions. These guys and their girls arrived in cars and must know other scenes where they can enjoy themselves. Be alone together. I'm aching, on the wrong side of the fence, overwhelmed with a longing to get up and walk over and talk to them, to hear their voices, their perhaps unclouded words, who they are, where they're from, what schools they went to, what dreams they have. Mae wouldn't understand that worth a damn. The girls probably wouldn't either. They might be birdbrains. Jesus, a fire I would happily leap into. A hand inside my throat clenches around my windpipe. I maintain my seat, hands folded on the table. Mae and the others at the table applaud some items passing up and down the runway, snicker behind their hands at others.

Sweat oozes onto my forehead. The trouble I'm in isn't clear to me yet, but I know I'm in trouble.

3)

"We'd have a place of our own," Mae says. Her eyes shine and her mouth stays open after her words end. Her aunt and uncle have bought a two-story duplex and offered us a bargain rent for the top floor, speaking to Mae, not to me.

"I thought we were going to stay here until I get out of school." Reading, study, writing papers, go well in our big room. Since I settled in, I've been an A student and maybe the top English major in the class. In case I need a job sometime—everybody asking, "What are you going to do when you get out of school?"—I'm taking enough education courses to get a teaching certificate. What I know, though, is that unless something that I don't plan on happens, I'll be going to the army as a draftee since I dropped ROTC.

"Auntie and Uncle Charles could get twice as much rent for this place, but they want to help us," she says.

"We're going to be really broke."

"We can make it."

Bargain rent will be a strain without the family utensils and appliances, but there's nothing to say, Mae in cahoots with this quiet nudge out the door by people who think it would do me some good, people who aren't sure that a grown person practicing trumpet exercises and reading and writing for hours every day is working. Early on, I noticed the rolled eyeballs when I took summer courses rather than accepting her father's offer of a full-time job cleaning office buildings at night that would have eliminated my parking lot job that eked us by during the school year.

"And besides," Mae says, "we might not be able to find anything as good as this place when you get out of school." She never seems to absorb the plain fact that after graduation I'm sure to be drafted.

My books and a couple lamps were the heaviest things we had to move. A gas range and an old frigidaire come with the apartment. It's the middle of my junior year. The family digs up a used bed and chest of drawers for us. We eat lots of rice and beans and have no record player or television set, but reading and study are easy, and in the bathroom with a mute I practice my horn, sometimes in the bathtub, without disturbing the house.

Maybe it's the water makes me think about the ocean of air we live in the way fish live in water. Everything depending on it. I breath in, my blood gets oxygenated and whips around my body, I'm alive. But more than that, I take in air and sculpture it into sounds through my horn and nothing feels better.

Mae's father has a five-passenger Chevy coupe that he doesn't need any longer and he offers to sell it to me. Some transportation would be a good idea. "I'll let you have it for a hundred and fifty dollars."

"I haven't got the money."

"You can get it down at the finance company," he says. "Go down there and talk to them."

Sure enough, down at City Finance they give me the money that I will later squeeze out to them in twelve fifteen-dollar payments.

After work, Mae often goes to her parents' house where I pick her up after finishing at the parking lot. She eats dinner there, helps her mother around the house and watches television. Near the end of the school year she says, "I'm tired of going over to mother's all the time after work. We need to get a television set."

"What with?" I say.

She plops herself at the kitchen table, elbows on it, cheeks between the heels of her hands. When she comes straight home from work, there's that time after she has had something to eat, the light chores are done and she has taken a soak. The people downstairs have a television set, but we saw right away that we would do best to keep a polite distance from them. The guy is about thirty, medium height, very dark and good-looking but edgy and shy acting. She has a blank yellow face with a few freckles and sounds as if she came from deep in the heart of Louisiana or Texas. We begin to hear him come in drunk some Saturday afternoons or nights and beat her and curse at her until he gets tired and things go silent. A lot of this takes place while their television set is on.

"You could make some money working for Daddy," Mae says.

"What?" This is a hookup she knows I'm leery of.

"You could make some money working for Daddy. You'll be out for the summer pretty soon, and he's going to need somebody to fill in for Uncle Charles when he goes on vacation."

That's how we became owners of a Sylvania television set. During school spring vacation, Mae's father arranged a shift for me in a downtown building that began at ten-thirty, after I finished at the parking lot, and ended at four-thirty in the morning. I pushed brooms, emptied wastebaskets, mopped, and buffed floors for ten days while her uncle vacationed in Louisiana. Mr Dupree slapped some extra onto my pay, "a little bonus" he said. "Yeah, boy, you a good worker," he said. "You could make some money in this business."

I said, "Thank you." He was cool when I didn't have anything to say about the work. Old Man Dupree is the stolid sort, the kind to cool it and wait for opportunity to come to him. I couldn't tell him how such work cramped my style, sucking up practice time and energy, and that I would never settle for it for any amount of money.

***

From working at The Horn Studio, I'm feeling more solid in the gut than ever, more power, and more fluent. Still, there's a simmering discomfort from the feeling that things keep happening to me, that I'm not really making things happen. I'm going to school and I've got my music, but this other stuff keeps pushing in, a discordant theme in my story, pushing against what I think is naturally growing in me, and which I'm trying to cultivate. I see it now. Starting with Sylvia difficulties. But the music didn't die. Falling into marriage pushes against my expansion. There's the car, then the apartment before I even have a real job. Then some work for Mae's father with that jivy bonus. The theme got to be major the afternoon I was looking for something in the top drawer of our chest of drawers and happened upon Mae's green plastic diaphragm case. Idle curiosity, I flipped it open and saw that the diaphragm had a neat slit across its diameter.

4)

The baby arrives a couple months before I graduate, rendering my body draft exempt. And numb. There it was, a baby boy, Mae happy. When I found that sabotaged diaphragm, it was already too late. I complained like hell and she went into a crying fit.

"Congratulations," people say. Mae and her family show him off at church, little Raleigh, named after an uncle of Mae. The diaper and bottle stuff crowds my time but feels natural though dissonant. You have to take care of a baby.

Mae has quit her library job to be home with the baby. With summer coming on, we figure we can make it until I start my teaching job in the fall if I do some summer work for her father. My juice is running low, though. Mae is all wrapped up in motherhood and doesn't pick up on much outside of that. I have to quit The Horn Studio and don't take out my horn much at the apartment. My thesis project, twenty pages on James Joyce as a poet, is past due, and I'm down to not caring whether I graduate or not when the head of the English department stops me outside the commons. He's a short, fat, peppery German, Professor Ehelebe, a Walt Whitman specialist. "Listen here, Mr Birdsong," he says, "you know you're more than two weeks overdue on that thesis project, don't you?"

"Yes, I guess so." My eyes won't come up to his.

"You guess so. Well, I think this is getting ridiculous. Don't you?"

"Sorry."

Air whooshes into his nostrils. "Sorry won't get it done, young man. I don't know what your problem is but I do know you could do the thing in a week if you wanted to. Now if you don't get it in to me by next week, I'm going to have to take action." He gives his briefcase a downward shake and walks off.

Panic yawns in my stomach and spreads upward, the first noticeable feeling I've had in a month beyond a low cooking lust for Margaret Strom who is probably inside the commons right now, waiting to have the coffee we scheduled. Ehelebe's attack was embarrassing, people passing by, looking. The man acted like he was really angry. All red in the face. He can hold up my graduation, and the school district has already hired me to teach next year, contingent upon my diploma. If I don't finish up things here, what a mess. Mae's father would no doubt be happy to give me a permanent job, but no, no, no, I ain't pushing that plow.

Margaret is at a table with a cup of coffee, zoned in on her copy of *Middlemarch.* I buy a coffee and join her. "Hi, Margaret. Sorry I'm late."

She takes off her glasses, puts her hands over her closed eyes and gives them a gentle rub with her fingertips. She draws her hands away and opens. Margaret's eyes are a blue you could fall into. "Don't worry about it, Joe," she says. "How are you?"

The English teacher speech that she's got already sends my imagination working overtime. We've talked easily and with heat about our studies. She knows I'm married, but we've never had time to talk about that. I can see all kinds of things swimming around in her eyes beyond her intelligence and habit of modesty. One thing I see swimming around is sympathy.

"Margaret, do you mind if I tell you the truth?"

"Why no, Joe. Of course not." She picks up her glasses and slides them back on.

"Well, Margaret, to tell you the truth I'm about at the end of my rope. I don't know what's the matter with me. I feel like I've run out of gas, or something. Most of the time, lately, I feel like flicking it all in. Everything. Starting with school. And I just got chewed out by Ehelebe. I haven't handed in my paper, you know. He practically threatened me."

"Threatened you?"

"He said if I didn't have it in to him by next week he was going to take action."

"I suppose he could hold up your diploma."

"Yes, he could. And the thing is I almost don't give a hoot. I've been feeling like walking away from the whole thing."

Her hand falls on my forearm, jostles it. I keep my eyes on the table. "Joe, you can't be serious," she says. "You're one of the very best students in the department. And you've already got a job for next year, right?"

"If I graduate." Her hand stays on my arm, fingers pressing. If anybody has a problem with that, it's just too bad. Her eyes barrel into my problem, whatever it is. I pull my chair in closer. "Margaret, I feel exhausted, like I've run out of gas but not necessarily physically, but in a way so that doing anything physically doesn't make any sense. Everything feels empty. Do you think I'm going nuts? Gone nuts?"

She draws back her hand, but her eyes stay on mine. Heat from her palm stays on my forearm.

"Don't be silly, Joe. Listen, I want to help you."

"Help me?"

"Yes. You know you were so much help to me on my paper." It is true she got her thesis idea from me, "Considerations Surrounding Desdemona's Marriage to the Blackamoor." She's been done with it for three weeks. "How far along are you?" she says. "You said you were almost done the last time I asked you."

"That's right, I am. I've got it all written out. I just need to give it a good proofreading, organize the footnotes and type it up. About twenty-four pages."

"Why don't you do the proofreading and the footnotes and then give it to me to type."

"I can't let you do that."

Her fingers on my forearm again. "Yes you can. I've got everything done and I have the time. I know you're a good typist, but so am I. I also know you must have a lot of things on your mind about now, with a new baby and all."

These last words come with a shiny new-baby smile, happiest damn thing she can imagine. But Margaret feels like a real friend, aside from any doggish fumes in my head, and I ain't about to be protesting against no such manna from Heaven. Me, man, on last legs in the damn desert?

"Well, thanks for the offer, Margaret. It really would be a big help right now."

She puts her hand on my forearm again. "I can see that," she says.

The black Ford pulls in a half-hour before I would shut down the lot for the night. I walk out and find Margaret Strom behind the wheel. Shameful imaginings flare along with the surprise of seeing her, imaginings that melt whatever restraints I might be supposed to have. "Margaret, what are you doing here?"

She laughs. "I hope you don't greet all your customers that way, Joe."

"Sorry. It's just such a surprise to see you, a pleasant surprise. I didn't know you had a car."

"It's my dad's car. I thought I'd better get this paper back to you today since I won't be at school tomorrow. Do you want me to park?"

"Oh sure, but you'll have to let me park it." I open the car door. She moves to get out, but I say, "You don't have to get out, just scoot over."

She sets the emergency brake, picks up the papers beside her on the seat and slides to the passenger side. I get in and drive up the slight asphalt incline of the lot to a space away from the street where I have a clear view of the shack. Going on ten o'clock, the street is quiet. I shut off the ignition and hand her the keys.

"Thank you, sir," she says.

"It's me who should be doing the thanking. You brought me my paper already?"

"I promised it to you tomorrow, but I won't be at school."

It's shadowy in the car, but light from the street reveals the shine in her eyes, looking at me. There's a shine on her lower lip too. My face must appear about the same way to her. Eyes shiny, mouth half open, almost panting, gasping a little as I speak. "Margaret, I can never thank you enough for typing this thing for me." I touch the folder in her lap.

"It's not necessary, Joe. I got a lot of pleasure out of reading it and learned a few things about James Joyce too."

"Ah, Margaret." I pick up her hand and kiss the back of it. Margaret has, I've observed, as now, a way of studying things with her lower lip drawn slightly back, mouth half-open, not committed to frown or smile. She withdraws her hand into her lap, watching me in that way of hers. "Look, Joe," she says, "I'm sure you understand that I like you a lot as a friend. I'm sorry if I've misled you into thinking something more has been in my mind. Well, even if, to tell the truth, things have passed through my head, I know it would be foolish to cling to them. I've never known anyone quite like you before, and it's true that I've been excited by that and by the opportunity to communicate with you."

"You mean you've never known a colored guy before?"

"Well, yes. But that's not the first thing I think of when I think about you."

"Really?"

"Really, Joe. What has always struck me with you is our common enthusiasm for literature."

Her words take me back to the piano bench, sitting beside Sylvia wrapped in our common enthusiasm for music. Margaret could be Sylvia.

"Yes, we do seem to have a lot in common literarily," I say. "Do you enjoy music, Margaret?"

"Yes, I do. Very much," she says. "I don't play all that well but I've had years of piano lessons.

I take her hand again and study her fingers, long and pale in the dark car. She doesn't draw it back.

"You're a musician, I know," she says. "A friend of mine plays clarinet in the symphonic ensemble—she says you're very good."

"What's her name?"

"Laurie Flowers. Short blond, long hair. She's a biology major."

"Yes, I know who she is." I have noticed her friend among the clarinets.

Margaret squeezes my hand and slides hers from my grip. "You really are a nice guy, Joe, and so talented, and I'm grateful to have made contact with you, but I intend to keep my wits about me."

She clasps her hands before her chest.

"Wits about you." Bumping against the wall of Margaret's words and body control, my wits are a bunch of spooked mice.

"That's right, Joe," she's saying. "I'm a normal twenty-one-year-old woman and I have emotions, but I haven't been going to school for nothing."

"I have noticed that fact." The overwhelming thing I first noticed about Margaret was her quick grasp of the structure of things, and I could see her easily taking apart any little project I might have in mind.

"Yes, I'm very interested in thinking and when I think about what you seemed to have in mind just now, all I get is confusion."

No use in jiving with Margaret. Her words are heavy and true.

"There's no reason for either of us to complicate things, Joe. I'm about to get my bachelor's degree in a subject I absolutely love and go work on my master's next year. From all I've ever read or understood, for us to get involved would be wrong, and in addition to that, it would be stupid." She unclasps her hands, takes my hand between hers, jiggles it, and says, "You can see that, can't you?"

Talk about feeling reduced. Or maybe it was that she kept growing as she laid out the A B Cs for me. Talk about feeling like a tinhorn, a half-ass kazoo blower.

"Yes, I can see it. You're right, Margaret, but at least you know how I feel about you."

Her fingertip brushes across my nose and my lips. "Shush," she says. She opens the glove compartment and fishes out a Kleenex and dabs the corner of each eye. We sit in the dark quiet like at the end of a movie where you might feel stunned for a moment but clear about what you just experienced.

"Well, sir, before we got sidetracked," she says, "I was going to present you with this. You know, you should seriously consider becoming an English professor, Joe." She hands me the folder that has been in her lap with my thesis paper in it.

The feelings that rush into my chest for the favor she's done me are more than I can tell her. I think she gets it when I look hard into her eyes and say, "Thank you, Margaret. You're a life-saver."

With Margaret's push and first aid, I graduate. She got a fellowship at a college in the Midwest to study for a master's degree in English. Impossible to have such an idea in my situation, married with a kid already, grounded, in a fulltime job, army time hanging over me if I weren't married with a kid. Margaret left me with a low-burning longing, agitated, or agitated longing. As in "left behind" from a possibly defining enterprise.

Stacy

1)

English teacher at Calvin Coolidge High School: People told me because I looked eighteen years old and was colored that my chances of landing a high school teaching job in Portland were scanty. There were only two colored high school teachers in the district. But it was a time of teacher shortage, and I was hired because my student-teaching went well and, I think, because I was a strong French minor. In a pinch, I could fill in for a French teacher. I put a suit on layaway and wouldn't be dressing like anybody's kid. I always thought I would get a job, not that I'm a big believer in justice, but I've started to notice that being a misfit, sometimes irregular stuff comes my way that's not so bad.

A few weeks after school started, my sometime teacher at The Horn Studio called me. "Do you know that City Arts Opera Company rehearses at that school where you're teaching?" he said.

"Nope, didn't know that. I'm still finding my way around the place."

"Well, look, they need a trumpet player over there, and I told the manager about you. It's not a paying gig, but it'll be good for your chops."

"How often do they rehearse?"

"One night a week. Thursdays, I think."

"Sounds cool enough."

"Go see them."

"I shall. Thanks, Jim." And that's how I hooked up with the opera company orchestra. They were beginning work on the score for Gounod's *Faust*.

"Opera?" Mae laughed and bounced the baby on her lap. "What do you want to do that for?" she said.

"It'll give me a chance to keep up my playing. I am a musician, you know." Mae had experience with a lot of my practicing but she'd never heard me stretch out in performance. Her response to music of any kind is about the quietest I've ever seen. In church she sings straight and quiet from the hymnal.

"Are they going to pay you?" she said.

"No. This isn't a paying job."

"Then why do it?"

"Why do it?"

"Yes."

"Because like I just told you, it'll give me a chance to keep up my playing." The other half of the truth is that I love to play. Most of the time I think it's my only hope for keeping my marbles.

"And you'll be out every Thursday night."

"That's when they rehearse. Seven to ten."

"I thought you had stopped playing."

"What made you think that?"

"I never heard you practice all summer." It was true because for most of the summer I was working for her father and at the parking lot about thirteen hours a day. No buzzing my lips, feeling the mouth-piece, no air rushing into my nostrils, filling my torso so that I could fill the horn with sound—without all that, I had to remind myself what my name was.

A few times on Sundays, while the family was at church, I took out the horn, took some deep breaths that got me into myself.

"You didn't hear me practice because I was working so damn much. And did you notice how depressed I was?"

"You don't have to curse."

"Well, there wasn't a whole lot of time for practice last summer, or for playing a gig."

"I don't know why you want to be running out of here at night, instead of spending time with your family, not getting paid for it."

"Maybe it's because the music is more important than money."

"I don't know what you mean by that," she said. "Poor as we are. Can't hardly afford to go anyplace."

"One thing I mean is I'm going to do it. It might keep me from going crazy."

Mae's instincts weren't wrong. Working in the silence of my classroom after school, reading and checking papers until the start of rehearsal was a big refreshing inhale, a time to mull my situation and stray in dreams. Mae and I weren't growing closer after the baby, even after I'd got what everyone seemed to think was a good job. Working with kids, teaching English classes, was all right, but we were broke before the end of every month. Our bargain rent, payments on the TV set and car, and the usual household stuff leveled us every month. Money might have been part of our problem, but I could see that I could be earning five times as much as I was earning and still feel as if I were getting nowhere. Mae enjoyed the idea of more and better furniture, but having more stuff and better stuff never seemed to me like something to work my ass off for. She dreamed of having a house, too, something that never took shape in my thoughts. What did begin to take shape was a sound out there and that feeling I sometimes got a taste of, in practice or performing. Contact with City Arts Opera and the chance to play regularly felt like the arrival of better weather, the possibility of sunshine.

***

I'm sitting out in the middle of the empty auditorium during a rehearsal break, checking papers, when this dark-haired young woman moves into the row, her thighs rubbing past laminated wooden seatbacks. Ponytailed white girl, looks twenty or so, carrying a thick black book. I've noticed her in a couple crowd scenes in Act Two and Act Four. Light, audible rubbing all the way down the row to where she slides into a seat four or five away from me and sinks into reading her book. There wasn't time to finish the papers in my classroom so I'm doing them now, until the young woman's friction jerked at my sensors. A quick eyeball to the book spine: *e.e. cummings* in white letters.

At break time the next Thursday I'm sitting in the same seat. Girl's thick, shapely body comes down the side aisle and enters the row, *e.e. cummings* in her hands. A wise-guy smirk tilts her lips as she rubs along the seats, closer and closer. I should yell "Boo," see if she spooks, but I don't. Two seats from me, she sits, places the book on her lap, and exhales.

"Hi," she says. "Same scene as last week." Her caramel-colored eyes play at my knees.

"Yes, it seems that way, except that this week I'm not checking papers."

She giggles. "You a teacher?"

"Yes, I am."

"I'm sorry, sir, but you look too young to be a teacher."

The fake "sir" gives her some kind of age edge. A mist of perspiration she probably can't see dampens my forehead, causing a pinpoint itch, but I keep my hands folded in my lap to maybe look older.

"People do say that," I tell her. "It's my first year."

"Where do you teach?"

"Right here."

"Here? At Coolidge?" She taps a finger on the *e.e. cummings* in her lap.

"That's right, luckily. If the company didn't rehearse here, I wouldn't be playing."

"So you teach music? You're sure a groovy trumpet player," she says. She flicks her hand toward the orchestra pit. "I've been listening."

The girl's words sail out with a jivy liquidity not like anything I've heard offstage. A different key from Sylvia's emotional modesty or Margaret Strom's diction. She could be a crazy talker, or maybe just daring.

Groovy. I keep my facial stretch down to Aw shucks and say, "I teach English."

"Oh, really?"

"Yes. At the college they had a symphonic band but no real music department. I enjoy reading, so I majored in English and minored in French." Let her think about that.

"Oh, *oui, oui*, English is my favorite subject," she says. "My mother used to be an English teacher."

"Ah. Is that so?" Mother not around anymore. Dead, perhaps. Sometimes I feel like a fatherless child. I am a fatherless child. Our father who art not... I ride herd on my voice that it isn't too loud or harsh. "I noticed your book. May I have a look at it?"

She gets up and sidesteps to the seat next to me, puts the book in my hands. In high school, Sylvia and I discovered a couple cummings poems that made us feel as if we knew something, and at college I went through a period of cummings love, that now looks like a pitiful attempt to restore my lost equilibrium. In the girl's book I find the page of "somewhere I have never traveled." She doesn't try to keep her upper arm from pressing warm skin against my shirtsleeve, leaning across to see, a touching that puts a trill in the air next to my ear. "Do you know this one?" I say.

"No, I don't think so."

"Listen." I read a couple stanzas to her, falling into the smooth *sotto voce* music of the lines which purls between us in the high hollow of the auditorium. She ought to be able to handle it, coming in with this big book two weeks in a row.

"You really like it, don't you?" she says.

I set the book in the girl's lap and say, "Thank you. Yes, I really like it."

She sits back and rests her hands on the book, lips together, silent, eyes eating into the space before her longish nose. The snap of the conductor's baton against the podium signals "places".

Getting up, we brush arms. "What's your name?" she says.

"The name is Birdsong, Joe Birdsong. What's yours?"

"Stacy. Stacy Kuhn. K-u-h-n."

In my classroom a half-hour before rehearsal, I push the stack of student journals aside, done reading them. The custodian swept through B Wing two hours ago. Except for my room, B Wing is deserted, and it's time for a deep quiet inhale before moving into rehearsal noise. I take out my horn and blow long tones and some lip slurs. *Pianissimo.* A knock on the door interrupts my chromatic runs, light knuckles. I hop over and open it.

Stacy Kuhn stands there, white arms shining out of her sleeveless dress, a twisty smile just below the skin of her face. I blink and swallow a couple times. It is true that during the week the memory of her arm touching mine in the auditorium seats, the trilling air next to my ear, and her eyes lit by the cummings poem, came to me a few times. Her naked arm sparkles against the dark cover of the book. She carries a pink sweater and the book.

"Hello. I was early so I thought I'd see where you work. Am I interrupting?" She takes a step back.

"Oh no. No. Come on in." She moves close enough that I inhale the scent of her hair and body, which sets off a chain of calculations I couldn't classify as thought. Taking the quietest deep breath I can manage, I shut the door and switch off the lights. We can still see one another in the faint outside light that comes through the windows.

"Oh." Her sound carries the tonic security of the words *I see*.

She lays her sweater and book on a desk and extends her arms to me. I set my horn on her sweater. We kiss and tongue and rub against each other, move into shadow by the filing cabinet where she hikes up her dress and turns to brace herself.

Every Thursday until the orchestra finishes rehearsing *Faust*, Stacy Kuhn slips through my classroom door a few minutes after six o'clock, and we repeat the filing cabinet dance. During rehearsal breaks, we sit and talk crazy about the opera's plot, joke about the conductor's frown and his cursing in German, which she understands, I find out, when she tells me she spent several of her early years in Germany where her mother taught English and was married to an army captain.

"Was wunchen Sie zu essen?" I say, fooling at the limit of my few German phrases.

"*Sie,* huh?" she says. "Sounds to me as if you could use a lttle help with your *Deutsch, Mein Herr.*" She rattled it off in German first and then translated for me, looking me in the eye in a way that slammed the door on my playing at German.

She says she works in a used bookstore in Sellwood, in far southeast Portland. When she discovers that I like Emily Dickinson's poems she brings me an old paperback selection of Dickinson. In the car, under the street light outside her mother's apartment, I read to her from the book.

Stacy makes herself comfortable against the passenger door, eyes closed, and listens to me pour the great Emily's verses over her. Mere existence feels so *understood* here in the car. My detachment from what people would call my responsibilities—I seem to exist like a spectator of it. Mae hasn't given sign of noticing anything yet. I close the book, thinking about when we might do this again, and try to impress the girl by reciting a few of the Dickinson poems lodged in my head. Stacy lets out a long breath, opens her eyes, puts one arm around me and eases the fingers of her other hand through my hair. "How come you're so interested in poetry, J.B.?" She has taken to calling me JB, sometimes John the Baptist.

"How interested am I? You seem pretty interested yourself."

"Yeah, but you seem majorly interested. More interested than any-body I know."

I could have said the same words about her, said how I've never felt so word-comfortable with anyone. Stacy, some kind of natural. "Well, let me remind you that I am a certified teacher of English," I tell her. "It's a part of my job."

"Yeah, but you seem more interested than that. I think it's in your blood." Margaret suggested Birdsong as English professor.

"Yuh know I got black blood in me, dontcha?"

"Stop. Don't go stupid on me," she says.

Then: "You know, you really are one spooky guy. Cold enough to make money haunting houses if you gave up crippling young minds—and why don't you play jazz?"

I pull back, let the "cold" remark slide. One of Mae's complaints. Stacy sees what's wrong with me. So what.

I say, "Now what do you know about jazz? You think just because I'm colored I should be playing jazz?"

"No, no, you know better than that. But I do hear a lot of it—Stan Kenton, Dave Brubeck, Count Basie, Miles Davis. My mother listens to it."

"Oh really?"

"It seems like something you might do. Like poetry."

"Do you find something wrong with my trumpet playing, Miss Kuhn?"

"No, no, now don't get testy. You know you play great. I was just wondering why you don't play jazz. You seem like you've got it in you."

Jesus.

Playing what I play got me a lot of attention, though, all through school. More than the sports that I played as a diluted version of my big brother. Got me love, too. Got me three years of band and orchestra with Sylvia, got us all kinds of precious moments at the school piano where she demystified the keyboard for me.

Stacy's remarks showed me something, though, projected a me looking different from the way I thought I looked.

Stacy lives in a big apartment building downtown by the stadium with her mother, Audrey. "We fight all the time," she says. "I hate her. Her ritzy family disowned her for screwing herself up, drinking like a fish. I don't see much of them. She's got a colored boyfriend, too, a married guy named Eugene that's got a place on the coast where they go to drink and screw on weekends. He's got a laundry business. The only good thing she ever did was name me after Eustacia Vye. You know Eustacia?"

"Sure. She's a Hardy girl, in *The Return of the Native*."

"I like my name."

"I like it too. It's got four beats in it."

"I give it three," she says.

"Boom-BOOM-boom," I say. "Cool enough."

The first time I go up to their apartment with Stacy, and Stacy introduces me, Audrey has a couple drinks in her. "Oh, Stace, he's a doll," she says.

She puts her hand on my shoulder, massages my upper arm. Audrey is tall with dark reddish brown hair like Stacy's and skin still working, thirty-eight years old, Stacy told me. She's leaner than Stacy and doesn't have her daughter's generous chest and *Birth of Venus* middle parts or fresh complexion. Audrey pats my cheek and puckers her lips, but Stacy jumps between us, bumps me backward with her butt into my crotch, and gets nose to nose with her mother. The air around her body gets cold. She snarls, "You keep your hands off of him."

Her mother wavers back a step and, hands on hips, says, "Well, listen to you, Miss High and Mighty Seventeen-Year-Old."

Audrey spat out the number, a hardball smack against my forehead, aimed at Stacy. I try to keep a neutral face while seeing stars and attempting to swallow.

Stacy's words bite the air. "You're just a real bitch, aren't you."

In the hall, she says, "Well?"

I say, "God damn, Stacy. What in the hell do you think you're doing? You're a high school student, aren't you—I thought you were at least twenty. You could get me hanged with what we've been doing. Why didn't you tell me how old you were? How the hell old are you, anyway?"

"You didn't ask me, JB. You heard her. I'm seventeen." The hall is empty, but for some reason we're whispering.

"Jesus H. Christ, what am I supposed to do now?"

She moves against me, arms around my waist, cheek against mine. "You're supposed to realize I love you, JB."

"We can't keep doing this. My wife is going to get suspicious sooner or later."

"Yeah, JB, you never told me you were married when we got together, and I've never seen a wedding ring on you."

It's true I don't wear a ring. I have one, but rings or metal watchbands make me itch and cramp. A nice loud Bach partita would help put this mess in order. Stacy, so seasoned. I take her hand and hold it against my cheek.

"You're not mad at me?" She says.

"No, not really. I'm more pissed off at myself. This is insane."

Silence, and then she says, "Listen, JB, I'm going to be eighteen in two-and-a-half months and out of school. You don't have much to worry about."

"Easy for you to say, baby." We've never talked about the fact that I'm married and have a kid. We've never talked about what we're doing together. We've never talked about the older guys I saw picking her up after rehearsal before we got together. And now this. Still, her flesh against me and breath next to my face, her eyes and her voice, push back questions that don't seem to need talking about. And the girl has been writing things like *Boy, you/don't know how/the Woman in the Moon boogies/when you're not watching* on pieces of paper that she slips into my pockets. Inside my trumpet case, I found a page from the little notebook she carries

j the Baptist,
my brown
bear
whose black
tongue finds
honey
in my trunk
, so that
i spill at
the least push
of yr hairy
paw
, so that
at yr slightest growl
i come

2)

People waiting for the musicians sit in the shadow of the balcony over-hang and watch the orchestra rehearse. They're too far away from the orchestra pit for me to make out features or to identify their clothing, but a figure sitting in the back row could be Mae, judging from size and contour. If she would move, I could be sure, but the figure sits motion-less. At home, I've had the feeling that she's laying extra eyes on me. If I'm stuck late at school, she's got questions she didn't used to have. And she has never been able to swallow the idea of my playing in the opera company orchestra for nothing. I've accepted that we've got some antipodal ideas about life that have caused my feelings for the marriage to go flat. If I felt the same way about music, I wouldn't be able to play my horn. I wouldn't be surprised to see Mae pop up anywhere about now. Pop out from under the manhole cover outside Stacy's apartment. Something told her having a baby would solve some kind of problem for her. Somebody might have given her some bad advice. She might have done better to ask me a few questions. My stomach jiggles like an egg yolk. Stacy and I had better not sit face to face or side by side, bumping our gums and nodding toward each other during the break that's coming up.

Break time arrives and Stacy motions me to the edge of the stage. "I've got to go to the little girls room," she says. "I'll meet you out front in a few minutes."

She heads for relief before I can say anything. The temptation rises to take a hike to the boys lavatory and stay there, tell Stacy I was feeling ill, but the next time I look toward the rear of the auditorium, the figure is gone. I don't say anything to Stacy about it.

Lights are on in the apartment when I pull up to the curb, following a late session in the car with Stacy. Mae is usually in bed asleep at this time, but tonight she's at the kitchen table, smoking. Kitchen full of smoke, three jammed-out butts in the ashtray. Beside the ashtray a wrinkled notebook page with Stacy's writing on it that was once in one of my pockets. Mae's eyes are red behind puffy, slitted lids. She should be in bed. No chance for me to bathe, get the Stacy smell and fever off me, get connected with the floor before Mae walks over and puts her face against my chest. She sucks in a fast breath, steps back and smacks me across the ear and jaw with her open hand. A head turner, that burns and rings in my ear. Might have to go to school tomorrow looking lopsided.

What happened to your jaw, Mr Birdsong? You in a fight?

My wife socked me.

Tee hee.

He said his wife socked him.

"You dog," Mae says. "Just what do you think you're doing now?"

"Dog!" Our ears are so far apart. My own, haywire at hearing somebody seriously snarl *dog. Je m'appelle Dog.* And I hear Charles Laughton, rasping, *Mr Christian, you're a mutinous dog.* Very fine in the old movie.

I move my jaw against my palm, checking the hinge, and say, "Doing?"

Mae is five inches shorter than I, but when her eyes flip haywire, like now, all considerations of dimension evaporate. The girl has ripped pajamas off me more than once when worked up, and now has my shirt front twisted in her mitts about to tear. Her lips push out into a tight little megaphone: *"Doing!* Yes, *doing!* Don't try to play dumb with me, Joe. You see what I been finding in your pockets." She whips her hand toward the table. Pieces of paper from my pockets. "All that nasty writing. I know something is going on. It's somebody in that music thing, isn't it?"

She wrenches more shirt into her grip. "Isn't it?" she says. "Look at you, coming in here smelling like you been out—out fucking, or I don't know what."

My eyes, side to side, don't pick up any hardware within reach that Mae might forget herself with. Ashtray plastic and too small. Mae has never hit me with anything, but we've never gotten this far before. Deep breath in, trying to get some kind of purchase on the situation. When the oxygen hits my brain, I remember how Mae didn't even know the word *fuck* when we first got together, though she'd done it. She said, "Funk me." I was greener, but I had beaucoup vocabulary.

Her grip strains the buttonholes and threatens to ruin a good shirt, and I'm ready to tell any kind of lie to get her off me. "I'm sorry, Mae. I'm sorry. I made a bad mistake."

Another try to breathe myself back to earth, to be serious, but when the oxygen arrives this time it's the back-home voice of Kayakaw kids: "Lyin' poor monkey and your feet smell funky."

Mae gives up her grip on my shirt and shoves me into the wall. My trumpet case butts the plaster loud enough it could have wakened the baby or the couple downstairs. She crouches back to the table with her eyes burning on me. She could spring at my lying throat or rip me with a left hook like one of those New Jersey lightweights on the Gillette Friday night fights, but she sits down and takes a cigarette from her pack of Viceroys and tamps the unfiltered end on her thumbnail. Couldn't get her to quit. She thumbs her lighter alive and starts the cigarette. All Mae wants is to be comfortable, relaxed and smoking in a little nest where she can fuss over babies, curtains and rugs, keep house, and go to church on Sundays. Zounds, man! The picture turns me to ice.

Before she says anything, Mae tightens her lips around the filter, takes a deep drag and lets smoke out toward my face. "Well," she says, "what are you planning to do?"

"Get through my first year of teaching" is the formulation that doesn't reach the tip of my tongue.

"Do?" I say out loud.

She takes a long, sniffing breath through her nose and lets it out. Her cheeks redden. Her free hand doubles into a fist on the table. "Listen here, Mr Man, after what you been pulling, don't think you're going to just march back in this place like nothing happened."

My face is still tender where my fingers touch, and there's sneezy weather around my head from her smoke. "I said I was sorry."

"No you're not," she says. "You need to talk to Reverend Bell."

Mae sees the truth about me not being sorry, something wrong with me, she thinks, but she thinks I can be fixed.

"Listen, Mae, you might as well forget about me talking to Reverend Bell. I ain't talking to nobody's ding dong preacher."

Her head jerks up at me, her mouth shocked half open. The Devil pushes me to go for the full opener. "What in the hell would I want to talk to Reverend Bell for? And what in the hell can he tell me? Get down on my knees and pray 'cause I been a bad boy. People can believe what they want to believe. Believe whatever you want to believe, but let me tell you I had enough of that Come to Jesus stuff a long time ago and I ain't interested in hearing any more of it. I stopped believing in Santa Claus when I was eight years old." My eyes pop wide, strain with my outburst. I press them shut. Sweat runs down into my eyebrows.

Mae jams her cigarette into the ashtray and throws her head onto her crossed arms, bawling, tears running across a forearm and puddling on the table. I take in as much air as my lungs will hold.

The tear tracks on her face when she raises it look like lacerations. "You ought to be ashamed of yourself," she's saying now. "I can't stand to look at you. You don't believe in nothing, and I wish you would just take your behind out of my house."

First night back in my cousin's basement, wide-eyed awake, can't blow my horn, I sit for hours scribbling designs on notebook paper, pages and pages cover the bed. If I could read my markings from all this motion, I might understand something, but I can't. I do understand one thing: I'm eligible for the draft.

My note to the draft board in Kayakaw:
"To Whom It May Concern:
This letter is to inform you that I am no longer living with my wife and that in due time I expect to be divorced. Sincerely, Josephus Alexander Birdsong."
Army must have needed more cotton pickers in a hurry because my note hardly has time to hit the bottom of the mailbox before I get an answer, telling me to report for induction in two weeks. True, I'm ready to escape into the army, get in there, find out how far gone I am, and reorganize myself while things settle down locally, but I hadn't contemplated being sluiced away so fast. My principal, a survivor from the second wave of marines onto Okinawa ("The guys on either side of me got it"), looks at the induction notice and restores me somewhat with his words: "Don't worry, Mr Birdsong, we'll get you off at least until the end of the school year."

***

Stacy gets drafted for a minor male role in *The Abduction from the Seraglio,* a Mozart *singspiel,* the company's next production. She's one of the small chorus of janissaries that follow the protagonist around. She's an alto so can sing tenor parts and in uniform makes a pretty cute chap. *Seraglio* will be my last trumpet gig before I go into the army, light duty percussive stuff.

Her graduation exercises come up just before school lets out while we're still rehearsing *Seraglio,* and she says, "Audrey isn't going to be there. Will you come?"

Studying her eyes, I see they are dry and that we both understand the wound from life's irrationality is so deep we don't need to talk about it. "Sure, Baby, I'll come."

Toward the middle of the alphabet, Stacy crosses the stage in her red robe, receives her diploma, and waves it at the crowd, at me. She is eighteen years old and out of high school.

3)

"Now that school is out," Mae says over the phone, "maybe you could find a little time for your son. You haven't bothered to see him since you left, you know. It's been four months. He's walking now." She's past railing and crying, but I can tell the woman is still a Christian incendiary, and I watch each word I say. The boy is walking who was a fixed lump of healthy babyhood, and he must be saying a few words.

"Is he talking too?"

"He says a few words."

"That's good."

"Listen," she says, "why don't you pick him up at mother's one of these afternoons and spend some time with him. You don't have a summer job yet, do you?"

"No, not exactly. And yeah, why don't I pick him up and take him to the park. The wading pool ought to be open."

"No, you keep him out of that water. I don't want him going in the water."

"Well okay, whatever you say."

"Can you do it this Wednesday afternoon," she says. "Say two o'clock? You can keep him an hour or two."

"Sure, I can do that. Pick him up at your folks' place?"

"That's right."

Her words are a curt burst that still wait for an answer, perhaps, an explanation from me of whatever happened to us. If I knew how to explain, I would tell her.

I say, "Hey, I haven't told you, Mae, but it looks like I'll be leaving for the army in a few weeks. I got a draft notice back in March, but the school district got me deferred till the end of the year."

She doesn't say anything. I'm about to ask if she's still there when she says, "So you'll be gone for a while."

"Yes, two years. You'll get an allotment check every month." Again, she takes a break. I picture her nostrils flattening with an angry inhale.

She says, "What is this I hear about you running around with some white girl?"

"What?"

"You heard me. Some of you guys need a good beating, and you're one of them. A couple of people have told me they heard you were running around with some white girl."

Wisecracks jam my circuits, ones that could get me in trouble, but I keep any of them from getting through. I say, "Wow, now there's some real hearsay. I don't know where that could have come from."

And I don't. No one except my cousins and Stacy's mother and her mother's boyfriend knows that Stacy and I spend any time together. Somebody must have got a glimpse of us cruising in my car, which we haven't done much, and usually at night.

"All you do is lie," she says. "You ought to be horse-whipped."

Dumb slave stuff, beating people with whips. Mean white men beating Negroes, got slaves thinking they should be treated that way. The image of a sweaty, dick thick whip handle rises between me and her, trying to choke me. My eyes burn. I could choke her for thinking and saying that. Her belief in the old-time shit, stuck in the old-time shit. Trying to make people behave, passing on your own self-hate. And Daddy, from down yonder too, he used to beat me and my brother for being bad. Me more than Zeke. When I got big enough, I was going to punch Daddy out. I strangle my voice again. "Okay. I'll pick Raleigh up at two on Wednesday."

Heat rises from the grass at the park. No clouds in the blue, so that where the boy and I play on a grassy slope near the camellias under which his mother and I first fiddled we can see Mount St Helens, covered with snow halfway down, and east of St Helens the white tip of Mt Adams peeps out of the Cascades. Adams—if I were in Kayakaw, two hundred miles away, standing at Second and Walnut streets where Sylvia and I walked that one time, I could see more of the mountain, the other side, white and blue in the distance.

Cold, impossible ahead
Lifts the mountain's lovely head

Here, there, elsewhere. Pretty soon I'll be someplace else. But I'm here on the grass, rocking baby boy in my lap and listening to him jabber. Every once in a while he touches my arm with his finger and says, "Dadduh."

We face Mount St Helens and I point to it and say, "Mount St Helens." He's bright-eyed, but I'm not sure he gets it. I have no memory of ever walking with Daddy. Busy on the job, he was, or working in the garden or studying the Bible.

We walk and toddle past rhododendrons and azaleas that stop us every few feet so that he can point to a red blossom and say, "Da."

I say, "Flower" each time, biting my lip on the f until he begins to say "Fowa."

The sight of the wading pool starts him toddling fast toward the water, but I hold him back. Several children his age, a couple in diapers, stand in the water near the pool's edge. I sit down and take off my shoes and then remove his. The sun is hot and things will dry out fast.

"Do you want to go in the water?" He starts toward the pool again. I catch him and guide him into the shallow part where we study wetness, and he pats the water before I deliver him back to his grandmother's house.

Brilliant Corners

1)

The audience claps long enough to let us think we weren't too rough on Mozart, singers up there onstage bowing and grinning. Next stop for me is Fort Ord, California, in three days. Then it's eight weeks of basic training. If I'm lucky, I might end up in an army band. One of my studio mates from The Horn Studio is doing his time in The Seventh Army Concert Band in Germany, right now. That would be some luck. Too cool. Over there, learning German.

This will be the first time I've stopped playing the horn since grade school. I open the spit valve and blow out the moisture. I've got to sell the horn because I'm so broke, mailing most of my paycheck to Mae. It's not a great instrument, and I've never had a really good trumpet, so my heart isn't breaking. Stacy is going to take care of selling it for me. I'll hang onto a couple mouthpieces. I'm betting my next horn will be an army one. People are putting away instruments and folding chairs, but I'm heavy in my seat until a hand touches my shoulder.

"Hey," she says. "The party's over."

"Oh, yeah, sorry. Sitting here daydreaming." I get up and put away my trumpet. Stacy's teeth and eyes shine. Music still surrounds her, garlands winding about her thighs and hips, her stomach, forms that I swear undo man's reason. In three days I'll be a few hundred miles away from her too, too solid flesh. There are still people around, but I sit back down and take her hand, tug on it. "It could be dreamy in a chair, Baby."

"JB, you are so bad. Get up, and let's go. I should report you."

"I don't give a shit."

2)

We creep out of my basement room after midnight with empty stomachs, light-headed and unwound, printed on each other, not ready to separate. "Why don't we go by The Porters Club and have a snack before I take you home?"

Going to The Porter's Club never seemed like a good idea before Stacy graduated and while she was seventeen. But she's out of school now, doesn't look like anybody's teenager with her size and in the clothes she has on, and the Porters Club is one place where I've seen mixed couples hanging out together. The woman who runs the café serves a light, creamy sweet potato pie at all hours. Stacy is all for the proposition. The veteran tone of her agreement causes me to ask, "You've been up there before?"

"A couple of times, with Audrey and her friends."

She doesn't look up from slipping into her shoes. I give my acceptance a casual, veteran tone. "Cool."

Somebody who knows me might be in the place and see me with Stacy and contribute to the rumor that reached Mae's ears, but so what. In three days I'm gone. And we're hungry.

The Porters Club is smoky and crowded with mostly colored people. We find a table against a wall on the café side and order two slices of sweet potato pie and tea. Brook Benton is crooning from the jukebox between the bar and the café. Stacy moves her shoulders and eats her pie in time with it. In a few minutes, though, a jazz tune comes on than which I have never heard anything more free, quirky and cool, that mocks my misery, I swear, tune saying Here's how you handle all this mess and don't care what any of y'all think.

I say, "Excuse me a minute," and walk over to the jukebox to discover "Brilliant Corners," by Thelonious Monk, Sonny Rollins on tenor saxophone.

At the jukebox, I also notice out of the corner of my eye one of my wife's brothers and two of his buddies, looking my way, a sizzling instant of contact between our glances. I walk back to the table filled with the punchy, eccentric pulse of "Brilliant Corners," six eye prints on my back.

"Have you ever heard this tune before," I ask Stacy.

"I don't think so, but it sounds like it could be Thelonious Monk."

"Jesus, how did you know that?"

Her eyes fall upon me full of sympathy for the hick. "Listen to how weird it sounds," she says. "I told you Audrey and whatshisname listen to jazz all the time." Audrey and Whatshisname, we might have run into them in the place. Might have been all right. The air is thick enough, though, with Mae's brother and two buddies sitting over there in the bar, looking evil. Three days, though, I'm gone from here.

Closing time, people mill out of the place, down the wooden stairs to the sidewalk where a light rain has started.

At the bottom of the stairs, a rabbit punch staggers me forward into a second fist on the jaw. The fist to the jaw was flush, but the thrower wasn't a puncher, and I keep my feet. Stacy shoves somebody and screams, "Stop it!"

A tough-looking brownskinned middleweight moves in front of me, a protector, or just somebody ready to join in a free for all, but my attackers have scrambled away and disappeared after getting their point across. People around us freeze for a moment, and not seeing more action, move on out of the rain.

"Y'all all right, man?" the middleweight says. A Negro I've never seen before.

"Yeah, thanks, man."

"Them was some hit-and-run motherfuckers."

"They sure were," I say.

"Yeah."

"Well, good night, man."

Stacy and I trot to the car, jump in and exhale big. There is still some stun from the rabbit punch, but my jaw doesn't hurt. The guy couldn't hit. Like to get his butt inside the ropes. In three days I may be aching somewhere else, but I'll be away from this nutty stuff. A wave of mad laughter gushes out of the tickling around my heart as Thelonious Monk's music from the jukebox fires off somewhere in my cortex. Thelonious Fucking Monk! Some real jazz.

Stacy lays her palm on my cheek, puts her face nurse close, trying to see into my eyes in the dark. "Okay, JB?"

"Yes, I'm fine." What was most fine was how close and humanly fresh she was, her warm fingers on my face, and her eyes and the music.

"Those bastards," she says.

"Yeah, lucky that that one guy couldn't punch."

3)

Outside her apartment building, Stacy settles back in the passenger seat, holding my hand, and studies the lit-up windows of her mother's place before she gets out of the car. We know Audrey isn't waiting up for her daughter.

Stacy says, "Would you mind waiting a minute because I'm not sure I can be here. She's having one of her damned parties, it looks like—she never warns me—and I don't like some of her friends."

"Sure, I'll wait." What she has in mind she doesn't say before she lets go my hand and gets out and goes inside. School is over for both of us, *The Abduction from the Seraglio* has finished its run, and my body already feels like the property of Uncle Sam. Stacy will be here in Portland doing I don't know what.

She comes out of the building with her head down, wearing a baseball cap and the letterman jacket I gave her with the big chenille K on it. She opens the car door and looks in. "I'm sorry," she says. "I can't be in there. Can we drive around for a while?"

"Sure we can. Is everything going to be all right, Stacy?"

"It will be if we can get away from here. Do you need gas? I've got some money."

"No. I've got gas." The fewer stops, the better for Stacy and me. We've already made one stop too many. "Brilliant Corners" was a find, though. I start the car and ease away from the curb, letting a route emerge in my head.

We drive out of downtown, west along the river for a stretch and over the St John's bridge into north Portland, listening to the car radio. Homeless but not alone after midnight, after the glow of our last performance of Mozart's little *singspiel*, after much hot limb tossing and twining in my bed, after pie and Monk, and getting punched, rolling through empty streets, all ours under wet Portland trees. We drive past the high school, dark now except for security lights. Good-bye, Coolidge High. We park on a side street beside a power station with a block of transformers behind a storm fence. The rain has let up. I shut off the engine and the radio, and we lean against the seat, holding hands, half asleep, talking.

The police cruiser slides alongside my window with its lights off and stops. Up on me like a throat-closing ghost before I knew it. Its engine must have been shut down because I didn't hear a damn thing. My hand comes away from Stacy's. A short thick policeman swings out of the passenger seat and flashes a light on me, settles on Stacy. He walks around to her side, opens the door and says, "Over there, please." He steps back to the cruiser and opens the rear door for her. She gets in and he shuts the door, cooping her in there with no handles. She puts her face to the window and waves to me. I take a deep slow breath into my diaphragm and breathe out hard and slow, a high high note. The policeman moves back to my window and says, "May I see your driver's license, please."

"Sure." I dig for my wallet. The cop's voice sounds young, relaxed, his language local and moderate. Same as my own. "Look, officer," I say, finding thought and voice for a verbal broad jump, "we just finished a musical performance over at Coolidge High tonight, and I gave the young lady a ride home, but her mother was having a wild party and she didn't want to go in. We were just trying to wait out the party. I'm a schoolteacher here."

He takes the laminated card I hand him and holds it in front of his flashlight. "Oh?" he says. "What school?"

"I teach at Coolidge. Actually, I just got my draft notice, so I won't be teaching there next year, but I'm under contract until September."

He puts his light on me, back on the driver's license.

"Ah, too bad," he says. He passes me my license and moves to the cruiser where he leans in and talks to his partner. Then he opens the rear door and says something to Stacy, and out she floats in my letterman jacket. The cop climbs back in the cruiser and says, "Take it easy," and they roll away, lights on.

The honks, squeaks, rushing, tugging, offbeat explosions of "Brilliant Corners" go off in my ears with the gendarmes' departure. Stacy gets in beside me and watches the cruiser turn out of sight. "What did you say to him?"

"I just told him what we were doing. Waiting for your mama to get through with her wild party—the truth has set you free, baby."

She slides herself against me, puts her arms around my neck, and lip-smacks the side of my face. "John the fucking Baptist," she says.

Countermarch

1)

My Dear Eustacia,

Like I said in my last letter, I'm still living off the time we had together during Christmas leave. Swinging into spring, you should see the iceplant around here, juicy green plant hugging the sandy ground with pink and red flowers. Dewy in the mornings. Coast liveoaks cover the hills where we did basic training. Mossy buggers. This is a beautiful part of the earth. Playing war here seems kind of crazy.

And thanks for sending those two cans of figs. How come you're so sweet to me, baby?

The Band Training Unit is a better deal than I ever expected. Everybody says "BTU." Lots of good musicians here, and it seems like all these Thermal Units have been to college except the old regular army guys, like the old master sergeant cornetist that plays first solo. Old Eddie can play. Several of the guys in the unit are concert pianists, and one of them studied with Darius Milhaud at Mills College (look up Milhaud if you're not hip)— really nice guy. Another guy, a colored pianist from Brooklyn, studied at the Julliard School of Music in New York. And there are some good jazz players around here in the BTU and a there's a big jazz rehearsal band. I sat in the trumpet section the other day, and it showed me something. It seems like jazz leans into everybody's language around here, talking about "cool" and "hip" and "fucked up." You even hear it from the symphony-type guys.

My roommate is a French horn player who graduated from USC. He writes poetry that he recites to me regularly since he found out I'm an

English teacher. His stuff is mostly sad stuff about his adolescence, not bad though. (But not as good as yours) I think the cat is a bit on the swishy side, like a number of guys in the unit seem to be, but old Eugene is very cool.

Yes, we've got rooms! And in the latrines, stalls with doors on them. I mean to tell you, this is a far cry from basic, baby. The bandleader is a warrant officer, Mr Bertucci—did you (with yr European military background) know they call warrant officers "Mister?" Sounds peculiar to me, like a British surgeon. And I'm telling you, you wouldn't believe this Bertucci, waving the stick and singing parts solfeggio during rehearsals (The guys call him "Ol' Sol-Fa-Mi"). Says he believes musicians should be treated like gentlemen and keeps the non-music duty as light as possible. Believe me, I can dig six months of this. (Shoot! Leave my ass here for the duration!)

This is a place where I fit in for now. We've had lots of interesting jobs around the area, parades and concerts, like the other night in Salinas, John Steinbeck's old stomping ground. A lot like Kayakaw and the Valley. I could feel the dewy early mornings, all that soil-turning and irrigating and pulling, picking. Breathed it in.

I didn't realize there were so many Mexicans in California. But why not? This used to be Mexico.

So what have you been up to? Are you still working at the coffee house by the Hawthorne Bridge? I hope you're not going to forget about trying to go to college. There's always a way. You could do it, baby. You need to do it. We know you could get pretty far on your looks, but you need some organized learning to fill out your talent and back up your jive. Remember what the man said about your writing. Listen to what I'm telling you.

Your Loving Thermal Unit,
Joe

2)

At Transportation, the crewcut specialist 4th class says, "They gave you a compartment." He says to the clerk at a desk behind him, "Hey, they gave him a compartment." The other clerk gets up, gets me in focus, runs an eye over the document, says, "Yep, compartment," and sits down.

After the music and easy living at the BTU, the air-conditioned, private, overnight trainride from Monterey to El Paso continues a level of ease I would never identify with soldiering—thank you, Mr. Bertucci.

The train is in Arizona when I open my eyes and think I'm still dreaming. Row after row of grey, mothballed warplanes, P-40s, Mustangs, Thunderbolts, Wildcats, Hellcats, F4U Corsairs, and bombers too, B-25s, B-26s, B-24 Liberators and B-17 Flying Fortresses, the core of my World War Two elementary school vocabulary fleshed-out and roaring through my head, passes on the silent desert outside the train. I close my eyes and take a deep breath of cool train air and feel this giant grey metal scab of World War Two through my skin, slipping past.

For the rest of the trip I swig from the pint of scotch I bought in Monterey and read Kerouac's stony little story of an interracial affair in San Francisco, *The Subterraneans*. Screwed-up couple. The beatnik girl, Mardou, is colored. The guy sounds like Kerouac.

***

So I'm standing outside the train at El Paso, home to Fort Showalter. It's Memorial Day. Heat comes off the metal side of the car, feels like a stovetop. People notice me in my heavy dress uniform, dumb Negro GI out here in wool in all this heat. First mistake, sending the duffel bag ahead with all my light clothing in it, and being stuck here looking extra-planetary and ignorant on the boiling-ass border. Naked in full dress. No horn, only a mouthpiece in my pocket.

A shower of self-pity and loss lets loose on me, the family break-up, my classroom, the opera company orchestra, my horn, spring in flowery Portland, the snowy torso of Stacy, down on me, but sizzles to nothing in the heat. I move away from the side of the train, locate the station entrance, and go inside to find it not much cooler with two ceiling fans going.

At least I'm unencumbered. But If I had a horn I might be able to find a place to practice, a church basement maybe. The mouthpiece is almost hot against my lips. Back outside, I buzz into it, *pianissimo*, some lip slurs and tonguing, and then I pick a road that looks like a straight shot to the center of downtown El Paso and start walking.

The street, parts of streets and low rusty red brick buildings roast between me and the downtown skyline to the east. A sign along the top of the tallest building over there reads "HUMBLE" in giant red letters. The uniform keeps the sun from broiling my ass, but it's weighty. After six months in the BTU, sitting around, blowing an army trumpet, I make a piss poor warrior. An alien, soft, horn-happy, used-to-be English teacher, that's what I am. I probably couldn't break eleven seconds in the hundred. By the end of a dozen hot blocks, my throat and mouth are dry, and at the next corner I stop at a place.

The wooden sign above the door says "Manolo's"—a Mexican café. A screendoor with a tin Pepsi Cola sign nailed across the bottom half covers the open entrance. I step inside, tightened by heavy history and current event of refusal I always feel on approaching eating places I don't know. The counter and several square wooden tables are empty. Fly-buzzing afternoon quiet. Faint whiff of meat history. A short Mexican in a white shirt leans against the wall behind the cash register, one foot hiked up against the baseboard. Next to him, a swinging door hides the kitchen. His hands are halfway in his pockets, and his eyes are trained out the window all the way to Cape Horn.

"Can I get a Pepsi, please?"

In about three seconds, the Mexican's daydream cracks and his eyes focus on me, customer on the other side of the counter in front of him. The man's eyes wobble side to side across me, and he wiggles his head fast, more like a shudder than shaking it. His voice is a loud whisper: "I'm sorry, man, I can't serve you."

"What?"

"I can't serve you." He strains upward on the word *serve* and throws his empty palms out to each side. Ten feet inside the border of Texas and this Mexican cat is saying he can't sell me a Pepsi Cola. Myself, slung with my bayoneted M-1, a grenade in hand, sprouts as the latest movie of my rage. Had I had the stuff, I might have forgotten my home training and my reading.

"All I want is a Pepsi."

The man shakes his hands in front of him like hefting a bowling ball in each one, and his voice becomes an embarrassing yelp. "I can't serve you. It's—it's not my law, man. It's not my law." He's sweating and rolling his eyes from side to side to not look at me, the cat does not want to see me, even if I'm not all that big and black. He's a featherweight and alone in the place, and I could probably pound his insignificant ass to a pulp, but I back out, sweating, my eyes on him.

The screen door slides off my butt and claps into the doorframe. I take off my cap and wipe my forehead with my sleeve. Small pebbles, dirt, and bits of concrete lie in the sidewalk's wider cracks. Nothing hand-sized in the gutter. If Booker Bain and the boys were with me in there, I could understand fucking the place up. I could understand not fucking it up. Take a vote. I walk a block with my eyes on the pitted, hot rectangles of concrete, heat coming through my thin soles, straining to find two rectangles that look identical, trying not to step on the lines between rectangles, trying to maintain an even, thirty-inch stride. If I had a piece of chalk, I could do some hopscotch. It is so hot. Hot scotch. Hotch scop. I could be delirious.

People with the same dark hair and same dark eyes walk past me. Mexicans. Mexican-Americans. Amero-Mexicans, Confusion-Americans, American-Confucians. Whoever the hell they think they are, they can eat where I can't with their straight-ass hair. Brown people segregated from Negroes. I see it, man, turn these poor motherfuckers against each other. Keep 'em confused. Shit. A woman who could be fifty years old comes toward me, heavyset, streaks of grey hair, a dark mole on her left cheek. Passing me, she looks just like Aunt Malinda, Mama's younger sister, but I can see she's Mexican. *Buenos dias,* Auntie. If she spoke a little Spanish, or didn't say anything, Aunt Malinda could buy a Pepsi.

The red, white, and blue sign over the door says "USO", that we heard much of during the war, Bob Hope and a flock of pin-up girls doing USO gigs for troops all over the world. So used to seeing white people I never noticed the absence of colored in the pictures.

Through the window I see young people inside. All white. I also see a big red and white Coke machine standing against a wall opposite the entrance. My fingertips play along the edge of a dime in my pocket, hot pocket, roasting my coin, my thin, trusting-in-God dime where the profile of my favorite president has usurped the place of Liberty. Should have a Statue of Roosevelt in the harbor. He could be in some robes, getting up out of his wheelchair, lifting his cigarette holder. I pinch the coin between my thumb and fingers, hulk myself into a mad, drink-seeking robot, and march into the USO, across the floor to the Coke machine.

Along my robot corridor flash impressions of color, flesh, stretched-up eyebrows, dark hair, light hair, lips frozen in O. One body moves. A spindly blonde woman with too much red lipstick flutters beside me, itty bitty eohippus foot noises from catching her toe against her heel, almost tripping, as if she would like to get in front of me, but I might touch her. Might trample her ass. I put a dime in the machine. The woman's lips part on some large teeth with specks of lipstick on them, and out comes her chilly, flaked voice. "Excuse me."

A Coke bumps its way down to the outlet. I jam the frosty bottle against the opener, jerk the cap off and drink. Everybody watches the first Negro in the world to drink a bottle of soda pop.

"—we don't have colored in here," the woman is saying.

I lower the bottle and hold it before her nose. "I am not seeking colored, madam. I only wish this bit of refreshment."

Her hands fly up like kitty paws, and she falls back, as surprised as I am by my word burst. Cold Coke down my gullet sends a brief ache, centered like a dime-sized caste mark, to the bones of my forehead. A titter escapes one of the girls. I take another swig and, looking around, notice two of the four girls are light Mexicans, not white, teenagers. High schoolers. Standing there like a mute musical ensemble. One of the white girls looks like she's fourteen or fifteen. All five of the GIs are white. A pool of ignorance here.

Two of the guys move toward me, both about my size, one of them well-built with brown eyes and kind of a boy scout look, the other one wiry and blond with a fox face. If I had my M1, I could take care of these fools with a couple butt strokes.

The hostess, kitty paws beside her cheeks, says, "You have to leave."

The two white soldiers move up to flank her. The blond one's accent is Deep South. "Yeah, boy. You know you don't belong in here."

Hands grab my arms and shake me back to the wood, metal, flesh and heat of the scene, to the two GIs pushing me toward the door. Comrades in arms. I go stiff and try to drain the bottle without breaking my teeth. They have the weight advantage, pushing me, and at the door the blond one grabs a pitcher of ice water from the counter and pours it over my head as soon as they muscle me out the door. The other one snatches the Coke bottle from me. Ice cubes slide off my cap, hit my shoulders. The USO defenders jump back inside.

I take off my cap and shake water from it. The blond fox-faced one sticks his head out the door and says, "That'll cool ya, boy." My kick against the door is a grace note to the loud slam. Memorial Day, hell, it's *El Dia de Espulsione.* I put my cap back on and move down the sidewalk. If I had a grenade, I'd give their pitiful asses something to remember. I take out my mouthpiece and buzz into it. The thought that atrocity is possible is delicious, even if I don't have the nerve to do it. It will happen someplace. Don't do evil for evil, Daddy said. A grenade might not be evil enough. Fuck this place.

Up ahead, GIs in civvies are hopping off a city bus labeled Fort Showalter at the curb of a small park. Convenient without a duffel bag, easier than calling for a base taxi, but I let the bus roll away without me. The park turns out to be a block square of grass with an old concrete pond in the middle and trees around the perimeter. The GIs take off south in clumps of two white, three white, five colored, in their short-sleeved shirts. Smoking. Laughing. Headed for Juarez. Fixing to get fixed up in Juarez. Dancing—I see it—separately toward the same funky hell.

I'm still thirsty and the sun has blazed hotter. The drinking fountain in the park appears to be for everybody, and I get something rusty-tasting but wet out of it. The water running over my hand doesn't turn cool like water from the street fountains in Portland. Try to get a cool drink in this fucking place. Heat and ignorance have taken over the world. I take off my cap, clap water onto my face.

Whoa, man.

When I first see him through my watery eyelashes—down here, standing over there—I think, "Damn, it's the heat and that USO jive."

Standing under the spreading red-leaved tree at the corner of the park, a corporal, dressed in a World War One cavalry uniform, saber, boots, leggings and all, leaning on a Springfield rifle, the way he used to stand in the garden after work with his shovel or hoe, whistling "Precious Lord" or some other old church tune.

Daddy.

Close my eyes. Open them. Still there. I put my cap back on and look around. The soldiers headed for Juarez dance along loose as puppets, still in sight. Nobody but me seems to notice the colored corporal standing under the tree in his antique cavalry uniform. I cross the field of sunlight between us, into the shade where he stands.

"Daddy?" I put out my hand, but he holds up his hand like *noli me tangere.*

"Yep," he says. He drops his hand and looks at me as if we've been talking all along. He points toward the river. "We spent a lot of time chasing old Pancho Villa right down over yonder," he says. "In weather like this too. Old Pancho liked to ride in hot weather. Boy, I'm tellin' you, them horses got hot. Yessiree. General Pershing in charge down here."

His coffee-colored face looks just about the way I remember before the stroke killed him. Willie. Willie Birdsong. Brother Birdsong, people called him. Sometimes, "Elder Birdsong." My father, the preacher. But I don't see the cords that had started to show in his neck, and his teeth look whiter than I ever saw them.

"Daddy, you never told me about that, that you were in El Paso."

He stays leaning on his rifle, hands piled over the muzzle, eyes toward the river. "Lotta things I never told you, son. Lotta things I spoke to you but you hadn't ears to hear. You been finding out a harder way."

"I have?"

He's facing me now, rifle at his side. "Be finding out more, too, having chosen the path of tribulation," he says. "People never can leave well enough alone. Think they can outsmart the Devil. But then that old temptation comes slidin' through the weeds and gets 'em. It's bigger than they is without some help."

"What? What are you talking about?"

A hopeless case head shake, and he goes back into his farmer pose, leaning on the rifle. He looks off in the direction he said they chased Pancho Villa, not at me, to say his next words. "Ain't you lived with a woman under false pretenses? And ain't y'all had a child and you forsook them?"

"What?

"You walked out."

My stomach pulls at my throat. "Well, I wouldn't exactly call it walking out, Daddy."

His eyes bead on me, then back toward Pancho Villa territory. "And I suppose you wouldn't call it false pretenses, neither," he says. "You call it what you want, I'll call it what I want."

I start to open my mouth, but he's gone. God damn! My jaw is quivering like it doesn't have any muscles. My whole body gone shakey. Sweat on sweat heavies my uniform. A sickly grinding at the top of my stomach tries to force its way into my throat. I have never fainted before. I take in a long breath, pull out my mouthpiece and buzz into it, eyes closed, a long slow buzz until all my air is expressed and I breathe in. I open my eyes. Dark red tree leaves, sparse green grass, movement of cars and people, sink in. Daddy's appearance sinks in, and I get a repeat of the shakes but am able to breathe it away. Doesn't feel like the last of it, though. I press my forehead against the narrow trunk of the tree to feel something against my skin before starting out again.

At the bridge, the stream of people clots up because they have to stop at a booth and pay three cents to cross. The man in the booth slides back two pennies change. Most people are throwing their change off the bridge.

In the brown trickle under the bridge, small boys jump and splash about, catching the falling pennies. Cooked brown, shirtless boys, most with skin as dark as mine. They hop and slog through the water, whooping, bumping each other, catching pennies in cone-shaped cups rigged out of cardboard. Muddy water shines on their bodies, dries up, shines. The mighty Rio Grande of the social studies books, the border.

Into *Ciudad Juarez.* A trio of Negro troops stays on course in front of me. There haven't been any colored troops in my Cold War experience, so far, no colored buddies. During basic at Ord, I and a light Negro from Los Angeles with a French name were the only colored in the company, but we seemed to belong to different parties. The pianist from Brooklyn and I were the only ones in the band training unit, and we were friendly but we didn't need one another. In dress greens, in this border heat, I'm sure I look like a man without a country. *It's me, Joseph, Joseph the soldier.* Words and music float up from "The Soldier's Tale." Good trumpet stuff. *L'Histoire du Soldat,* fun, sunny, dusty, struggle with the Devil. Struggling with that motherfucker right now down here in this heat.

My scouts turn west and finally go into a place that has "Copacabana" painted across a wide front window. On the sidewalk, near the window, people press past. Vendors at the curb sell juicy green, orange, and red melon slices and fruit drinks that I've been warned against, bright colors carrying misery to the gut.

Inside, the Copacabana is dark after the sunny street. It's a large barroom with many tables where young men in civilian clothes sit drinking, laughing, talking together and to women. All the men are Negroes. No one else is in uniform, but my entry doesn't turn any heads or stop any talk in the big shadowy room. Ceiling fans stir cigarette smoke that rises from the tables.

The bar stools are all empty until I settle on one. Settle, but still too damn shakey to dwell on what befell me in the park in El Paso.

"*Buenos dias,*" the bartender says. His eyes favor something just over my shoulder. Smoke from the cigarette in his hand scrims up across his European-looking face.

"Hello. I'll have a tequila, please." I'm not loose enough yet to respond in Spanish.

"You want Pepsi or lemon with it?" He has hardly any accent, except when he says "bebsi."

"Uh, Pepsi." This tequila is a first, and I don't understand the lemon.

The bartender, cigarette between his lips, sets a whiskey glass half full of chipped ice on the bar, pours a shot of tequila, and returns the bottle to the ledge behind him. Squinting against smoke from his cigarette, he brings a bottle of Pepsi from under the bar and tops off the glass. He swings the cigarette away from his mouth and says, "Ten cents."

"A dime?"

"*Si.*"

One thin dime, a Liberty head that I lay on the bar. Fuck the USO. Across the room, a woman in a light blue dress eases through the curtain. Her eyes tap me, move on. She sits at a table by herself with hands folded like a counselor, no drink, not smoking. Enough hips and breasts. Nothing in her tan smooth face puts me off. She looks clean.

My first tequila goes down cool, Pepsi-sweet and strong. I order another and watch the clear cactus alcohol turn brown from the bartender's shot of Pepsi. I give him a Roosevelt dime. Good Neighbor Policy at The Copa, yes. The first drink starts to churn in my head but leaves my gut alone. The woman in the light blue dress plays her easy part, studies her hands. I take a sip of the fresh drink and walk over. "Hello," I say. "May I sit down?"

Her lips curve up at the corners, my uniform the mirth-causer, maybe, and she extends her arm toward the chair across from her. "*Bienvenido, senor.* Welcome."

3)

At Fort Showalter I locate Building 1013 which houses the 72nd Army Band and find a note pinned on the orderly room door that says, "CQ back in a few minutes." About the time I finish reading it, the outside door of the floor below bangs shut and footsteps hit the stairs. A spec 4 in khakis bounces into the hall. "You waiting for me?" he says, coming my way, key in hand.

"I guess so. You the CQ for the band?"

"Yeah. Joel Levinski." He shifts the keys and puts out his hand. His dark, almost black, eyes stick on me like headlights.

"Joe Birdsong." We shake hands.

"Come on in." He unlocks the orderly room door and we go in. Two desks sit in front of the window wall before us, the one on the left with a wooden nameplate that says MSgt Howell. Levinski slides into the office chair behind the other one, the clerk's desk, on which lies a clarinet in an open case. On the wall behind me are the usual photos of

President Eisenhower and the rest of the Chain of Command. Levinski leans back in the chair, one knee bouncing. "You just came in from Fort Ord, right? The new trumpet player?"

"Right."

"Where you from?"

His fuzzy final r-sounds are easy on my ear. "Oregon, I'm from Portland, Oregon. You, you're from New York City, aren't you?"

Levinski's mug splits into a grin that draws the tip of his nose close to his upper lip. "Yeah, you could tell, huh?"

"Oh yes. In high school I worked for some people from Brooklyn."

"Yep," he says, "bet they were Jews too. Right?"

"Right. They were." Nat and Sarah were the only Jews I ever heard of in Kayakaw, and I never thought about them being Jews, or knew what that meant when I first worked in their grocery store. But they talked about it, how they missed life back in Brooklyn, the museums, events, and foods that couldn't be found in the God-forsaken burg of my birth. Just about everybody in Kayakaw was plain old white American. I wasn't aware of anybody who worried much about the few Negroes, Indians, and Mexicans that might be around. Never thought much about what I was, before high school, unless somebody brought up the subject, and then it was hard to say what I was, something wrong with being different from everybody else. In school, the subject came up only when we passed through slavery in social studies or when Dr. Ralph Bunche won the Nobel Peace Prize. People couldn't stop talking about it when the Brooklyn Dodgers signed Jackie Robinson to play baseball. Nat and Sarah, especially Sarah, talked about race any time they felt like it, about how racially prejudiced Kayakaw was, compared to Brooklyn, and about being Jews. And here was Levinski that I just met, that I could see now was Jewish, saying, "bet they were Jews."

"So what were they doing out there in Oregon?"

"They came out to Portland to work in the shipyards during the war. After the war they moved up to Kayakaw in Washington. That's where I met them."

"I see, I see." He pushed back from the desk and stood up. "Where's your duffel bag?"

"I sent it ahead. I hope it's here."

"It's probably down in supply. You can pick it up in the morning—come on, let me show you your bunk."

"Cool, but give me a minute. Where's the latrine?"

"Oh sure." He steps past me to the door and points across the hall. "It's right over there." *Right ovuh theah.*

"Thanks." I push through the swinging door of the latrine. Amber-colored tiles cover the walls and floors of the space, and the porcelain urinals and sinks and chrome and stainless steel fixtures look new. Clarinet notes ripple from across the hall. Levinski can play. And I'm thinking latrine is not the word for this place. *Salle de bain,* man. *Salon de lavage!* At one of the spotless urinals I examine my penis for the first time since my maiden voyage to the Copacabana. Some kind of remote control experience, that was. More than the spasm, I remember the woman's bare arm across the small of my back in a brief warm squeeze.

Back in the orderly room, I ask Levinski, "What's the CO like?"

Levinski lays his clarinet on the desk. "Mr. Tappendorf? The guy is nuts. You'll see soon enough." He motions me into the hall and we walk down to the large bay at the end that is divided down the middle by a double row of green metal army lockers just like the ones at Fort Ord. We veer to the right. "The band side," Levinski says.

"Who's on the other side?"

"Signal corps guys and clerks from headquarters mostly." The band side is partitioned into cubicles with two bunks each, footlockers at the foot of each bunk. We go to the end of the row where the next to the last bunk is unmade, the black and white striped mattress folded double with sheets, blankets, and pillowslip stacked on top. Levinski points, "There's your bunk. That's mine over there." He flips his elbow toward the last bunk in the row.

"Cool enough." A piece of good luck, Levinski for a cubicle mate.

"Yeah, old Collins got out last week," Levinski says, waving a hand toward my new bunk. "Collins was going crazy. He got married on his last leave and he couldn't stop talking about how much he missed her. Talking about her all day and running off batches every night."

Levinski's words put a few pinpricks of perspiration on my forehead. Outgoing mate running to a wife. Incoming mate running from a wife. He sits on his bunk and watches me take off my coat and start to arrange my new lair. "Well," he says, "you didn't exactly luck out, man."

"How's that?"

"You could have got assigned to the 224th."

"The 224th?"

"Yeah, the other band on post. Up at Bolden Heights."

"Oh, I didn't know there was another band here. What's better about the other one?"

I'm smoothing my top sheet into place. Levinski gets to his feet and paces a couple steps. "What's better about it is they don't have a band-leader," he says. "Theirs got sent to Southeast Asia. We're stuck with a nut, an incompetent, scared shitless of Headquarters."

"Really?"

"You'll see what I mean pretty fast. We have a combined gig with the 224th tomorrow up at White Sands."

"I can't wait."

"Well, I better get back to the orderly room. If you need anything, just holler."

Hollah.

After breakfast with Levinski in the mess hall in Building 1012, I'm trying to digest the sight of so many men of approximately my own physical description, Negroes in their late teens or early twenties, most of them dressed in green fatigues and combat boots. Half the troops in the place, looks like. The space bulges with the noise of silverware, metal trays, water spraying in the dishwashing machine, voices rising and falling. My dress green uniform with no rank on the sleeves passes through a gauntlet of eyeballing, snickers, suppressed howls and junior high somersaults. Walking back to the supply room in the basement of Building 1013, I'm still stunned from the energy in the mess hall and the sight of all the colored soldiers who looked alike, and the icy fact that my eyes readily picked up individual features of the white soldiers.

Levinski introduces me to the supply sergeant who issues me a horn and hefts my duffel bag over the counter. I sling it over my shoulder, and we stow the trumpet in the rehearsal room and head upstairs. A trio of white privates, Hiebert, Jarboe, and Muccigrosso, according to the name patches on their khaki shirts, are standing inside the entrance to the bay. Levinski fans his palm toward me. "New trumpet player."

The two southerners say, "Hi," in their flat accents from behind their invisible walls. I recognize them, and their faces redden at the same time. I drop my duffel bag and aim a left hook at the fox-faced blond one's jaw. He half turns away from it, but I got good leverage and my fist reaches bone under his eye. I'm coming back with a right, but his two buddies jump between us before I can come across with it. We go to shoving, and I feel pain in the knuckle of my middle finger. Levinski clamps his arms around my chest and pulls me backward. "Wait a minute. Wait a minute," he says. "What the hell is going on here?"

He lets go of me, and I shake my shoulders, grab a deep inhale. My knuckle burns, but the weight of my hot heavy uniform gives me power, and I point at Hiebert and Jarboe, who fingers his cheek where he's going to have a mouse pretty soon. "Ask those assholes."

Troops coming back from breakfast stop, bunch together to see the show. Levinski looks from Hiebert to Jarboe. Jarboe takes his hand away from his reddening cheek and gives a single slap at the air. "Li'l misunderstanding," he says. His partner Hiebert stands back, sizing me up—unless he knows some special shit, I could murder his ass. Jarboe's lips twist up to one side, and he cuts his eyes toward me, and I see all kinds of trouble in him before he looks at the floor. Levinski grabs the sling of my duffel bag and starts toward our area. "Come on," he says.

Behind us, rising and falling, What happened What happened What happened. Levinski sets the duffel bag on top of my footlocker, goes over to his bunk and sits watching me pace. I undo my tie and snatch it off. The hardness of the floor beats through my thin soles, and my hand is beginning to throb. Levinski sits, all ears while I dig khakis out of the duffel bag and change out of my greens. I tell him about meeting

Jarboe and Hiebert at the USO, which draws quick nods from him to the beat of my story. "Yeah, I went there one, and one time only, myself," he says. "The USO is no fucking where."

"Bet they didn't throw you out."

Levinski runs his hand through his black hair. "No, but it wasn't all that comfortable. Nothing there you'd want."

"All I wanted was a fucking Coke."

"Well, those guys aren't all that bad, you'll see."

"Yeah, we'll see." The reservoir of ill history and derangement I saw in Jarboe's look toward me was something new to me in person. *You know you don't belong in here, boy.* Like who in the fuck does he think he is? Somebody my own age. Of course I've been reading about such shit for a long time.

"They are where they're from, though, Texas and Mississippi," Levinski says.

In Kayakaw, a few white kids from Texas, Oklahoma, Arkansas, showed up after the war, and I played basketball and baseball with some of them. They weren't breezy friendly like the guys I'd known since grade school. Always, around the southerners, seemed like a huge subject hung over us, behind the body motions, tightening the silences, just beyond the fingers of my vocabulary. I see the Cotton Curtain now. "Fuck it. I'm not looking for trouble," I say, "but seeing those bastards after what happened downtown really snuck up on me."

"I saw that."

"I'm not one of your violent Negroes, Levinski." I pull on fresh black socks, slide into my shoes.

"I have only the testimony of my eyes," he says.

Rough physical contact is something I put up with on the field or the court, but otherwise I try to avoid it. After the trouble opened up around me and my high school girlfriend, I was angry a lot of the time and went to the YMCA and worked on boxing for months. It helped. Only got popped in the mouth a couple times, and not seriously. In Portland I never had time for boxing. Since becoming a *soldado,* however, it begins to feel like an additional weapon that I should maybe cultivate, apart from the rifle, bayonet, and trumpet.

The skinny young guy with the nametag that says "Muccigrosso" peeks into our space and then bops in. He waves a finger at Levinski. "What's happening, Joel?"

A featherweight, he dances his feet toward me, dipping his shoulders left and right. "Say, man, I'm Dino." He throws out his hand and we shake.

"Joe. Nice to meet you."

"Hah. Joe and Joel. How 'bout that?" Muccigrosso skips around, going noplace, thumbs hooked into two of his belt loops. Watery brown eyes bounce back and forth past my face. He looks like a fugitive from the eleventh grade. "Say, man," he says, "the fellahs want you to know they don't feel good about what happened."

"What do you mean?"

"At the USO, right?"

"You weren't there?"

He straightens, throws his hands out to the sides. "No, man, I was someplace else."

"Well, I was at the fucking USO. Briefly."

Muccigrosso ducks his head again, bobs and weaves. "Well, they said they didn't know you were in the band. The bastards are embarrassed, I guess."

*Didn't know I was in the band...*some lame shit. I push back an urge to mount the pulpit and really get into it. "Well, I guess I was pretty fucking embarrassed too. And somebody could have got hurt."

"Yeah, man. I can understand."

"You can, huh?"

"Damn right, man. I'm from Philly, where you from?"

"Portland, Oregon."

"Oregon?" Muccigrosso shouts the word as if he just got something mucho hip out of a fortune cookie. "An Oregon Bastard," he says. "First one I ever met."

He pumps his shoulders and throws out his hand to shake again.

I say to him, "You tell your buddies I'm not interested in trouble. As far as I'm concerned, it's over." I've sent thoughts up and down the chutes of my feelings and on the surface it's the truth, but that shit from the USO is in the bank and I know I won't forget it.

The big tanned head of the master sergeant behind the first sergeant's desk is hairless except for a retreating cuff of blond going white. At the clerk's desk, a redfaced sergeant first class fights a typewriter with a form and several carbons in it. Sounds of trumpet noodling come from the office next door, the bandleader, loosening up. We walk over to the master sergeant. The mild look he raises to Levinski has respect in it, and I don't see a whole lot of trouble in his face when the sergeant's brown eyes focus on me.

"Good morning, men."

"Good morning, Sarge," Levinski says. "Sergeant Howell, meet Private Birdsong, the new trumpet player."

The first sergeant focuses his thick-featured face on me and reaches his hand across the desk. "Clem Howell," he says. Sergeant Howell's chubby hand has a Masonic ring on the third finger. "And that's Sergeant Barnstable over there," he says. He dips his head in the clerk's direction.

"Good morning, Sergeant. Joe Birdsong." I give the clerk a little wave. No scent in the air of my run-in with the southerners.

"It's good to meet ya, Birdsong." The first sergeant's deep southern accent aims close to the ear, round and mellow, doesn't sound poisonous, here in the orderly room, but one never knows. *On ne sait jamais. It's good to meet ya, Birdsong.* He sounds like a pretty good old bear even if he might join up with a Klan lynching party if he heard I was messing with his daughter. He sounds close to the ear like an undertaker. "Now what you've got to do, Birdsong, is report to Mr Tappendorf. You got your orders there—yes. I'll just step over there and tell him I'm sending you in."

The sergeant's knock on the bandleader's door carries through the hall. The trumpet noodling stops. Sergeant Howell comes back to the orderly room and says, "Go on over, Private."

Just under the nameplate, I knock on the bandleader's door. A tight-throated tenor voice. "Come in."

I step in, close the door, move up to the desk at attention and salute. "Private Birdsong reporting for duty, sir."

He throws me a two-finger salute and says, "At ease." I step forward and lay my orders on his desk.

Mr. Tappendorf's long pale face hasn't shown any expression yet, though his eyes suggest he's still in the process of arriving at his office. Not quite warmed up. The trumpet in his hands is a good one, a Selmer, whose lacquer has gotten dull around the valves. His uniform is fresh from the laundry and starched enough so it's hard not to think cardboard. Pants look like they could march by themselves. He sits down and lays the horn in the open case in front of him, picks up my orders and runs his eyes over them. A couple times, little humming noises come from his throat.

"So you were a teacher," he says. "You're a college graduate." His blue eyes show tiny pupils.

"Yes sir."

"Music teacher?"

"No sir, English teacher."

He exhales. The skin around his nose and mouth pales, flushes, pales. "That's very good, very good. You've got very high scores here."

"Yes sir." I flex my toes against the confines of my shoes.

"What's this O-two-one-six? What's the six for?"

"That's for French, sir. French is my secondary specialty."

His eyes stay on the paper. "Oh. Good. Good," he says. He talks to the paper or to my belt buckle, and I remember Levinski speaking of the man's phobia about unshined belt buckles. The flesh around his nose and mouth turns from pale to pink to pale again. "Well, Birdsong, we rehearse every morning at 0900 unless we have a job."

"Yes sir." I'm sure his eyes would follow my belt buckle if I moved a foot to the left or right.

"While you're here, just practice your instrument and listen to the first sergeant and you won't have any trouble."

"Yes sir."

"That'll be all, Private."

***

In the soundproofed basement rehearsal hall, Mr Tappendorf fumbles with a stack of six by eight cards on the podium in front of him. Copies of the band's march music are glued to cards like those. Levinski said Mr Tappendorf himself designed the leather pouches that hold our one hundred marches, and we are to always have all the marches in pouch. Keep all marches in numerical order in pouch. Always bring pouch along on jobs unless ordered not to do so. If in doubt, bring pouch. Bandsmen do not lose pouches. Think of losing your love finger before losing pouch. Levinski said all that. It seems that Muccigrosso earned Tappendorf's undying hate by losing a pouch with marches on a job at Carlsbad.

The bandleader's baton lies among the jumble of cards on the stand and interferes with his sorting. He picks it up, clamps the middle of it between his teeth, and keeps on sorting.

Helzer, a red-haired draftee is a new guy too. He sits down next to me, trumpet across his knees. "Hi."

"Hi."

Brass players begin to blow long tones, run up and down scales, play snatches of tunes. Helzer sounds like a high school-level player. I don't hear anything hip. A master sergeant sits at the upright piano and plays to himself with one hand, a glockenspiel across his lap. Helzer says, "White Sands job today, huh?"

"Yes, that's what I hear, a missile firing."

Mr Tappendorf takes the baton out of his mouth and raps twice on the podium. Horn and drum noises halt. A couple islands of chatter keep going. Sergeant Howell stands and raises his voice. "At ease over there."

The talking stops. The bandleader's voice struggles out of his throat and wavers to the back row. "All right, let's begin. Get out your pouches." Pouches come out from under the chairs. "Okay. You have your 'Men of Ohio,' Number 20. You have your 'Washington Post,' Number 32 and you have your 'Hands Across the Sea,' Number 76." He pauses, studies the cards in his hands. "And you have your 'Garry Owen,' Number 43. Now let's get those up on your stands."

Before he lifts his baton, Mr T moves around like he's trying to bump his way out of an invisible telephone booth but can't get out. Ready to snap. He waves a shaky baton when we start into "Men of Ohio," but it doesn't make much difference because it's a simple march that anybody can play in his sleep. Something is wrong, though. After four measures, he waves the band to a stop and jams his fists toward the floor, elbows into his sides as if he's bound but not gagged. "Muccigrosso," he yells, "how many times—if you don't raise that goddamn stand, so help me Christ I'll court-martial you."

Muccigrosso gets busy, squeezes the telescoping post of the stand between his knees and pulls it up to what I gather is an acceptable level. Tappendorf's eyes rake the high school dropout like two thirty-caliber machineguns. On checking the relaxed bodies around me, I see I must be watching a familiar routine. Dino gets the stand adjusted, and we play through "Men of Ohio," "Hands Across the Sea," and "Garry Owen." Mr T has the supply sergeant pass out copies of the Jordanian national anthem, which we play through until the band-leader considers it pouch-worthy for the job.

During a short break in the rehearsal, Muccigrosso, down front with the reeds, stops noodling on his sax and says in our direction, "Hey, Helzer, you Wisconsin Bastard, you going with us tonight?"

Helzer's face breaks into a shine at Muccigrosso's fraternal probe, and he looks around like Who me. He says, "Yeah, I'll go with you."

Muccigrosso snaps his fingers. "All right then," he says.

Hiebert, wrapped in his sousaphone over in the corner, and Jarboe with his trombone, right in front of me, say, "All right."

It would be good if I didn't have to sit so near the trombones. Jarboe is within striking range. I don't believe I'll do it, but thoughts well up of beating him over the head with my new army trumpet, beating him bloody. In games, I've tried to bash other guys, beat them into the ground, but after the game it's over, like a ritual. This Jarboe thing is hanging on, though, like a fever in which I'm experiencing historical roots.

Sergeant Howell gets up at the end of rehearsal and says,"All right, Everybody listen up. Y'all know we got a White Sands job with the 224th this afternoon. We'll meet them up there. Everybody fall out at thirteen hundred hours in the courtyard. Uniform will be khakis with tie and dress cap. Make sure them shoes and belt buckles are shinin'. The bus will load at thirteen-thirty hours."

Outside the rehearsal hall, one of the sergeants' voice:

"What happened to your eye, Jarboe?"

"Nothin'."

Swink

1)

"The River Styx must be nearby."

The voice behind me when I turn around is someone in the band from Bolden Heights, the 224th, a slim, pasty-faced private in sunglasses, a silver trumpet under his arm. It's at least a hundred degrees, but this private talking about the River Styx isn't talking about just the heat, but fishing for an ear, letting whoever can hear know that he's a reader, is cool, and not all that impressed with the scene. River Styx Boy has a way of slouching even when standing more or less straight.

"Yeah, really hot," I say, "but I haven't run up on any three-headed dogs yet."

River Styx Boy allows himself a short laugh. The nameplate on his shirt says "Swink." *Swink. Swincan,* one of the Old English verbs I found so good to chew on back in school. *Swincan.* Toil. Labor. Swink's small head fits his body just right, and his pink lips stand out in the pale face like watercolor on white paper. "Yeah," he says.

The lenses of his sunglasses blank out any clue about how his eyes work. I ask him, "How long have you been at Showalter?"

"I've been here awhile."

The bandsmen aren't moving around much or noodling on their horns in the heat. Not supposed to noodle anyway, Levinski says, unless you want Tappendorf on your ass. The men talk and smoke. Sergeants bunch together except for the one whose nameplate says "Vogel." He stands apart, cradling the glockenspiel and studying the hot white sand through sunglasses. I've also learned that this is the 72nd's first combined gig with the 224th since their bandleader got assigned to Southeast Asia.

The metal of my trumpet has picked up noticeable heat. I put the horn under my arm. "So how do you like the 224th?"

"It'll do."

"Where are you from?"

"Connecticut. New Haven." He lets his horn dangle from two hooked fingers toward the packed white sand.

"How old are you? You must have joined."

"Yeah, you're right. I'm nineteen."

Jarboe and the group he's chatting with have drifted close enough that I feel my animus rising, so I walk off a few steps, drawing Swink with me. "How come you joined? How come you didn't go to college?"

"Needed to get away," he says. "And I wasn't ready for college."

Then: "Or college wasn't ready for me." His voice is quiet and even, then flares: "Have you read *Howl?*"

"Read what?"

"*Howl.* Ginsberg's poem." Allen Ginsberg, friend of Jack Kerouac, big marijuana smoker. That's all I know. When I say I haven't read it, Swink's shoulders come to attention and he says, "Really? You've got to read it, man. It's great."

Chaucer is great. Spenser is great. Shakespeare is great. Milton is great. Wordsworth and Coleridge are great. Keats is great. Walt Whitman is great. I am not sure there are any great living poets in English. I say, "*Great,* huh?"

"I'm telling you. Listen, can you come up to the Heights this evening? I'll turn you on to it."

"Can't make it tonight, man. But as soon as I get straightened out down at the 72nd?"

"Sure," he says. "You've got to read it."

Sergeant Howell gives the order to fall in, and we get into marching order. The small prince that Jordan sent to watch its troops fire this missile is on the reviewing stand in an oversized fancy uniform, a flyweight among the bigger American officers. We march into position and play "The Star Spangled Banner." We follow that with the Jordanian national anthem in which I hear Jordan's country-love story, a message I always got from "America, the Beautiful," singing it in grade school, when I knew America was the greatest amber waves of grain country in the world, beating Hitler and Mussolini and Tojo.

After the anthems, high in the blue south of us, a red-tailed drone buzzes into sight, and from somewhere out in the white dunes, Jordanian troops fire their missile.

2)

Levinski is getting up from the table to bus his tray, and I'm gathering my silver to do the same when two colored GIs in fatigues stop at the table. A couple privates first class, bigger than Two Jay. The more massive one, whose nametag says "Washington," taps me on the shoulder and says, "Excuse me, brother, could we have a word with you for a minute?"

The blank faces of the two nor the voice give any hint of the nature of the proposed word. I wave to Levinski and sit back. "See you upstairs," he says.

My "brother" and the other one take the chairs on either side of me, pulling in close, heavy forearms on the table. The less bulky one pushes a hand forward to shake. "Polk," he says. It sounds like "poke" but I know from his nametag it's Polk.

"Birdsong. Nice to meet you." I shake his hand and do the same with Washington who seems to be leader of the expedition. Washington has smoldering eyes.

He leans in and, quiet, says, "Here's what it is, man. We heard you had a little trouble with a grey boy in the barracks yesterday."

Tobacco scent floats on his breath. His *we* sounds like something beyond the two of them. "Oh yeah? What did you hear?"

"We heard you swung on the paddy," Polk says.

"Yes, I did." Closing my left hand still causes pain in the knuckles.

"We heard it started from some mess down at the USO downtown," Washington says.

"Yeah."

"Motherfuckers don't want us in there," Polk says.

"I sort of got the idea—man, news travels fast around here."

"Yeah, it do. Especially if you got your eyes and ears open." Can't tell if Washington intends humor with his *it do*, but his partner's head rocks in agreement.

I say, "Yes, it certainly looks that way."

"Look here, bro, you let us know if there's anything you want us to do about this paddy."

"Do?"

"Yeah. You know, touch him up a little bit. Let him know we ain't down with no paddies fucking with the members?"

"Members?" The wild possibilities of the word stump me. Their eyes do a quick bounce off each other.

"Yeah, *members,* man," Polk says. "You know, spooks, splibs, jigaboos? Us."

"Oh, okay. I'm hip." A new one on me.

"You need us to do anything, you let us know."

"Well, what do you do? And who are you?"

Washington's eyes narrow in support of his words. "We're a concern that does whatever needs to be done to straighten shit out."

A *concern.* Another surprise word here, so old-fashioned-sounding in his usage that it might be hip. "You've got some kind of organization?"

Polk draws his elbows from the table and sits up straight, eyes on his partner. Washington's lips come together in a near pucker. "Maybe," he says.

"Well, I think I got the fool straight yesterday that I'm not taking any shit."

"That's what we're talking about, bro." They get to their feet, both a couple weight classes or more beyond me. We shake hands. They say, "Later, man," and walk off.

Jesus. *Member.* So now I'm a *member* and didn't even know it. The cats were pretty cool about it, though. So unhip, me. Serious cases, especially Washington, all that zeal behind his eyes. The heaviness the departed brothers brought to the table leaves me feeling the table might rise from the floor. I press my elbows into it.

***

Their big bodies ease into the dayroom and sit down. They wait for a commercial break, and then Washington says, "How's everything going, brother?"

"Everything's cool." Late evening, we're the only ones in the dayroom.

"Say, why don't you come take this ride with us," he says. "You're new around here. We want to show you something."

"A ride?"

"Yeah, man, a ride. Don't worry, you ain't in no gangster movie. It won't be long." They're already on their feet. I get the feeling that any refusal of their offer might not be understood.

Polk says, "Be good for you to see a little more of El Paso, man."

The trip downtown in the backseat of an older Chrysler New Yorker at ten-thirty at night doesn't show me much of El Paso, and we end up at a house in a neighborhood east of downtown. I follow the two heavy brothers to the back of the house where they knock and a door opens into an unlit porch.

Whoa. In the almost-dark I can see that whoever let us in wears a hooded robe that covers his face except for eye holes. He hands Washington and Polk similar hoods that they slip on.

"Him too," Washington says.

"Here, man." The doorman pushes a bundled hood against my stomach. No way out of whatever the shit is at this point, I take it, shake it out, and pull it over my head. The weave is loose enough that inhaling is easy. Exhaling heats up my face. A costume party of some kind, but I ain't gettin' no sounds of merriment.

We go through a kitchen into a dining room crowded with eight or nine robed figures at a round table that's got a candleholder in the middle, three tall white candles burning, throwing loony silhouettes on the walls.

Nobody is saying anything until somebody's bass growl: "When these motherfuckers goin' get here?"

"They be here any minute."

All of the bodies at the table are much bigger than I, as large as Washington and Polk or larger—Heavy Brothers all right, with their jive-time hoods. They sit with hands folded on the table. I sit with hands folded like everybody else, waiting for I don't know who or what. A knock on the back porch door, footsteps and bumping, and all eye holes train on the door at that end of the room.

First, half-way falling into the room from a shove, is a pudgy young white guy, a red necktie blindfolding his eyes, with bruises about the face. His fall is checked by the rope around his neck, a noose, held by one of the three hooded people who crowd in behind him. Someone trains a strong flashlight beam on his face. Another yanks off the blindfold. The prisoner's eyes blink then go wide with an instability like egg yolks before he squints against the light. Struggle is nowhere in the question. His torn shirt and welts and bruises about his face tell too much story. The way he winces with slight movement, he's got injured ribs. I close my eyes. Never seen anybody in this condition outside the movies. Heat inside the hood steams my face. I open my eyes. The fool probably tried to run, but the brothers ran him down and worked him over. His clothes are full of dirt. Two of them hold him up. He's pretty good-sized, taller than they but limp and looking ready to throw up or pass out. My stomach turns over and a greenish, sick taste creeps into my throat. The captor holding the noose jerks it and says, "Stand up, fool. You going to get to lay your fat ass down in a minute."

One of the hooded figures at the table rises. It's Washington. "All right, your attention, brothers," he says. "You ones that was there—is this one of the individuals that was doing it?"

"Yeah, that's one of them motherfuckers," somebody says.

"Yeah, he the one was swingin' a chain when they beat up that boy and run him out the place."

"What you got to say now, faggot?" The guy holding the rope gives it a couple rough jerks.

Washington and Polk don't strike me as Southern Negroes. More like the thugs in stories and rumored stories about tough colored gangs back East that I heard of once in a while, growing up in Kayakaw. Hard cats, their rage focused on each other as well as white people. Their language doesn't sound southern. *Faggot,* he called the guy, something that escaped me. He obviously didn't mean one of a bundle of twigs.

This stagy hooded gathering has a whole lot of theater in it, but these cats are not playing. A couple slow, deep breaths and I'm able to swallow, able to keep my stomach from sticking in my throat.

Washington: "All right, y'all, you got the thing in there?"

One of the figures ducks to the door of an adjoining room, looks in, and says, "Oh yeah."

Washington says, "Take him on in there."

Two of the captors replace two heavyweights at the table who get up and go into the adjoining bedroom with the prisoner and the other two captors. They close the door. "Shut the fuck up," comes through, and sounds of thrashing, bedsprings. Groans. A weak, swallowed cry, "Fer God's sake, please. No-o-o...."

While all that is going on, Washington gives a report that consists of a description of my humiliation at the USO and the little fracas in the barracks, noting that the culprits of interest, especially the one from Mississippi, are receiving special surveillance. Washington's report comes through like looking in the wrong end of a telescope and hard to hear with what's going on in the next room. My face is sweating and beginning to itch and my stomach doesn't feel so good, and there's that taste at the base of my throat. I can't imagine him getting the facts from Levinski, but his report is accurate in the main parts. He had to have got it from someone Levinski told it to, especially the USO part. He makes no mention of my name or presence.

The group from the bedroom comes back out with their bent blindfolded prisoner, pants halfway on, face red and wet, his mouth slack and drooling. Grunts of approval and snickers rise from the table. My stomach gathers into a tight, hot ball, and I think I might vomit, but I close my eyes, think high notes, and breathe into my diaphragm until I feel woozy. My gut calms. They take the boy away.

People leave the gathering in the order they arrived, through the dark back porch where they take off hoods. I don't get a look at any unhooded brothers other than Washington and Polk. Dropping me off at Building 1013, Washington says, "You know you got to keep this to yourself, don't you?"

"Yes, I know."

Back in the barracks it's too late to write a letter to Stacy. Past midnight but impossible to lie down and sleep. Tortured. They tortured the guy. It wasn't a movie. If I knew where to go to get a couple shots of whiskey or tequila, that's where I'd be. Too late, and except for heading south, I don't even know how to start toward Mexico from the barracks yet. The guy looked awful, a broken guy, when they brought him out of that room. The boy stepped in some bad shit for sure. My stomach turns over and pulls on my throat. Poor sucker looked so bad, so broken. Obscene. Damn. Took the cat behind the wall and fucked him up. I creep toward my bunk in the dark bay.

Whoa. Funny how I see him in the dark. Daddy, like in a black and white movie, sitting on the side of my bunk in that cavalry uniform, palms pressed into the blanket on either side of him the way Coach used to sit on the bench during ballgames. "Things sure can get ugly sometimes, can't they? And not just in some them books you been reading."

"You saw all that?"

"Oh yeah. And you thought it was some real bad doin's."

"Yes, I did."

"It was evil enough," he says. "'Vengeance is mine saith the Lord.' Vengeance don't belong to man."

"I know that."

"Oh yes, you think you know. Revenge don't get people noplace, just treadin' a whole lot of sad water."

My weak convictions on the subject glow in the dark.

He rises to his feet and glides past me to the aisle. "If you ever become strong enough and deep enough," he says, "you may understand in your soul what I'm saying."

Scrambled eggs, bacon, toast, and coffee don't erase last night's heavy imagery. It's Saturday and the 72nd has no gig. In the latrine, brushing my teeth, I'm a sink away from the tall sergeant who plays glockenspiel when we march, a piano player. His nametag says "Vogel." Kind of a loner, I've noticed. Brown hair and a mustache—in a stage play or modern opera he'd be a British air force officer. Royal Air Force, finishing up his shave. The sergeant's reflection nods good morning from the mirror over his sink. He's patting a dime-sized piece of toilet tissue onto a razor nick.

"Morning," I say when I locate my voice.

He doesn't seem like a guy who talks much so I'm surprised when he finishes his shave and sticks out his hand. "Herb Vogel," he says. "Getting things figured out?"

Last night's outing looms. A ball of sick feeling stirs in my stomach. "I'm trying," I say.

"Well, good luck." Towel over his shoulder, he picks up his shaving kit and walks out.

I finish brushing my teeth. Back in our space, Levinski is lying on his bunk reading, something with a thick dark cover that looks like it came from a library. I could go to the post library if it's open on Saturdays. Should be open. Levinski waves and keeps reading. Says he went to the USO once, but he never leaves the post as far as I've seen. I stow my toothbrush and toothpaste in the footlocker and head downstairs to the rehearsal hall.

The army horn isn't bad, a new Conn trumpet, a solid band instrument, but this morning with my shaky insides, it's a long time before I get with my breath, feel it coming in and issuing out, doing me some good, and before I start hearing myself. Closing my eyes is good sometimes, but closing my eyes now I get pictures from last night of that guy looking so pitiful after they got through working him over in that room, the way he was groaning in there and the way he looked broken into two mismatched pieces of soul and body, slobbering and freaked, when they came back out. And all those big cats in black hoods. I blow some jagged phrases, loud, that don't bring relief.

Building 1013 is air-conditioned like everything on the post seems to be, and down here in the soundproof rehearsal hall, below ground level, no windows, I start to get the shivers. I put away the horn and go upstairs and outside where already in the middle of the morning the sun is a screaming hot bright note. Every day since I got to El Paso has been a hundred degrees or more. Standing in the sun, the heat on my skin, is an improvement. Take off my shirt, get barefoot, run around the courtyard, get busted. In my pocket I've got a few coins and in my wallet a few bills. I ask a couple GIs where to catch the bus downtown.

Sunlight rules the street outside the Copacabana. Light in such a high key I never experienced on the West Coast or in midsummer Kayakaw, light here in the street bouncing off glass, off colors in clothes, off the dangerous red and green and orange slices of melons on the street vendors' stands. I go inside and sit at the bar. Same bartender, Senor Remote. "Tequila, please. With Pepsi."

Things don't lighten up after a couple tequilas, so I try a third. Sunlight splashes in through the open doorway. The complaining sound and rhythm of Mexican trumpets over the loudspeakers plays above the three girls that come out of the curtained entrance I went through on my first day in Juarez. The woman I met that day is not one of them. These girls strut in like a stage act in their shiny dresses, size up the joint. The well-stacked one in blue, hands on her hips, stops and ices me with an exaggerated stare. I've been gawking, I think, like some joker from the hills who ain't never seen nothin'. I close my mouth and put the back of my hand to my lips to check for drooling. Damn. Her breasts threaten to pop from the top of the tight sleeveless dress, and her hips and thighs challenge the fabric also. She's a fair-skinned girl with high cheekbones that make me think Eskimo. Her black hair is cut short, bobbed. She comes to the stool beside me, close enough to sniff her. Her breasts rise like two yeast rolls. "You see something you like, Senor?"

The words deposit themselves like individual coins in my head. She is speaking to me. Big dark eyes reinforce her voice. From the pit in which I've been sitting it's not clear what I should say to this shiny, muscular girl who eyes me without smiling. I say, "You look very good."

She tosses her chin with a light snort, but her eyes are tank treads running up and down my front.

"Can you go in back with me?" I say.

"Come on," she says. Just like that. I'm jerked, on a leash.

I suck the last tequila out of the glass along with a few ice chips and follow her through the curtain where I pay and the "nurse" inspects me.

Watching her muscular flanks wind toward the room, thought wavers into my head this girl probably sees ten guys or more every day she works. Let's say she works three days a week, or five days. Over a hundred guys a month. New troops coming all the time, year after year. I'm just a speck in her experience, a specimen, pinned and wriggling on her belly for a few seconds. Oh, man. Inside the room she hooks the door and takes off everything but her bra. I take off my pants. Her body is golden, curvy, smooth-muscled perfection that she sells, and I'm lusted up at the sight. Lusted up and head going round. She puts her hand out behind and lowers herself to the mattress on the floor. Her polished red nails dig into the sheet. I kneel beside her and touch the mesh of her bra with my finger. "Could you please take off your brassiere?"

She bats my finger away. "You gonna fuck me there?" she says.

Concussion grenade, dry ice, I don't know what, but the effect kayos my erection, and a deposit of shame, embarrassment, self-pity, darkness, fear, and confusion thumps into my stomach. Shoulders, arms, legs, breath feel as punchless as my outdone penis. I fumble my pants and shoes back on. She rolls onto one elbow. "*Que pasa,* what are you doing?"

"I'm not doing anything—I think I'm going to leave."

"We don't give no money back, *Senor.*"

"I don't care. I just want to get out of here." I unhook the door and leave her with her easy money, putting her clothes on.

Outside the Copa on the uneven sidewalk the air is hot but fresh. I should be able to walk in a military manner or at least without lurching like a drunk apple knocker from nowhere. Start toward the bridge. Hip hoo, hip ha. It's a swim upstream against the troops invading *Ciudad Juarez.* Better luck than I had, boys! My step goes off. Things going fine until I lost my step, not easy to get it back, weaving against the grain. Hut, two, three, fo'.

In the latrine of Building 1013, chrome and porcelain make a bright cold music that has nothing to do with the heat outside. Air conditioning cools the brightness. I splash handfuls of cold water on my face, close my eyes and let music play, high notes probing for some pure place beyond this earth, I swear, from Telemann's D Trumpet Concerto.

Something bursts in my chest and I'm sobbing. Sore grabbing in the throat, so I put my face in the sink, run more water, and massage my face in case somebody walks in. Nobody walks in. I keep my eyes closed and let the sore currents run through me till I feel washed out. Still got some booze in me, though.

Coming out of the latrine I see into the orderly room and that the red-haired guy from Wisconsin is on CQ duty. I stick my head inside the door and say, "Hi, Helzer, how's it going?"

He looks up in his easy, small-town way, good-looking young white guy, but he's behind the Cotton Curtain now, that we pretend is not there. In grade school we would have been buddies on the playground. "Hi, Joe," he says. "It's a quiet one."

I weave my way to my bunk and lie down until chow time.

After an hour of long tones and exercises from the Arban book, my head and gut settle. I put my horn away and leave the basement. On the first floor landing, outside the windows of the double doors, Washington and Polk stand smoking. They've been watching the door and never would have missed me. They see that I've seen them. I stop. No use jiving around. Washington drops his smoke, grinds it under his foot, and brings his tree stumpy two hundred pounds through the door. I've never seen young guys outside of church look as fervent as these guys. All those hooded cats were about Washington's size, except for the one other guy my size. Felt like a featherweight in there. Washington puts out a thick paw and we shake. "How you feelin' today, bro?"

"I'm fine," I say. "How about yourself?"

"I'm good." He stays in his serious business groove, dark meaty-faced bishop. "Listen here, bro, we just stopped by to see how you doing with what you saw going down other night."

"I'm doing all right."

"And we want to make sure you understand the confidential nature of the proceedings. What I'm saying is you don't say nothing to nobody."

The cat's presumptuousness regarding my understanding is almost enough to make me break tone and say something ridiculous. "I think you got that across."

"That's good, that's good. Understanding saves a whole lot of trouble," he says. "See you later." He backs out the door and joins his partner who waves to me, and they walk off.

***

Dearest Stacy,

Hard to believe that this time last year I was still in the classroom, trying to teach, and we were doing the opera and you were getting ready to graduate. It's real different down here in the desert, baby.

Except for the guy I share the cubicle with, the 72nd Army Band looks like some kind of a desert to me, so far. Except for a few of them, most of the guys in the barracks seem to take off for Juarez damn near every evening. Maybe because it's early in the month and they've still got money. I never see any of these cats practicing, usually have the rehearsal room all to myself. It's a cool place to write letters, too, like now.

Down here at Showalter is the first time I've seen so many people from the South, white and colored. And they stay separated except at work on the post. I'm the only colored guy in the band right now, except for one sergeant, a French horn player who lives off post. The First Sergeant is from Louisiana and the clerk is from Tennessee, cats that have been in the army since it was invented. They know how to act, but there are a couple punks in the barracks that cause me to think evil thoughts. The one from Mississippi especially gets on my nerves and I regularly have shocking thoughts related to his destruction. He and I have already had a run-in, and it's like every time I see the guy all the poisonous stuff I ever heard about Mississippi is right in front of me—Senator Bilbo talking shit about "nigras," lynching, Emmett Till. Never felt so awful toward a person. You don't want to feel that way toward another person, but at the same time the idea of pulverizing the motherfucker is delicious. I'm telling you this, baby, because I know you understand. It's not a good way to feel. It's a good thing I've studied some Faulkner, although he is a strange cat.

One good thing here is that I share a cubicle with a clarinet player from Brooklyn who plans to be a music professor. Levinski has a degree from NYU. He is plain nuts over Mozart and can't believe I don't share his enthusiasm. I told him about Seraglio. Nice guy, though.

Baby, you wouldn't believe how hot it is down here, over a hundred damn near every day. I do believe the River Styx is nearby. And if it ain't a hundred, it's ninety-eight or ninety-nine. Hot and dry. I like the warm nights and think a lot about how cool it would be walking out in the desert with you, rollin' in the dust. Gets me to salivating (till I starting thinkin' 'bout them scorpions and rattlesnakes, my tongue dries up). Bye, bye.

Much love,
JB

3)

CQ duty for the first time, I'm in the orderly room at the clerk's desk, reading *The El Paso Times.* Foot noises and voices bounce off the hall surfaces. Two monkeys the army sent into space have been recovered in good condition down at Cape Canaveral. Got a couple monkeys right here I could recommend for the next flight. Every once in a while, somebody sticks his head in the doorway, sees me, and goes on. I'm still a new guy, no buddies. Not much in the paper, I set it aside and pull the cover off the typewriter. It's a big black Remington, looks new. In one of the desk drawers I find some typing paper and roll a couple sheets into the machine and begin a letter to Stacy, getting the feel of the keyboard back in my fingers. The middle finger on my left hand is still a little sore, which shakes loose a couple puffs of hate.

I'm rambling mostly about nothing when Sergeant Vogel walks in, stops, scans the room and clears his throat. Back to World War II and the RAF. He's smoking a pipe with a curved stem and carrying a folded newspaper. "Excuse me," he says.

I swing away from the typewriter. "Hi, Sarge."

"You're a typist, eh?"

"I know how to type. I don't call myself a typist."

He draws on his pipe, lets out the smoke and says, "Hmm ." The way he's holding it, the newspaper looks like the main reason for this visit. He lays it on the desk and puts his finger on a headline. "Did you see this?"

I stretch far enough forward to see what he's pointing to. It's an article that tells about Benjamin O. Davis, Jr, being promoted to major general. First Negro to get two stars. "Yes, I read that."

"What do you think?" He keeps his eyes on the paper.

There's something shellshocked and shy about the sergeant's manner that tells me I should keep my wilder thoughts about the subject out of the conversation. I say, "What do I think?"

"Yes."

"It sounds good to me. It's probably long overdue." At Fort Showalter, I haven't yet seen a colored officer. At Ord I saw one or two lieutenants. Benjamin O. Davis, Jr, is a name I've been seeing since World War Two, when he was leader of the Tuskegee Airmen and the 332nd fighter group. Davis's father was the first Negro general in the US Army, saw his picture in *The Pittsburgh Courier*. In all the news photos of him I ever saw, though, the old man looked white. Davis Junior is light too, but looks Negro in photos with his dark mustache and not completely straight hair.

Vogel draws on his pipe and lets out some smoke. "I was thinking the same thing. I followed what he was doing during the war."

"Oh really?"

He gives me a quick sidelong look and directs his eyes to the floor. "A kid I was friends with, growing up, was in the 332nd."

That straightens me up in my chair. "Where was that, Sarge?"

"New York. Brooklyn, actually."

"Brooklyn? Wow! I never would have guessed. You don't sound anything like Levinski."

He half snickers. "Brooklyn has a lot of different neighborhoods, and I've been away from there for a long time."

"Interesting. Interesting." That's all I can think to say in the space between writing to Stacy and Vogel walking in with this article. A childhood friend in the 332nd of B.O. Davis, Jr. Vogel from Brooklyn, like the Kesslers.

He rolls up the newspaper, his gaze toward the floor, but I dig that his mental eyes are on me. "Well, I'd better let you get back to your typing," he says. "See you later."

While I was chatting with Vogel I'm sure Washington and Polk passed the doorway. The thought of them in the building feels like weight, but they passed on by, making for easier breathing.

4)

"Welcome to Bolden Heights."

Merlin Swink waves me into the wooden barracks of the 224th, a structure tiny and light compared to the cinder block and masonry mass of Building 1013 that's as big as Kayakaw High. We haven't talked since the gig at White Sands.

"Thanks, man. I thought it was about time I took you up on your invitation."

"How're you doing?" he says. Without his sunglasses, Swink has wide-open blue eyes.

"I'm doing okay, I guess."

We walk down the middle of the room that has a row of bunks and lockers on each side until we reach Swink's area. No partitions between bunks. The walls are varnished plywood, the floor surfaced with black tile. Four windows on each side let in plenty of light. Swink reaches into his locker and takes out a slim, almost square paperback book, black and white cover, HOWL printed across it. "I got most of my high school education outside of high school," he says, shaking the book, and I think of my free-ranging Stacy and of my own junior year, working for the Kesslers when I read *Anna Karenina* and *Cry the Beloved Country,* and reading changed, and life started looking more layered and saturated in its colors. A photograph slips from Swink's book onto the floor. He picks it up and sits down, looks at it, and hands it to me. "My used-to-be girlfriend," he says. "And me, before *Howl.*"

Him, before *Howl.* In the photo, Swink and a girl in a sweater that could have been cashmere sit on a sofa in a living room. Part of a fireplace and a mirror above the fireplace show in the photo, and there's a Christmas tree behind the sofa. Swink's hair is longer than now, combed straight back. A guitar lies across his lap. He reeks of toys, birthday parties, bicycles, good underwear and socks without holes, a high school sweetheart he could visit any old time. The girl's arm is around his shoulders. She has long dark hair, smiling lips, and her breasts could occupy the male mind of a high school student body beyond the last bell of the school day. Her lips in the photo, the curve of her cheek and breasts and their known softness sharpen the presence of the steel cots around us with their scratchy olive green blankets, put a shine to the varnished plywood walls, put an ache in the air.

Swink says, "So you've never read this, huh?" He isn't with the photo of his high school sweetheart. He's with *Howl*. He opens it, jabs the page with his finger, conducting my eyes to the print.

"Nope, never read it."

Swink's watercolor face takes in my words without any raise of the brow or contortion of the lips. "It came out three years ago."

Which would have been near the time of the photo in his hand, the all-American boy and girl picture of Swink and his high school girlfriend.

He shakes the book at me, says, "Listen to this:

I saw the best minds of my generation destroyed by
madness, starving hysterical naked,
dragging themselves through the negro streets at dawn
looking for an angry fix

Whoa. His voice and the words bring me halfway back from my trip into the photo of him and the girl. Swink hisses the words, waves his free hand through the air, pounds the air. Gets louder:

who poverty and tatters and hollow-eyed and high sat
up smoking in the supernatural darkness of
cold-water flats floating across the tops of cities
contemplating jazz

Even the beginning of Swink's reading confirms possibilities just beyond the fog in which I stand, the fog of four years of square-ass study and work, denying my derangement in a job and marriage designed to make a bill-paying drone out of me, scratching out a dying while *Howl* was going on. Already I can hear it's a disgrace I hadn't even heard of this poem.

Contemplating jazz.

Swink's spiraling free hand lifts him from his seat and he paces away, a shirt-tailed street preacher in "poverty and tatters" shouting lines to the rows of cots and his audience of one. Cat is crazy with it. He spins and paces toward me. His esses are juicy, but he doesn't spit and foam at the mouth. Testifying. At home, my mother recited the couple poems she knew like that, not as loud, but serious, like she was in a trance, eyes locked in a stare way inside where the poem was coming from, like she was testifying, sanctified, at church. Swink's head bobs to the beats of the lines pouring through him.

I stand still, holding my breath, not to change the air. Swink breathes in through his nose, flips ahead in the book, chants a final spate of Ginsberg's words. He closes the book, holds it between his palms, and then sits, a skinny man down here on the border holding the last tortilla on earth. "Can you believe that," he says. "What do you think?"

"Man, I think I can't believe I'm just now hearing this. It's damn near like I haven't been alive."

"Yes," Swink says. He hangs onto the ess. "Yes."

Cooped up in Portland, nesting with unexploded bombs in my head, trying to teach school so I could try to buy stuff. Sidetracked and sore. Only by luck getting to play my horn, I never would have heard *Howl*. Never would have heard the alarm. This alarm against all the shit trying to come down on you—what poetry is. Righteous. In the air above Swink, I shadowbox for a moment. "Shit, man, I feel like I just got turned loose from a straitjacket."

The breath in the poem does, in this moment, in fact blow away the straitjacket offered by the army, the Heavy Brothers, marriage, school teaching, trying to be sane.

"Yes. Yes, I know," Swink says. "I know." He lifts his top hand off the book and passes it to me. The poem sprawls across the pages like Genesis or Walt Whitman. Who-clause begets who-clause up and down the pages. My eyes separate the poet's black words from the light pulpy pages like drink from a paper cup. I drink in relief from my stony introduction to El Paso, Juarez, the 72nd Army Band, and the darkness of the Heavy Brothers. *Howl.*

"You can borrow it."

"Oh, man, thank you. I'll study it." Swink's face floats in front of me, broken into colorful particles by the blaze of the poem. The girlfriend photo, burnt up by his reading, is still in my hand. I look at it again. "What's with the guitar," I ask.

"Oh, I used to screw around with it."

I shake the photo at him. "She's really good-looking."

Swink's wild blue eyes don't go to the photo, nor does he reach for it. "Yeah. Yeah, and she was supposed to be the all-time brain at our school," he says. "In the whole history of the school she was supposed to be the smartest kid that ever went there. But you know what? I was greater than she was."

At the moment, I could understand that. No doubt Swink was greater in his madness. Greater in his appetites. Greater in his burning for ancient heavenly connections that reading stuff like *Howl* set loose in him. And more expressive, wilder, in his reports. No doubt. He pushes the photo away, points to the book, and I slide it into the middle pages and tell him, "You know, man, you really are great."

5)

I drop back to let others in front of me because, walking behind Jarboe, I was becoming fixated on the idea of a rabbit punch. We're returning to the bus from the parade ground. A punch like the one I got that time coming out of the Porters Club with Stacy. Some contagious stuff. Not that I would have punched him with all these people around, but my stability don't feel all that stable when I get too close to the cat.

Sergeant Howell comes up beside me, clarinet in his hand. "So how you coming along, Birdsong?"

"So far, so good, Sarge."

"Good, good. You sound real strong up there with them trumpets," he says.

"Thanks, Sarge, I'm trying."

"Well, you're doing all right, boy." My impression of the First Sergeant from the first morning in the orderly room has been that he's a naturally friendly man, even if he is from Louisiana and white. There's the Cotton Curtain, but Howell's got a decent side that knows how to put people at ease. The man is all army and knows how to work with soldiers. The way he's hanging next to me, seems like he wants to ask me something which he finally gets around to. "Say, Birdsong, they tell me you know how to type. Is that right?"

"Sure, I know how to type."

At the bus, he pulls me aside before we get on. "Listen," he says, "we need somebody in the orderly room that can type. Sergeant Barnstable has been filling in just till we can find somebody, but really he ain't nobody's clerk-typist. Ya see, bands don't get authorized no clerk typists. When we get back to the building, put your stuff away and come see me."

The typing sample I hand Sergeant Howell is flawless, and he digs it. "I don't know what Barny called hisself worrying about, boy, this looks real good."

Barny, the nervous sergeant filling in as clerk, must have told Howell he wasn't sure the new colored private could type or type well enough. I had marked Sergeant First Class Barnstable's manner—"a Tennessee Bastard" Muccigrosso labels him—one of those cats that tries to be cool, talks the requisite shit, but he wants you Negro to understand that he's A White Man and then a sergeant. Some of that shit that's always trying to come down on you. He'd shown me the typewriter but didn't ask me to type anything, had only said "It's a ticklish son of a bitch" about the morning report I would have to type every weekday if I became clerk.

"You can't use an eraser on these damn things," he said. "See? It's four copies." He held up a form and pointed to some carbon sheets and matching onionskins on the desk.

"Yes, I see. An original and three copies."

"And you're only allowed three strikeovers," he said.

"Strikeovers?"

"Mistakes. If you make a mistake, you can cross it out with a slash, but you can only do that three times."

"That's a pretty nice typewriter there," I said.

He swiveled to the typing table and whipped the plastic cover from the glossy black Remington. His eyelids closed part way, and his face drooped when he looked at the typewriter. "It's a damn good machine," he said.

Then: "If Howell sees you messing up too many of these DD forms with strikeovers, he gets real nervous."

"Really?"

"Yeah. He can get to shittin' little green bullets about that." His eyes got wide when he said that, and I laughed. He didn't laugh. He said, "You report the wrong number of men on leave or use the wrong code and Headquarters will call down here in a minute."

"You've had the experience, huh?"

He gave me a short, sharp look loaded with color clashing, something I never used to think about but since I got down here I'm bumping up against all the time inside my head. It ain't something I'm reading about in books. My pigmentation can make for some crazy daily bread shit. Like in the troop information class yesterday, the instructor seemed to get an attitude because I answered a couple questions he was figuring to stump the class with so that he could give a big unnecessary explanation. After that, wouldn't call on me when I raised my hand. White cat from down in these parts. Barny took out a cigarette, lit up, and then offered me one. "No thanks," I said. "I don't smoke."

But he was still the sergeant here. He took a passionate suck on the smoke that ended with a tremor, and settled back. "Like I told you, boy, it's a ticklish son of a bitch."

What Sergeant Barnstable didn't understand, though, was that he was talking to the cleanup hitter of the '52 Kayakaw Boys' Typing Team.

At rehearsal, Sergeant Howell, down front with the clarinets, gets up and faces the band. "At ease," he says. "I want y'all to know Private

Birdsong, back there in the trumpet section, is the new band clerk. And thanks to Sergeant Barnstable for filling in—great job, Barny. We got somebody now that can make that old typewriter holler. Got here just in time too. Don't y'all be bothering Joe while he's working in the morning. He'll be doing the morning report. Y'all know that, but we got some new men in here. The clerk has got to get that thing done and then get down here by 0800. If you got business with the clerk, see him after rehearsal."

6)

At Bolden Heights, Swink says, "How're you doing?"

"I'm doing okay, I guess. You're looking at the new clerk of the 72nd."

Swink's eyebrows go up. "Is that going to be cool?"

"It should be. We'll see."

"You're a typist?"

"I can type. Took typing for the hell of it after I completed my graduation requirements when I was a senior in high school. It sure came in handy in college."

Swink says, "Let's go next door. I'll show you where we play." Leaving the barracks and closing the wooden door, I hear wood and smell wood, a friendlier resonance than what comes off the cinder block, mortar, clay tile, and steel down in Building 1013.

The brown trombonist standing in the middle of a scatter of folding chairs takes the horn away from his lips, and the drummer wearing a snap-brim cap stops playing when Swink and I walk into the rehearsal hall of the 224th. The trombonist's hornrimmed glasses give him a hip but serious look. He's dark chocolate brown and a little taller than I. Swink walks right up to him and jabs him on the shoulder. "Hey, Freddy, this is Joe Birdsong from the 72nd."

"Oh yeah, new man. I noticed him up at White Sands." The hand he puts out for me to shake has rounded, even fingernails.

The drummer adjusts his cap, revealing red hair, eases off his stool and comes over to shake hands. "Jerry Gilson."

"Nice to meet you."

Swink gives the trombonist another jab on the shoulder. "And this is Freddy Turner."

Freddy Turner shakes his shoulder and pushes Swink in the chest. "Motherfucker, you better try to find something else to hit."

Swink falls back, laughing.

The drummer returns to his drums and sits.

Turner says, "Nice to meet you, man."

"Likewise. You guys sound pretty good. We could hear you from outside."

Turner waves his horn toward the drummer. "We're working on it. Old Jerry here is getting good," he says. "Do you blow, man?"

"A good question. That's one thing I'm working on while I'm down here." My knuckle is still sore, and a cold tingle creeps under my skin when that Heavy Brother business and wearing the hood floats to mind, so that I haven't really settled down to practicing. Should have said "That's one thing I *plan* to work on."

The drummer, Gilson, says, "You play trumpet, right?"

"Right."

"Well, bring your axe on up sometime," Turner says. "Look at some charts with us."

Gilson taps a cymbal. "Yeah."

"Hey, thanks. I'll look forward to that."

Turner points his trombone slide at Swink. "So where did you meet up with this here juvenile delinquent?"

"Merlin and I talked at the White Sands job. He invited me up to read something."

"Reading or preaching, or looking to get high," Turner says. "That's old Merlin."

Turner might be twenty-three, but has the look of an old sanctified person at church. Sweet look. Looking right at you like you're the most precious thing on earth. He could come from a long line of preachers. He knuckles his glasses higher on the bridge of his nose, checking out my face, modulates, "So how you doing, so far, man?"

I shrug off the blues of the Heavy Brothers. "Well, it's really quite difficult to say, you know. I am in the fucking army."

The words reach Turner's funnybone, and he doubles over in a fit of laughing.

Swink says, "Christ sake, Freddy, it wasn't that funny."

Swink's words prod the trombonist into a second spasm, who, gasping, lays his hand on my shoulder. "I'm sorry, man. Caught me off guard. You know, most cats you ask them how they doing, they just say 'fine'." He takes his hand off my shoulder, squares up and says, "And the cat sounded so proper."

"He sounds like a schoolmaster," Gilson says.

Schoolmaster. With a soft New England *a.* I ask him, "Where are you from, man?"

"New Bedford."

"New Bedford. A very historic place. You're the first person I've ever met from New Bedford," I say. "And you're on the beam, man. Last year at this time I was teaching school."

"Oh yeah? What'd you teach?"

"English, high school."

Freddy Turner puts up his hand. "Didn't I say the cat sounded proper? Didn't I say it?"

"English, my worst subject," Gilson says. "Oh man."

Turner lays a backhand swat on Swink's arm. "Say, boy, thanks for bringing this cat over."

Swink says, "*De nada.*"

Then: "Hey, Joe, I've got something in the barracks I want to give you before you leave. Excuse me, I'll be right back." He's closing the door behind him before I can say anything.

"You guys been playing jazz long?" I say to the other two.

"Been playing at it a long time," Freddy Turner says, "but now I'm starting to get it, man. You know?"

Gilson says, "I got started in high school, listening to Max Roach."

Ancient heavenly connection, these guys inviting me up to do music with them, a way out of the lowlands of the 72nd, perhaps. An opening.

Swink comes back into the rehearsal hall carrying two record albums. He holds them up in front of me. "Here, take these," he says.

"You've already given me *Howl,* man."

"Yes, but you've got to have these too."

Swink disturbs the air around my face, waving the albums. "This is some of the greatest jazz trumpet playing you'll ever hear."

Turner says, "He ain't lying about that."

I take the albums. "Well, thanks, Merlin, I'll give them a good listen."

Swink stands by, springy in the knees with satisfaction. Boy really digs making an impression.

Down the hill, in the basement of Building 1013, I listen to *Study in Brown* and *Clifford Brown with Strings.* Swink was seriously right. I hear a trumpet voice full of color, direct, smart, husky, saying This is the way to do it, a way to stay alive while you're alive.

Closer Encounters

1)

After chow I go down to the rehearsal room to practice and to listen to Swink's records some more. I take a folded newspaper page that Sergeant Vogel gave me, saying I should read the article he pointed out. Before I start to practice, I read the article. Down in New Orleans a bunch of colored protesters were marching in support of a boycott against stores where they could shop but couldn't get jobs. The usual white yokels were yelling insults and throwing shit. The cops came and arrested the marchers, took them to jail. They all got hundred and fifty-dollar fines, two fucking times my monthly pay. I close my eyes, put the horn to my lips, and start blowing long tones. My breathing stays rough. I put away the horn and go out and catch the bus downtown.

Out of the country, *Ciudad Juarez*, at the Copa, I sit and drink tequila with Pepsi. The girls in shiny dresses loop through the room. They're like hard Christmas candy, the red and green stuff, in cellophane. That first woman, on Memorial Day, was pleasant. I was thirsty. But it's nothing like the real thing with Mae in the early days, or with Stacy, when your whole heart melts into it and you hang together keeping each other warm, feeling whole, and the morning after when you wake on a cloud. This business is closer to jerking off, woman not even half there and she's taking your money. And then you run into some tough Eskimex like Alicia. Alicia with her bold-ass chest is present and busy. At least twice, I see her swing through the curtain with a guy. Mean to me. Alicia was not a good representative of the sorority. I have taken care to avoid eye contact, kept my elbows on the bar and stared into my glass whenever a girl has come purring close.

It's late when I think about the hike back across the bridge and finally slide off the barstool. I find myself facing Washington and Polk, too-close walls behind me as if they had been attending me all along. Massive, darkly brotherly, opportunistic, the nearest to smiling I've ever seen them.

"You making your move now, bro?" Polk says. "You want a ride back across the bridge?"

A vision carriage with six white horses rises up, soars across the river, and fades. I say, "As a matter of fact, my good man, I am ready to go, and a ride across the bridge would represent a substantial benefit."

Polk's eyes examine the floor, and he bumps his partner with his elbow. Washington claps me on the upper arm, "Let's make the move, then," he says.

We move out to the sidewalk. Warmer night air than ever in Portland hugs my face. I look up into the starry dynamo of night, wait for stars to come into focus above the illumination of El Paso—Juarez. Washington leads us up the street to the weathered Chrysler. A light-complexioned cat the size of Washington eases off the front fender, walks around the front of the car, and gets in behind the wheel. Polk gets in beside him. Washington and I get into the back seat.

Washington says, "We're going to drop Bro here at the bus stop."

The driver twists his big body and reaches over the seat to shake my hand. "How you doin', man?"

"Fine."

"Let's go," Washington says. Washington's got the air of a field grade officer. Any time I've seen him with other people, he takes over. These cats with him know who's in charge. He ain't in charge of me.

The driver pulls out, swings around the block, and heads for the bridge. Through my pollution I sense that the brothers are out to do some business this evening, at least a meeting, and they're not interested in having me with them. I ain't interested in their agenda, I don't think, but there's at least a little bit of wanting to be wanted in everybody. No invitation of no kind here. Sombitches probably think I'm too drunk. Maybe so. They drop me off at Alligator Park where I catch the bus to Fort Showalter.

Crossing the parade ground in the warm dark, I break into a trot that I slow to a march after a few jelly-legged yards. My thirty-inch step wobbles. I start trotting again and running, try a little Doak Walker broken field run and end up face in the grass. Tackled by the ground. Dry grass against my cheek, could just curl up here and go to sleep. I roll onto my back and stretch out like Leonardo's man in the circle. See more stars here than downtown.

Whoa, man.

Something in a bundle of light floats down beside me, then looms over me. Daddy on that horse, in Technicolor this time, one hand on his hip the other holding the reins, his shadowed face on me.

"On your feet, Private."

His shout puts me to scrambling, drowning on dry ground, before I make it upright.

"Daddy?"

"You better believe it."

"Believe it?"

"Listen, boy, you need to get a thing or two straight or you not gonna last no time."

I shake myself and try to meet his pulpit tone. "What are you talking about?"

"I'm talking about forget not they is such a thing as disgrace."

"I know that."

"Then why you wobblin' here like you can't stand up like a man, down on the ground like some creeping thing.

"I fell."

He rides off a few yards and then back, scans me from under his brim.

"Ye-e-es Lord. You sure enough did," he says. "And can fall farther, too."

Off he goes, lights out, into the dark.

"You all right there this morning, Birdie?" Sergeant Howell has had his feelers out ever since I walked into the orderly room. My khakis are crisp, my belt buckle shines, but he probably noticed my eyes are red. Cold water and breakfast didn't help.

"Yes. I'm all right, Sarge." I get the DD Form 1 and the onionskins into the typewriter and knock out the morning report. Two damn strike-overs in it. I never do that. It'll pass with only two strikeovers, no need to waste paper. Howell will notice if I start a do-over ("Something wrong there, Birdie?"), and time is running out.

"Here you go, Sarge." I pass him the besmirched report.

He takes it, lays it before him and runs his eyes over it, lower lip pushing against his upper, thick hands framing the paper. I slip the cover over the typewriter. He says, "All right, Birdie. See you downstairs."

After rehearsal we have a ten o'clock review on the parade ground where I foundered in the grass last night. The 224th is joining us for the job because the commanding general will be there. Swink and Turner and Gilson already look like long-lost brothers when I see them. We slap fives, shuffle around, laugh.

Turner says, "Man, why don't you bring your horn up to the place this evening and fool around on some stuff with me and Jerry?"

"Sounds like a good idea." I haven't been up to Bolden Heights since Swink gave me the Clifford Brown records.

Since noon, the pall from last night, Daddy's appearance and all, has gotten heavier and heavier. There was the hangover, but it has passed into something else where I'm having trouble keeping hold of thoughts. Part of me is sinking.

We're through with work by mid-afternoon, a good time to finally visit the post library and see what's in there. I take paper and pen and make my way to the small wooden building, pre-fab and newcomer-looking among the sturdy old brick and stucco houses in the area, where officers and their families live in roomy pads with good plumbing, central heating and air-conditioning, close to the parade ground. Wives and kids can hear band music floating over the area.

The spec 4 behind the desk sits reading. The place feels empty. He raises his eyes from the book with an expression on his face that suggests he's really digging where he is. His arm comes up in a gesture that reminds me of my old buddy Luke, toward the rows of bookshelves and tables, and he says, "Let me know if I can help you with anything."

He's still with the dream in the book. I say, "Thanks," touched by his dreaminess and gesture in the quiet room with wooden walls, tables, chairs.

Oak library chairs like those in the public library in Portland and in the Kayakaw High library are a surprise here, like a nice cup of afternoon tea. I slide onto one of them and lay my pen and paper on the table. It would be easy to sit here in the quiet on this oak seat with its friendly contour for the rest of the day, be a statue with thoughts light and heavy falling down on me.

I get up and find the fiction shelves. Faint, dry, paper smell hangs distinct as smoke in the air. Some steady reading would help. I pull out two Thomas Hardy novels and take them back to the table. My thoughts jump between the print, the Heavy Brothers, the music I've been listening to, and the business that has been happening with Daddy. I push the books aside and start a letter to Stacy, describing a part of the situation at Showalter.

The clock on the wall behind the clerk's desk tells me I could get in an hour of practice before chow, after which I'm taking off for Bolden Heights. I'll put the finishing touches on the letter later. Nobody here watching, I close my eyes and take a couple deep breaths, feeling them all the way into my diaphragm and lungs, and let them out in silent notes. Throughout the dry, woody space, summer afternoon silence rules. I check out the Hardy books and head back to Building 1013.

The bulky sight of Washington and Polk standing on the concrete porch outside the building entrance, smoking, changes the weather. I consider swinging around to the other side of the building, but they've seen me, and seen that I've seen them, so I don't break stride. These big suckers ain't no way passive in they program. I step onto the porch, and they wave their cigarette hands. "How you doin' this afternoon, Brother Birdsong," Washington says.

Polk says the same thing with a head gesture.

"I'm doing okay."

"Look like you fixin' to do some heavy readin', man." Washington points his cigarette toward the books under my arm.

"Yes, I was just now over at the library. Got to do something to stay busy around here." My words are out before I really got connected with them. Something I need to watch around these guys.

"We got us a studious young man right here," Polk says. "Boy might help us out sometime. Real studious."

"That's a good thing," Washington says.

"I don't know if I'm all that studious, but I do enjoy reading."

Washington taps out his cigarette butt on the porch railing and field strips it. "Listen, man, you ought to come look at this movie with us tomorrow night. Smart fellah like you, maybe you already seen it," he says. "Anyhow, we studying some history."

"History, huh?"

"That's right."

"What's the movie you're talking about?"

He cuts his eyes right, then left, bends my way and mumbles, "It's called *The Birth of a Nation.* You seen it?"

I know about the film and the trouble it caused across the country right after World War One, but I've never seen it. "No, I've heard about it but I've never seen it," I say. "They're showing it at the post theater?"

"Naw, man, this is strictly on the QT for members in the know. Ain't nobody else suppose to hear about it. You dig?"

Washington underlines his last two words with light thumps on my chest from his heavy fist. I say, "I'm hip."

Washington's weight makes me feel like a benchwarmer even though I might have a better idea of the game than he. He says, "They tell me this motherfucker is the last thing they'd be showing down here at a army post."

A small sweat gathers on my forehead. "You're right, I'm sure."

"We be cuttin' out at eight o'clock," he says.

"Where is it showing?"

"It ain't at no theater, man. Some brothers are passing through with it and giving us this private showing so we get a better understanding of our situation."

"A better understanding of our situation" explodes on me like a poster for all my earthly yearnings. A better understanding of where I sit in time and space. A grip on my uncertainties, perhaps.

Polk says, "You coming with us, man?"

"Sure, I'll go. It's a film I've always wanted to see." A few fleeting announcements of showings of *The Birth of a Nation* are all I've ever seen. Whenever I've heard about it, I've felt something big and worrisome behind the paucity of discussion about a movie that was supposed to be so great in movie history. Some shit going on. Stuff being held back.

"Be out here tomorrow night at eight o'clock, man."

2)

"Hey, Brother Birdsong." Freddy Turner is oiling his trombone slide when I walk into the 224th rehearsal hall. The way he says "Brother Birdsong" has a resonance that I hear in his playing, something I don't feel or hear in my own playing yet. And it's a sound different from the "brother" of the Heavy Brothers in which I feel no brotherhood. One of these times, I should maybe talk to Turner about those guys. I haven't been able to bring them up. "I see you brought your axe," he says.

We slap fives. "Yeah, man, I need to get to work on the project."

"Good, good." He looks interested when he says, "So how you doing?"

It's an opening beyond music, but I'm not ready to enter. "Doing okay, man. How about yourself?"

"Everything's cool."

"Jerry and Merlin around?"

"Jerry said he'd be over after while."

We warm up together and blow through the melodies of a few tunes from Freddy's fakebook.

Gilson shows up shortly with Swink, who leaves when he, Turner, and I start to work. Swink says he's reading *The Seven Pillars of Wisdom*.

After we've played around long enough with some blues changes, getting acquainted, Turner brings out a chart for the tune "Moanin'." It's catchy and I've liked it the couple times I've heard it on the radio.

"Y'all want to try this," he says.

Gilson says, "Why not?"

I signal assent, and we play through the head a few times until it's tight. Freddy improvises a few choruses full of energy and good humor. My attempts are not as fluent as Turner's, but in the struggle to get beyond clichés I see possibilities. Stay loose. Listen harder. I'm feeling

I should write out some ideas and study them. When we get through, my whole body is tingling, and none of me really ready to stop.

Freddy takes out a pack of Chesterfields, offers Gilson and me smokes that I decline. He and Gilson share a flame.

"Your drumming really juices things up," I say.

Gilson laughs. "Yeah?"

"Yeah. It gets to feeling like church, man."

"A whole lot of that in it," Turner says.

"I sort of dig it." My head is light and my chest is stirred up from playing, and not ready to quit.

Turner takes a drag from his smoke, pushes his glasses up with the little finger of his cigarette hand. "You got a lot of technique, man, and you were starting to get it pretty good," he says. "You know about hard bop?"

"Hard bop?" The term is new to me, and Turner reads the expression on my face.

"Well, you know about bebop, don't you, man?" His ear tilts toward me.

The question is a quiet one, but I feel caught with my pants down. "No, man, not much, just heard a little bit of Charlie Parker and Dizzy Gillespie."

"Well you heard how those cats be going up and down the chords and a lot of that stuff is real fast?"

"Yeah."

"With hard bop it's more horizontal and you get to hearing more blues in it and you get some of that gospel feel." He taps the "Moanin'" chart. "Like in this thing here."

"I hear it." At the occasional sanctified church, or on records at parties I heard more of this other bluesy, gospel sound. Colored people sound. My playing has never had that sound. A wave of chill passes over my skin followed by heat. A lot of the stuff we sang in Daddy's Pentecostal church was lame hymns like "Just as I Am" and "Nearer My God to Thee", draggy moaners that I got out from under as soon as I could. "Amazing Grace."

"That record Merlin gave you to listen to, that Clifford Brown, it's got a lot of hard bop on it," Gilson says.

Turner finishes his cigarette and says, "That's right. Why don't we look at a couple more of these things."

We play through "Walkin'" and "The Preacher." Turner's sound is filled with voice I haven't got, a whole lot of color and seasoning from mucho practice and thinking. I can hear it.

"Oh man, yeah. Thank you, Freddy. Don't understand why they call it 'hard bop,' but I sort of get the idea now."

Making my way down the hill from Bolden Heights, humming, I feel saved though not yet secure on terra firma.

3)

Cigarette smoke fills the space above the heads of the men seated on folding chairs in the crowded front room. We're all brown of some shade, of all sizes, about the same age, and with haircuts that say Government Issue. This is the same house the brothers brought me to that other time. A white sheet I figure to be the movie screen stretches across the front windows of the room. The two members showing the film wear dark suits, white shirts, and ties, and are not much older than the crowd. On most of my classroom days I dressed as these two are dressed, suit and tie, shined shoes, trying to not look like a kid. The school district wanted teachers to dress like business people. My evaluation read, "Mr Birdsong is well-groomed." Both of the speakers sound college edu-cated. They say they represent an organization called The Group for Social Truth. "Our purpose," they say, "is to fight unfair, biased, and prejudiced portrayals of Negroes in film, radio, and, lately, television." Their enunciation is crisp and complete.

One of the men is as light-complexioned as many white people, and he has red, kinky hair. Reggie Fletcher was a boy in Kayakaw with such coloring. We called him "Red." Red Fletcher. The colored girls liked him. The other man is a regular brown Negro who wears rimless glasses. Their faces are smooth and freshly shaved. They dipped their heads in acknowledgement when we entered the room, but they didn't smile or grin. Before starting the projector, the darker one in rimless glasses, who is my height but heavier, stands in front of the sheet and says, "It's good to see all of you here in El Paso tonight. It's a privilege but it has also been something of an ordeal to bring this experience to you. I expect that you can't imagine the difficulty involved in laying hands on this particular film that a lot of people wouldn't want you all to see—getting hold of it and getting it into the form that we have it so that we can easily transport it. But get yourselves as comfortable as you can. This is a long story. I know it's hot in here, but we have to keep the windows closed because of the sound track music—you've got close neighbors here. It'll help if y'all don't smoke. We'll take a little break after the first reel."

The man's eyes behind the rimless glasses have a more than natural shine that gets the group's attention and adds heat to his delivery. He's young, but his words and thoughts have a seasoning that jabs at my lack of education and application. These are the first such young Negroes I've seen in person. Dead serious. Not boxing. Not swinging no bat, not singing or dancing or tootin' no horn. Jesus!

He's saying, "I expect you'll find this film different from what you're used to watching. It was made in 1915 by a film maker named David Wark Griffith, D.W. Griffith. You'll hear a musical sound track, but the action is silent. You'll have to read the writings between shots of action—we call those "titles." Now if you've never seen or heard of *The Birth of a Nation* before, it's because somebody didn't want you to see or hear of the shameful thing. This movie, this *Birth of a Nation*, poured more racial poison into the American system than anything ever manufactured here on this side of slavery. The lies and degrading images of Negroes conveyed by this film caused brainless and susceptible whites all over this country to attack and sometimes kill Negroes after seeing it. Just a little more than forty years ago. We're still fighting the evil effects of what you will see tonight. I expect some of you know that firsthand. This movie is the source of a lot of those evil effects that got spread around. Now we're not here for an entertaining night at the movies, you understand, we're here to get a better hold on what's been going on and what to do about it. Let's watch *The Birth of a Nation*."

The film gets on the Negro's case from the first title: "The bringing of the African to America's shores planted the seeds of division." The

whites look good and the Negroes look pitiful or childish. I feel the
crowded, hot room straining over the titles, consuming the pictures. In
the beam from the projector I see mouths hanging open, eyes locked on
original screen presentations of nappy-headed, bowing and scraping,
grinning, dancing, cotton-picking Negroes. Snickers, groans, every
once in a while somebody says, "Shee-it." At the end of the reel, windows and doors get opened, and half the crowd goes out to the backyard
to smoke. A few smoke in the room. The two men put the next reel on
the projector, thread it with the same kind of focus they've maintained
from the first. "All right, we're about ready to start again," the lighter
one says. "Will somebody tell the folks in the backyard. And let's shut
those windows."

I move to the window nearest me and pull it shut. Guys crowd back
into the room, smelling of smoke, that will mix with sweat during more
of the long, manic, dehumanizing portrayal of people like us. The bed-
sheet movie screen crawls and flashes with Civil War action, the hunting
down of Gus, the rapist, played by a white actor in blackface, Ku Klux
Klan antics, interspersed with vignettes of white gentility. A poison
pellet swallowed by a nation.

Smoke and a bristling silence fill the room when the triumphant Klan
rides off at last and the frame goes black then white from the projector
lamp. A couple windows and front and back doors again open to air out
the space. Some of us stand up and stretch, shake our heads to throw
off the bludgeoning, or to perhaps attempt to order the extensive and
awful shit we just took in. Everything the man in rimless glasses said
about the racial poison in the film has just been verified in black and
white. We've all been whacked in the head. At first, people study the
space in front of them, then they pick up the gazes around them, all in
heavy dark agreement.

The two men light cigarettes and smoke in silence for a few puffs. If
I were a smoker, I'd be puffing with them. They feel a lot like compa-
dres, teachers, though that identity feels thinner on me every day. They
are teaching, teaching something important. The one in rimless glasses
moves to the front of the room, in front of the white sheet where the

movie showed. He looks the group over, rocking slightly on the balls of his feet, before opening his mouth to speak. "Well, what did you think of *The Birth of a Nation?*"

"Man, that was a whole lot of shit in that movie," someone in the back says.

"Sure as hell was."

"When did they make that movie, man?"

"D.W. Griffith made the film in 1915," the man in glasses answers.

"All the niggers looking pitiful and stupid. Crawlin'."

"Most of 'em wasn't even niggers, man. They was white guys with black on they faces."

"Sure was."

"Sombitches looked silly as hell."

"Sure did."

"And old Gus he didn't look like nobody's brother to me."

"Couldn't be payin' no nigger for a big part like that."

"And that's all some of these motherfuckers can think of—Negroes raping white women."

The redhaired man moves to the side of his partner and says, "Gentlemen, one of the reasons we showed you *The Birth of a Nation* this evening was to acquaint you with one of the main sources of racial bigotry in the United States today. You saw it right here." He points behind him, at the sheet. "The black man portrayed as a cowardly, depraved rapist who becomes a hunted animal to be slain, to be killed like a hog. An absolutely cruel and ridiculous portrayal. You could even say a sick, insane portrayal, given the fact that every one of us in this room has likely got some white blood in him that started with a rape by a white man."

He stops to let the words soak in. Perspiration gleams on his smooth pink forehead. My fair-skinned relatives float to mind, and Grandma's "Keep the coal out of the family..." Stories from Mae's Louisiana family are even more present, the complications of preference for light skin and straight hair. His partner beside him takes a drag from his cigarette and blows out the smoke. The eyes of the room burn in their direction. Up front, in their suits and ties, young men bringing fire. The brown one in rimless glasses goes on, "Let me tell you, gentlemen, this was the first moving picture ever shown in the White House. *In the White House.* And the President of the United States, President Woodrow Wilson, praised it. Think about that. What we want you brothers to understand is the powerful way this movie and other movies have worked against us. But especially this one. Millions of white people in this country got their ideas of who we are from this movie, *The Birth of a Nation.* Some of them, maybe most of them, without even seeing the thing. Think of it—if your daddy's beliefs were formed by this film and you got your racial beliefs from your daddy. And think of all the guilt—they know they've been wrong—and hysteria down South and elsewhere about sexual relations. They cannot look at the facts. And living alongside the facts without facing them has made them act crazy and inhuman. Think of all the rapes of Negro women. Think of all the lynchings of Negro men. And boys—think of fourteen-year-old Emmett Till murdered down in Mississippi not long ago for whistling at a white woman."

There had been murmurs of "That's right." Now someone shouts, "No shit!"

The speaker gives the shout a couple of solo seconds and continues, "What we're saying is that material like this movie, this *Birth of a Nation,* puts poison in people's minds that is very bad for our survival in this country. When *The Birth of a Nation* was first shown in theaters, all across this country, not just the South, there were riots after showings. Negroes were attacked by mobs. There were killings. Now things may have changed a little bit. We might be feeling the first stirrings of the winds of change. We've had that Little Rock school case. We've had the Montgomery Bus Boycott that desegregated the buses down there. We're trying to make the winds blow harder by presenting this film to show the brothers and sisters too what we're up against, some of the background. Thank you all for coming out tonight."

The crowd exhales. Swelled up with it, I'd been holding my breath for a long time. Several people shout, "Thank you." There's clapping.

More deficiency in my education. At least as big as not knowing about *Howl.* Bigger. No way I would have seen it, cocooned in a classroom in Portland. I close my eyes tight and breathe to hold back angry tears.

Then it comes to me: my present deficiency will mean anything only if I don't follow the sound deep in my head.

Heading back to Fort Showalter after midnight, the Chrysler is full, six of us, me between Polk and Washington in the front seat. My fists are balled and I'm taking careful breaths. In the silence inside the car, I hear others breathing. There's a sigh. I never got a look at the members in the backseat, and nobody introduced me, but sense that they are sizable and disturbed. I also sense that we aren't headed straight back to Fort Showalter when Polk circles a dark block just off the center of downtown.

"Is that the joint," Washington says.

"Yeah, man, that be it." The backseat growl that answers Washington's question seems to refer to a closed café on the passenger side that we cruised by. Washington keeps his eyes on the outside rear view mirror. We're the only thing stirring in the area. Coming around the block a second time, Polk stops the car after we turn onto our original street, and one of the guys in back gets out. The car moves on and we begin to circle the block again, this time slowing and oozing along a few yards behind our man who walks opposite the café and heaves what looks like a brick through the large plate glass window with the name of the place on it. He's not working at the right thing, but the guy's powerful pitching motion sent a surge of envy through my gut. At the moment of shattering, he's opposite the Chrysler and he wheels and jumps in. Polk gooses it and in no time we're on Montana Street, headed for the fort. The thought of requesting such a service for Manolo's café came and went.

In the backseat, the thrower says, "One of y'all got a cigarette?"

"Here you go, man."

Smoke invades the air around my head.

"Shoulda had me a motherfuckin' Molotov cocktail."

"Maybe next time," Washington says.

Howl

1)

For the third morning in a row, I type in two entries on the morning report for the two men who are on leave. One of the guys is Master Sergeant Vogel. Actually, I'm reporting Vogel returned from leave. A nothing little typing job, but somebody has to do it. That's the band typing gig. My report has no strikeovers in it, and, if I do say so myself, I can't remember the last time one of my reports had a ding in it. I pull it out of the typewriter, clip the original and copies together and hand it to the first sergeant. "Here you go, Sarge."

"Thanks, Birdie." Sergeant Howell puts aside his cigarette and runs his eyes across the page. "Looks good." He rolls himself back from the desk, gets up, and takes the report nextdoor for the bandleader to sign. The swinging door of the latrine across the hall keeps a busy random beat with the in and out of troops getting ready to go to work. Morning voices in the hall stir the air like familiar horn sounds, warming up for the day.

Sergeant Howell comes back in the orderly room just in time to pick up his ringing phone. "Seventy-second Army Band, Master Sergeant Howell speaking."

He puts his hand over the mouthpiece and whispers, "Birdie, Birdie, pick up your phone." The Headquarters voice goes on feeding its procedure-loving sound to Master Sergeant Howell about inserting the latest changes in the band's copy of Army Regulations. Howell sits there, saying, "Right, right, you bet, Sergeant. Got it."

He hangs up. "You got that, Birdie?" he says.

"Yup, sure do, Sarge."

"Good boy." The mild rounding of the sergeant's bald thick head and the beginnings of jowls bring to mind Daddy preaching about "Forgive them for they know not what they do." Yeah.

The first sergeant lights up one more time before we go to rehearsal.

***

After chow, I take my writing stuff, my Hardy novel, and the *El Paso Times* to the orderly room where Muccigrosso is on CQ duty. "Hey, what's happening, Joe," he says. Muccigrosso's head and shoulders bob along with his words. I set my things on the desk.

"You can split if you want to, man. I'm going to work in here. I'll answer the phone."

"Okay. Deal, man." He picks up and heads for the dayroom where he'll shoot pool and watch television. Or he might split for town with the Southerners if they haven't left already.

I've just got my stationery, newspaper, and book laid out when he bops back in. He's got three dollar bills in his hand that he lays on the desk. "Here, man, this is yours," he says.

"What do you mean?"

"It's not really my CQ. Gonzales pays me to do his CQ for him."

"Really?"

"Yeah. That's what the guys that live off post do."

"No kidding."

"So you should get this." He holds the bills out to me and I take them.

"Okay," I say. Thank you, man. You didn't have to do it."

"Just don't want to feel like I was pulling some shit on you. All right? I'm hauling ass out of here." And out the door he goes.

I write a short letter to my mother in Kayakaw and start one to my cousin in Portland. My cousin's last letter told me that Stacy had called to say hello and tell them about my last letter to her.

Somebody stops at the orderly room door. I look up. It's the queer clerk from Headquarters, an overweight, fat-cheeked brown guy. He says, "Hi," and moves on, the only one among the other colored troops on the floor who has ever spoken to me. Most of them seem young, bouncing around in their fatigues and boots, What we doing Where we going When we leaving, busting over to Juarez evenings and weekends to jump into vice and sin.

I am into the *El Paso Times* when Sergeant Vogel walks in with his folded newspaper, containing my depressing social studies lesson for the day. He sets the paper in front of me and points to an article. He takes his pipe out of his mouth and says, "Did you read this?"

"Yes, I did," I tell him. He gives the headshake of disbelief in mankind and walks out, back to his room down the hall. The article describes a big mess at one of those lunch counter sit-ins over in North Carolina, a bunch of colored college students getting their heads beat by the police in the most beautiful amber fucking waves of grain country in the world.

The reports in the newspaper sometimes read like the description of a dream. Sitting here, in the orderly room of the 72nd Army Band, I can't locate much of a feel for the chaos of civilian life with all the army time I've got left and my cooking music project. The mad stuff with the Heavy Brothers feels extra-curricular. The army is full of prejudiced bastards from generals on down. What it hates worse than sin, though, is for things to be out of control and make it look bad. Like losing a battle. Stuff like the Heavy Brothers, who'd better watch their angry asses before they get smashed. I blame no brother for being a little crazy from living in the Untied Slates, but we can work on the problem, don't have to go completely crazy, and things do actually change. Daddy was in a segregated US Army.

The dreamiest stuff, though, is the stuff I've been hearing about people calling themselves Black Muslims who believe that the white man is a devil created by a demented black scientist in some past time. I heard that, I said to myself, "We've finally been driven off our rocker." What hurt was I could understand it, caught the *we* in my reaction, the need for even a cockeyed explanation for where some of this madness came from. If I never saw anything but mean and corrupt white people, abusing darker people, thumping Bibles, talking all kinds of ignorant shit, and lynching for entertainment to which they take their kids, my mind might be bent that way too. And these muslims change their last names to X. Dropping their slave names, they say.

Daddy, out of the deep cotton-picking South, the name Birdsong is one of those names for sure. I am who I am, whatever the name, but I've always enjoyed the sound of my name and felt connected to it because I never knew a time when Daddy's whistling wasn't a part of it. Working around the house or in the garden, or just walking to his job he was liable to be whistling. Old gospel tunes, same ones over and over. At church he was a strong singer. It was great luck, music forever stuck to the name. When kids made jokes about it, I laughed along with them. It got even richer when I began to see the name Vogelsong, the German version of it, and then I discovered *Chandoiseaux* in French. Truckin' with some poetry.

Can't say I'm untouched by the same history that disturbs the X people but I'll keep my name. In X, I don't hear no music.

2)

"Birdsong! Telephone," the CQ hollers from the orderly room. It's Mae, just as I'm about to take off for Bolden Heights to practice with Turner and Gilson.

"Hello, it's me," she says.

"Hello. How are you?"

"I'm fine," she says. "I'm just calling to let you know the divorce papers are in the mail." Her voice rises from the cautious flatness of her hello.

"Okay," I say. "And Raleigh, how's he doing?"

"He's doing just fine, no thanks to you."

"Now why would you want to say something like that, Mae?"

"Because it's true. You don't think about anybody but yourself."

I don't say anything, contemplating hanging up on her.

"And another thing," she says. "You're just a complete disgrace. I found out that girl you were running around with is underage."

"You don't know what you're talking about, Mae."

She slams down her receiver, and that's that. I hang up. Empty-handed. I go down to the basement rehearsal hall, take out my mouthpiece and buzz into it with my eyes closed. When I open my eyes, he's sitting on the piano bench across the room in his old-time fatigues. "Take note, Private," he says. "The woman spoke no untruths about you."

"So?" My voice is weak and overpowered by his delivery.

"So it might be time for you to start trying to act like a man."

He rises from the piano bench and is gone, leaving me with those words that said it all for Daddy, words that became heavier and heavier through a couple hours, pinning me to the chair like under a lapful of bricks. A lapful of bricks inscribed with English words I feel unable to decipher.

Approaching the rehearsal hall at Bolden Heights, I hear Turner blowing up and down chords, smooth and fast, around the cycle of fifths. He stops when I hit the door and walk in. "Hey, Brother Birdsong, how you feeling, man?"

"Sorry to show up so late," I say. "Where's Jerry?"

"He cut out a little while ago. I think him and Merlin went to the show."

"Oh."

He looks me over. "Is everything all right, man?" Freddy sets his trombone on top of the piano, rubs his hands together, and sits in one of the folding chairs.

"Yeah. No. I was late getting away because my old lady called from Portland. Divorce papers are in the mail."

"Didn't you say you got married while you were still in school," Turner says.

I pull up a chair near him and sit. "Yeah, man. Big mistake. I was a sophomore."

"And you got a kid?"

"Right. A little boy." Fatherhood, a civilian thing.

"What happened, man?" Turner says.

"What do you mean—you mean between me and my wife?"

"Yeah, between you and your old lady."

"Well, to tell the truth, I got to messing around. There was another woman. I got caught."

"Is that right?" Turner says.

"Yeah, my wife put me out and then got real upset when I wasn't interested in coming back."

"That sounds pretty cold, man." Freddy is looking at me with his ears wide open.

"Yeah, I guess it was. But what I discovered after I left was that I had never really been there, man, and had zero desire to go back. She wanted a regular tight little home scene with babies and all the household stuff, and, man, I just wasn't there. Am not there. Started feeling like I got married before I got born. I needed to get out of the womb. And one day I just popped out."

Freddy stands and takes his trombone off the piano.

"You feel better now, man?"

"No, man, I don't feel better. I feel like hell about the whole thing, but I feel clearer. You know? I've got a long row to hoe. Got to take care of the kid, got to do music, and there's all kinds of stuff I need to find out about, need more schooling, need to read more."

"Sounds like you got you some work cut out for yourself."

"Yeah."

Turner plays the slide of his horn out and in a few times. "Well, get out your axe, man. Let's look at a couple things."

We work out on blues changes for a while. Freddy digs into his choruses like sermons, building and building, elbows out, loose wrist shooting the slide out and in, hunching his shoulders and bending his knees, getting it out. In his creating I hear release and relief. I hear organizing. I find my way through some choruses and see I'll need a whole lot of time in the woodshed before I can come up with anything like the cool, shuffling, shouting, melodic stuff Turner is producing. He tells me again, "You got a lot of technique, Joe."

"Thanks, man, but I know I've got a long way to go."

"It'll come, it'll come." Turner pulls up a chair and sits with the trombone across his lap.

"Well, I'm trying."

He takes a long breath in, lets it out. "All you've got to do is keep working," he says. "You got it going on."

"Think so?"

"Oh yeah."

The quiet in the wooden building sinks in. "Were you in school before you came in the army, man," I ask Turner.

"Yeah, I spent three years at Northwestern. Ran out of money."

"Studying music?"

"No, business," he says. "But look at you, man. Got you a degree already, been teaching school. Maybe you ought to think about Chicago. Fresh start." Turner's voice and the casual velocity of his words create a banner that flutters by: *Goin' to Chicago.*

"You know, speaking of cities, El Paso isn't as bad as I thought it would be," I say. "Couldn't think about living down here, though." It's true that I dig El Paso's extreme position on the map, last place in western Texas, right up against New Mexico, right on the border with Mexico, and I dig the heat and hearing Spanish, learning Spanish. There's a college. But: "No, don't put me noplace with fifty thousand troops and I got fools telling me I can't come in some greasy little half-ass joint and buy a Pepsi." The brick through the window of that place after *The Birth of a Nation,* when I remember it, takes some of the acid out of my bad feeling. Blues come with it, though.

"That happen to you?" Turner says.

"First day I was here."

Turner runs his fingers into his shirt pocket and takes out a pack of cigarettes. He shakes one out and lights it. "It's a whole lot different than where I come from and the Deep South," he says. "Ain't that many members here."

"I expected it to be different from the Deep South," I say, "but I was surprised to find so many Mexicans. Been too locked-in to maps. Mexicans don't stop at the border. I never thought about what it meant being smack on the border till I got here. Even got their first Mexican mayor, I notice."

"Yeah, it's real different that way and not so mean," he says. "One time down in Memphis, before we moved to Chicago, this white policeman slapped my father for not calling him sir—my father was seventy years old."

Whoa.

"What?"

"Right there in the street, waiting on a traffic light," Turner says. "The cop told us to get back up on the curb, and Daddy said, 'Okay.' This cop—looked like he might be twenty-five, twenty-six, said, 'What you talkin' about *Okay*, boy? You better learn to say *Yes, sir.* Daddy looked at him and said, 'Son, I'm old enough to be your grandfather,' and that cracker hauled off and slapped him."

Turner's eyes keep their usual dark shine. He drags on his cigarette and blows out the smoke. "I was seventeen. I wanted to kill that cop."

At this cowardly distance, I'm ready to kill too, ready to call in the Heavy Brothers. Start us a fucking army. I swallow and speak. "Were there other people around?"

"Yeah, there was—it was downtown in Memphis. Spooks and 'fays, they just stood around and looked or walked on past. Somebody grabbed hold of my arms because I was trying to get around Daddy to get to the cop. Cop just stood there with his hand on his gun."

Turner, my size, trying to get at the cop barehanded. "God damn."

Turner that close to death. Seventeen-year-old boy dead in the street.

"Yeah. Daddy just said, 'Let it go, Son.'"

Turner, about my size, in front of me with his fresh haircut, clear brown face, who can really play jazz, telling me this, doesn't seem deranged now. Got past that helplessness.

"God damn," I say again.

"Yeah, for a while I didn't let it go," Turner says. "Me and my buddy tracked that bastard for weeks, man, watched him from a distance, looking to kill him."

"Really?"

"Really. I was close to doing it at first. Couldn't think about anything else, sick with the idea, man. But then I started thinking about doing all that prison time if they caught me—they probably would have electrocuted my ass. And my father is real religious, and I guess I'm kind of that way too even if I don't show it sometime. He showed me how these fools don't know what they're doing."

Don't know what they're doing for a moment grabs me like the deepest thing I've ever heard, like Turner's father, an old holy man, maybe understood something that really carries. Then it loosens, escapes.

"Did you have a gun?"

Turner looks down into his palm, hefting a memory. "Yeah, I had a gun—a sweet little old blueblack thirty-eight automatic." He stands and stretches, cigarette in one hand, trombone in the other.

"Man, that's a hell of a story."

Turner drops his arms and takes in a big breath, relaxed, deep smooth brown, in love with music and can express it, looking past me into the dark outside the window. A wooden barracks door slams somewhere in the area. "Then I graduated from high school," he says, "and we moved to Chicago. I really dig Chicago, man, and you would too."

3)

This time when he interrupts my after-work studies in the orderly room, Vogel isn't carrying a newspaper, and the look on his face could be interpreted as a smile. He isn't showing teeth, but his lips under the mustache look like they're trying to curve upward. "I've got something to ask you, Joe."

Something to ask me. We've had a few conversations about things in the newspaper, mostly repetitious talk about how fucked up and sad a place the world is, Vogel's curriculum. The cat is really depressed. He's all broken up about the way things are. The cat is forty-some years old and he ought to realize by now that, if you think about it, the worst shit you can imagine is happening to somebody, someplace, all the time. Hell, we dropped two atomic bombs on people.

"So what is it you've got to ask me, Herb?"

"Well, you see, I've been playing for this singer, usually on Wednesday afternoons, and she's from up in Seattle. I told her there was a man in the band from up that way and she said I should bring you by sometime. She'd like to meet you."

"You told her about me?"

"Sure. Why not? You are from up there aren't you?"

"I'm not from Seattle, Herb."

"You said you were from Washington, didn't you?"

"Yes, I am. Originally."

"Well, that's what I told her, and she said she'd like to meet you sometime." His eyes are on the floor as he speaks. "You said you played for an opera company."

"I did, I did. What kind of singer is she?"

"She's an opera singer. A contralto. She's a widow."

From Seattle, she could be cool, widowed old lady and all. Be just like old Herb not to mention that I was colored. "How do you know she wants an extra GI trooping through her place, man?"

Herb's voice focuses, comes at me with an edge. "Listen. She said she'd like to meet you. She's a very nice woman, Joe."

"I'm sure she is."

"So what's your problem? Come out to her place with me next week. Okay?"

Herb's got a good heart, but I'm not sure how hip he is, and I'm too chicken to say I'm scared this white widow might be shocked when she sees I'm a black Negro. You never know. And down here in Texas... It's a fucked-up feeling. Herb is flexing his fingers at his sides.

I say, "Okay, Herb."

The widow's house is not far from Bolden Heights. I've decided that Herb most likely told the woman about me being colored. Also, I've been telling myself she's likely to be fairly cool, coming from Seattle. And she's a musician, a contralto, who must know a thing or two about Marian Anderson. Marian Anderson sure couldn't live in this neighborhood. People be throwing shit in her yard, shooting at the house, blowing up her car. The wild-ass West.

Herb drives through the area of low ranch houses where rocks and cactus and yucca plants take the place of lawns. A few short, long-needled pine trees give a touch of brushy green to some of the yards. No grass. Not a whole lot of water for grass in this neck of the woods. People living on the post can't water their lawns or wash their cars any time they wish, but get assigned even- or odd-numbered days for watering. Orders from Headquarters.

Herb pulls into the carport beside a new black Dodge sedan, and at the back door screen, a tall young woman with dark brown hair appears.

"Is that her daughter?"

Herb's face comes close to admitting a grin, first time I've seen it. "No," he says. "That's Tanya."

"All right, Sergeant. I guess I was expecting a real widow."

"She's very real."

The woman steps outside and opens up on some perfect teeth when I come around the car toward her. Her reddish-brown hair is lighter than Stacy's, and she's a mite taller than I and well filled out. Her voice matches her smile. "Hello," she says.

"Hello."

"Tanya, this is Joe Birdsong that I told you about," Herb says.

Told her about. Her hand swings out to me and the brown eyes read my face. Her voice is not loud, but I can hear muscle in it. Her good-sized, confident body livens the air. "I'm so pleased to meet you, Joe. Do come in, and let's sit a minute before Herbert and I get started. Would you like a Coke, coffee, lemonade?"

"Thank you, I'll try a Coke." Dark-stained cabinets and a stone tile floor with a checkerboard pattern of charcoal and ivory give the room a quiet, cool feel. "Your kitchen certainly has a relaxing atmosphere about it," I say.

"That's because the children aren't home from school yet." Herb never mentioned children.

She sets a glass with two ice cubes in it and a bottle of Coke in front of me, and puts a cup of black coffee in front of Herb. Herb sits stiff, but the cat's eyes are wider open than usual, and he's smiling at his reflection in the coffee. The contralto sits down with a glass of water. "Herbert tells me you're a very fine musician."

Herb is still digging his image in the coffee cup. "That was nice of him," I say. "Didn't know he felt that way."

My words ring insincere, flat, and square as soon as they leave my mouth. I should have said "I'm trying to do the best I can." Her easy and musical burst of laughter blows away my concern. "Herbert also told me you were from Washington, but he didn't think you were from Seattle. I'm from Seattle, you know."

"Yes, Herb told me that. I'm from the other side of the Cascades," I tell her, "born and raised in Kayakaw."

She remembers fruit blossoms from family trips to the Kayakaw Valley in early spring and says she once did a recital there. I would have been in high school. We finish our drinks. Tanya Mendel doesn't seem to be rushing but sweeps my glass and Coke bottle and Herb's cup and saucer to the sink. "Time to get to work," she says.

She takes up her glass of water, and we walk down a hall into a room with an old walnut Steinway sitting in the middle of an oriental carpet. A large abstract painting hangs on the wall in front of the piano. In the opposite wall are French doors with drapes she pulls back. The doors open onto a patio.

Tanya checks her watch. I sit on the bench beside Herb and read along and turn pages. Tanya Mendel's contralto voice is a fresh flavor after hearing so much band music since I've been in the army, and so much soprano at the opera company where the contralto was weak. She produces powerful low tones and buttery trills that take all the soldier out of me in a hurry. Her eyes go liquid and somewhere else as the notes pass through her lips. She is way with the music, reminds me of Turner when he gets it going, creating, so fluent and expressive. Her voice is strong enough to put pressure on the walls. In the opera company orchestra, my view of the singers was never so intimate, never got a whiff of them. Every once in a while Tanya comes to the keyboard to look at the music. She is careful with her hands, only lightly touching Herb's shoulder while pointing out something in the score.

Her grade school daughter and son rattle into the house as Herb and I are leaving. "Michael, Marian," she says, "say hello to Private Birdsong, an army friend of Herbert."

The children have strong voices and smiles like their mother. "Hello, Private Birdsong," they say, watching each other's lips move in unison, and fighting to keep straight faces when they say "Bird song." Their teeth shine when they look my way.

"Hi, Herbert," the girl says. She's older of the two.

Herb says, "Hello, Marian," in a tone full of woodwind notes.

It looks to me that in the desert of his heart old Herb thinks he's come upon an oasis. The man has spent too much time isolated in his own personal wasteland, though, it seems to me, and is most likely seeing a mirage. If I had to guess, I'd say Tanya is about thirty-two years old and so naturally cool and mature that I find myself looking up to her the way

I used to look up to older athletes. The woman is trained, heavy, works like she's preparing for a world championship, and she has enough voice and looks to knock out a whole lot of people. Every time her lips part in a smile directed at me, I'm a happy puppy. At City Arts in Portland, her voice and figure would have been big news. Every couple months, Herb tells me, she takes a flight to San Francisco for sessions with her coach, and during the coming Christmas season she's scheduled to do a performance there.

If her husband's death left any noticeable print on the widow, I don't see it unless it's in the tough artist I feel under her classy surface. It was a drunk driving crash, three years ago, Mr Tanya the missile engineer, drunk. Herb's case has got to be hopeless, but I can see the man's hopes flaring whenever Tanya comes close. And I don't blame the cat. The woman is f-i-n-e. But Herb is out of touch. He's in the army since before WWII. He's too old and cranky. I bet she can't imagine how depressed Herb is on an average day.

4)

"It's the only integrated club in town," Swink says, talking about The Box, the place where Freddy has been playing. "And you should know it's on account of the jazz."

We're on our way there after a brief ramble in Juarez where we smoked a couple joints. Freddy has Gilson with him on the gig tonight. Turner hasn't bragged about it, but he seems to have caught on playing regularly at The Box. I haven't been there yet because I usually feel too broke, and weekends are when I do my reading and write letters. Also, tripping out to Tanya Mendel's house with Vogel has taken up some slack in my social life, and filled in some music too. Tanya has turned out to be as nice as anyone I've ever met and like someone I've always known. Watching her commitment to singing, I see that her devotion to music puts things in order for her. Or maybe it's that the woman just naturally has good sense.

And I haven't seen the meaty forms of the Heavy Brothers in a while, which I don't miss.

Swink and I are in the groove with the stream of people in the street. The fan of gold and amber and blue from the set sun shrinks to silky dark. Winking neon bars of blue, green, red and yellow saturate my eyes as if it's their first time seeing color. *Tres different* from the first feeble smokes at Fort Ord. A hummingbird flutters in my esophagus. We fall into a parlor where Swink plays a pinball game, crouching, jerking in front of the lights. Bells go off. Swink leaps and leaps onto the air. "Free games," he sings out. The words evaporate into the night, but I hear them as his one desire, from childhood, for life. For relief from life and its schools, armies, heavy brothers. "Fool" Turner calls Swink, and I'm amazed at Freddy's consonance with Shakespeare where I hear man's situation as "fool" echoing through the whole works. Landing splat on me. On all. No such thing as free games. Bargains, maybe, but no free games. Shit follows. My insides tickle and the tickle bubbles out till I'm laughing like a fool at nothing.

In The Box, we can't find seats anywhere, so we stand against a wall, controlling our fragile faces, and dig Freddy and Gilson with the quintet, playing "Pennies from Heaven." Guys on the stand really together, weaving beaucoup righteous music, testifying and listening to each other. No conductor. No bandleader. A table of shiny young women sits in front of the bandstand, drinking in the musicians. Nobody down in the square-assed 72nd ever mentioned The Box. Heavy as he is, Levinski is missing it, locked into Mozart and the rest. And hopeless Herb. If I hadn't found these guys from Bolden Heights, no telling how long it would have been before I discovered The Box. Wouldn't be standing here watching Freddy Turner, his head bowed deep and eyes closed like praying, soaking up the solo of the alto player, a white cat Swink tells me is from New York who can really play, a GI not in either one of the bands at Showalter.

The skinny waiter with bleached blond hair comes over, eyes lit up, with an order pad and pencil and taps Swink on the elbow, face lit up at the sight of my lean buddy. "There's a table opening up right over there, Merlin, if you guys want to sit down."

"Hi, Zaza," Swink says. "Sure, we'll sit." We follow the waiter's twisty steps to the table.

"So, guys, can I get you something to drink?"

"Yes, I think so," Swink says. "And hey, Zaza, this is my friend Joe. Joe, this is Zaza."

The waiter draws himself up next to Swink, relaxes hipshot, and says, "Nice to meet you."

"Likewise."

"Joe's a trumpet player," Swink says.

"Oh, that's nice. Are you going to play tonight?"

"Nope, not playing tonight." I don't know where the cat thinks my horn is. The question is a surprise spotlight, though, exposing where I am not. Me, the trumpeter, not playing here where I think I'm on the verge of having the language.

"Well what can I get for you guys?"

"Coffee for me," Swink says. I order a 7UP.

Swink tells me Zaza the waiter's name is Robert Esparza, but nobody calls him Robert or Bobby. "Yeah, he thinks he's in love with me," Swink says. He's really screwed up right now. I like Zaza, but I'm not that way."

Swink doesn't seem to be trying to shock me. He forms a leaning tepee with his fingers and plunks them around the tabletop, underlining his talk, his voice below the music, words level and intense with a lot of saliva around his tongue when he says the long word. "I had sex with him a couple of times," he says. "They were homosexual acts, but I'm not a homosexual."

There were those pictures with the girlfriend, but just like that, the cat is reporting to me he had sex with this other guy like he's explaining what makes triangles congruent, or something. Swink. I breathe it all in. It balloons cartoon-like in my imagination and I'm whooping inside.

Zaza is half Mexican, his father a gung ho master sergeant, Swink says, his mother a *gringa*. He appeared white when I first saw him in his horn-rimmed glasses with his bleached blond hair and pale pimply face, and I dug that the cat was some degree of androgyne. "He's an art student at Texas Western and he can really paint," Swink tells me.

Swink and Zaza, a couple veering beanpoles having sex, I see erector set pieces trying to copulate and have to fight the giggles. All those long bones, elbows and hairy legs, extra penis and balls, bony hips. The redundance! No breasts to jelly against your palms or slap against your face, globes with nipples to suck. None of my business.

Zaza comes back with our drinks on a round tray. He sets the mug of coffee in front of Swink and the bottle of 7UP with a glass and a cocktail napkin before me. "Okay?"

"Great," Swink says. "These are on me." He pays and Zaza takes off. I say, "Thanks, man."

Swink puts his lips against the rim of the coffee mug and takes a sip, and then a bigger one before setting it down. Through talking, he settles back, digging the music. I'm digging it too, even with Swink's words clanging, hearing Freddy weave solutions on his trombone.

5)

Ciudad Juarez: At the Copacabana, Washington and Polk ease in on either side of me at the bar and park themselves.

"*Dos cervezas,*" Washington says to the bartender. He points to himself and Polk. I'm nursing a tequila with salt and a slice of lemon.

"What's happening, man," he says to me.

"Nothing much," I say.

"Haven't seen much of you lately."

"I've been real busy with practice lately." It's the truth. An effect from visiting The Box and from spending time at Tanya Mendel's place too. I've gotten into a heavy practice groove in the basement of Building 1013 and at Bolden Heights with Turner and Gilson.

"Oh yeah?"

"Yeah."

"You one of them serious musicians," he says.

I lick my knuckle, sprinkle salt onto it, and sip some tequila. "Yeah, real serious."

Polk winces, watching me bite into the lemon slice.

The bartender sets beers and glasses in front of Washington and Polk. Washington takes a swig from the bottle. Polk tilts beer into his glass, says, "You a trumpet player, huh?"

"Yes."

"I used to play the trumpet when I was in school." He actually says "schoo'."

Washington wipes the back of his hand across his mouth and says, "Look here, man, we need some help from you."

My eyes focus on the drink in front of me. "Some help?"

"Yeah man, some help. Here's what it is. That grey boy from Mississippi in your unit. We got another report about him and some shit down to the USO and some shit over here."

"You mean keeping members out of the place?"

"That's what I'm talking about," Washington says. "The boy has got a whole lot of mouth. We need to straighten him out."

That first trip with Washington and Polk, the hooded robes in the candlelit room, drifts up from my tequila glass, Jarboe in place of the big tubby guy, moaning, battered and bruised and I don't want to guess but I've an idea what else in that bedroom. "What are you thinking about," I say.

"We're thinking we want you to finger this cracker for our people who will take care of him."

"Finger him?"

"Yeah, you know, point him out."

"Why don't you do it yourself?"

Their heavy bodies get heavier on either side of me. These cats intend some serious dealing with Jarboe. Jarboe getting his smug Mississippi ass bruised by the Heavy Brothers flares in wild colors, appealing for a moment. But then the image of the blindfolded boy and what they did to him and his pitiful body comes back, depressing and obscene and, man, my stomach feels like it's got an overdose of something too rich to keep down. I salt and lick my knuckle again and take a sip of tequila.

"We don't know what the boy look like," Polk says. "You the only one we know for sure know what he look like."

It's possible but it doesn't sound convincing, sounds like these cats just want to get me involved in their shit.

"We'll let you know when," Washington says. "In the mess hall. All you got to do is stand in back of the boy for a couple of seconds like we tell you to."

"I'm not going to do it, man." The words are out. I bite into the lemon slice and study my tequila glass.

"What you mean you not going to do it," Polk says.

"Yeah. What you saying, brother?" Washington leans in on me, big and sweaty.

"I'm saying I'm not going to do it. I am not one of your guys and I don't want anything to do with this."

Smoldering beers on either side of me. Me, a middleweight in the middle, quaky because I might get mashed all to hell between these two meat grinders. These cats don't get it, but I know which picture makes me sicker. Think they can manipulate me with their size and color. Some primitive shit. If I don't keep these guys off me, I'll end up not being able to breathe.

They finish their beers and rise from their stools, ascending bulls. My fingers hug the tequila glass. I wouldn't get in a car with these cats now. Washington puts his face to my ear and says in a low undertaker's voice, "Talk to you later, man." He underlines the words with three heavy taps of his fist against my shoulder blade.

My walk back across the river to Alligator Park is more like a march, Daddy pacing me in full field gear, whistling.

Step to the Loo

1)

Coming out of the mess hall, no chance to dodge them. These cats might as well be Siamese twins. I've never seen them apart.

"Hey, bro, how you feeling today?" It's Washington, Polk at his side in the courtyard near the entrance to Building 1013.

"I'm fine, man. How are you doing?"

"Good. Good," he says. "You was a little bit tore up last time we talked over in Juarez."

"You think so?"

"I'm just saying you looked like you was closing in on your limit, man." Might have been a good time to tell Washington and Polk that I'd reached my limit with them.

"Might have been," I say.

"You remember what we was talking about?"

"Yes, I do."

"So what you think?"

"I told you what I think."

"Aw, that was then, man." Washington's words and toss of the head slap away my answer.

"Well, I'll tell you again, today. I'm not down with it. Count me out. I don't want anything to do with the program."

"So you telling us you in favor of letting the paddies run all over people and not saying nothing?" he says.

"No, man, that's not what I'm telling you. I'm just telling you that I don't want anything to do with the kind of operation you guys seem to be running. I don't dig the violence."

Polk gets in my face. "Nigger, what you talking about? That's the only thing these motherfuckers understand."

I put my forearm against his chest. He doesn't budge. I step back and take a deep breath. "Maybe it's the only thing they understand, but it's not the only thing I understand. It doesn't get anybody anywhere, man, just keeps getting people hurt and killed. People have been doing the same shit for centuries and getting nowhere. Too fucked up and stupid to see that we're all the same laughing, crying, pissing, shitting, fucking, dying-ass thing."

Out of breath and dizzy, I lean against one of the doors. Polk's clamped teeth harden his face. He turns to Washington.

Washington looks like he's taken a hit but he says, "Fuck that history shit. We got ourselves some problems right here in front of us."

"Well, I believe you have to fight sometimes, for the right thing, but I'm not into all this revenge stuff."

"Okay, brother, have it your way—you think we shouldn't be straightening out some these crazy paddies around here. But you know what? You better watch your step. And don't come looking for no help when you have some more trouble with these fools."

They walk away, faces swung back at me like the sullen barrels of two howitzers, but things feel clearer. And lonelier. I imagine they've got brothers who might do me in. Polk would like to do me in.

2)

The combined 72nd and 224th passes the reviewing stand, playing Sousa's "Washington Post" that will remain in my head for the rest of my life. Ritual for a retiring colonel. We're in our fresh, starched khakis, bright strains of the march out of our horns and drums going out of hearing over the parade ground's acres of grass. This is the most regular type of band gig.

Walking back to the bus, my recent head-butting with Washington and Polk in mind, I decide to lie low all week after work. After chow, nothing but woodshedding and a little reading. I'm working up a few surprises for Turner and Gilson the next time I go up to Bolden Heights.

Some stuff I've picked up listening to Swink's Clifford Brown albums. Got to soak in more Clifford and some of the other stuff I'm studying. I've always been good at playing off classical charts, what I grew up with, but playing alongside Turner I feel certain old habits getting in the way of grooving with him.

Wednesday, Vogel asks me if I want to turn pages for him while he plays for Tanya Mendel's workout. I say, "Sure."

Sitting in the middle of Herb's playing and Tanya's singing, drinking up the score is the usual pleasure I've had from this music. The pleasure is still there, though the fresh love of jazz has sprouted alongside it.

My own Eustacia, in her feeling for me, opened a heavenly musical door. Reading *The Return of the Native* for the enjoyment of Hardy's Eustacia, I feel for both mixed-up girls. I hear her name throughout the sad story. The music rises.

Listening hard to Clifford Brown, Lee Morgan, Donald Byrd, and others, I hear the expression I'm trying to grow in. In Miles Davis, I don't hear what I need right now. Got to study Miles, but the groove I'm looking for is clearer in the hard bop players. There's the gospel, blues, and hard-times emotional roots, but it comes down to technical command of the ecstatic moment. Or technical facility, mastery, that gives way, disappears into ecstatic musical moments. Bringin' all you got to the altar. Something like that.

***

Because we're the 72nd Army Band under the command of Chief Warrant Officer Tappendorf, it seems that we might be under the command of Mrs Gordon O. Tappendorf too, who has caused us to have a Saturday afternoon gig. Mrs T is a Girl Scout and Brownie official, and the woman has arranged for her husband's army band to provide music at a Brownie Fly Up ceremony.

Nobody is charmed by such a Saturday afternoon prospect. "It's probably fucking illegal," Muccigrosso says. Nevertheless we pile onto the bus at fifteen hundred hours without a whole lot of inspection and ride to a neighborhood elementary school in El Paso, one of those standard red brick schoolbuildings, looked like it was built in the late twenties.

The auditorium where we start setting up has the usual school-type stage with curtains.

Three semicircular rows of folding chairs to the left of the stage is where we sit, looking across the Brownies, all white, and their parents seated behind them. Each one of the girls holds a small unlit candle in her hand. Little blondes and brunettes in brown cotton dresses with buttons down to the waist, brown anklets with a trefoil woven into the sides, brown and black oxfords, brown skullcaps. Sitting there twisting and turning, waving to grandma or somebody. The job takes on an unexpected charm when I spot Tanya Mendel among the parents, her son beside her. Her daughter then will be one of the Brownies flying up.

Sergeant Howell, in front, is counting heads. "Where is Sergeant Vogel?" he says. "Anybody seen him?"

Everybody blank, including me until I'm stung with remembering I was supposed to wake Herb at fourteen-thirty hours. One more piece of evidence for Herb that the human race is no fucking good. My forehead gets hot. If he was expecting to see Tanya...

Tappendorf, standing behind the first sergeant, narrows his eyes, and red spots come into his cheeks.

A couple minutes before the program is about to start and Tappendorf is standing up front with his bushy black eyebrows making a V from frowning so hard, that's when Vogel comes rushing through the door nearest the band, carrying his pouch and mallet in one hand, the glockenspiel in the other.

He takes half a dozen long steps right up to me, lips worming around under his mustache and eyes blinking fast, about to come apart. He could screaming tattoo me with one of his mallets. Or brain me with his glockenspiel. Or cry. What happens is all the wind goes out of him. Weak pipe tobacco breath comes at me.

"I thought I could depend on you, of all people," he says.

Me, now a loser, now part of Herb's disappointment world. Cats are looking at me like What happened.

Before I can open my mouth to say, "I'm sorry," he's heading toward his place in the percussion section.

The band opens with "The Star Spangled Banner." Mrs Tappendorf tells the audience the Brownie seated behind her onstage will lead us in The Pledge of Allegiance. Everybody stands and faces the flag at the edge of the stage. The girl leads in a strong clear voice.

Mrs Tappendorf announces the special treat of the afternoon, the 72nd Army Band from Fort Showalter, playing *In the Hall of the Mountain King,* from Edvard Grieg's Peer Gynt Suite. It's a fairly simple band arrangement that we rehearse regularly which Mr T can almost handle. We work our way through it. Many of the little girls throw their heads from side to side to the bump of the music. The applause is generous.

Tappendorf doesn't smile or wink at Mrs T who now sits onstage beside the minister who will be addressing the girls.

Mr T looks like Jack Sprat beside Mrs Tappendorf. She is hefty, big round face and heavy arms and legs. Her voice has a bowl-full-of-jolly sound. She introduces the speaker who gives the girls a short talk on the theme of how to soar like eagles. After their candlelighting ceremony, Mrs Tappendorf leads the group in reciting The Girl Scout Promise.

In the percussion section, Herb moves sideways to the aisle, brown hair furrowed as if he combed it with his fingers. He appears to know where he's going, and I notice for the first time a dark upright piano sitting at the back of the stage. Herb has walked this walk a thousand times and does it so slim and easy he's onstage seated at the piano before the audience notices him.

At the podium, Mrs Tappendorf pats the edges of her papers to even them up. "Ladies and gentlemen," she says. "The girls will now sing for you 'America the Beautiful.' They will be accompanied on the piano by Master Sergeant Herbert Vogel of the 72nd Army Band."

Something I haven't figured out yet. Why I get a big-assed lump in my throat when I hear young kids do something like this, really pure. Especially young girls. All these pledges and songs give me gas when I start thinking how people and countries really act. But something about kid voices pricks the old water bag. It's the worst if I hear a young girl singing with a really great voice.

After the singing, I look across at Herb Vogel, back at his seat now with the glockenspiel against his troubled bony breast. His playing made a sparkling melodic nest for little girls' singing. So easy for him.

Dizzy from the narrow avoidance of organizational, emotional, and mental calamity, I dig out my handkerchief and wipe sweat from my forehead.

Program over, people are milling. Tanya Mendel with her new girl scout and her son has spoken to Herb and is now stepping my way with an embracing smile, her hand extended. "Joe," she says, "so good to see you."

"Likewise, Tanya." I take her hand, give it a shake. "Hi, kids. And congratulations, Marian."

Marian says, "Thank you."

"Having the band here bolstered the program quite nicely," Tanya says.

"Yes, it did seem to go well. Herb certainly did his part."

Tanya is standing close, her fingertips in light friendly contact with my forearm as she often does at close quarters, and I'm aware of Jarboe and Hiebert, frozen, watching us from near the stage.

"Are you coming over to the house with Herb next week, Joe?"

"I'd like to, Tanya, but I can't say just yet." Got to find out what level of hell Herb has consigned me to.

"Well, it's always good to see you."

"Thank you. You too." We all wave good-bye and they move on.

I sling my pouch over my shoulder so as not to forget it after being bolstered by the contralto's presence, put my horn away, and join traffic out of the building. Good that Herb raced to the job in his car. He won't be on the bus.

But the narrow escape from humiliation that I caused him hits me, gathers around me in an oppressive cloud. Accusing fingers point from it, and my unsteady guts shrink. I let the man down.

The Attack

1)

Back into Building 1013 after the evening working out with Turner and Gilson at Bolden Heights, first time in a couple weeks, it's Jarboe's voice coming out of the orderly room. "And these four big niggers jumped us as we was coming out. Hiebert and me hauled ass, but they caught ol' Dino and started whalin' on him."

"Watch your language, Private." An official-sounding voice. "The word is Negroes."

The doorway is jammed with guys in their skivvies and shower shoes, straining for a look into the orderly room. One of them sees me, elbows his neighbor, and says, "Here's Birdsong. Hi, Joe."

Between the heads and shoulders, I see an MP helmet in the room. The group shifts enough so I can see Jarboe with his ass on my desk and Hiebert leaning against the first sergeant's desk. They don't see me. There's a second MP near Hiebert with a notepad and a pencil, jotting. "Did you recognize any of the attackers," he says.

Both of the Southerners whinny at the question and say, "Nope."

Hiebert bursts out with something close to mirth, "They were wearin' fuckin' ski masks."

I edge to the back of the group and ask, "What the hell is going on?"

"Dino got beat up downtown. He's in the hospital."

My stomach turns over and I feel pinpricks all over my body. So the incompetent creeps got Dino.

One of the MPs is asking, "How do you know that these individuals were Negroes?"

"I didn't see any white around them eyeholes," Jarboe says. "And you know how they sound."

Eyes near me look straight ahead or study the floor tiles.

The pinpricks turn to sweat and dry mouth and awareness of the weight of my horn at the end of my arm. Getting a deep breath dizzies me, but I manage not to wobble. I lift the trumpet to my chest and embrace it with both arms to test the possibility of moving. Inside my clothes I'm drenched and gravity wants to take me to the floor. I back away from the group and head for my bunk. Never felt anything like this before. Churning squall in my gut, pulling at my throat, taking my breath. Levinski isn't in the area. I melt into my bunk and wait for my breathing to return to normal.

***

At the base hospital: "Man, look at you," I say to him. "What the hell happened?" Muccigrosso's cranium is a dome of cotton, gauze, and tape. A couple bandaids on his cheeks. He's lying on his back. I peeked at the chart to make sure it was Dino. The room has four beds in it, his the only one occupied.

"Some fuckers jumped us over in Juarez, man."

Four big niggers...

"Jumped you."

"Yeah, four colored cats. Big motherfuckers, man. Had fucking ski mask things over their heads."

Rolling onto his side to face me, he groans.

I say, "Cracked some ribs, huh?"

"Fuckin' ay."

He points to the pack of Kools and the lighter on his bedside table, and I hand them to him. He lights up, passes the pack and lighter back to me, and lies back.

"You said some guys jumped *us*. What happened to Jarboe and Hiebert?"

"Those two bastards got away clean. They grabbed me first and didn't even try to chase those other two fuckers. Started punching me, threw me down and kicked the shit out of me." He draws on his cigarette.

"Hiebert and Jarboe took off, huh?"

"Hell, I don't blame 'em. You'd of took off too if you saw the size of those bastards, except one of them was about your size."

"Did they say anything, man?"

"Oh yeah, a bunch of shit. 'Take that you motherfuckin' paddy.' One funny-sounding thing I never heard before, called me a Bilbo-assed son of a bitch'. Bilbo? What the fuck is that?"

Right now my mercury is so low I can hardly pull up any words, only shake my head. Inhale. Exhale.

"I'm sorry this happened to you, Dino."

"So am I, man." He takes a drag on his smoke. His cheeks would be red and shining at his faint witticism if he felt better. The urge to put my arm around his shoulders is strong, but I know he's sore all over and so am I.

"What has the doc told you?"

"Told me I'll be all right, back to the band on Monday. Said he'd put me on light duty. Fucking Tappendorf will love that."

"You say all you've got is cracks in the ribs? No concussion?"

He presses a fingertip to the edge of the bandage near his ear, scratches back and forth. "Nope."

"All that shit on your head and you don't even have a concussion?"

"Nope. Just nicks and bumps."

"Tappendorf must be right—you got a hard head, Dino."

"Hey, man, where I come from we call it tough."

2)

Freddy Turner and I put away our horns after a session where I struggled. Gilson is packing up his drums. Part of my struggle is the still-fresh sight of Muccigrosso at the hospital. That, and what to do about the Heavy Brothers.

Turner gets comfortable in one of the folding chairs, shakes a cigarette from the pack, and offers one to Gilson who pulls a chair up next to him and sits. They light up. I take a seat opposite them, my horn on the floor beside me, and try to think how to talk about the trouble I was having during the session. Swink pops in, having heard us stop playing. He looks us over and pulls a chair next to mine.

"Hi, Joe, how's it going?" he says.

"I've seen better days."

Turner rocks his head, timed to agreement with my words. "Better days," he says. "So what you got on your mind, man?"

Turner's question budges open the heavy gate behind which I stow fears, uncertainties, shameful desires and cravings, needs. Six eyes focus on me, fencing sword points.

"Listen, you guys..." My mouth is dry, cottony. "I need your help with something, help with figuring out what to do about something."

Swink says, "What is it, man?" He's bent forward, twisted my way.

Turner and Gilson say, "Yeah, tell us."

I unload the whole story of my contact with the Heavy Brothers and their operations, and the shock of their attack on Muccigrosso that was meant for Jarboe. "The whole fucking thing makes me sick," I tell them.

"Some real evil stuff," Turner says.

"Heavy," Gilson says.

"I feel a whole lot better, telling you guys about it because I know those guys are pissed off at me and probably figure I know too much because they misread me. Don't forget their names in case something happens to me."

This last is bravado. I'm really saying it out of superstitious belief that maybe if I mention it the deadly shit won't come down on me.

"Nothing's going to happen to you, man," Swink says.

"You never know. I'm telling you, these are some hard cats." I still see the blindfolded, blubbering, violated guy, rope around his neck, in that candlelit room.

"What are you thinking about doing, bro?" Turner says.

"I'm thinking I'll keep feeling sick if I don't do something. I don't know how many of them there are or who all of them are, but I'm pretty sure I know the main cat and his boy, like I told you, Washington and Polk. I'm going to turn their asses in. The army is full of prejudice and shit, but this is some special poison that I can't promote." My eyes water up, and I believe what I'm saying.

Swink says, "Amen to that, Joe."

Then: "Especially that the army is full of shit."

"Hey, man, seriously, we all dig what you're saying," Gilson says.

"Where would you start if you were me?"

"I'd go to the MPs," Swink says.

"Really? Directly?"

"Yep."

Turner says, "Naw, man, you got to talk to your first sergeant before you do anything."

"I agree," Gilson says. "Tell your first sergeant about this and what you want to do."

Swink says, "But isn't it a fact your first sergeant is an old boy from down South?"

"Howell? Yeah, he's from down in Louisiana."

Swink throws his hands out, palms up. "Well?"

"Howell and I get along just fine, and I don't think he's poisonous," I say. "He likes me, and the cat has been in the army since the year One."

"You'd trust him?"

"In stuff related to the army? Yeah, I think so."

"What makes you think so," Gilson says.

"Howell is all army. The way I figure it, army doesn't want to self-destruct," I tell him. "This is some self-destructive shit we've got here, and I think Howell would be interested in clearing it up."

"There's one thing I don't think I'd tell him or whoever you talk to," Swink says.

"What's that?"

"That those guys intended to get Jarboe when they beat up Muccigrosso."

"Oh yeah?"

"Yeah, I'll bet you five bucks by now everybody in the band and your whole damn building knows you slugged Jarboe that time."

Turner puts out his hand. Swink gives him five. "Yeah, I think old Merlin got that right," Turner says.

"Yes, I think so too. Good chance it won't come up. I don't need any more pressure than I have on me already."

"Stay cool, man," Turner says. "We're behind you."

Gilson and Swink slap me on the knee. I take a deep breath, blow it out, and pick up my horn. "Thank you guys for letting me unload on you. I don't mind telling you I've been feeling shaky about this whole damn thing for quite a while. It sure helps to have somebody to talk to."

Swink says, "Washington and Polk, is that right?"

"That's right," I say.

He throws his hands out. "A couple of fucking presidents."

"By George, the boy is right," I say. "I haven't been properly appreciating their attention." Swink and I slap five.

They get up and walk out the door with me. Outside, Turner says, "Wait here a minute, man. Let me get my keys."

"Your keys?"

Yeah, man, we're going to give you a ride down to your place."

***

At The Box, Zaza delivers Swink and me two coffees. I could use a couple shots of tequila and Pepsi, but The Box is a coffee house, the only thing like it in town. Gilson is on the stand with Turner and the others. They swung by Building 1013 in Turner's Plymouth after chow and picked me up. Their protectiveness since I told them about the Heavy Brothers is something I hadn't expected.

Turner says, "You got to be careful, bro."

I haven't said anything to Sergeant Howell yet, still thinking about it. Washington and Polk haven't brought their heavy-duty asses into the area lately, and after what they did to Muccigrosso, they might be steering clear of the 72nd. They've got nothing brotherly to say to me, nor I anything to say to them. Turner, Swink, and Gilson seem like precious battlefield comrades right now.

Two fine Mexican women, occupying a table smack in front of the bandstand, catching the light, bring things back to smoke, my scruffy clothes, my nerves. Most beautiful girls in the world, though, right here, girls made out of star stuff. The one in the gold-rimmed specs, the way she looks and listens trips me into visioning her as a young psychiatrist or maybe an astrophysicist. Tell me something, *Querida*, my mind is lost in space.

Lonely interstellar meat distance between us.

I flex my toes inside my cheap shoes, roll my ragamuffin shoulders.

Swink beside me is as still as he ever gets, on account of the music. Turner bends his knees now, working the slide, commanding, charming the attention of the place with ideas I've heard him practice at Bolden Heights, outside himself, swinging, approaching the starry dynamo with stuff out of the midnight mathematics of the sky. We'll talk about it next time we get together.

Freddy should be asking me to come up there and blow sometime soon. Gilson is up there. Troubles lately, but I'm ready. The Devil tries to tell me Freddy doesn't want people to hear me, doesn't want to share any spotlight. I kick the doggish thought away. Losing my mind in all this fucking stew. Freddy is not like that. He's generous like a best brother, and the scene is bountiful down here at The Box, so different from cowering in front of a conductor pushing some composer's notes, or in front of Washington and the brothers—down here with my boys, these girls, with jazz, that weaves life's shit and roses into my Fort Showalter blues.

3)

Sergeant Howell empties his desk ashtray into the wastebasket at the side of his desk. We're about to shut down the orderly room for the day.

"Sarge, can you hang on for a couple minutes? I need to talk to you about something."

He swings his chair in my direction and rests back. Brown eyes in his big tanned head study me. My tone here is new to him. "Yeah, Birdie, what is it?"

I stand up. "Is it okay if I close the door?"

"Go ahead."

I close the door and sit down again, elbows on my desk, not looking at Howell, taking a couple good breaths. The sergeant pulls the ashtray to him and takes out a cigarette.

Swink's question about the first sergeant being a good old boy from the South is faint in my ear. Louder is the suggestion that no mention be made of Jarboe as the real target of the attack on Muccigrosso.

I give Sergeant Howell the lowdown on my contacts with Washington and Polk, minus the *Birth of a Nation* program and any mention of

Jarboe. He's all ears and solemn, taking in my report with his cigarette smoke. Every once in a while his chin rises and falls. "This is some real serious business, Birdie," he says when I finish. "We're gonna have to report this."

"To the military police?"

"Maybe, maybe not." He taps his cigarette on the rim of the ashtray.

"Why wouldn't you?"

"Looks to me like there'll have to be some kind of investigation. You don't know how many people might be involved in this thing. I remember one time in Germany we had something like this come up, and they was six months investigatin' that sucker. You know yourself this is a touchy damn subject and it best be done quiet."

"For sure, Sarge." The idea of myself walking around during a loud, public examination of the gang gives me a moment of hot pinpricks.

"So what we got to do is turn this information over to the CID. Investigation is what they do."

"I see."

"I'll make contact with them, and they'll probably want to talk to you pretty quick."

Pretty quick turns out to be the next afternoon. Howell and I go to a CID office downtown where I give my story to a couple warrant officers. I'm satisfied with the seriousness of their approach, though at first I miss the possibility that part of it is because I'm a Negro informing on Negro miscreants.

On our way back to Building 1013, Sergeant Howell says, "Good job, Birdie. Now let's see if they can get this thing cleaned up."

4)

"Birdie, your cab is here."

Clerking and the Heavy Brothers mess don't get me off the bugling roster. It's my turn to go to the cemetery and blow "Taps." Tie in place, I pick up my horn and move away from the mirror.

In the hall I almost bump into the driver who fills the space just outside the orderly room. He looks at my horn. "You the bugler," he says.

What else he thinks I could be, I don't know. Sounds like a Southerner, a stout farmer build, but jelly-bellied and soft, a long way from basic training. His wide blue eyes roll as if damn near everything they light on is Man, I ain't never seen nothing like that before. Don't know if I can tolerate this cat. "Yup, I'm the bugler."

When he says "Let's go," I hear a faint lisp. His nameplate says "Bonebrake."

I get in behind the passenger seat, horn in my hand, ready to contemplate Muccigrosso's pain and feel the absence of Levinski on the drive to the post cemetery. Bonebrake gets behind the wheel and turns halfway around to me. "Where you from," he says.

"Portland, Oregon."

His voice goes falsetto. "Ooowee. Gits cold up there, don't it?" He starts the car and we pull out.

"Not too cold. Mostly cloudy and rainy when the weather's bad."

His voice drops way down in his throat, intimate confession voice: "Me, I'm from Memphis."

Memphith.

"Is that so?"

"Yep. Went to Ole Miss for a year-and-a-half. Got to fucking around too much, you know?"

"Yeah, I know."

Fucked around too much. Can't wait to get out. We're in harmony there.

"But I'm going back to Ole Miss," he says. "I know I can make it."

Levinski with mucho theory in his head just headed back to Brooklyn, to graduate school, to study musicology, ain't gonna study war no more. With months to go, I'm headed for the cemetery with Bonebrake. We, the funny people of the Untied Slates. I say, "You probably can make it."

I say that, but I don't believe it. This cat doesn't seem evil but looks to me like he couldn't think his way out of wet paper bag. Easy for people to lead him into the ways of unrighteousness, all that Southern Way of Life shit that keeps lynching Negroes. Easy material for the system, this boy.

"What you gonna do when you get out? You a perfessional musician?"

Hell, I could say, "Yes." I can play. I am contemplating jazz. I'm getting paid to play. "No, I'm a schoolteacher. I'll go back to teaching, I guess."

He takes his eyes off the road for a quick look at me in the backseat, big-toothed blond smile on his face, slaps the steering wheel with the fat of his hand. "Boy, you don't look old enough to be no teacher."

"Yeah, well I've got one whole year under my belt."

We drive through the gates of the cemetery, small cemetery with no gravestones, only marble slabs marking the graves.

"You know, back home we got separate but equal," Bonebrake says. *Thepprit but equo.* Man.

Not sure what to say to this here happy Southern white boy slapping me in the face with his separate but equal. Thinks maybe I'm separate but equal. Whatever the fuck makes him think I'm interested in talking about that suggests we have a problem here. Got to know somewhere in his noggin my equal ain't the same as his equal. Believes that shit. Don't know whether to get ignorant or icy with this peckerwood, or what, from down there where they slap Turner's seventy-year-old father. Be thoughtful, instructive, exemplary in my commitment to brotherhood, explain that *thepprit but equo* ain't constitutional no more, since 1954 because it's a big-ass lie. That the Constitution is the law of the land, if you can dig it, and probably our only hope if we aren't a hopeless-ass case.

we doctors know a hopeless case when we see one

A trio of white helmets, the firing party, stand at parade rest with their M-1s across the field.

"You can pull over right here," I tell Bonebrake.

He does it, and I get out and walk across the grass to my spot near the firing party.

A black Cadillac hearse eases along the curb like the head of a snake attached to the matching limousine and a dozen cars behind it. Men get out of the limousine. They extend their hands to women who twist their way out of the big car. Colored people. I spot the widow, a big brown woman, a young man on either side of her, maybe her sons. Could be brothers. A veil veils her face. Mama didn't wear a veil at

Daddy's funeral. The pallbearers pull the casket draped with stars and stripes out of the hearse and lead the next of kin to the grave behind the commander of the funeral detail and a colored chaplain. This gig is starting to look almost separate but equal. We is here on account of The Great Equalizer. The young men help the widow to one of the folding chairs facing the grave, the firing party, and me. Two white couples in the crowd, the men in uniform, sergeants.

The chaplain holds up a book, has his say, and steps to the side. Two soldiers lift the flag from the casket, fold it by the numbers, and pass it to their commander. The casket goes down. The officer says a few words and hands the flag to the widow who holds it to her bosom.

The sergeant in charge of the firing party says, "Present ARMS. Firing party, FIRE THREE VOLLEYS." Three shots crack the air. Smoke swirls away from the rifle barrels. I bring the horn to my lips.

"Taps" for the dead Negro soldier.

The widow looks up in my direction, sees me. She throws back her veil as I'm coming down from the high note that I hung onto for a sweet liquid moment because I actually dig playing "Taps," and since our souls are like water and all our names are "writ in water" that finally goes into the air, I try to send that baby way out beyond hearing. Yeah, the widow sees my color. Young Negro bugler. She drops the flag onto her lap. Her hands go to her face and her body begins to shake. She falls forward like she wants to go into the grave in front of her, but the men grab her in time, and one of them catches the flag before it goes into the hole.

I could see it. Seeing me, young colored soldier like her man once was, live muscle and bone, playing "Taps" at her husband's funeral, was a final shot to the heart the woman just couldn't stand. Could've been that. So much mystery and sadness in the world.

Now it's back to the barracks and how to stop the Heavy Brothers from hurting people, hurting more people than their ignorance can imagine. I do a left face and march to the curb where my fat-ass Huckleberry Friend waits.

Bonebrake. Big pink defenseless baby, too soft to be a farmer, arms crossed high on his chest, crowds the space behind the wheel, asleep. Deep in the dream forest, he is, an easy lunch for lying witches, goblins, devilish wizards. "We got separate but equal," somebody told him. I bend to his ear, say "Back to Building 1013," and get in the back seat.

Bonebrake stretches a thick arm out the window. "A-a-ah," he says. "Out too late last night."

He starts the car and pulls onto the road out of the cemetery. "You go to Juarez much?"

"What?"

"I said, 'You go to Juarez much?'"

"I've been over there."

"You got a girl over there you like?"

"No, I don't have."

"I got me one. And, boy, I'm telling you she is hot." He gives me a loose-lipped profile of his big blonde baby face. I have read that sex is one of the approved topics of conversation between colored and white men in the South. *Voila.*

"You're lucky."

Then: "So hey, Bonebrake, you went to those separate but equal schools down there in Tennessee?

"Shore did."

"You think the colored schools were as good as the schools you went to?"

The pink in Bonebrake's ears deepens. "They tell me they was separate but equal."

"Did you ever go inside one of those colored schools?"

"No, there wasn't none of that?" He presses the steering with the heels of his hands, flexes his fingers.

"You must have passed by some colored school buildings sometime or other. Did they look as good as the white buildings?"

"Wait a minute. What you tryna say, boy?"

Jesus—what was it Washington said, "What you sayin', brother?" Same opening notes in defense of an indefensible pile of shit.

We coast to a stop at the entrance to Building 1013. I get out and step up to the driver's window. Bonebrake is gripping the steering wheel with both hands.

"One thing I'm saying, buddy, is that separate but equal is a thing of the past. It's not legal anymore. And it's not legal because it's bullshit."

Bonebrake's face is red and damp, his blue eyes bright with disappointment and confusion. He doesn't look at me, but straight ahead. I believe I can see that he came from a proper Christian upbringing. "Thanks for the ride, man."

He drives off without a word.

Vogel

1)

Herb Vogel, a sad heron, shoulders all steepled up and cymbals pressed against his long legs, on the chilly morning parade ground, looks worse than red-cheeked Muccigrosso with his shaky cigarette. It's easier to face Muccigrosso, bad as he looks, now that I've talked to the CID. Dino seems like his normal cheerful self but still winces and walks stiff from the beating, not back to walking with his Philly Pump. Vogel has the more battered look, that comes from the inside, and for damn good reason. My view of Herb all shriveled up is colored by knowledge of the meat part of his problems.

Last time at the contralto's house, she'd just come back from a session with her coach in San Francisco and from rehearsing for her holiday performance. Tanya's got the large, warm, personality, but she always keeps things professional. However, seeing her just back from the coast, refreshed, her smooth moves limned with subtle satisfaction, I dig that the big fine widow most likely has something in addition to singing going on out in the Bay Area. Ain't no way in the world cats are going to leave a woman alone that looks as fine and ripe as Tanya, don't care what kind of suits they be wearin' or what kind of shit they be talkin'. And it ain't like the woman has been a nun up to now. But old Herb would be one of the world's last cats to pick up on the reality of all this.

I was on the patio reading to her children when the music stopped way before the end of the hour, and through the French doors I see Herb get up from the piano and walk over to Tanya, moving his arms in a good old-fashioned pleading manner and saying something to her. Her surprised mouth is open, and her hands are up like she's about to catch a chest pass. Herb comes at her to give her a hug and no doubt try to get at her lips, but she blocks him with her forearms. I keep reading to the kids, louder, who are facing me, and do my best to follow the action behind the French doors. This is nobody's jive-time opera. Herb has worked his arms around her, but Tanya rips her forearms upward like breaking chains and catches him hard beside the ear. Herb falls back into the curve of the piano, elbow on the rim, eyes on the floor, mourns his way back to the bench. Tanya's eyes are wide and, even from where I sit, full of lightning. Her shoulders pump up and down, lips contract, stretch, baring teeth, a sexy contralto into a heavy recitativo. The rise and fall of her voice comes through the closed doors, but the sound doesn't break into syllables I can riddle. If they can hear it, the kids probably take it in like opera. She stops, waits for Herb to say whatever he is saying or not saying, sitting at the piano like a statue of shame. Herb's face is so broken and dumb sad, Lord help me if I ever look like that.

Tanya exits. I go on reading to Michael and Marian, digging Herb's rigid body at the Steinway. By the time I've read a few sentences, he sags, closes the lid on the keyboard, and quits the room.

Tanya Mendel comes around the side of the house to the patio, wearing a white blouse with billowing long sleeves. She stands behind her children until I finish reading. I close the book and raise my eyes to smooth, composed features, to eyes that give up *nada*. "Thank you, Joe," she says.

"You're certainly welcome." My feelers detect nothing wavery in her, though in my movie she might say to the children, "Excuse us a moment, I need to speak to Joe privately," and we would go into the studio, close the drapes and she would fall sobbing into my arms and I would apply myself to inhaling her heat, massaging and comforting her, and she would melt all over me. Oh, man.

"Thank Joe for reading to you," she says to the children. And they do. To me she says, "I believe Herbert is waiting in his car." She hands me a note-sized lavender envelope that I tear open as soon as I get to the barracks after our silent ride back to Showalter:

Dear Joe,

If this seems like abrupt notification of our departure, forgive me. After Christmas and the New Year, I and the children will be living in Seattle. We probably won't see you again before our move, but please know that Michael, Marian, and I shall miss you. You've been a good friend and I hope our paths cross again someday. I should tell you that things have become uncomfortably complex between Herbert and myself—perceptive as you are, you might have observed this. This is not the total reason I'm returning to Seattle, but now happens to be a very good time to leave El Paso.

Good luck with your music and the remainder of your military duty. If you wish to look me up in Seattle, you can find me by contacting the Cornish Institute.

Fondly,
Tanya

The music of Tanya's letter, her attention to me, makes my head swirl for a couple minutes. She's big and gorgeous and tough but she has always been kind and had the feel of a natural friend. Seeing her daughter's name written—Marian—I perspire with embarrassment at my slow-wittedness that I never once considered the possibility that the girl's contralto mother named her after Marian Anderson. I never noticed it, never made the observation. What a dunce. And she wrote me this sweet note that breaks up clouds of Heavy Brother presence, them with their grisly shit, and what's going to happen with the CID's investigation. There is a world of trouble out there, but there is also the music from Tanya Mendel's existence.

***

Down in the rehearsal room, Herb's eyes are on his feet, standing over by the drums. But he ain't seein' nothin', he's all up in his head, face clenched, strangling positive thoughts. Since that last day at Tanya Mendel's house, two weeks ago now, I haven't heard a peep out of him.

I sit down at the unoccupied upright and peck at the chord progressions Freddy Turner and I have lately been exploring. At the sound of the piano, Herb's eyes lift from his shoes, and his posture becomes less like something rejected by Madame Tussaud's. He comes over to the piano, and I move to get up and let him sit down. His hand on my shoulder keeps me from rising. "No, no," he says. "Stay there. I heard what you were doing. Why don't you try this?" He reaches across and whips through the progression in all the flat keys. Pipe tobacco smell mixes with the music.

"Jesus, Herb, how come you keep saying you can't play jazz?" When I look up at him, his eyes go sideways.

"Because I can't," he says, "but that stuff you're doing there, those chord changes, it's in darn near every tune that was ever written."

Wait a minute. Tunes start going off in my ears. "Really?"

"Really." He goes to the music rack by the door, comes back with a floppy book of Rodgers and Hart tunes and sets it on the piano, open to "I Could Write a Book." "Look here," he says. "Practically the whole tune is two-five-one progressions. Seven of them in this one tune." He flips through the book, jabbing at other examples.

"Man, oh man. I see what you mean."

He goes on talking, slapping the book, pressing the keys, showing me ways to work on chords to put color in my trumpet solos. And I'm hearing half-thoughts how James Joyce used the chords of the *Odyssey* to build his big work—something like that. I could always hear chord moves in tunes, but I never consciously identified them. "Wow, Herb, that's heavy. Thank you, man."

Some kind of retarded I am. Herb's eyes examine the floor, and he makes a sniffing noise against his knuckle. He says, "You're doing right, working it out on the keyboard."

"I really appreciate the help, Herb."

A low grainy hum in his throat acknowledges my thanks, I guess, and he moves on, leaves me breathing deep, salivating, with my head full of new light about the progression, and musical hope.

2)

Swink's dope dealer steps in the door as I'm munching on a taco at the cafe counter and fingering through an issue of *Contact* magazine.

Waiting to hear something from the CID about their investigation of the Heavy Brothers has started to become a strain. In halls, I walk close to the wall and look behind me often. I approach corners with hands out from the body, feet ready to fly. The back of my head twitches, waiting...

On top of that, Herb Vogel and I are still not exactly back in the groove since I forgot to wake him, which made him late for the Brownie job. Herb is a backward-looking cat, hangs onto stuff. I told the first sergeant Herb's lateness was my fault. "Herb is really one depressed guy," I said.

The first sergeant said, "Well, Birdie, the man is a master sergeant. He's supposed to be able to take care of hisself."

When I told him about Vogel's funk, Swink said, "Forget it, man. And forgive him—he's a sergeant. You need some relief. Let's go across the river." No sympathy nowhere in this man's army.

Barr, Swink said the dealer's name was. Barr slides himself onto the counter stool next to Swink, his feelers out, and elbows himself into position. A short, brown-skinned Negro with broad shoulders and long arms, Barr spreads his eyeballs over Gilson and me. Swink never mentioned that Barr was a member. He has on a blue work shirt, tail out, and Levis with some of the biggest most countrified cuffs I have ever seen, above some scuffed-up work boots.

Swink says, "Hi, Barr. How are ya?"

Barr sprawls onto the counter on one elbow and grins down the line of us. "I'm doing fine, man."

Though he comes on casual, he's on alert, I can sense from my own months of watching for trouble to pop up from shadows, broad daylight, anywhere.

"Hey, Barr, meet Joe and Jerry. Okay?"

Big white teeth, yellowing in between when he smiles, look like they could eat anything. In his first sniffing glance, Barr makes his appraisal. "Cool with me, man. How y'all doing?"

Gilson and I throw up our fingers in little V-for-victory signs, twin Churchills, cool with whatever is going down.

"So what's been going on, Barr?" Swink says.

"Nothing much. You cats about ready to go?"

I shake a jet of hot sauce onto the last of my taco and stuff it in my mouth. The tabasco blazes up into my sinuses. Whatever happens next is not going to catch me hungry. Barr's wide mouth twitches like fixing to chew along with me to make sure I chew right, same kind of signifying my brother used to do when we were in grade school. Some kind of joker, this cat is, sniffing out a sense of who Gilson and I might be. He needs to wash some of that sweat and dust off his face, but I give him credit for knowing Swink.

Swink told us Barr would be taking us to his crib in Juarez. Behind his hand Barr speaks into Swink's ear loud enough to make sure I hear.

"Bro here is copping some serious *alimentacion*, man."

His sound and image ruffle a layer of experience in me that I could call *colored*.

I wipe my lips with one of the unbleached paper napkins and say, "Hey, man, you know signifying is worse than lying, don't you?"

Barr's shoulders bounce, and he lets his head fall to his forearm on the counter. He pushes a hand toward me, past Swink, to shake. "Man, you know I was just jiving," he says. His thick hand is tough but uncallused.

"No sweat, man. I know how you people are."

He runs a hand under the front of his shirt, scratches his chest, pats himself, a picture of inveterate confidence in his muscular-assed body. A smirk remains on his mug. "Now who's tryin' to signify—you got to admit though, man, you was hurtin' that taco."

"Well it's beyond pain now," I say, veering away from a temptation to try The Dozens. Gilson slaps me on the shoulder.

Barr's face gaps into a grin, fronting a gravelly rumble in his throat. He slides off the stool and pushes away from the counter, ready to go, but his eyes go to the issue of *Contact*, lying between Swink and me. "Let me see that," he says. Swink slides it over in front of him, and Barr picks it up and fans through it. Stops. "Will you look at this shit," he says. "'How to Be Sane Though Negro.' Man, is this your book?" He pokes the spine of the magazine into Swink's ribs.

"No, man, it's mine," I say.

Barr holds the small journal between his thumb and one finger, the way he might hold an angleworm, and makes like he's going to fling it over the counter. After the fake, he shows his big teeth and passes it to me.

"Here, man. *How to Be Sane Though Negro.* Ain't that a bitch?" Barr's voice is hard at the center when he recites the title of Hayakawa's essay.

I squeeze it in one hand until the cover bends. "It's a bitch all right. Cat that wrote it thinks Negroes ought to try to forget they're Negroes and try to make white people feel more at ease in our relations with them."

Swink and Gilson sit with backs against the counter, taking in the show. Barr's eyebrows writhe with his frown. "How I'm supposed to forget I'm a jigaboo, man? Shit. What the hell am I supposed to be?" He brings his hand down on the counter like a hot gospel preacher. "Who is this stupid Negro writing down this shit?"

"Ain't no member, man. He's a Japanese-American professor."

Barr slaps himself on the head and shakes it. "Lord have mercy Jesus," he says. "You cats about ready to cut out?"

Barr's crib is a mile into Juarez, no whorehouses and honkytonks, no American *soldados* and their kind of noise around, just adobe houses up against one another. We walk down a narrow street of uneven bricks and broken concrete sidewalks that I try to imagine having once been new. An old green Chevy with black fenders, like the one Daddy used to own, our family car, bumps along toward us. Four kids playing in the street jump to the curb. Bent fenders, rust holes in the doors, faded and chipped paint, a ghost of a car, a dark driver with straw hat low on his head. The kids run back into the street as soon as the Chevy passes.

Barr's big fake farmer strides lead us off the sidewalk into his living room. Just like that. Sidewalk, living room with a couple dusty throw rugs on an adobe floor. Gilson and I sit on a couch covered with a sheet worn grey and thin. The couch sags low enough that our knees are almost even with our heads. House here in Juarez, Barr must know how to do some maneuvering. I say, "Cool pad you got here, man."

Barr looks at me and tosses his head as if he thinks I'm jiving, which I am, but I do find the austerity familiar and precious like the worn wood floor with no linoleum back home. Somehow it feeds me, puts me more into the groove than Tanya Mendel's lovely pad or the middle class stuffing of the Dupree house in Portland. Wild groove, close-to-the-bone groove. Barr says, "Y'all make yourselves comfortable. I got to get the stuff ready."

He puts his shoulder to the door of a room or closet next to the one we're in, a door with years of puffed and chipped enamel coatings and no knob. The door doesn't open. Swink stands behind Barr with his hands on his hips. He's been here before. "Open up, motherfucker," Barr says and gives the door another bump. The door opens and Swink follows Barr into the space. Barr comes back out carrying an armload of dried weed, arms around the bundle like a peasant in a Van Gogh drawing, humping an armload of something peasants would be working with. Gilson and I sit with our arms crossed. Swink comes out behind our host carrying a thin stack of newspapers.

Barr says, "Spread some that paper on the floor right here." Swink lays out several full pages, and Barr starts shaking the stalks and beating them against the newsprint. He crumbles bits of leaf onto a brown cigarette paper and rolls a fat joint. "Here, bro," he says. He passes the joint to me along with a book of matches.

"Thank you, man." I take it, but have never lit one of these things before, and pass it to Gilson. "You light it, Jerry."

Gilson lights it, sucks in a drag and passes it back to me. I pull in a weedy lungful, hold it, and let it stretch my chest. Gilson takes the cigarette and passes it to Swink who sniffs in some smoke before he sucks in a drag. Barr takes a hit.

Barr's dusty pink walls are Mother Hubbard bare except for a cardboard calendar, tear-off paper months, 1959 getting thin, but I've got a thick stack of days and weeks into the next year to get through. Heavy ones, if I last. A throb of blue wobbles my insides. Thick stack to get through before Stacy and the rest, papery days between my thumbs and fingers. Barr, on the floor in front of me, crumbles leaves on the newspaper, separates the olive-colored beebees. Seeds. Dates circled on Barr's calendar could be deals. Today's date circled. Year running out, the end of "a low dishonest decade." I am far from the madding crowd out here, far from the hateful brothers, smoking in Juarez. Far from home. Barr, master preparer, in his levis with six-inch cuffs, now on one knee, now stepping over spread-out pages of news heaped with dried marijuana leaves, living room farmer now on both knees, folds quantities of his product among articles about Soviet space satellites, Eisenhower's golf, civil rights mess in the U.S., parks in El Paso, jive in the Congo. Black and white and read all over. Teach, brother.

Barr looks at me and says, "Cat got one thing right."

"Who?"

"How to Be Sane Though Negro."

"Oh, yeah?"

"Yeah," he says. "If you ain't white, living in the United States of America has got to make you *some* kind of crazy."

Barr's words come on like gospel.

Swink says, "That's because of all the crazy fucking white people."

Barr keeps folding and talking. "That's what I'm trying to tell you, bro."

I say, "That why you're living in Mexico, man?"

"Es posible, hombre," he says. A stack of newsprint packages of marijuana has risen beside him.

From Barr's broken-down sofa, Gilson and I inhale the righteous music of the scene.

> *While still a child nor yet a fool to fame*
> *he lisped in packages for the packages came*

Lingerie ads, letters to the editor, sales, headlines, editorials, Barr talks himself through, creasing newsprint pages into neat square packages of pot. It's some somnambulistic jive. I myself a current event, a whale under the sea, Barr's wide-mouthed words wavering through water. *Barr's a Mason jar.*

I start to laugh and can't stop. Barr's big mustache and colossal chops come at me like a Chrysler grill, him squatting there in his workboots beside his pile of packaged pot. "Looks like bro here is getting his kicks this evening," he says.

Barr's big teeth, the Pancho Villa mustache spilling off his lip over his booted saying, his clodhoppered utterance. No man in the world funnier than Barr.

"Yes," Swink says. "I think Joe is still somewhat new to this."

Barr says, "Oh, my goodness."

Barr's words are a funny finger in the ribs. Sound like my mother's "Oh, my goodness." I see Barr's goodness, a white dishtowel floating from his hand. My goodness. Surely goodness and mercy shall follow him all the days of his dishes. Here comes the fiery, wrinkly-papered torpedo again. A long pull, smoke in my lungs. Just what old Herb needs, smoke some this shit and get loose. Washington and Polk smoke their share, I bet. But they remain suicidally angry. Got to corral them cats. Between my head-high knees, I scope Barr on the floor, scooping and folding. Who in "potters and taverty and hollow-eyed and hip" sits up smoking. Footsteps and voices of children bounce on the sidewalk outside the skin of door and windows. Cars up the street, down the street. Heavy old chevies. Adult voices. A car door slamming separates itself from other sounds. Metal against metal. Adult voices. We should be scrambling, cleaning up. The cops must know what's going on inside Barr's place. Barr continues to move fluidly through his priestly duties. Underwater motions.

Wade in the water, chil'ren
Wade in the water
God's gonna trouble the wa-ater

Men talking Spanish outside the window. Got to be the cops, those guys in blue caps, getting ready to bust in on us. Not even a screen door on this place. Just a wooden door between us and the sidewalk. Us and the cops. *Yo soy* innocent, *hombres!* Gilson sitting with his head against the back of the couch. The matter with him? Swink puffing and gassing with Barr. These cats don't see what's happening. This is serious. But I can't move if they don't do something.

"How many do we want," Swink says.

What want who?

"Let's get twenty," Gilson says. "Okay, Schoolmaster?"

"Oh. Yeah, yeah, let's get twenty of them mothers."

By myself, Swink and Gilson gone to Bolden Heights, I'm weaving my way, watery-legged across the parade ground to Building 1013. Ain't about to stumble, ain't about to fall, and ain't no Heavy Brothers going to catch my ass between here and the door. I've been practicing my ass off, and Turner told me yesterday, "You got it goin' on, man."

The infernal blast of heat blows down on me. Coming at me, up ahead, Daddy's horse gives a whinny, springs across the fifty yards between us, and plops down like a slinky off the bottom stair, surrounded by hot bright daylight. Daddy swings his leg over the horse's neck and slides out of the saddle.

"Feeling pretty good, huh?" he says.

"I was starting to feel all right. What is it you want?"

"Well, for one thing, you been thinkin' I didn't know what I was talkin' about, sayin' you was headed for trouble. How many times you got to be told? I'm tellin' you again: You better look out for what you need to decide on, boy."

Standing there under the moon in his own daylight, middle of acres of night grass, talking this stuff.

"What are you talking about?" I start walking again.

He in his Buffalo Soldier outfit, and that damn horse, pacing me, he says, "Now you want to act simple. Fact may be you ain't acting."

"Fuck it, I'm just trying to get home."

"Oh," he says. "Trying to get home."

"Yeah."

"I'm not going to ask you where that is and how that relates to what you got to decide."

"What are you talking about?"

"Like I said—I'm talking about you got a long way to go, boy."

"What?"

"You want me to give you some examples attached to your person?"

"No, man, no."

"All right, then. Act like you got some sense." He puts his boot in the stirrup and swings himself onto the horse. I don't look up to see which way they went. They just went.

3)

"Okay, men, you got fifteen minutes here," Sergeant Howell says from the front of the bus. "Smoke 'em if you got 'em. I want to see ever last swinging Richard lined back up here in fifteen minutes."

We sit in the bus outside the 224th barracks in Bolden Heights, meeting them for a combined Santa Claus gig. That's right, Santa Claus. A gig that smacks of the bandleader's wife. The winter sun, a fried high yellow egg yolk behind thin clouds, warms things a little, but you can see your breath. The band is in dress greens, mine fresh from the cleaners. Inside my uniform, inside my ribcage, my knowledge of the Heavy Brothers and their crimes lies, extra, disturbing weight only half-lifted since I reported it to the Criminal Investigation Division. I buzz into my mouthpiece. Behind the windows of the rehearsal hall, 224th guys move around, getting out instruments, warming up. Cats bump their way off the bus for a smoke. After a long, low G-flat on the horn, I hop off and go into the rehearsal hall.

Freddy Turner is in a corner with his trombone, blowing long tones. I walk over to him and blow the first four bars of "Jordu." Freddy throws his head back like Lookee here, and comes in on the next four, then says, "Let's do it again, man. Whole thing?"

"Yeah."

We blow through it again. Turner puts out his palm. "That's a gas, man."

"Yeah it is." I slap his palm. "Solid."

The front door opens and Swink and Gilson come in. Swink says, "Hi, Joe, what's going on?"

"Nothing shaking but the leaves. Hey, Jerry."

"Hey, Schoolmaster."

"You cats best get your butts moving," Turner says. "We're leaving in a minute."

Gilson gets his snare and a pair of sticks. Swink takes his trumpet off the shelf, the old silver Benge he blows. The sergeant's whistle sounds and we go outside to line up. Santa Claus is doing his act in a field close by, and we're supposed to march to the place.

Before joining the trumpets, I drift over to where Herb stands. "How are you doing, Herb?"

What I get out of the master sergeant is a solid grunt.

I say, "By the way, Herb, did you see that article on the *Times* front page about Governor Long and the chick over at Ruidoso?"

"No."

He's lower than a turtle's belly because a couple weeks ago he asked me to type up a 1049 for him, which I did, but Mr Tappendorf hasn't responded. I don't blame Herb for wanting to get the hell out of here even if it won't solve his basic problem, whatever that is. Since his defeat at Tanya Mendel's house, he's been keeping to his room even more than his regular hermit habit. When he comes out, he says nothing beyond yes and no, and his belt buckle hasn't been shined.

"Shit," Muccigrosso says. "Marching to see Santa Claus. Ain't that a bitch?" He tosses the cigarette he's been puffing to the ground and steps on it.

Barny has been watching Dino and playing sergeant, says, "Dino, you know better than that. Pick that sombitch up and field strip it." Muccigrosso has just become able to march again and it's still an effort for him to bend over, so I pick up the butt and hand it to him. He does a weak Philly shoulder pump, takes it and says, "Thanks, man," shreds paper and tobacco over the ground.

Another whistle blast. Everybody falls in and we march to the sandy dirt field at the bottom of a slope where Mr Tappendorf waits in his dress greens, first time I've seen the cat unstarched. We halt. Sergeant Howell approaches the bandleader with a salute and a "Morning, sir." A hundred or so kids bunch in the middle of the field, swinging their arms, hopping around, with half a dozen women wading among them, arms out like wings. They know that Santa is on his way. Primary schoolers. I notice that I'm noticing all the children are white. No members. Could have been a Mexican or two. Innocent little army brats.

Santa's helicopter boomerangs up from behind the hill and hovers over the field. The beat of its rotors shudders the air. There's nothing to show where the thing will land. "Ya-a-ay," the kids shout. They jump and point and clap.

Somebody didn't know how to organize worth a damn. A landing area should have been marked off, and an area for the sprawling group of kids too. They look up with mouths open. The copter starts to swing down. Inside the plastic bubble in his red suit, Santa waves a white-gloved hand. The draft from the rotors beats down on us, and dirt flies. Kids break out running toward the descending helicopter. One little boy in a green jacket is faster than the rest and runs nearly under the copter where sand and dirt are churning. Sandy dirt spews into the band and we don't do no British at Bunker Hill, we bust ass in all directions without an order. Women scream at the kids, grab at them, pull them back, as many as they can corral. I run for the boy in the green jacket and bowl him over and cover him before he gets a mouth full of dirt or blinded or worse. The draft from the rotors beats on my back, presses me down and blows dirt into the kids who got too close and fell in piles, hollering and crying. Damn thing so close I can smell hot oil. Women's hair and scarves fly every which way in the blow. They bat their arms at the sky. The helicopter sails upward and hovers like a dragonfly. The kid under me is hands up to the wrist in sandy dirt, wet lips bent like a bawling tragedy mask, nose running mud, but he isn't crying, he's toughing it. Muddy saliva and snot rope across his chin.

I heft the boy under one arm and carry him to the nearest woman and set him down. The woman's blue eyes are wide and somewhere else, but she grabs the kid's wrist and hurries away with him. I walk back to where the band is milling, my fresh uniform packed with grit. "A fucking enemy attack," the wounded Muccigrosso yells. "Fucking Santa Claus."

"Isn't it great," Swink says. "Just too perfect."

Herb Vogel's mustache trembles. If he were at the controls of a Spitfire, he'd deal with that fucking helicopter.

The helicopter poises on high to begin a second coming, a clattery elevator with no building around it. It could be an exotic and maybe dangerous animal the way the kids hold back now, at a safe distance, watching it descend, muddy tear tracks on their faces, instinctively aware of the controlling prohibition behind this jive experience but with no defense against its allure. Women run around beating dust off clothes and wiping noses, mouths, cheeks. The skids of the helicopter touch the ground with a little bounce and the rotors puff to a stop.

Santa's plexiglass door opens. He hauls a red leg out in its black shiny boot, swings himself sideways in his seat beside the pilot and brings out the other leg. Still seated, plastic boots on the ground, he throws out his arms toward the kids and goes to ho ho ho-ing to beat the band. They creep toward him. Santa rises, reaches into the copter and tugs out a large, lumpy canvas bag. He sits back on the edge of his seat with the bag between his knees, holds out a gewgaw so small you can't tell what the thing is. The little suckers run toward him like water rushing down a drain. Hurrying among them, the women wrestle the disorder into a scruffy line.

The reassembled and combined 72nd and 224th Army Bands strike up "Jolly Old St Nicholas."

***

Hiebert's Texas twang bounces off the tiled floor of the bay, the metal lockers facing the band's bunks, and the windows. "Birdsong, Fultz, Garrett, Muccifuckingrosso, y'all got mail."

I close *Far from the Madding Crowd*, roll off my bunk, and skate in stocking feet to the doorway. Hiebert gives me my mail. "Here y'are— boy, you're popular today, Birdsong."

"Yeah, thanks." I have come to accept the Texas Bastard as the more incomplete villain, far from a friend of mine, but less poisonous than his oblivious running mate from Mississippi.

Four letters: my cousin Estella, Mae, Mama, and Stacy.

My mother's pencil writing says there is snow in Kayakaw like I never saw "when you all were kids." Almost two feet.

Looking out at blue sky over the desert, over miles of dry asphalt and concrete, there is no echo of home here at the fort. Every weather going on someplace. Just like every thing that people do, going on someplace. Lovemaking. Lying. Murder. Torture. Theft. Betrayal. I take a deep breath and close my eyes tight until the swirling downward stops. Somewhere there's music.

Mae's letter says she's now recovered from the "terrible thing" I did to her and Raleigh. A long slow motion clash of breaking glass from her words showers into space I don't know where. She's right. It was a terrible thing. Terrible, though I am unable to imagine it not happening. She also informs me that she's planning to remarry in a few months. Hallelujah.

My cousin's letter says she hasn't seen much of Stacy.

Stacy's letter is postmarked New York, New York. She says she's had quite a time in New York and that she's planning to stop in El Paso to see me on her way back to Portland. She says she'll be in El Paso sometime after the first of the year, says she'll call when she arrives. Bringing her little white ass to El Paso, as if she has no idea of history or geography, as if Portland wasn't bad enough with people staring their asses off and ready to stick their noses in your business. Down here, all these Southerners around, no telling what could happen. None of my fears, however, are as pressing as my appetite for her face, the jivy smirk she puts on, her slick wisecracks, and the luxury of her snowy torso. Stacy. Colored men with white women doesn't happen in El Paso, but I'm thinking Juarez for this chunk of my civilian life that is falling out of the blue.

I talk to Turner about it. Turner knows places to rent by the hour across the border.

4)

Quiet in Building 1013 with damn near everybody on Christmas leave who can afford it, or out for the evening. I'm in love with Hardy's girl Tess, reading through her troubles. Soaking up her life in the silence of the orderly room. Her body is young and full like Stacy, who is coming, and I'm ravishing the hell out of her story when a heavy firecracker goes off across the hall in the latrine. Some immature bastard's idea of Christmas fun.

The sound, too big for my ears, spirals through my head. I jump across the hall to block the door because this fool is not getting away if I can help it. I crouch with a knee and both hands against the door and yell, "A little help on Two," but nobody runs against it. And nobody shows up in the hall.

I go in, all eyes, in case the cat is hiding and hopes to make a run for it. Gunpowder smell gives body to the silence. Nobody at the sinks. I go to the shower where the sight that fills my eyes is too much for my stomach. I vomit.

Herb Vogel, his body, in only skivvies, is down in a corner of the shower. Bony shoulders jammed upward, bloody head fallen against his left shoulder. Blood and bits of fresh pink matter mark his height on the shower wall, and there's the smear of his descent. Blood runs over the floor tiles and under Herb, blood still oozing out of the hole in his temple, over his shoulder, into his armpit. At the end of his jammed right arm, on the floor, is the .45 he used. His bent knee falls against the other leg. Hairy lower legs. Black specks surround the mean little hole in the side of his head.

"Ho-ly shit." I back to a sink, stepping over the lumpy puddle of vomit, and wipe tears out of my eyes with the back of my hand, throw cold water over my face, and rinse my mouth. My stomach shakes, my hands shake, but I go over to Herb and get down on my knees to feel for the pulse that I know will not be there. Blood has run down Herb's shoulder, arm, hand, to the floor in a smooth red puddle my knees edge up to. The arm is still warm and limp, and the hand too, but there's no Herb in there. I roll the fingers between my own, heat leaving them like a sound that will never come back.

Granite jaws of the absolute fact clamp shut: Herb gone, myself still here, shaking, out of breath, teetering beside the crater where Herb used to be. Pistol heavy at hand, loaded. Somebody pushes the latrine door half open, and I jump up. The round brown head and one shoulder of the queer clerk nudge into the room. "Did somebody set off a firecracker?"

"No firecracker, man." I point to the shower.

He peeks into the shower, clamps both hands over his mouth and looks at me. The clerk's stretched white T-shirt is grey-brown over the live swell of his gut. His eyes above his clamped hands narrow into whatever figuring he's doing. He speaks into his fingers, half to himself. "That's that sergeant, isn't it?"

"Yes. Sergeant Vogel." Talking to the clerk's shocked watery eyes I lose the shakes. "Watch here while I call the MPs. Don't let anybody touch anything if somebody shows up. Got that?"

One gingerbread-colored hand grips the corner of a sink, the other still over his mouth. He drops the hand from his mouth and stands straight. "Sure, I'll watch," he says.

A tall specialist sixth class with a neat mustache shows up, two spec fours with him, all wearing black MP armbands.

"Private Birdsong, I'm Specialist Anderson, patrol supervisor," he says. "You reported a shooting here?"

"Yes. Right in there." Specialist Anderson follows the line of my arm to the latrine, does an about face and goes in, leaving his two men just outside the door. I go back to the desk and put my head down on my arms. I hear the windy swing of the latrine door and the clerk and Specialist Anderson coming out.

"Clear the building and collect dogtags," Anderson says to the two MPs in the hall. The boots double-time off to execute the order.

Footsteps and voices beat in the stairwell. Specialist Anderson makes himself comfortable at the first sergeant's desk and asks me a few general questions, including the name of the individual whose body lies in the latrine. The two MPs come back, one of them with dogtag chains looped over his forearm. "The building is cleared," he says. "They're all in the courtyard."

The MP lifts the dogtags off his wrist and hands them to Anderson. "Good," Anderson says. "Posts."

The MPs post themselves on either side of the latrine door like wooden sculptures with .45s hung on their hips. Wood. Cigar store MPs. *Wood* used to mean crazy, way back in the language. It is crazy, Herb's body inside, gawked up in the corner, grey-fringed hole and black specks on one side of his head, signifying death, bloody crater on the other side saying, "Yes, indeed."

The patrol supervisor is saying, "The CID should be here any minute," when two men in civvies appear in the hall, the acronym become flesh, carrying what look like small suitcases.

Anderson knows the investigators pretty well by the way he gets up, throws an easy salute, and says, "Hi." Their faces are open and they are loose in their bodies and their whiteness. My existence is not recognizable yet. Anderson talks, the CID men look into his face, black cases swinging alongside their pantlegs. Anderson extends a hand in my direction and their eyes follow, their faces blank white. I remain seated. "Private Birdsong here heard the round go off and discovered the body," he says.

The investigators, warrant officers no doubt, look me over. One of them wears colorless plastic-rimmed army spectacles that give his face an albino look. These two give me colder looks than the people Sergeant Howell and I talked to downtown. I have no sponsor here.

"We'll want to talk to you after we process the crime scene, Private Birdsong," the one in glasses says. *Crahm, Prahvit* Birdsong.

"Okay."

Their stiffened spines suggest that I should have said "Yes, sir." But what the hell, Herb just shot himself and these cats are wearing civvies, and they flashed their credentials on Anderson, not on me. The one in specs is into some movie version of looking inscrutable. And he's got a serious case of whiteness. He turns to Specialist Anderson and says, "Have him wait down in the courtyard."

"Yes, sir," Anderson says.

The CID men go into the latrine with their black cases.

"Okay, Private, wait down in the courtyard," Anderson says. "I'll be down in a minute. We'll get you all back into the building as soon as we can."

"Right."

"Oh, and Birdsong..."

"Yes?"

"Let me have your dogtags."

I pull them off and hand them to him.

"And I noticed," Anderson says, "somebody vomited in the latrine."

"Yeah. That was me. When I first saw Herb, the body."

Anderson's head goes up and down. "Yup, it's a pretty tough sight to look at."

Then: "You can go on downstairs."

Whoa ho.

Heat against my face in the hall, and on the first landing in the stairwell it's even warmer. Daddy is standing there in a dress uniform at attention. "Your friend killed hisself," he says, "but you could of got on your feet in there and give the institution its due."

"Aw, man, what are you talking about?"

"I'm talking about this whole thing is bigger than you, Private."

"Well, they weren't in uniform."

"That don't make no difference. You knew they was commissioned or warranted."

"You saw what kind of attitude they had."

"Don't make no difference. Your duty is clear. Your attitude is what you got to worry about."

"My attitude?"

"That's right. A wrong attitude will keep you from seeing things you ought to see. There is a place for order. You don't want to undermine the means of your preservation, boy—maybe you can understand that. And everybody don't have to please you. You let every last little thing somebody do shake you so you stop thinking, you be in big trouble."

"I know that."

"Listen here, boy, what you don't seem to know is that there is an order here bigger than you and all other individuals within it, in which your hope lies. You violate it, you weaken it." He takes a step back, salutes, and disappears.

In the chilly clamp of the outside air, a dozen or so soldiers under the night light smoke cigarettes. The ones in T-shirts draw their shoulders up toward their ears and tuck their free hands into their armpits. Duty-bound American soldiers. Their eyes locked on the door when I came out. Except for two men from the band and the clerk, Reed, I don't know anybody except by sight. In the smoky half-light nobody's identity is sure. I'm not looking for anybody to talk to, but they all look at me, a fellow broke-ass GI, who couldn't go home for Christmas or didn't have home to go to, eyes black holes, faces of no content but light and shadow, their mouths empty black holes. Jesus Christ, faces of the whole wasted human race, *starving hysterical naked*. Waiting for the word. Reed must not have told them. I say, "Sergeant Herb Vogel, on the second floor, shot himself. Through the head. Suicide. MPs said they'll get us inside pretty soon."

"Shit. I thought that was a firecracker."

"Wow."

"Blew his brains out!"

"Merry fucking Christmas!"

A blond shivering smoker moves close enough to see that his eyes are brown. "Hey, man," he says, "what'd he use?"

"A forty-five."

He moves back into the smoky troop. "Jesus, a forty-five. Those things really make a mess."

The men kick at the ground, cigarettes between their first two fingers up to their mouths, down at their sides. "Hey, how come they took our dogtags?"

"I don't know. Ask the big MP. He'll be down here in a minute."

In the mess hall of Building 1014, Specialist Anderson gets up in front of the group. He brushes his mustache with the sharp knuckle of his forefinger. Herb brushed his mustache with his finger extended, front of his fingertip. "Okay, men," Anderson says, "sorry for the inconvenience, but I imagine you all understand by now what's going on." Hands on his hips just above his forty-five, he looks us over. "The CID has your dogtags. Soon as they finish processing the crime scene over in Building 1013, they'll call you in, individually, and return them."

"All right," somebody in back says, "I was starting to feel sort of naked." *Nekkid.*

"Shut up, fool," a neighbor says.

Specialist Anderson scans the jumpy, uprooted group with a half-smile on his face. He could kick ass if he wanted to. The army. "Okay, at ease, troopers. If the CID has any questions for you, they'll ask at that time. But unless you were an acquaintance or friend of the sergeant, I don't imagine they'll question you."

Although I stood at attention when I collected my dogtags, the CID officers hardly let their eyes fall on me and assumed I knew nothing of interest about Master Sergeant Vogel. I did not volunteer anything. In my bunk, trying to sleep, my unsettled stomach radiates uneasiness so that my arms feel weak, hands shaky under my head. Before sunup, the draft of Herb's death sucks at me that brushed against me when I knelt beside his pistol on the latrine floor. I'm falling through a scoured-out cylinder, stainless steel, no handholds. My sheets are damp from sweat. I sit up and take deep breaths until my insides stop quivering.

***

"Ever one of y'all just as well go on about your business 'cause Birdie's got a long report this morning. Go on down to the basement and get ready for rehearsal."

Everyone who was on leave is back on time, which I'm typing into the longer than usual morning report. A couple guys have already asked me about Herb, and I can hear the fever of questions in the air before rehearsal. Muccigrosso, the Southerners, and some others are still hanging just outside the orderly room, talking. Sergeant Howell gets up from his desk, goes to the door and says, "Go on. Git!"

The sergeant's phone rings. He steps back into the room and picks up. He says "Yes, sir" a couple times and hangs up. "That was Mr Tappendorf. He wants to see you when you finish the morning report."

It's close to 0800 when I finish typing. Sergeant Howell says, "I'm going on downstairs and get the band started, Birdie. You can take the report in and have him sign it and see what he wants."

"Okay, Sarge."

He stabs out his cigarette and leaves for the basement.

Mr Tappendorf grazes his forehead with the forefinger he flips out, answering my salute. "At ease," he says.

I lay the morning report next to some other papers before him on the desk. He looks at it like a surprising plate of eggs, recognizes it, and reaches into his desk for a pen. He signs the report and pushes it aside.

"Uh, Birdsong," he says, "I think it might be a good idea during rehearsal this morning if you tell the men exactly what happened with Sergeant Vogel while we've got everybody together in one spot."

"Sounds like a good idea to me, sir."

I stick to the essential facts. Some guys want to know how naked was he and how much blood was there and what did the bullet wound look like and how did you feel. "Please don't ask me for all the bloody details," I tell them. "I haven't got the stomach for going over that stuff." I could tell them you don't want to get too close to the draft from a suicide. Don't want to get that hollow cylinder feeling, with the endless hurtling downward. Swink and Gilson might help me digest the story, but Herb didn't have friends down here. They look more confounded than stricken with sadness for Herb, and when I think my recitation has been sufficient for the reasonably curious, I go sit in my place in the trumpet section.

Tappendorf picks up his baton and shuffles the sheets of music in front of him. He brings his eyes up, looking just over our heads, for his finest moment: "Things happen in life," he says. "We've just got to go on. Okay, you've got your Number Forty-seven and your Number Eighty-two. Let's get those up on your stands."

Part Two: Ornithology

Love, from New York

1)

Two o'clock, I'm sitting here. The library is empty except for the clerk and me. I told Stacy I'd be sitting at the table next to fiction, which is out of sight of the clerk's desk and counter. Told her we'd have to be real cool. This is Texas. I don't have to worry about Stacy getting to the library. Stacy wants to be someplace, she gets there. Gets there, like being down here in Texas to see me.

Sitting next to fiction, rereading a few pages of *On the Road*, I feel her tiptoe around the corner bookshelf, trying to slip up on me. She gets to the end of the table before I look up. I know she planned to swing around behind me and put her hands over my eyes which would disturb my stomach more than she could imagine. Stacy. Crooked little smile on her mouth and in her eyes. Down here to see me. She has on a white windbreaker over a drawstring white blouse and light blue pedal push-ers. Cost me some nerves not to jump up and hug the hell out of her.

She whispers, "Hi."

Stacy can act like a dipshit sometimes, being young and screwed up, but she has these eyes, caramel-colored and transparent, that have everything in the encyclopedia in them. *O, the cruelty of putting me into this ill-conceived world! I was capable of much; but I have been injured and blighted and crushed by things beyond my control!*

Ill-conceived, oh man, Eustacia. It's all in the books, I swear. My voice is as quiet as I can make it. "Hi, baby. Sit over there."

She sits across the table at an angle from me. I look around. Nobody else in this part of the room. I slide *On the Road* across the table to her. "Here—your favorite book. Make like you're reading it."

She straightens her back, draws in her chin and opens her mouth without saying anything like *What's going on here?* This is the post library, but I'm remembering things Richard Wright and Carl Rowan wrote about not being allowed to even check out library books down in Mississippi and Tennessee. One of those dog-bite things, Heavy Brother material, this trickle of terror memory, way back in the woods of my psyche, full of members castrated, lynched, getting the Emmett Till treatment for doing less than nothing with ignorant-ass white women down South. And this here Texas is South enough for me.

I get up and pull the first novel that comes to my hand out of the bookshelf: *Random Harvest.* Read it a long time ago when I worked for the Kesslers.

The front door of the library clashes and girl voices get louder in our direction. A couple with two wiry, sandy-haired girls, fourth or fifth graders that look like the kind to eat books, come in and set two shopping bags on the table across the aisle. Not interested in a colored soldier and a white girl sitting at the same table, reading.

I take my notepad and pencil out of my pocket, tear off a sheet and write: "Let's write." *How did you get down here? When did you get in? You look good.* I shove the note and pencil over to Stacy and look at the open pages of *Random Harvest.* Across the aisle, the family pulls children's books from a shelf.

Stacy pushes the paper and pencil back to me without checking to see where the other people are located. I bug my eyes at her and look halfway over my shoulder. She wrote: *Got in yesterday morning. This place wigs me, man! What do people do here for fun? Can't we go some-place where we can talk? You look like something happened to you what is it. You should see New York!!!*

I write: *Something did happen to me. One of my friends blew his brains out on Christmas Day, and I found the body. What the hell were you doing in New York? How did you get there? How long you gonna be in El Paso? Where are you staying? Let's shack up tonight. I can find a place across the border after we leave here.*

Yes, I am cool, armed with Turner's intelligence regarding cheap trysting spots across the border. Yeah, man. *Adieu, tristesse.*

She writes: *Oh, poor you, I'm so sorry. You're okay now aren't you? I love you, JB. I love your letters and run to the mailbox every day in Portland. Do I have some waiting there now? Drove to NY with these friends in a VW. They got me a job in a coffee house. I was a waitress. I quit, so I'm heading back to Portland. We're leaving here tomorrow some-time. Yes! Yes! Yes! Please let us shack up tonight!! How about right now? On this table? Oh I want to rub your fuzzy butt right now.*

She looked around this time before she slid the note across the table. The two young girls across the room finger through a stack of books. Stacy takes off her windbreaker. Neck, shoulders, arms, full of curves. Curvaceous, Eustacia is. My mouth waters and my stomach is hollowed and tugging. Fourteen months. Impossible Stacy. And me without a pit to hiss in. Nothing I could give her. And she doesn't care. No right to make any demands on her, screw-loose as I was since breaking with Mae. Then there's Herb and the Heavy Brother mess jarring against my rivets right now.

I turn the paper over and write: *Seeing you makes me feel a whole lot better, baby. Listen:*

> *Whispering neighbors left and right*
> *Pluck us from our real delight*
> *And the active hands must freeze*
> *Lonely on the separate knees*

Yeah, that's Auden—ain't it cool—but I wants to git between yo knees, Eustacia. Not on this table, though (it's past lunchtime, anyhow). We'll find something in Juarez tonight. You didn't tell me where you were staying.

She writes: *You are so bad, Josephus! I don't know where I'm staying. It's a house. Some friends of the people I'm riding with live there, let us flop there. How long are we going to sit here?*

People she was riding with. No telling what story she's giving them about visiting El Paso. I never ask Stacy too many questions because I don't own her and because, it seems to me, the answers could range farther and farther from the truth if I kept asking. Like I thought she hitchhiked to New York. Cool enough that she came down here to see me. I write *Let's do this: It's about three o'clock now. I've got to go back to the barracks. Can you kill time until six? I'll meet you at Alligator Park at six. Everybody knows Alligator Park—middle of downtown. We can walk over to Juarez from there. You'll have to walk in front of me like we're not together, at least until we get across the bridge. This is Texas and I ain't ready to get lynched down here in this motherfucker. You understand, sweetheart.*

Bad shit could happen in Portland too. Happened in Kayakaw. National poison, but people don't get so anthropological up there, don't have so much of that Southern mad dog shit working when they see colored and white close together. Stacy closes *On the Road,* pushes back her chair, and stands up, looking at me, in my eyes, with her transparent caramel-colored irises. She breathes in, breathes out, stretches her arms out to the sides like she's pushing back walls. Almost nineteen now. Face, arms, and hands could model for a Raphael virgin. So jail me, motherfuckers.

In the four-hour room Turner suggested in Juarez, Stacy undoes my belt buckle, and I work her windbreaker off her shoulders. I pull my sweater over my head and throw it on the chair while she slips out of her white cotton blouse. Hard breathing, at the sight of her neck curving down to her bare shoulders and arms.

"Hey," she says. "Unhook me."

She gives me her back, and I unhook her brassiere and slide it off her shoulders. She tosses it onto the pile of clothes on the chair. Her back under my hands is not so adolescent firm as I remember. My hands feel their way around until I hold a breast in each one. A holy bleeding emperor, got me a blooming orb in each hand.

She bumps me back with her hips and slips her pedal pushers down to her feet, pulls her panties down and steps out of them. The sight of her breasts, curving downward, lifting out, nipples at attention—oh man, let me be a pencil running along those lines, down, around and up the curves of her legs into the lips of her vagina. And her colors in the half dark of the evening, her dark dark red hair, her ivory and pink, colors without edges, liven the air. I take off my pants and shorts.

"Stacy, you are chiaroscuro."

"What?"

Words hung in my throat. I straighten up in front of her and stretch my arms out to the side. She does the same. We interlock fingers, press foreheads together. She pushes her belly against me, rubs side to side. We roll onto the bed. Directions like *meno mosso, andante, andantino*, guide our hands, lips, noses, tongues into mouths, along skin, through hair for a long time before she puts me in. We come like we always did, and I'm so grateful, lying between Stacy's thighs, sweated to her belly and breasts, that water runs out of my eyes over her neck. All this fucking crying, crying before I knew it when I saw Herb's body. But this is relief.

"There, there," she says like I'm somebody's baby, patting me like putting me together out of clay. Her hand, warm, slides up and down my back. So old, she is, doing that. Like she knows some woman thing about me I'm not so sure I know myself. That's a main feeling I've experienced with Stacy. She crosses her legs around my buttocks and wriggles her crotch against me till I could cash it in right here. We stay like that for awhile. Until I hear that bastard Iago back in the trees, yapping, trying to start some colonial shit, "The black ram is tupping the white ewe." We roll over, her on top of me, dipping to let a breast fall in my mouth, nipple riding my tongue, the beat of blood in her neck against my face. I gasp against her, trying to keep the crazy laughter down in my throat.

She sits back and slides down onto me. Her hands cup my shoulders, heels and fingers printing my skin and whatever is beyond. Our eyes pool together and we go way way away, or we fill up the universe, and I would die happy right now, but I'm still alive with depression and threat and death lurking, and I hear the Raylettes chorusing "How true-woo can this be" and I see Herb, his head crooked like his neck is broken, fallen bloody in the corner of the latrine, brains all over the wall and floor. Emptied out mortal coil that I saw for real.

Across the bridge in the night air, in El Paso, Stacy walks ahead of me among a few other nightwalkers. But behind me three young guys talk loud, laughing and grab-assing.

They could have seen Stacy and me over in Juarez. Could be trouble. Maybe this is it. Three of them. They wouldn't fuck with Washington and Polk. I could probably outrun them. Run where? They might mess with Stacy at the bus stop. I walk faster, but they keep their same pace, their voices harder to make out.

When I reach the corner I take a quick look back at the three coming across the street behind me. Three looped eighteen-year-olds, happy as they can be. Got drunk, got fucked, got each other, got the week to talk and carry on about it. Down the sidewalk from me, reeling, talking loud, laughing together.

Stacy and I look across the corner of meager grass that separates our bus stops. Going in opposite directions, we are. No idea when I'll see her again. None of the few citizens and GIs waiting with us knows she's got traces of me inside her, that I can smell her on me and ain't hurrying to shower again. She looks off and thumbs her ear at me. Pink lips arc into her crooked grin. Looking nowhere in particular, I roll my eyes and rub my stomach wide down to my crotch. She sticks out her tongue and pulls her jacket down from her shoulder.

Here comes her bus. This is it for now. Big long green and yellow thing, all lighted up inside, idling at the stop. Idling in my nerves. Stacy stands to the side of the door until everyone else gets on. She's not grinning now. She pats herself over the heart three times, waves her hand like a hankie, and gets on.

Whoa hee ho.

A wave of heat breaks against the skin of my face and hands, and I see him when I raise up from the drinking fountain. He's riding back and forth under the same tree where he was standing that first time I saw him—Chinese elm, I found out. That first hot day in *Ciudad El Paso*. Night now, and he and the horse are something out of a black and white movie this time, back and forth under the tree. I cross over to the area. The horse is clopping toward me without a sound. Inside me, though, the sound happens like fiction. Daddy reins up and looks down at me. "You seem to be feelin' pretty good about yourself right now, Private," he says.

He thumbs his hat upward on his forehead. The scent of Stacy is still in my nostrils. "I feel all right," I say.

"I would say you even feel the pride of conquest at this moment."

"I don't know why you want to say that."

"Then you should be trying to find out."

"Think so, huh?"

"Yes. Prideful and unseeing in your present satisfied condition, that is you." His words bring sweat to my brow, and I remember learning the word *discomfited.* "Remember, boy, pride goeth before a fall."

He rides off a few yards, swings around and rides back past me, studying. Rides back in front of me and stops. He points down like he used to do from the pulpit. "Look here, you've had your little accomplishments and you may have more if you survive your foolishness, but you have done some wrong you will never outrun."

Sweat. Pinpricks overrun my skin and my throat tightens so that I have to force out the words. "I'm trying to learn to do better. I'm studying now."

"You best keep studying, boy. And understand you always going to come up short."

Gone.

2)

A big cold draft hangs around from Herb shooting himself, from the Heavy Brothers and their big bodies creeping around the area, and then comes this letter from Cousin Estella, a month after Stacy left, with a cold-ass haymaker in it.

Cousin Estella writes that she and Richard got a phone call from her at three in the morning one Saturday. Seems that Eustacia needed a rescue. There had been a big beatnik whing ding in a building downtown in Portland. "Old, spooky place," my cousin wrote. The police raided the joint, people scattered, and Stacy, hiding, got left behind with no clothes on for some reason. She asked Estella and Richard to bring a coat. Estella said when they saw her Stacy was indeed naked, and her body was covered with soot. That just about choked the breath out of me with questions that could go nowhere. My cousin didn't help, said she didn't ask Stacy any questions, just put the coat on the girl and gave her a ride home. I lay on my bunk studying the perforated ceiling tiles for a long time after that one. The weeks after my cousin's letter, I'm getting the usual letters from Stacy: the scene is cool in Portland, she's thinking about taking a guitar class or hitching to New York, wishes we could be together again.

***

Dear Stacy,

Sorry for this tardy response to your last few notes. What's going on in Portland? I've been doing a lot of work on the horn-playing lately, gettin' with it, you know. Baby, if I forget to say it again, let me say it now. Thank you, thank you, thank you, for pointing out the possibility that I should be playing jazz. You can't know how right you were when you said, "You seem like you've got it in you." Out of the mouths of babes, etc. And I'm saying jazz has got me in it, too. I'm at home with it. Seems like there's a whole world of stuff that wants to come out. I feel like I'm on the highway to somewhere. Hard to describe, but maybe someday I can tell you about it. You started something.

I wish I could make as big a smudge on you, baby. Like make you stop screwing around and go to college and develop that bright mind of yours. You've got more imagination than anybody I know.

Be good.

> *Much love,*
> *JB*

Fowler

1)

Herb Vogel's replacement is Cedric Weems, a staff sergeant who wears a mustache and has lightbrown skin and hair that suggests some usual American racial mix-up. Two members in the band quarters now. No private room available for a staff sergeant, the first sergeant assigns him to my space. I move over to Levinski's old bunk against the end wall and Weems takes my former bunk. Weems is jumpy, and his life looks like an agitated sack of Negro woe. He's always going on about it, ready to fire on white people that strike him wrong, pretty much hates the Southern ones before they say a word to him. Short and stocky like he's made up of knots, Cedric is the one the word *pugnacious* was derived for. Still, he doesn't have the heavy, brutal feel of Washington and Polk.

Jarboe came in one night after lights-out, talking and giggling in a normal voice, and Weems yelled, "Knock that shit off down there."

Jarboe says, "I wasn't making no noise, Sarge."

Weems jumps up and busts barefooted down to the Mississippi Bastard's space, gets all up in Jarboe's mug. "Don't fuck with me, boy," he says. "I'm forty-three years old and I will kick your ass." Jarboe had enough sense not to say anything.

Muccigrosso knows how to talk shit with Weems, doesn't try to get too wise with him or jive around out of his own depth. Hiebert and Jarboe— *immured in frosty whiteness,* I imagine Shakespeare saying—the closer in proximity to Weems, the quieter they get. In my trite, evil movie, they would murder Weems and themselves end up stumbling off a railroad trestle into a rocky torrent at the bottom of a dingle.

Weems has got scars on his brow like you see on a veteran prize fighter. He told me he was a kid in the same Chicago neighborhood as Nat King Cole and that Nat ran home fast after school every day to stay out of fights and to practice the piano. I can see old Weems wading into the rough stuff every day. It's apparent that Cedric didn't dedicate his youth to practicing the pianoforte. Cat doesn't play piano anything like Herb Vogel. Or Nat Cole. A big-knuckled blues player who plays by ear, that's Weems, but he doesn't have to worry about playing much piano for the 72nd. He plays the cymbals or the glockenspiel when we march, just like Herb did.

We're putting away music, chairs, instruments, done for the day early in the afternoon, when Weems comes over to me. "Man, come go downtown with me."

"What are you going to do downtown," I say.

"I'm going to see a cat I know here in El Paso, a musician—come on, man, make this run with me." Weems's eyes bug out more than normal so he looks urgent and more jumpy any time he stares at you. Sort of crazy, so his craziness puts pressure on you. I hate for Negroes I don't know to be grabbing onto me to do shit with them just because I'm a member too, like the mess with the Heavy Brothers. But I know this cat a little bit, and his eyes are bugging. I could hang around the barracks, stewing, and read or practice, waiting for Stacy's naked body covered with soot to come and go like malaria or a migraine. What's been happening is, before I can read or practice my horn or the piano, I fall into stewing over images of her naked, soot-powdered body in all kinds of black dusty positions. My stomach wants to come through my throat.

She's a thousand miles away. Weems's *ojos* are bugging at me.

"Okay, why not?" I say. "Who is this cat you're looking up?"

"Mercer Fowler. Blind cat. Real good trumpet player. Plays piano too, and can sing. The cat is bad."

"You mean the guy that made the record they're playing all the time on the radio here? And he plays at that spook joint they talk about?"

"Yeah, that's him, and singing 'Sherry Pie'."

The street is wide and not busy. The adobe houses sit in yards and not right up against the sidewalk like the ones in Juarez. No kids out playing.

Only a few days left in the school year. In Portland, kids are in school too. I'd be in there with them, lunchroom duty, under that low ceiling, before rushing back upstairs to meet the one o'clock class. "Okay, ladies and gentlemen, let's open our books to page two hundred seventy-two where you all should have read by now 'The Cask of Amontillado'."

But I'm here, bright sunshine, middle of the afternoon, walking around in El Paso, Texas, with a regular army sergeant of marginal stability, months to go before I get out, to look up a blind musician. We go in the wooden gate of a house set back a few yards from the side-walk. Weems opens the screen and knocks on the front door. It's an old varnished door that has a leaded window in the upper half with a shade that's drawn. Smaller panes of red, yellow, blue, and green border the clear center pane of the window. "He's home," Weems says. "I know he's home."

He raises his voice. "Hey, Merce. It's me, Cedric."

From behind the door, across a room, perhaps, a big gravel voice. "Who is it?"

"It's me. Cedric, man." Weems looks at me, shakes his head. His lips press together to keep his face from splitting into a grin.

The door opens. A big cinnamon-colored man in dark glasses fills the gap, looking straight ahead. Big cat with good hair, about Weems's age, got on a short-sleeved gray shirt, and huaraches on his feet. Weems's clamped lips give up the grin, and he steps close to the big man, hand on his arm. "Merce, man, it's me. Cedric, Cedric Weems."

The big man dips his knees and laughs, puts out his arms and gives Weems a bear hug. And then holds him away by the shoulders as if he could see him. "Cedric. Got damn, man. You gettin' fat, boy. How you been? I thought you was still in the army."

Cedric ducks his head, still grinning, with the big man's hands on his shoulders. Prodigal-ass Weems. "I'm still in," he says. "Just got sent back out here to Showalter."

The big man takes a couple careful steps backward. "Come on in here," he says. "Who this you got with you, man?" Weems and I shuffle into the tobacco-tinged air of the room. I slip toward the back wall to take a peek at the old upright there, a big mahogany thing with fancy carving on it. And resting on the piano lid is a French Besson trumpet in an open case, shiny gold and perfect against the red velvet.

"This my friend Joe, Merce, from the band out there." Weems knows I'm Joe, the band clerk, the cat he bunks across from, but I'm not sure my last name has got through the barbed wire in his head. I step away from the piano, and the big man sticks out his hand toward me, so I figure he must have a slight bit of vision or he's got sonar.

"Welcome, Joe," he says. "Merce Fowler."

Fowler has a big warm hand, long fingers, with softness and strength that come through his grasp. "Joe Birdsong," I say. "I'm pleased to meet you."

"Joe's a trumpet player," Cedric says.

Fowler's huaraches slap the bare floor over to the armchair between the piano and the sofa. He keeps a hand out before him until he touches the chair arm, and sits down. "Y'all make yourselves comfortable."

Then: "A young trumpet player, huh?"

"Well, I try."

"He can blow." Weems.

I sit on the piano stool, an old one with a round seat that spins and eagle claw feet gripping clear glass balls. Weems moves to the sofa. Merce Fowler shakes a cigarette from the pack on the end table next to his armchair. He takes the silver lighter next to the pack and lights up, lets out a cloud of blue smoke. "You gonna have to come see me now, Cedric, now you stationed down here."

Fowler's heavy saxophone voice rings in the room, and there's rhythm in it. Weems pulls out a cigarette and joins him in smoking, says, "Oh I'll be by, man."

Smoke spreads out like cirrus clouds with our heads up in them. Might as well be puffing one myself.

"Come on over to the club once in a while and play some of that mess you play," Fowler says. "I won't work your ass too hard."

Weems's laugh down in his chest is half grunt. "Yeah, man."

"And don't be spendin' all your time and money over there in Juarez with them whore-ez." Fowler slaps himself on the leg and rocks forward and back in the armchair.

Weems draws his knees together, takes a squint-eyed drag on his cigarette. "Man, you know I'm getting too old for that shit."

"Boy, tell another one 'fore that one gets cold."

"Naw, man, serious business."

Fowler's ear must tell him that his jive has pinked Weems. He says, "You know I'm just kiddin' you, Cedric. You know how I am."

"Yeah, you just as full of shit as ever."

Fowler whoops and laughs until he starts coughing, fist up to his mouth, shoulders up and down. He mashes out the cigarette and waggles his hand toward the door next to the piano. "Man, get me a glass of water, will you?"

Weems puts down his cigarette.

I say, "I'll get it, Cedric."

"Oh. Thanks, man." He picks up his cigarette.

A row of clean highball glasses lines the back edge of the kitchen sink counter. I fill one with water and take it to Fowler. "Here you go."

His hand finds the glass. "Thanks, Cuz."

"*Nada.*"

He turns the glass up, drains it in one long draught, and sets it on his table. I sit back down on the piano stool. "Say," Fowler says, "have you cats heard my new record?"

"I've heard it a few times on the radio," I say. "Getting played a lot." There isn't much to "Sherry Pie," but Fowler's voice and clowning on the lyrics make it catchy.

"Yeah. Just tryin' to pick up a few extra pennies, you understand. That's not my real groove."

"Naw, man, Merce is jazz," Weems says, "from way back."

"Way, way back," Fowler puts in. "Farther back than I want to remember now." He laughs, but in his "way, way back" I see a grainy newsreel of gigs in lowdown places, zoot suits, low lights and booze, conked heads, messed-up women moaning over *love*, hopeless hopes, sooty blues.

There's a light triple knock at the door, and a good-sized young Mexican woman with wavy black hair down past her shoulders comes onstage when Fowler says, "Come on in."

Her smooth, tawny arms are impossible not to look at, flowing out of a white sleeveless blouse. She scans the room as if to check whether anything is missing or out of place, and Merce Fowler gets the same kind of going over. She checks out Weems and me. "Hello," she says.

Weems and I say hello at the same time.

"MJ," she says, "I'm going down to the store. Do you need anything?" Her bright colors, like a tropical bird just flew in, and the way her eyes touch everything in the room, they take over, outnumber us three cats. I don't hear any accent in her speech except for a slight hanging onto the r in store. Her voice is a strong alto. Her eyes lock on Fowler, who I don't think can see me gawking.

"Yeah, bring me a pack of Luckies when you come back, baby," he says. "Hold on a minute. Meet my friends here."

She takes a smooth step over to Fowler, and his big arm slides around her waist. I beat back a swarm of shameful, thieving impulses.

"Y'all, this is my girl, Corazon," he says. "I don't think you remember Cedric, baby."

I get up from the piano stool and half bow. Corazon is only an inch shorter than I. Her chest reaches out toward me. Her eyes are so dark I have to look hard to see her pupils, and her bare arms—they're as loud as Fowler's French Besson. "Joe Birdsong," I say.

Corazon's face looks like the face of somebody whose mind is still on her errand, but I figure I might be seeing here the famous veiled look of women. Weems shuffles his feet under the coffee table, waves to her from the sofa. "Cedric," he says.

"Nice to meet you," she says. She gives us a crumb of a smile, kisses Fowler on the cheek, and moves from his arm to the screendoor. "I'll see you around six, MJ."

"Okay, baby." His girl. She couldn't be much older than Stacy. Bad old cat. Her ankles in retreat set off a fanfare in my ears that Fowler's voice cuts short. "You cats want a beer or something? Look in the frigidaire and get yourself something."

"Yeah, thanks, Merce," Weems says. "You want a beer, man?"

"Sure."

Weems gets up and goes in the kitchen. The heavy door of the refrigerator smacks shut, bottle caps rattle against the drainboard. Fowler sits easy in the big chair, can hear him listening to the music inside himself, soaking up footsteps, breaths, creaks, knocks, music of the bottle. He says, "How long you been playin' the horn, man?"

"Going on fifteen years."

"You must of not been nothin' but a little bitty boy when you started."

"I was going on ten."

"Humph, that's about what I was when I started. Picked up the piano later." Fowler presses his elbows into the fat arms of his chair, taking some load off his spine.

I say, "What do you think of Clifford Brown's playing, Merce?"

"Pure genius, Cuz. You heard him."

"Yeah. I've got a couple of his albums at the barracks, *Study in Brown* and another one."

"It's a damn shame Clifford had to die so early," Fowler says. "Goddamn cars, for sure, will kill you."

Weems comes out of the kitchen with a brown bottle of beer for each of us. He sets one on the table next to Fowler and hands me a cold wet one. I set it on the coffee table.

"What do you think of Lee Morgan?" I ask.

"Outstanding. The boy can play. Right up there with the best of them."

"Yeah, that's what I think too. I've been listening to him a lot lately. Have you heard *Blue Train?* He's on that one with John Coltrane."

"Ain't heard that one yet."

"Coltrane is bad too, isn't he?"

"Oh yeah, bad as he wannabe." Fowler eases his hand around the beer bottle and raises it to his mouth. Runs the back of his hand across his lips. Overtones from the girl's visit hang in the room.

"If you'd like to hear it," I say, "I'll bring the album by sometime."

"Cedric says, "I'll bet old Merce would enjoy that."

"Yeah, I would. Bring it on by, Cuz. Love to hear it." His aloneness in the dark spreads out around the words, and I dig the way words and music must soak into the vacuum left by his gone sight. A chance to deliver a truckload of groovy sound to the man.

I say, "One day next week, maybe?"

Fowler sets his beer down, takes another cigarette from the pack, and picks up his lighter. "That'd be fine. Come on over. I ain't goin' noplace, just be here punishin' the cushion."

Then: "And bring your axe, too. Let's do some investigatin'."

Weems did say, "He can play," talking about me.

The air is hot and bright in Fowler's bare living room, and the tangy cool beer goes down as if my mouth were made of sand. Fowler and Weems pass memories back and forth. I lean back, light-headed with the blind man's invitation, and listen to the hoarse voices, rise and fall of sound from chamber music-making ravens.

***

Wednesday afternoon I'm on Merce Fowler's doorstep with my trumpet in one hand and *Blue Train* in the other. Boy oh boy, get in some licks with Merce Fowler, could be something different. Seek and ye shall find. I knock on the screendoor and listen.

"Who is it?" Fowler's voice.

I raise my voice like Weems last week. "It's me, Joe Birdsong. Remember? I was here with Cedric."

"Yeah. Yeah. Oh yeah. Come on in, Cuz, it ain't locked." The screendoor needs a little tug, but the door to Fowler's living room opens easy as an eye. Opens on Merce Fowler in his blind man glasses, sitting in his chair, a glass of whiskey in one hand, half a bottle of Jim Beam on the table beside him. He sets down the glass and sticks out his big paw. My hand, not that small, is no match for his.

"Ay, my man, I never expected you to come back."

"Really? I said I was coming back."

He elbows himself straighter in his chair. Fowler's voice is a baritone saxophone against the walls of the room. "You know how cats are, man. Most cats anyway."

"Really?"

"Swear to God. Take old Cedric. Joker won't be by till he gets in trouble."

That's water I don't care to wade in. I lay the album on the coffee table beside my trumpet and sit down. "I brought my horn with me. And that Coltrane record I was telling you about."

"Good, good. Go get yourself a glass, Cuz, and some ice out the kitchen. You drink, don't you?"

"Yes, I have a little taste now and then. Thanks."

At the back of the drainboard against the wall, a line of clean highball glasses just like last week. The food and bottles and dishes in Fowler's refrigerator are lined up in neat rows. Whites, reds, greens, fresh in the light. Half a bottle of ginger ale stands behind a bottle of milk. I get two ice cubes and drop them in a glass. "Say, Merce, is it okay if I use some of this ginger ale?"

"Help yourself, man, bring it on in here." Fowler is sitting at the piano, big on the stool, when I go back in the front room. "You got what you need?" he says.

"Yes, thank you."

"Boy, you sure are polite."

"Way I was raised, man."

"Well, that's good. Must've had some good people."

"Yeah."

"Your daddy still around?"

"No. He died my last year in high school."

"That so?" He takes a swallow of his drink that he refilled while I was in the kitchen. The Jim Beam is my first whiskey since California, and its cool sweet burn loosens the joints of the afternoon.

"Well, I never knew *my* daddy," Fowler says. "Where you from, Cuz?"

"Oregon, Portland. But I was born and raised in Washington. My mother still lives there."

"That so? Never spent much time up that way. Played a job in Seattle once back in the thirties when I could still see." Back in the thirties. Fowler was probably remembering what Weems told me about. Told me a woman Fowler was messing with threw ammonia in his face and fucked up his eyes. Back in the thirties. Must have burned like holy hell. He must think about that every day.

I say, "You want to hear this record?"

He motions with his thumb toward the stereo set next to the piano. "Yeah, go ahead and put it on. You know how to work that thing there, don't you?"

"Sure. At least I will in a minute."

The album starts with the title track that first got me hooked on Coltrane and then on Lee Morgan, who was only nineteen, Swink's age, when they cut the record. Stacy's almost-age. We sip and listen, chins on our chests. "That's real hip," Fowler says at the end of the tune.

Listening to "I'm Old-fashioned," a later track, Fowler hums along and hits a chord on the piano with his left hand every now and then. On Kenny Drew's solo, he comps all the way through, big fingers floating down on the black and white keys like they've got radar. It's a live conversation with the piano on the recording. Sitting here soaking up whiskey and ginger ale and music, master musician in front of me being his blind cool self, I hear the music like I never heard it before.

Three light knocks on the door and Fowler's girl comes in, wearing shorts and a halter top, and I am back in the meat world, eyes peeled on her smooth, muscular legs. Corazon. She's carrying a book with a plain black cover, tiptoes through the music into the kitchen without saying anything. The refrigerator door opens and shuts, and there's the gentle clash of aluminum, ice, and glass. She comes back to the front room, carrying a highball glass with three ice cubes in it, and lays her book on the coffee table. Seating herself an arm's length from me on the sofa, she reaches for the green ginger ale bottle and pours a glassful. A whiff of bath soap joins the music in the air.

I get my eyes to close, and my listening posture stays cool with her settled at the other end of the sofa. Elbows on my knees, hands clasped, patting my foot. The cats on the record are cooking, but it's harder now for me to hear what Coltrane and they are saying, Corazon on the sofa with her bare legs. It's for Merce, anyway.

The music ends. Fowler swivels around toward us, his black specs aimed off in space. "Righteous," he says. "Thanks for bringin' that over, Cuz."

"It's my pleasure, Merce. I'm glad you enjoyed it."

"Better believe I did—say, I heard my girl come in."

His girl. I look across the sofa at her. She takes the glass away from her lips. "Yes, you did," she says, and then turning her deep brown eyes to me, "Hi."

"Everything all right, baby?" Fowler says.

Her upper lip shines with ginger ale. "Sure, MJ. Everything's fine."

Corazon rises from the sofa with her glass, steps past me and puts her hand on Fowler's shoulder, pats him, and then picks up his ashtray and takes it to the kitchen. I hear her glass go "pock" against the counter, hear the trashcan open, hear tapping, hear water running. She comes back with the clean ashtray and sets it on the table, exactly where it was before. "Need anything?"

She's talking to Fowler, not addressing the needs of a hungry, anxious *soldado* from nowhere, trying to get the soot out of his head, trying to stay clear of ambush, so hungry he don't know where to start chomping. Her eye whites are clear and moist as she picks up her book that I don't catch the title of and gives me and the room one of her inspecting looks.

"Don't need nothin' right now, baby," Fowler says.

Need anything. Oooh, baby. Her back, bare between halter top and shorts, pulls my eyes along, moving to the door. Do she know what she got—she must know.

"Well then, if you don't need anything," she says, "I'll see you later, MJ."

"Bye, baby."

At the door, she swings around. The corners of her mouth lilt, heisting dimples into her cheeks. "Goodbye, Joe."

Yes, she remembered my name. "See you, Corazon."

Fowler at the piano starts fooling with a blues scale in his right hand, rippling up and down. I finish my watery whiskey and ginger ale and suck on an ice cube. He starts plunking out phrases, kind of lowdown bluesy stuff that stirs up words, clichés about hard times. Man, I have to admit, this kind of down-home blues stuff doesn't usually do much for me, but Fowler's playing insinuates words into my head

You rolled your body in soot
And you hid beneath the stairs
You ordered a coat at midnight
Baby, you act like nobody cares

He goes on with both hands, rocking and humming along. "Get out your axe, Cuz. B-flat."

I get out my horn, lick the mouthpiece, and listen to Fowler rock himself through a couple more choruses. "Come on," he says.

I blow for a while, some of it moves I've practiced with Freddy, soot and Stacy words pushing me. Some dregs of Heavy Brother blues dogging me. Ideas from the mystery of Corazon. Fowler's fingers across the keyboard work like a big truck, carrying me and my elementary exertions. Generous. I'm hacking away, sounding pitiful, I know, but I'm getting looser. Old Fowler grunts and laughs. The cat really does have a lot of gut bucket in him, but then the next minute he'll come up with some of the most hip, surprising stuff you ever heard. He plays on while I lay out. I play some more till my cupboard is bare. Fowler keeps on, it's a lecture. He plays some of the clichés I just finished playing, messing with them, disguising them with alterations so cool I just sit there and watch and listen with my mouth open. His feet dance under the keyboard. The cat has got a metronome inside him. Time, the beat, is these ancient pillars he plays among, slapping ideas off them like some kind of blind, possibly demented, burly-ass Bach. He rocks back on the stool, laughing out loud. Every once in a while he croaks, "Lookee here," as if he's tripped over a groovy surprise under his hands. When he stops, it isn't like he's played out. Just through for now. "All right, Cuz. That's enough of that mess for today. You got a good ear. I can see you ain't done a lot of this, but you got a nice sound and plenty technique. Just listen and trust yourself."

Trust yourself. Listening to Fowler, the power in his playing and the heaviness of his voice, I feel small and shaken for a moment, tugged at by guilty thoughts of Mae and the boy. Merce, in front of me, massive on the piano stool, is smiling.

"Thanks, Merce. That's the most fun I've had in a long time."

"Look out, now."

"No jive, man. I've never played with somebody able to do the stuff that you do. I must have sounded real pitiful there a few times."

Fowler laughs and reaches for his cigarettes. "Boy, what you talkin' about? Come on back over when you get time, and let's make some more noise."

Back at Building 1013, Weems: "Naw, man. What you talking about? Ain't none of his old lady, that's his daughter. Chick is still a schoolgirl, I think. Yeah, she's fine, but that's jailbait, man."

2)

"Close the door a minute, Birdie," Sergeant Howell says, and motions me to my chair across from him.

I close the door and sit. "What is it, Sarge?"

"Well, I don't know exactly, but you got someplace to go this afternoon."

"CID, huh?"

"Yup, they want to talk to you some more. They're sending a taxi at 1400 hours."

"Did they tell you anything? Like maybe they caught those creeps and sent them to Siberia?"

"Naw, that's all they told me, 'We want to talk to Private Birdsong this afternoon.'"

"Shit. I wish they would hurry up and come down on those cats so I could stop looking behind me every time I walk out of here."

"Yeah, I know ya do." He lights a cigarette and takes a couple silent puffs before he reaches over, pats my knee, and says, "Well, go on down there and see what they want, Birdie."

At the CID office, two investigators tell me they've had Washington, Polk, and several other individuals under surveillance and that while their movements suggest that something might be going on, nothing really incriminating has come to light. "Have you had contact with any of these individuals lately, Private Birdsong?"

"No, not that I know of."

"Not that you know of?"

"That's right. I believe I told you the one time I was with a group of them everybody had on hoods. I only know two of them for sure."

"Yes, you did tell us they were hooded." The way he says it and pauses makes me suspect that he might think I'm not telling everything I know.

His partner says, "This is a real sensitive situation, Private, and we know it could be a little bit dangerous for you, but if you can remember anything at all you haven't told us, we'd like to hear it."

"I've told you all I know at this time."

Across the table from me, they sit quiet with their hands folded in front of them. I feel their expectation, or hope, that I'll let loose with some jabber. There's nothing to dislodge. I don't know the names or ranks or serial numbers of the brothers in the car after the *Birth of a Nation* outing.

The silence stretches out, becomes unwieldy. The first questioner withdraws his hands from the table. "Look," he says, "one thing we'd like you to consider, Private Birdsong."

"What is that?"

"It might be helpful if you renewed contact with the two individuals you've told us about."

"Washington and Polk."

"That's right. It doesn't sound like you burned any serious bridges behind you."

"I don't know about that." Trying to picture myself crawling up to Washington and Polk doesn't work. Especially since I blew up at them last time they leaned on me. Nauseating to think about, and the cats would be suspicious. I could see myself getting pounded to mincemeat.

"It's not something we can force on you, but it sure could help out."

I don't say anything.

"We understand things could get a little ticklish, but if you were to feel at any point that your safety at Fort Showalter had been compromised, we could probably work something out in the way of a quick transfer away from here."

A transfer. The word knocks the air out of me. Away from Showalter and El Paso. Away from Swink and Gilson and Turner. Away from the gold mine I've stumbled into at Merce Fowler's house. A wave of heat and pinpricks laps against me. I take a deep breath and flex my fingers to see if I can still move.

"Would you like some water, Private?"

They noticed. It ain't no stone—he's holding a paper cone of water out to me.

I drink.

"Thank you." I hand him the empty cone. He crumples it and tosses it into the wastebasket beside his desk.

"Sure," he says.

Then: "Think it over, Private. I'm sure you can see the sooner we get to the bottom of this business the better."

Jesus. Go hang out with the Heavy Brothers some more. From the gold mine to the fucking coal mine. Maybe get hurt. Maybe have to move away just as I've found me somebody who can show me some real stuff. Old Merce.

No, I'm staying here with the music, facing it.

***

"I came to see Merce." I raise my trumpet case in front of me.

Corazon curls her finger under the hook, pulls it out of the screw eye and pushes the screen open. "Come in," she says.

The few steps behind her into the front room let me dig the muscular way her neck and shoulders connect, the way her hips move, her bare arms and unmercifully fine legs. Hefty girl but not fat. Lots of her. Oh yes, I came to see Merce.

In the middle of the room she spins around. The hem of her skirt swirls outward, her hair swings, and a fruity perfumed draft passes my nostrils. Too close to her, almost bumped into her. She doesn't give ground, looks right at me with her hands together in front of her, fingers laced just below her middle like a debutante. I sidestep to the sofa.

"Oh, don't sit down," she says. "Come in the kitchen. MJ is sleeping right now."

I slide my trumpet under the coffee table and follow her into the kitchen. "Is Merce all right?"

"Maybe, if you call drunk all right. He's been drinking too much." She says this in a low, even voice, hips against the counter, a glass with two ice cubes in it in her hand. Her face doesn't give up much, either, except for the clear wet blacks and whites of her eyes, looking at me, and then out the window of the breakfast nook. Back at me. "You want a soda or beer or something? He's got lots of beer here."

"Thank you. A beer would be great."

Corazon opens the refrigerator and brings out a stubby and a large bottle of ginger ale. She presses the beer bottle against the Coke opener screwed to the counter edge and pops off the cap, which she catches in her left hand and sets on the counter. "Do you want a glass?"

"No thank you. This will be fine." Her fingers touch mine when she passes the cold stubby.

She pours ginger ale over her ice cubes and returns the bottle to its place in the refrigerator. "Let's sit here," she says.

On opposite sides of the table in the breakfast nook our knees don't touch. She stretches to the holder at the end of the table and pulls out a light green paper napkin. Her skirt hem brushes my pantleg. She lays the napkin next to my bottle, and the glide of her arm and hand sweeps me into a dreamlet where I'm yelling to Merce Fowler to stay in bed, man, where it's safe, and let this movie run on.

"Thanks," I say and take a swig of cold beer. "Do you think Merce is going to get up?"

"Oh yes. He always does." Her golden arm slides toward the napkin holder again to get one for herself.

"Where do you live?" I ask her.

"Across the street."

"Your family lives over there?"

"Me and my mom." She wipes under her glass with the napkin.

"Really?"

"Yes, we always lived there. My mom and MJ used to be girlfriend and boyfriend." Her eyes go to her hands and the glass of ginger ale she caresses. *Ain't none of his old lady, that's his daughter.*

"And you look after Merce?"

"Yes, well, sort of. He can take care of himself—he can see a tiny bit, you know."

"That must be why he hasn't burned the house down."

She laughs. "Adobe houses don't burn down."

"I'll bet they can burn out, though."

"Well, maybe so," she says, "but MJ can take pretty good care of himself."

"Doesn't look like it right now."

She sits up straight, away from the back of the bench, and combs loose hair away from her face with her fingers. Corazon's mouth is on the wide side with a curvy upper lip, a hint of dark fuzz above it. An upper lip ready to spread into a feature-length smile or twist into a moody snarl. Could pucker into a kiss. Her forearms rest easy on the table. The way her fingers curve around her ginger ale glass, she could grip a ball and really heave it. I say, "How old are you?"

"Going on nineteen."

"You mean you're eighteen. Are you out of school?"

Sylvia. Mae. Stacy. An eighteen-year-old has never worked out.

Corazon's look, black irises right into my eyeballs, underlines her words. "I'm just now graduated."

Stacy, sootless, graduated last year.

"That's good. What are you going to do next year?"

"I'm going to college. I want to be an eye doctor." Fingers form a tight collar around her ginger ale glass.

"Wow. That's great. Is it on account of Merce?"

"Maybe so. It just seems like something I would love to do, from when I was even a little girl."

Ain't giving no achievement tests right here, but looking in her eyes and listening to her voice, I get the feeling Corazon is serious and might be a pretty good student. "And you," she says, "you must've graduated."

"Yes, I did."

"How old are you?"

"Twenty-three."

Her chin draws in, her eyes widen, and she laughs.

"What's the matter," I say.

She swallows and sits back on her bench. "I'm sorry. I thought you was maybe nineteen or twenty. You graduated a long time ago."

"Only two years ago."

"What?"

"I graduated from college two years ago."

Corazon puts both hands on the table and studies me with cartoon-wide eyes. Her lips shine into a grin. "You're lying."

"Wish I were. That's why I'm in the army. I broke up with my wife and they drafted me."

"Really? You were married?"

"Yep."

"How long were you married?"

"A little over three years." I turn up my beer for a couple swallows.

She takes her hands from the table, lets them drop to her sides on the bench. "Three years," she says. "And you didn't have no kids?"

Her double negative heavies the simple question. "We have one, a son."

"Oh." She looks at me as if she's trying to make out some hiero-glyphics.

Then: "How do you call him?"

"You mean what's his name?"

"Yes."

"His name is Raleigh."

"Oh, that's a nice name," she says. "But I can't believe it. You look younger than some kids in my class, like you could have eighteen years, maybe."

"I could still have a child."

"You're a father." The girl's words fall in my lap like an anvil.

It's like coming into a clearing, though, talking to this girl to whom I'm not a number, to be contemplating something other than the thicket of Heavy Brothers, army, time, death, and soot. Yes, Lord.

She says, "And your name is Joe what?"

"Birdsong."

Her mouth gets wider, turns up at the corners. "What?"

"Birdsong. Joe Birdsong."

She puts her hand over her mouth with her shoulders up. I say, "You think Joe is a funny name or something?"

Her hand drops away from her mouth, but her lips squirm for control of the grin that's trying to break out. Her chokehold on the ginger ale glass whitens her knuckles.

I say, "I see all kinds of Joses running around down here. Isn't that the same thing?"

She stiffens her shoulder muscles, trying not to giggle, until her eyes fill up with tears.

"Come on, what's so funny about the name Joe? Or Josephus? Shoot, it's right out of the Bible." She registers an aftershock at *Josephus*, slaps at my hand on the table.

"Stop, stop. I'm sorry. I didn't mean to laugh at your name. You're silly, though."

"Me silly? I'm not the one giggling and carrying on."

"You know what I'm talking about. I know it's not nice to laugh at nobody's name, but I never heard of nobody named Birdsong before."

"Well, you have now. So get used to it. There are a few of them around."

She presses her napkin to her eyes a couple times and then folds her hands on the table, wet eyes on me.

"Y'all seem to be having a good time in here." Fowler's voice jars the air in the room, big notes from a baritone saxophone. He fills the doorway, blind man spectacles aimed nowhere, heavy arm raised against the jamb.

"Oh, MJ," Corazon says, "I didn't hear you get up."

"Too busy lollygaggin' in here. How you doing, Cuz?"

"Fine, Merce. How about yourself?"

"I'm doin' all right. You been here long, man?"

"Just a few minutes. Waiting for you to wake up."

Fowler hunches his shoulders till he finishes a yawn big enough to air out his belfry. "You bring your horn?"

"Oh yeah. Wouldn't come without it, Merce."

"Well, one never knows."

On sait-on jamais. I stretch my ear, looking to hear if there is any double-entendre in his attitude. He didn't sound angry when he spoke to Corazon, but I thought he was perhaps a degree stony toward her. Corazon makes herself smaller and quieter and clears the table. Fowler says, "You can go on home, baby. Me and Joe got work to do."

Her lips don't part but curve upward just enough to accentuate the positive, and on her way to the sink while Fowler heads for the front room she silently springs toward me and plants a gingery peck on my lips, then fills a highball glass with water. I choke down an impulse to wig off into crazy laughter, compose myself with a deep inhale, and follow her and the big man into the front room. He gets comfortable in his chair. Corazon sets the water on the end table and lines up his lighter and cigarettes. She kisses his forehead. "All right, MJ," she says, "I'll be back at six."

"All right, baby."

With a wave to me, out she goes, and the room is quiet and colorless until Fowler drains his water glass and lights up. He takes a drag, blows out a stream of blue smoke, and clears his phlegmy throat. "What you want to work on today, Cuz?"

The next time at Fowler's house, Corazon asks me what I was doing before I came into the army. When I tell her I taught English in a high school, she gets quiet and looks at her hands. She says, "You mean if I was in your town, you could have been one of my teachers."

"Sure, why not? You don't think I could teach you anything?"

Still studying her hands, she says she's sorry for getting fresh with me and that her English is terrible.

I say, "What is this? First you're telling me I look like I could be in your high school class and now you're acting like I'm some old, square teacher. You're out of high school, aren't you? Or were you lying?"

"No."

"No what?"

"No, I wasn't lying, I'm graduated."

"And your English ain't all that bad, baby, but you could lighten up on the double negatives."

Her eyebrows drift down and inward, her face reddens, and her eyes get watery. She folds her arms under her breasts. I pull her hands away from her body and draw her into a clinch. Her body does a marble statue number at first, then softens, till her head falls against my neck. She pulls away when we hear Fowler come out of his room.

Fowler says I've got to go through the blues if I want to get anything out of him. Stuff that sounded too basic and greasy to me at first. "The blues is in your body," he says. "You got to start with the blues." He plays music on the piano and horn that sounds a long way from the blues, but he keeps telling me the blues is the well where the water is at, that it comes out of "whatever you been had around you." Whatever

I been had around me. Blowing with Fowler, I begin to hear things I heard but didn't really hear in the chord changes of spirituals and gospel music and rhythm and blues, a connection with the hard bop tunes I've worked on with Turner and Gilson. "Moanin'." "Sermonette." "The Preacher." You listen to some of those hard bop tunes you hear voices moanin', shoutin', pleadin', praisin', askin' for mercy, and all the time swinging. Daddy's whistling had some of that.

Fowler says, "You got to know the keyboard, Cuz, if you really goin' to do somethin'." We spend a lot of time with me playing blues chords on the piano while he blows all kinds of ideas on his horn, showing me.

"But then you got to get away from just tryin' to play the right notes, you got to go for the feeling. And that comes from shit you seen and heard and thought and read about. Dreamed about too. You understand what I'm sayin'?"

Whatever I been had around me.

At Bolden Heights, Freddie Turner says, "Damn, man, you sure are getting into it."

"Yeah, Schoolmaster, you're getting there," Gilson says.

"Well, thanks. I sure don't know where I'd be without you guys, though."

But I do know things would look much sootier, more threatening, and more military without this music we're swimming in. At Fowler's house, Corazon's presence adds a growing tingle to the music. And my gut is feeling calmer about Stacy. Daddy used to say, "Time heals all wounds," but time can stretch them out too, preserve them, like with Sylvia, Stacy, like with Mae, like with this CID investigation. A couple times, I see Washington and Polk across the mess hall, but the CID can forget about me initiating contact.

***

Freddy encourages me down to The Box for my first real jam session. There's some B-flat blues to start, and I do all right on that. People clap loud. "Bernie's Tune" didn't go all that great. Cats, including me, having trouble with the tempo, but I can see what I need to work on. Sitting out, I salivate to get back on the stand, back in the game, just like when I was on the bench in high school. Put me in, coach. I get to play again when a singer does "My Funny Valentine." Colored woman, smooth and dark chocolate brown, around thirty, Nikki Nanette, a woman with bountiful curves along her body. I get in some nice intimate licks on the tune, trying not to blow too many notes. "You don't need to show out," Fowler says. "You just need to say a little something appropriate." Must have said a little bit of something because this Nikki Nanette slides over and squeezes me around the waist, right in rhythm, moving back to the microphone with her juicy voice. You don't get nothing like that sitting in front of nobody's conductor.

Gilson, Freddy, and I, we babble about the session. "Man, did you hear what I put in on that one chorus of 'Blackbird'?"

"You blew some real down fours, Freddy."

"Drummer messed me up, didn't know the cat was goin' to start double-timin'."

"That cat from Houston was playing too loud."

"Old Nikki can blow, can't she?"

We run out of talk, look at each other like climbers who just reached the top of a minor peak, and lay hands on our instruments again.

***

Swink says, "You could be a really good jazz player. You're good already."

He's through with working at trumpet playing, but my ears are open to Swink because he brought *Howl* to my attention, and Clifford Brown. And he listens and he reads. He points out a whole raft of great trumpet players that I never heard of or have barely heard of. Fats Navarro. Kenny Dorham. Art Farmer. Freddie Hubbard. Blue Mitchell. Nat Adderly. Still, Swink seems way off the beam when it comes to seeing himself. Maybe. He's old in some ways, but the boy should be in college someplace, getting himself organized. He's not comfortable anyplace, though, doesn't want to be in the army any-more, he says. He's taking himself apart, not going to school, seeing big lies behind everything, looking to do dope all the time, says he's going to get himself kicked out on a Section Eight, a bad conduct or undesirable discharge. Tell the army he's a homo and get kicked out. Still, I haven't had a closer army friend.

"Man, you ought to stop talking that shit," Turner says to Swink. "Don't even talk to me about that queer shit, because you ain't for real. You signed up, now you got to serve your time."

"Not necessarily, Freddy. I can just leave. And that's what I'm going to do."

"Listen to this fool," Freddy says to Gilson and me. "They'll slap your ass in the stockade when they catch you, boy."

"They won't have to catch me, I'll come back when I feel like it. I don't give a damn about the stockade."

"Oh man." Freddy's neat brown paw bats the air. "Somebody tell me this motherfucker ain't crazy."

"What's crazy?" Swink says. "The army is what's crazy. An organization dedicated to killing human beings. It sucks, and I'm getting out."

"Look here, man," Turner says, "you get yourself a Section Eight and you won't be able to get no kind of job when you get out."

Swink looks at Freddy like a wise-ass reptile. "Don't make me laugh," he says. "I'll bet I could go to your little old hometown right now, Freddy, and get any number of jobs you couldn't get, even if I had a Section Eight."

Freddy gets an outdone grin of recognition on his brown mug like Where in the hell did this kid come from, up in my face, handcuffing me with this shit. I dig how Freddy feels, having Swink slam him with the truth, same truth that applies to me as a citizen of the greatest amber fucking waves of grain country on earth. The discussion ends on the same cadence Turner and Swink discussions always end on. "Man, you're crazy."

3)

Turner and I play through "Misty" a few times. He's been playing it with Nikki Nanette at The Box, and he says she asked him to bring me along to their next gig so I can sit in on a couple tunes with her. That would be tonight. "She says she likes your sound, man."

"Tell Miss Nanette the feeling is mutual."

"I'm going over to her crib right now," he says. "Come on with me, man. You can tell her yourself."

We pull up in front of Nikki Nanette's place, which is a wooden house, one story, with dried siding that looks like it needed painting last year in all this hot dry air. There's a wire fence bordering the yard, and a lemon tree between the house and the street on the north side. Don't see any colored people on the street. I still don't know where the Negroes are in El Paso.

A dark brown boy, maybe nine years old, comes running into the front yard with a faun-colored Great Dane and a brindle boxer, both of them bigger than he. Heavy dogs. They halt, jostling in the gate entrance. The boy yells and slaps at the dogs who seem to be used to the game, Eat the Visitors, or whatever it's called. Turner gets out of the car. I stay where I am.

"Hi, Freddy," the boy says.

Turner walks up to him and gives his hand and arm a floppy shake. The dogs act like they know Turner, and he pats the Great Dane on the skull. "Hey, Marques, how you doin', my man?"

"Fine," the boy says.

Turner lays a wide grin on him. "How come you aren't in school?"

The boy is prepared and throws the words at Freddy like a handful of marbles: "Because it's Saturday. Ain't no school on Saturday."

"Whoops," Freddy says, "it sure is, else I wouldn't be here myself. Lookee here, is your mama home?"

"She's in the house."

Turner waves to me to come on, but the ghost of a long ago panic from a dog bite keeps me studying the bony-headed canines with their wet, floppy jowls. Voices in my head have already designated the dogs "Washington" and "Polk." Turner says, "Hey, man, you gonna get out of that car or what?"

I take a long sniff and recall the warmth of Nikki Nanette's arm around my waist at the jam session.

"Come on, Joe. These dogs don't bite." A confident croon informs Freddy's declaration. Getting past this obstacle will bring me to Nikki

Nanette, up close, and I really do like dogs if they're not so damned big and I know them.

I push open the car door. "Well, they may not bite," I say, "but they look like they might eat."

On the sidewalk, the jowly canines pay me no mind. Freddy says, "Marques, this is Joe."

Marques's round brown face still has baby lips and his eyes are quick-shiny. "Hi, Marques. Nice dogs you've got there," I say. His arm lies across the Great Dane's shoulders. "How do you spell your name, M-a-r-c-u-s?"

"Nope." He takes his arm off the Great Dane's back and claps his hands for each letter he chants: "M-a-r-q-u-e-s."

Then: "And this is Thor and this is Buddy."

"Cool dogs," I say. And, happily, some laconic sombitches.

Turner says, "Let's see what old Nikki is up to."

We bump our way between dog ribs and Marques to the screen door. Freddy knocks and calls out. The door to the living room is open. "Anybody home?"

The woman's voice inside, farther back than the living room: "Freddy, is that you?"

"Yeah, it's me. Can we come in? I got that cat with me you liked."

I slap Turner's elbow. "Man, what are you talking about?"

"I told you she dug your playing the other night, man."

"Come on in." We walk into the front room and wait for Nikki Nanette to appear. There's an old upright against the wall in front of us. The round coffee table in front of the sofa is fitted with a plate of glass that covers a collection of family pictures, mostly black and white, some sepia ones, and a couple in color. Several photos feature Marques in baby stages. Across the room a large, framed oval photo portrait of a woman hangs above a wicker captain's chair. She's a young colored woman looks like she's got some Indian, Mexican, white, or all of it, in her.

Nikki Nanette cruises into the room in a powder blue housecoat followed by a breeze of lotion, powder, perfume. Again, I'd guess that she's three or four years older than I. Could be thirty. Her wide umber eyes click past me and beam on Turner. "Freddy, I'm so glad you could come over. Sorry to keep you guys waiting."

He slides into the fleshy dark arms she holds out to him and puts his arms all the way around her so her healthy breasts squash against him. The light smack of his lips on her cheek sugars up the air. Deficit eats on me till Freddy lets go of the woman and stretches a hand in my direction. "Well, there he is, your trumpet player."

Nikki turns her wide, healthy-lipped smile my way. The slight gap between her two front teeth make you expect a lisp, but her esses issue clean and sibilant. "Oh, Joe, I'm so glad to see you. I really enjoyed your playing the other night and I said to Freddy, 'We gots to do that one mo' time." Nikki is a clean pronouncer, something between Sarah and Ella.

She unreels her hand to me like if she had a real hip ring on her finger I should kiss it. I dig that the woman can talk as much mess as any bishop, so I take her hand, nod into the surrounding bouquet, and kiss it. "The greater part of the pleasure was mine, I'm sure, m'am," I say, "and I certainly do hope we can work together again soon."

Nikki separates from Freddy, pats my cheek, and rolls her eyes toward him. "Lord, listen to the young man. Do he talk that way all the time?"

"He can get real proper," Turner says. "My man's a schoolteacher. A English teacher."

The woman, palms on her flanks, elbows back, glances me up and down. "No he ain't. He too young. Who he gonna teach?"

"Ask him."

She narrows her eyes and makes like she's scrutinizing my molecules, talks to Freddy. "Well, I do know he could teach somebody how to blow the trumpet."

"Thank you very much," I say. "Nice of you to say that." Her words do pump me up.

She reaches her arm around my waist and pulls me to her, hip to hip, like she did on the bandstand, leans her head against mine, so I'm all up against her. Her good size feels bracing and comfortable. "I mean it," she says. "It's really good to see you again, Joe."

She emphasizes her words with an extra squeeze that makes a willing-ass believer out of me, says, "What was your last name, again?"

"Birdsong."

"That's right," she says. "Joe Birdsong." She lets go of me, leaves me floating up off the floor. "You fellows want some coffee? I just now made a fresh pot."

"Yeah, Nik," Freddy says, "lay it on us."

"Come on in the kitchen then."

Fresh coffee smell in the afternoon, sunlight in the kitchen, two dogs and a boy in the yard. Boy in the yard, blues rising around him.

Nikki takes out two white cups and saucers from a windowed cupboard. "Have a seat," she says. "Freddy likes his black. How do you like yours, Joe?"

"A little sugar, thanks."

On the kitchen table are a couple charts that Freddy picks up when he sits down. "We gonna do these tonight?" he says.

He turns them so I can see them: "Misty" and "Bye Bye, Blackbird."

Nikki sets the cups and saucers on the table. She fills our cups, gives me a spoon and slides a glass bowl of sugar cubes in front of me. "Yes, how about those," she says. "And Joe, you're going to do them with us?"

"Sure. I'll give it a try."

Her palm floats to rest on my forearm. "Oh, good," she says.

Freddy says, "How you wanna do 'Blackbird'?"

Elbow on the table, Nikki swings her hand from side to side and snaps the off beats with her fingers. "About like that. Nice easy medium swing."

"That's cool," he says.

Nikki gets up from the table and takes a cigarette from an open pack lying on the sink counter. She strikes a book match and lights up, snuffs the match with one shake. On her third finger left hand, I dig three narrow gold rings.

Steam plays the smell of Nikki's good-tasting coffee around my nose when I turn up the cup. Corazon doesn't do coffee that I've ever seen. Drinks ginger ale. Fowler keeps Jim Beam in business. Nikki is acquainted with Fowler but doesn't know him well. "Quite the fellow," she says. She and Freddy Turner laugh and talk about some of the people they've played gigs with. They're pretty careful about putting down other cats, I don't hear anything mean. Nikki fills our cups again.

"So where did you say you were from, Joe," she says.

"I don't remember saying but I'm from Portland, Oregon. Born up in Washington, though."

"Aha. You sure don't sound like somebody from these parts."

Freddy says, "I hope not."

Nikki backhands him in the ribs. "Wait a minute, boy, you're not trying to make some kind of remark about the way I talk, are you?"

"Now what would I want to do that for?"

"That's what I want to know," she says. Her eyes shift my way. "How do I sound to the professor?"

"You sound fine to me," I say. "Actually, ever since I first heard you, I've been impressed with your articulation."

"Listen to this cat," Freddy says.

Eyes on me, she pats him on the shoulder and goes into a squeaky falsetto beside his ear. "You know he be tellin' the truth, baby."

We laugh big together, but I'm still the new boy, some kind of outsider. Nikki asks me, "Did you start your music in church?"

"No, I got started at school in the fourth grade."

She and Freddy got started in church, in the South, where they heard nothing but gospel music. "My mother played piano for the church when we lived in Shreveport," she says.

There wasn't all that much gospel music in Daddy's Pentecostal tabernacle in Kayakaw where half the people were white. "Just As I Am" and "Are You Washed in the Blood" were big tunes— "The Old Rugged Cross."

Nikki in profile has a rounded chin and a hint of an underbite that along with the gap in her front teeth keeps me watching her, in hope she won't stop talking. However, Private Freddy Turner finishes his coffee, stands up and sets the cup in the sink. He puts his hand on her shoulder, which I don't feel eligible to do yet, and says, "Nikki, me and Joe got to think about splittin'. You're straight about tonight, right?"

"Right."

"We'll pick you up at seven-thirty."

She gets up, takes her and my coffee cups to the sink counter. "Right, seven-thirty," she says. "Thank you, baby."

At the front door, Nikki says, "And thanks for bringing this young man by, Freddy."

"Yeah, thanks, Freddy," I say. "I feel like some lucky groceries that just got delivered."

Nikki does a little do-wop step at that and loops an arm through mine. "Lord, will you listen to this child?"

Turner says, "Yeah, he's pretty funny sometimes."

She wraps her arms around Freddy and me in turn. I stifle additional jive percolating on the tip of my tongue and say, "It really is nice to see you, Nikki. And thanks for the coffee."

Turner cruises onto Montana Avenue, heading west. I say, "You and Nikki seem pretty tight."

"Yeah, we tight. Nothing special, though."

"She's married, right?"

"Separated. Her and her old man been separated more than a year now."

"Is he bad?" I don't have enough nerve to say "big and bad."

"Naw, he ain't bad. Quiet kind of a cat. Works over at Biggs."

"She ain't too quiet. She always that friendly?"

"Yeah, she's friendly, about like you saw, but she ain't nobody's fool. She likes to clown, but the chick can get real serious."

Watching Nikki swing her fine hips up there at the microphone, listening to her phrasing, I am back in school. Her sense of time and swing keeps me on edge to match it. We get through our tunes with no trouble, and I feel how much good stuff Fowler has been putting in my mess kit. Riding back to her place after the gig, Freddy at the wheel, Nikki in the middle, nobody talking, not needing any talk, she gets comfortable against me with her body English. I'm close to feeling in my gut that everything is all right.

The music is still expanding when Nikki kisses Freddy on the cheek, and I help her out of the car and she pecks me on the chops and hugs me good night at her front door.

4)

Corazon holds a white towel wound into a turban around her hair so I am warmed by the blue-white flash of her shaved armpit. Her free hand unhooks the screendoor and pushes it open for me. Corazon's eye whites match the towel. The print of her gingery lips last time flutters back onto my mouth like a movie shot that is still happening. I hand her the sack with the bottle of ginger ale in it that I brought for her. "A little something for you."

"For me? Oh thank you." She takes the sack, her eyes shining as if it's an event.

"It's nothing, but I've noticed you like ginger ale."

"I do. And I think it's so sweet for you to do this."

Then: "*Pajaro.*"

"What?"

"*Pajaro*—it means 'bird'." A soft puff from her lips, breathy word like wings against air. *Bird. Pajaro. Oiseau. Pajaro. Vogel. Pajaro.*

"It's my new name for you," she says.

"Well, may I call you Cory, then?"

"Yes, sir, you can."

"You don't call a private 'sir', baby."

She giggles with her mouth closed. "Okay, *Pajaro.*"

"Is Merce home?"

"Yes, he's home. He told me to wake him up whenever you got here." She studies me, her foot holding the screen open, the sack with the ginger ale in her hand, she with that white towel around her black hair above her honey-colored face with the rose red lips. My feet stuck at the sight of her.

"Come inside, sir." My feet switch on. I step past her into the front room and she guides the screen to a silent closing with her foot.

"Like I said, you don't call a private, 'sir', girl."

"Oh, I'm sorry, Joe."

I ignore the grin that denies her words. "That's better," I say. "What are you doing?"

"I just started to wash my hair when you knocked at the door."

"Oh. How long has Merce been down?"

"Not long—maybe fifteen minutes."

I move in and put my arm around her waist, her flesh against my arm where her blouse separates from her shorts. Her skin feels cool and smooth. She doesn't pull away but sinks against me, thick and sweet-smelling, damp hair and towel against the side of my face. "Why don't we let our man sleep a little longer," I say.

"Well, we could."

I slide my horn under the coffee table, straighten up, and run both arms around her, lips against her ear. "Could what?" I say.

She puts the ginger ale bottle against my chest and pushes me back. "Silly," she says, "let's go in the kitchen."

Corazon sets the bottle on the table in the breakfast nook. A wash basin full of water sits in the sink, a bottle of Drene shampoo on the drainboard.

"So you're washing your hair?"

"I told you I was just starting to when you came to the door."

"Let me help you."

Her eyes widen and her chin jerks back. "What?"

"Let me help you shampoo your hair."

"Do you really want to?"

"Sure I really want to—why would I ask? Come on."

She unwraps the towel from her hair and gives her head a fast swing so that her hair bushes up and falls in all directions, a wild black bush to jump into. I put my fingers into it and push it back from her face. Midnight umber eyes study me, shining, ready for a communion wafer. My dog blood gets me watering at the mouth. I take her arm and turn her toward the sink, stick my hand in the water which feels not warm enough. I run some hot water into it. "Feel that," I say. "How is it?"

She puts a finger in the water. "A little more hot, please."

I run the hot tap with my hand in the water, turn it off. "How's that?"

"That's better, *Senor Pajaro.*"

"Here we go." She bends over the basin, her bare elbows and forearms against the sink counter. I gather her hair into the water, my fingers into the shiny black curls at her neck, muted traces of Africanicity. A few drops of shampoo make a cloud of lather I work through her hair. Her back arches against my chest and then sinks from a long exhale. I run my fingers back and forth in the soap slip over the curve of her skull.

I say, "Is this the way you do it?"

"Oh, Joe, this is so fine. I never had a boy to wash my hair before." The way Corazon holds her r's makes a small music that tests my defenses against going maudlin.

"Well, maybe you should hire yourself a boy to do it regularly."

She giggles into the basin, catches herself, and puts a finger to her lips. Oh yes, we are in the bear's lair, and this is some fine porridge I'm working with here, breathing deeper, standing behind her, her buttocks bumping the hard front of my pants that she must feel, her hair and skull soapy in my hands. Heat from her neck and head come up through my fingertips. I slide my palms back and forth across the muscles of her neck, digging all the life and heat under my hands, and sounds inside her that she's holding in.

Corazon dips one shoulder, breaking my dreamy motions, and slips her head out from under my hands. She twists around to face me, gets her arms around me, and through water and shampoo running across our noses and mouths, brings her lips against mine. Not an experienced kiss, lips tense, pressing. We've got sweet, soapy, cheap perfume smell up our noses, bitter seep of shampoo on our lips. I've got water and girl all over my shirt. She keeps her eyes closed and clamps my leg between her thighs, moves against my leg. Hard to hold back, but getting some in Fowler's house with him napping in the next room, I don't plan to wear out my welcome that way. Corazon breathes harder and harder, and we're bumping against each other's lips in a way unhealthy for my embouchure. I go to kissing her neck, and the sniffing rush of air in and out of her nose comes faster and faster until I see her eyes roll upward, and she slides halfway down my leg. I hoist her up and hold her against me. Her arms come to life around my neck. I take the towel from the drainboard and pat her face dry. "Are you all right, Cory?"

"*Si,* yes, I think so. Oh, I'm so sorry, *Pajaro.*" She burrows her head between my neck and shoulder.

My ears stretch to the limit on a long inhale, for the humming of her cells, for any sounds in the house. "Nothing to be sorry about, baby. Everything is all right."

Corazon's wet hair cools my nose, her middle, still hot, rests against the hardness in my pants. She whispers, "I don't know what to do."

I exhale. There's nothing for Fowler to interrupt now, and I feel no Heavy Brothers lurking. Corazon's body is a warm armful. My lip is in good shape. We breathe together, letting the event soak in and cool until I turn her to the sink. "Let's rinse your hair, Cory."

Fowler, awake and heavy in the post-shampoo air, stretches his hands above the keyboard as if preparing to give a blessing. First time I notice his fingers are manicured. "Look here, Cuz," he says, "this is what Bud showed the cats to help 'em keep up with them horns."

"Bud?"

"You know, Bud Powell."

More deficiency in my history. People talked about Bud Powell back at Fort Ord, and Turner has mentioned him. His brother played piano with Clifford Brown, killed in the same car crash. Bud, one of the guys who invented bebop.

"You got to listen to Bud if you want to know what's happenin'," Fowler says. "Watch this. This is the raw basics." He drops his hands to the keyboard and goes into "How High the Moon." His right hand ripples through the melody while his left hand plays just two notes, a two-note chord, on each chord change. Sounds lean but good, the way Fowler does it.

"See what I'm doin' with my left hand," he says. He comps louder with his left, two notes each time he hits the keys.

"Yes, I'm looking."

"Shell voicings, that's what you call them," he says, careful to enunciate the whole noun. "You just got the shell of the chord down here. See? You leave out everything between the root and the seventh. Just play the root and the seventh with your left hand." Fowler's big perfect fingers come down like the law in the middle of each black or white key. Stuff just a little outside Herb Vogel's orbit. Out of nowhere, a sob wavers through my chest. My face might show it, but Fowler can't see.

"Wow, Merce. That's really hip."

"That'll get you started," he says. "You can get cute later on if you want to play more piano. But this'll help you learn them chords and a lot of tunes, too."

Three light knocks on the front door and Corazon comes through, quiet steps, bare arms and legs, small rosy smile on her lips. Her hair jiggles in damp black ringlets. The large bag of groceries in her arms bulges as if it's got a melon or John the Baptist's head in the bottom. Something wrapped in butcher paper sticks out of the top. The look she lays on me is a head to toe paint job.

Fowler gets up from the piano, takes two steps to his armchair and lowers his bulk to sitting. "Put your horn down and take my place there."

I lay my horn on top of the piano next to his French Besson and take his place on the stool.

"Now," he says, "you know 'All the Things You Are.' Right?"

Grocery bag sounds come from the kitchen, the refrigerator door opens and closes, a can of food clicks against the counter.

"Yeah, I guess so."

"What you mean, you guess so? Man, if you don't know that tune, you don't know nothin'." His voice gets a growl in it like he's fixing to get pissed off.

"Okay, I know it," I say.

"This ain't guesswork, Cuz. You know what the hell you're doin', or you don't. You don't know what you're doin', you fuck everybody else up."

Didn't know what I was doin', fucked everybody else up. Loudest thing he's said yet, though the cat has no idea.

"Sorry, man, I know you're right." Fowler faces straight ahead in his dark glasses behind my back. His words thud between my shoulder blades.

"So play the song. And I want you to do the left hand like I did on the chords—just the root and the seventh."

Fowler hums it. I work my way through "All the Things You Are." Hell of a song his radar picked up, considering all the things going on in his kitchen. I get to the end of the tune, and Corazon sings out, "MJ, you and Joe want a tunafish sandwich?"

"Sure, baby," Fowler says. "You gonna have a sandwich with me, ain't you, Cuz?"

"Oh man, yeah. Thank you."

He claps his hands together and rocks forward. "Righteous," he says. "Now play that thing again. Slow it down a little bit and give me some better time."

He says, "Slow it down a little bit, some better time," I hear a stony command and just know that way off in his mind someplace it's *This cat's time is fucked up something terrible.*

He counts out the tempo he has in mind. The first snap of his fingers beside my head makes my ear ring. I get into the tune again and get through it. I don't feel Fowler flinch or hear him growl while I'm playing. "How them sandwiches coming, baby," he calls out.

"Just about ready."

Fowler moves his butt around in the armchair and rolls his shoulders. "Do that on all the tunes you know," he says. "It'll be good for you."

"Yeah, I can see that already."

"And if they got words, learn the words if you don't know them."

"And sing them?"

"That's right, Cuz. Sing the damn songs. Everybody ought to sing. It'll make a better man out of you."

Sing. People sing in Hardy's novels. Daddy sang at church. Nikki Nanette sings.

Corazon, in the kitchen doorway, speaks to Fowler, studies me. "Excuse me, MJ. What do you want to drink?"

"You can send in Mr. Beam with my sandwich. You gonna have a little taste with me, Joe?"

"Sure, why not. With ginger ale, please."

Corazon smiles herself back into the kitchen with her eyes on me. The only thing as fresh, full of color, and direct that I can think of are the early daffodils back in Portland. Innocent in the weather, too.

Fowler says, "All right, one more time." The words to "All the Things You Are" mouth themselves in my ear after the cat's dictum about learning the lyrics. Cool enough, I dig lyrics. I'm playing the shell voicings, Fowler is snapping his fingers and humming, and I'm not trying to sing the song yet because those lyrics are just too mucking fuch right now. I mean spring is actually here and the song is talking about "you are the promised breath of springtime" and Corazon is in the kitchen with her lips and eyes, shoulders and legs, too meat-ily, sweetly what the spring and the song are about. Stacy used to be about spring. All of these damn songs. So I'm really into moving the chords to Fowler's beat and keeping the melody going with my right hand so I'm getting some good grunts out of the cat. Fowler growls or says "Damn," it's a kick in the stomach, I'm a lost or abandoned child who'll never be found. It's awful, worse than any threat from the Heavy Brothers or the misled fucking world. But I get through the tune.

Corazon comes in with a blue and white plate in each hand with a sandwich on it and sets one on the table next to Fowler's chair. She sets the other one on the coffee table in front of the sofa. She goes back in the kitchen and brings out napkins and Fowler's whiskey and one for me that she sets beside the sandwich on the coffee table. Slices of tomato and lettuce layered above the tuna fill the sandwich. Long time since I've seen a sandwich like this, not Juarez or army food. Impaled against the top slice of bread by a toothpick is a healthy slice of pickle. Don't know whether it's dill or sweet, but I'm ready to bite it.

"Ahora," Corazon says, "it's time to eat."

Fowler slides his hand onto the table, fingers find the whiskey. "All right," he says. "Thank you, baby."

I move from the piano stool to the sofa and taste my drink, which has just the right amount of ginger ale in it. The girl's eyes are plaster-ing me with domestic tranquillity. For a moment Mae's face covers her features, and there's wrenching at the top of my windpipe, but a gulp of whiskey restores Corazon's eyes, mouth, hair. "Thanks, Cory," I say. "It tastes perfect."

She ducks into the kitchen and comes back with her own sandwich and this time sits next to me, hip touching mine. A whiff of her hair speeds up my pulse, and the bread and tuna and mayonaise and tomato and lettuce all mixed up in my mouth feels like more than food. Feels possible I could blow till I was beyond confusion. The pickle is a sweet bread and butter pickle.

Fowler swallows and smacks his lips, runs his tongue over his upper teeth. "Now like I said, Cuz, after while you might get where you want to put in a third with some of them roots and sevenths, leave out the root sometimes. You'll see."

Daddy and the horse pose under the Chinese elm opposite the bus stop at Alligator Park. On my way from Fowler's and full of what happened there, I'm singing to myself. Daddy straightens up from leaning on his Springfield rifle, farmer-like, except for the cavalry corporal uniform. I walk up to him, feel him bristling.

"Well," he says.

"Well, what?"

"What you goin' to do now?"

"What do you mean, what am I going to do now?"

He pounds the rifle butt against the ground. His eyes pop wide. "Boy, you sure can act simple sometimes. You mean to tell me you can't see you started somethin' that could singe all the feathers off your behind? Again?" He gives the ground another blow with the rifle butt and exits. The surface under my feet rocks.

Here comes the bus to Fort Showalter.

Corazon

"You could still come by next week, you know." Corazon's lips are close to my ear. We're standing at the front door of Fowler's house before my session with him, looking out at the street. Next week Fowler will be gone for a gig in San Antonio. My stomach shimmies at the picture fleshed up by her invitation, but the truth is that it took a while for my nerves to settle last week after I dug how much this feels like the way things started with Mae. Corazon looks down at her hands and says, "MJ has a girlfriend that he visits when he goes up there."

"Well, I don't imagine he'd get much out of just poking around in the Alamo."

She slaps me on the shoulder and draws in a breath I can hear, still not looking at me. Her chest rises and falls. I need to stand close to her so I don't see her bare legs that I swear can make my jaws quiver. For sure, Corazon is packing all the necessaries, but she's a virgin, I think, and serious, and she's the man's daughter, and I do not have any honorable intentions to lay on her, and I got no need to be stirring up dissonance and confusion in the bear's lair, fucking up what I'm here for. Daddy is right. Perspective. I keep my eyes on the street, studying. I could tell her the 72nd and the other band are going to be gone to New Mexico for the gig in Silver City on Wednesday, a couple days earlier than the truth.

Corazon moves in front of me, face to face, and taps my chest with the fingertips of both hands. Ten hot pennies across my chest. "Will you do it?" she says.

Corazon wants to do it. Her eyes, parted lips, nose, are a half-dozen fragrant inches from my face. Something grabs in my throat so I can't say anything until I've swallowed. "No," I say. "I don't think I should do it. Merce won't be here, and I have to practice for a gig Wednesday night."

Her eyelids flutter, and her mouth opens as if somebody surprised her with a punch to the stomach. My gut is clenched in surprise too, hearing myself say *I don't think I should do it*. She sucks in her breath, her shoulders go up, then down, and she takes off out of the house with quick hard steps.

I sit down at Fowler's piano and wait for him to finish his nap. Corazon's ideas of order in the furniture, the kitchen cupboards, the refrigerator, dominate the place, but at the piano my fingers carry me farther and farther away from the house and her hard-heeled exit, and from time to time patches of notes make clear sense, like colors of houses, trees, coats, in grey weather.

Fowler and I are playing when she comes back through the front door, without knocking, and crosses into the kitchen. Water splashes in the sink. She comes back out and sits on the sofa. Fowler says, "Hi, baby," and keeps on playing. I stay with the music. Her eyes and the tip of her nose are red. Too much of this shit with women. My eyes are on her while I'm blowing, and, again, I see Mae's unhappy head on her body. She sits there, hands in her lap, taking deep breaths, eyes straight ahead, making like Whistler's Daughter.

Her hand goes in the pocket of her shorts and she takes out a small white envelope that she lays on the coffee table. Again, she gets up and leaves the house. First chance I get I check the envelope, which has JB printed on it, and stick it in my back pocket.

Fowler is acting as if he wants to make himself memorable before leaving for San Antonio, on me about keeping the beat and knowing where I am in the beat. "No, man, no," damn near breaking my eardrums. "Like this." Fowler really is a thundercloud when he doesn't like my time. I'm fighting to keep from being drowned.

We get done, he's in his easychair with a cigarette and a glass of whiskey, the cat becomes Old King Cole, one merry motherfucker again, laughing and talking like everything has always been cool. He says, "Lookee here, Cuz, you hear about that plane they shot down over there?"

"You mean the U2, the spy plane?"

"Yeah, you got it. I heard it on the radio. Sombitch flyin' sixty thousand feet up in the air—all up out of sight—and them damn Russians shot his ass down with a missile. Boy, I'm tellin' you..."

"Yeah, I wouldn't want to be in that pilot's shoes right now. No telling what the Russians are liable to do with him."

"I hear ya. They already talkin' about a trial. What was the boy's name?"

"Powers. Francis Gary Powers."

"Man, just goes to show you. Never know what these sombitches is up to. Airplanes flyin' all up out of sight. Spyin'." Fowler takes a stately suite of puffs on his cigarette. We've gotten so we can sit for minutes without talking, just digging the music in the air and me letting his teaching sink in. "Yep, Cuz, goin' up to San Antone. Now you come see me when I get back, boy."

Fowler's voice amped up a few notches when he said that, like a substitute for eyeballing me, if he could see, and maybe poking his finger in my chest. Like it was important to him, as if I might desert him. I could have hugged Fowler for that. Like he didn't know all the great stuff he was putting in my ears, the big joy painting my entrails, breath, and fingers, even with all the wreckage I've got going on. Me, with no money, a broken life, nothing, getting the best lessons I ever got. No reason for this G.I. to be fucking up.

Wednesday. Fowler is in San Antonio. And I'm sitting in the rehearsal room, trying to think through why in the hell I ever told Corazon I couldn't come by while Merce was gone, jiving myself with some kind of half-assed idea of being noble or good. When she said "Will you do it," hot to have me come over and initiate her, giving me all that power over her golden nubile pulchritude, it was more power than I could say yes to under the circumstances. It was a moment of drunken power, instant corruption, with a few grains of perversity from I don't know where. Also, plain scared is the truth. Plain scared of all the misery that could erupt out of opening a can of worms disguised, once again, as a luscious and true sweetheart. Jesus, there it is. It ain't like I've been getting some regularly, though. And here's

Corazon's maximum-type anatomy twisting through my head. Her note said she felt terrible and embarrassed that I didn't want to see her after what happened in the kitchen. She thought I liked her. "I thought you were nice and that you really liked me," she wrote, "which is why I let you touch me." What a fucking amateur, me, sitting here with my tongue hanging out. Hard, grinding through this thing, the girl's need for trust that, after Mae, I know damn well I am not ready for, and the sight of Corazon's fine body wearing out my eyeballs. Merce's daughter she is. I really must keep the big thing, the music, in focus. Merce is keeping the faith in San Antonio tonight, and he wants to check me out when he gets back. I have to practice for tonight and playing with Nikki Nanette.

On top of that, the first sergeant ties me down with a funeral job, and, in the middle of the afternoon, I'm in fresh khakis at the post cemetery, blowing taps for a dead veteran.

***

Nikki Nanette's body is doing some sinuous and sweet lady jive in front of me, singing "Misty," and my soul feels on the way to restoration since last week's contretemps with Corazon. After the cemetery gig, I practiced on the piano before chow, chord changes and lyrics from the American Songbook. Thought about singing. Fowler would dig how I'm going with the music here behind Nikki, working to get below the skin of the obvious without too many notes. Keeping my ego out of it, supporting the singer. "It's about the music, man, it ain't about you. Let the music out!" he yelled at me once.

Nikki's mouth shines when she hears something she likes, hears me talking to her. Might even hear some yearning. I'm into the tune pretty well when Corazon walks into the place with another girl, Mexican girl about the same age I've never seen before. Both of them looking slick. Corazon's eyes are on me right away. I don't look up but stay with the music, stay with Fowler's blind attention to the music, listening to Nikki and the rhythm section with my eyes closed.

We finish "Moon River" and Nikki bows, thanks the clapping people, and backs away from the mike, stumbles into me, recovers, and laughs into her hands. She puts her arm around my shoulders and kisses me on the cheek. "Excuse me, baby," she says.

Corazon's eyes drain the bandstand. No doubt about I was telling her the truth when I said I had a gig for this evening. She sits beside her friend with her hands folded on the small table, listening and watching. Her chest swells toward escape from the sheer top of her black dress.

I stay loose under Nikki's arm, keep both hands on my horn. I say, "Nice job, Nikki."

Corazon and her friend have a couple ginger ales, it looks like, with slices of lime, in front of them. I smile in their direction. Her lips make a small tight stretch toward reciprocity, but she ain't turning 'em loose. Nikki lifts her arm off me, and Freddy Turner counts off the next tune. Got Clifford's solo in my head. Can't skip and blip like he does, but he's a beacon that lets me know how far off the coast I am. Most of my blowing is stuff I've practiced, or very close to it, but here and there something fresh hits me for a few out-of-my-mind measures until I have to find my way back to familiar territory through some cliché or other. I don't care, I'm studying, and I've had a taste of something that keeps me going, something almost as good as water. Nikki dances at the edge of the bandstand beside me while Freddy solos. We're all into the work, stitching together a dream, an explanatory dream, a planetary dream, a swinging, centrifugal dream that carries our whole excuse for living.

Nikki sings the last number of the set, and I've got my eyes closed, listening hard to her, trying to talk to her lyrics with my notes. When I open my eyes, Corazon and her friend are gone. The last set starts around midnight, and Nikki isn't doing it since she's got to get home and release the babysitter. "I'm sorry I forgot to ask you earlier, baby," she says, "but could you run me home. Freddy said it's all right."

She hands me Freddy's car keys.

"Sure, Nikki. Be glad to."

Nikki Nanette sits close to me on the way to her house. Man, woman, sit close. Natural to let her head fall on my shoulder and shut her eyes. My nose immerses me in the night's perfume and smoke she carries in her hair. We arrive at her house and she sits up, stretches her arms in front of her, swings them up and around my neck. I work my arms around her and, cheek to cheek, fall into listening to the night with her, listening to the conversation between our jazzed-up bodies, unwinding together. She kisses my ear. "I've got to go, baby," she says.

"Thanks for the great set, Nikki. I really enjoyed it."

She puts her parted lips on mine, thick, soft, perfumed, brief. A taste of jazz. I'm having an ecstatic choke, trying to breathe and keep cool. I hop out of the car, stand at attention and gulp some air, then walk around to let her out. "What a gentleman," she says.

"What a lady."

At her front door, she gives me another hug that's got thighs and stomach and breasts in it, gives me another, longer sweet one on the lips, runs a finger along my cheek and says, "Come see me when you all get back from New Mexico, baby."

All the way back to The Box, I'm salivating and running through priorities and the calendar. A week, at least, before I can get loose. When I walk in, they're getting ready to do "Bye, Bye, Blackbird," this time without a singer. I jump in.

2)

On the bus ride to Silver City, I fake sleeping so I can lie in peace with fresh thoughts of Nikki Nanette's cushiony body molded against me. Ain't studying war with no Heavy Brothers or nobody. If we didn't have this parade to play, I could be jamming at The Box, Nikki there, swinging. *Come see me when you all get back from New Mexico, baby.* Miss Lady and me. Could happen. And Corazon, in that black dress with the sheer jive covering her shoulders down to the bloomings of her bosom. Rocka my soul. And there's a soundtrack of tunes, chords, lines of melody under my earlids, some applied mathematics ain't nobody ever heard. Sippa dippa deebop.

Swink's elbow against my arm breaks into my picture show. The bus has stopped, guys are in the aisle yapping and moving around. We're in the mountains, low mountains with long-needled pine trees, in front of a whitewashed stucco veterans' hospital. Midday. Chowtime.

After we eat, nurses wheel a bunch of the old guys out under the here and there shade of the ponderosa pines around the building. They wheel them down the improvised board ramp laid across the steps next to where we're sitting. The nurses and the old men leave a trail of tobacco and disinfectant smell when they pass by.

Seems there are four female nurses working this part of the building. Each woman wheels one of the vets out of the big double doors and goes back and wheels out another one until they have four ranks of four lined up on the grass. A bunch of battered rowboats, seasick soldiers, oarless, out there on green water, ready to sink. Sinking. Oh man.

Sergeant Howell comes out of the building and stands next to where I'm sitting on the steps.

"How are ya, Birdie"

"Fine, Sarge. How are you?"

"I'm doin' okay." Howell pushes out his lips and sucks on his teeth for a minute, runs his tongue along his teeth, bellying out his upper lip, studying the flotilla of wheelchairs on the grass. None of this for Howell, all his years in the army, master sergeant, retire before long. His brown eyes in his big round face look quieter than usual, darker, not so ready to fire off some countrified jive or holler a command. Got some chow in him, looking like he could use a toothpick. He gives himself a couple pats on the stomach, and his hand with the bulky masonic ring comes close to my head. He eases down the steps, stops at the bottom. "All right, men, everbody fall in over there beside the bus."

Everybody gets up from where we're sitting and mumbles across the grass to the bus. Mr Tappendorf is there waiting for us, red splotches on his face, blue beard shadow like Vice-president Nixon on TV, and no smile. I still have never seen this cat looking as if he's happy to see the band. Sergeant Howell approaches him with a salute. Tappendorf hits the bill of his cap with a couple fingertips, turns his back to the group of us gathered at the side of the bus, and talks low into the first sergeant's ear. Howell stands with his fat forearms at his sides. He gets through lending his faithful ear and walks over to us. "Okay, at ease," he says. "Mr Tappendorf has arranged for the band to play a couple of numbers for these people. You won't need your pouches. You have your 'Men of Ohio' and you have your 'Garry Owen.' Them's what we're goin' to play. So y'all get your instruments and form up over there in front of them steps."

Muccigrosso limps sleeve to sleeve with me for a few paces. The bandleader decided that his gait wasn't impaired enough to excuse him from this gig. Dino didn't complain, happy as usual grab-assing with his buddies. He says to me, "You hear Howell? 'You have your "Men of Ohio" and you have your "Garry Owen."' Louisiana Bastard's starting to sound like Tappendorf." He punctuates this with what I'm calling a Willy Pump, a Weak Philly Pump, on account of his ribs.

"God help us, Dino. You're right."

The driver's crank rattles in the lock of the luggage compartment, and the lid opens out of the side of the bus. Khaki and brass, we swarm at the compartment, pulling out instruments, and then away, noodling on our horns. Tappendorf doesn't raise any hell about noodling before an impromptu gig like this one. I take some slow, deep breaths and buzz into my mouthpiece. Corazon's note, folded in my back pocket, burns. "I thought you were nice and that you liked me. I let you touch me because I thought you liked me," she wrote. Corazon is a good girl. Dog, me. She also wrote she felt embarrassed and terrible I didn't want to see her on Wednesday. If the girl only knew. "I let you touch me" tugs at my sentimental bone. It grates, though, that she seriously says "you was" when she's talking. I take out her note and look at each word, and it's true, she wrote "you *were*."

"Okay, men, over there by them steps where I told you," Sergeant Howell says.

We head for the spot, still unwrinkled in our khaki short pants and shirts with our knee stockings and black army shoes. On the bus and in the dry heat of the hills here, the uniform is comfortable except for the shoes. Inside army shoes, my feet never get a good grip on grass or concrete or wood or asphalt.

Swink punches my shoulder and jerks his head toward the old men in wheelchairs on the grass. "What do you think about this," he says.

"I think it's not too uplifting."

Swink doesn't laugh. His eyes blaze madder blue than usual, as if he'd like to do something drastic. "I think it sucks," he says. "This place is a fucking meat locker."

And when he says "sucks," the word has a juicy, sucking sound but acts the opposite, like you might get sprayed if you stand too close in front of the cat.

"Yeah," I say.

Anything army, nowadays, that's all Swink has to say about it. "It sucks."

All I could say was "Yeah," fresh from what I saw in the empty corridor I came out into after taking a pee: No nurses or doctors around, an old soldier in a wheelchair, left out in the hall, his munching grey monkey face covered with white stubble that yellowed around his mouth, no teeth. The seersucker robe was open, and the fly of his blue pajamas. He fingered his penis and grinned till his gums and tongue showed. One foggy blue eye half-closed, the other bulging and runny didn't register me as I tipped through his pissy bouquet. Maybe tell Swink and Gilson about it later, but right now too hard a subject. I'm in the wrong damn place, me and my desperate pussy thoughts and dreams of a voice. Old man soldier, drooling, mush-brained at the end of his life, homeless in a wheelchair, playing with his weenie, is what's real.

Out on the grass, some of the old soldiers in wheelchairs puff on cigarettes, loose-lipped leaky smokers, killing themselves faster, puffing on those motherfuckers. Bet you could measure their days in smokes. "Joe Dokes had a seventeen-smoke Thursday." Half of them look like they're asleep, sitting out there in their pajamas and robes. About the same shape as the old guy in the hall. The bullshit white heroes the nation claims to care so much about. Tongues stuck halfway out their mouths, no good anymore for tasting or talking or French kissing. Skin flaking, disappearing flake by flake. Nobody cares. What a piece of work is man, man.

"Two of these guys have been here since World War One," Swink says.

"Oh yeah? How do you know?"

"That nurse over there told me." He points to a heavyset woman with grey hair, standing behind the wheelchairs on the grass.

"Damn—forty years. I told you my uncle was in World War One, in France?"

"Yes."

"Yeah," I said. "Uncle Ulysses told me one time that the biggest battles he saw over there were the ones he and other colored guys fought against crackers from the United States that kept fucking with them." Swink's eyes stay wide, studying me. He puts his hand on my shoulder, his long light fingers and thumb. I understand it as ministerial. I took his advice about my skirmish at the USO with Hiebert and Jarboe and slugging Jarboe, not tell the CID about that, my biggest battle of the Cold War. And about the Heavy Brothers. Ain't seen a Russian yet. Only *loco americanos*. Jesus—me and the Southerners at the USO, a continuation of the shit in France, I see now. And Washington and Polk, creations from the same shit. My son could be looking at some of the same do-do in the next go-around. "You wouldn't believe some of the stuff the army put out about Negroes over there, telling people Negroes had tails and all other kinds of shit. Did it in the last war, too. Advised the French to keep their women away from Negroes."

Swink takes his hand off my shoulder and makes a laughing noise that doesn't sound funny, like maybe he takes this shit harder than I do. The cat is sensitive, and back East he's seen more heavy racial shit than I ever saw, growing up in Kayakaw. Externally, that is. I really believe Swink has been driven more out of his mind by it than I have, so far. Less sane, though white. Then again, maybe it's true the boy has been driven into his mind. Maybe it's me that's out of his mind with my habitually well-adjusted ass. Maybe heavy brotherhood makes more sense, even if I can't be that way. Eye for a fucking eye. Swink says, "I'd believe it."

Our eyes are on the old men on the grass in front of us. A forgotten, ass-whipped platoon.

"The only thing was, my uncle said the French are smarter than Americans and didn't swallow all that shit. Said the French people he met treated him real normal."

"Yeah, man," Swink says. "This country is really fucked up." His words rattle figments of my blind love of the red, white, and blue before World War Two ended and just after, before high school, before women. The greatest amber fucking waves of grain country in the world, we had all those P40s, Mustangs, Thunderbolts, B17s, B29s. We had the *U.S.S. Missouri.*

We had the bomb. We beat Hitler and Tojo and Mussolini, won the big war, strongest best country in the world, Jackie Robinson in the majors, "young and easy under the apple boughs," me, rolling around under the trees in Kayakaw, till the complications set in. "Yeah, tell me about it," I say.

Back on the bus, Turner gets out of his seat next to Gilson, comes over and taps Swink on the shoulder.

"Say, boy, go sit next to Jerry, I need to talk to my man here." Swink closes his book on a finger, pulls himself up and across the aisle to the seat Turner left. Turner swings in beside me.

"You've been up this way before, Freddy?" I say.

"Yeah, we came up here last year with the other bandleader we had then." Other bandleader—this is the first time I've heard the phrase *other bandleader*. Mr T's stiff pants, leather pouches choked with marches, his scowl and his shaky baton, are not eternal.

"How was it?"

"Nothing to it, nothing happening."

Then: "Say, man, you thought anything about what I said to you about Chicago?"

"You mean about living in Chicago?"

"That's right."

"No, man, I haven't really thought about it."

"So you're thinking about going back to Oregon."

"I guess so."

"You guess so?" Turner's eyes on the side of my face I feel like flashlights, zeroed in.

I say, "Yes."

"Teaching school?"

"Yeah."

"Don't make much money teaching school, do you?"

"It could get me by." Child support will put a dent in that slim, second-year teacher check, though. Turner, with his old man thoughts, could have thought of some of this.

He rubs his hands together. "Man, how many members did you say there was in Portland?"

"Around ten thousand."

"Out of about four hundred thousand, huh? Man, that ain't no kind of numbers for a city."

"What do you mean?"

"Well, what can you do?"

"Do anything I want to do." The empty nature of my statement bounces back at me. Portland is a tight-ass little city just like I realized Kayakaw was a tight-ass little town, after I got old enough, that was all I ever knew. It was a big deal if a member got a good steady job. You can't get an apartment or live anywhere you want. It would be a front page deal if my trumpet teacher slipped me into a symphony chair for which I wouldn't be paid enough to afford haircuts. I never saw a colored school teacher or doctor or dentist or insurance man or even a bus driver until I visited San Francisco once in high school. And downtown in Portland, they wouldn't even let Mae and me and two other couples into a supper club to hear a colored tenor who was going around the country doing gigs like that because he sure wasn't going to sing at nobody's Metrofuckinpolitan Opera.

"They got lots of clubs and bars for members in Portland?"

"No, not a lot of them. Pickings are sort of slim."

"Man, I'm telling you, you ought to come to Chicago when you get out."

"Yeah?"

"The way you're blowing already, you need to be where you got some audience and where you can hear some bad cats and run up against some bad cats."

Clifford Brown died in Chicago.

Only months ago, my trumpet teacher, a cool white cat from Los Angeles, was pushing to get me into the symphony. There was resistance. The usual color shit. "We've never had one in the symphony before." *One.* But I'm someplace else now, listening to Clifford and all the rest, getting attention at The Box, breathing in Nikki's phrasings, working with Merce Fowler, making music as well as playing it. I say to Freddy, "I've got a lot to learn yet."

And I could have told him I still have to decide how sane I'm planning to remain.

"We all got something to learn yet, but we still play, and we learn a lot of it on the job," he says. "And, shoot, there's all kinds of places to study in Chicago. Bet you ain't got that out in Oregon."

"There are places to study."

"Jazz?"

"You said places to study."

"Okay, places to study—Portland got anything like Northwestern, Loyola, DePaul, Roosevelt, the University of Chicago? And that ain't all?"

"Man, Chicago is way bigger than Portland. What do you expect?"

"That's right. And what I expect is more opportunity to do your thing. There's about two million members in Chicago, man. Now for a cat like you, with an education and some talent..." He let the words hang and then went on. "Think about it, man. I'm gonna be out of here, back in Chi-town in a few weeks, and I can fix you up."

"Fix me up, huh?"

"Yeah, man, more fine chicks up there than you ever saw in Portland, I bet."

"Not looking for no more woman trouble right now, Frederick. Got to work on my music."

"That's right, that's what I'm really talking about, Joe. Come to Chicago, we could find us a rhythm section, get something started. Wouldn't that be cool?"

Turner's idea snapped out like a fresh white tablecloth. A team, weaving sounds, lighting things up.

I say, "Oh yeah. Set the table, man."

"What?"

"I mean that sounds really cool, Freddy."

He relaxes back in his seat, wordless for a moment. He rocks his head, agreeing with himself, says, "You know I'd be glad to help you get situated, man. I know a whole lot of people, and so does my family."

"Thanks, Freddy. That's real down of you. I've got a lot of stuff to think about, though."

"I understand, bro, but put some Chicago in your thoughts. It could be righteous."

***

Inside the armory at Silver City, a national guard sergeant in short khakis leads us to a roomy bay. Looks like all they do around the place is wax and buff the black tile floor. Twenty bunks in the room, uppers and lowers. Squared away. The sergeants and Mr Tappendorf go to other quarters. Rank, like whorehouses and lunch counters, must be segregated. Turner and Gilson throw their duffel bags onto an upper and lower, and Swink and I claim the next pair in the row. Farther down, Hiebert bounces his duffel onto a lower bunk. "Hey, Jarboe," he says, "what's the sound of shit hittin' the floor?"

Jarboe takes up the tired-ass cue: "Wop!" Muccigrosso yells, "You can kiss my ass you nowhere bastards."

"AT HEEZ!"

Sergeant Howell bulges in the doorway, Mr Tappendorf behind him. Tappendorf, a smaller more tentative bear, shifts his feet. The two of them step inside the room. Sergeant Howell looks over at me and says, "Birdie, I need to check with you about the morning report after chow."

He would just be reassuring himself that I'd reported the band TDY—temporary duty—to Silver City for two days on this morning's report, one of the things he knew the clerk should do.

"Okay, Sarge."

Swink whispers in my ear, "Ya got that, Birdie?"

I breathe back, "Kiss my ass, Connecticut Bastard."

To the group, Sergeant Howell's voice comes from deeper in his throat and chest. "All right, listen up now. Chow is at seventeen hundred hours. The mess hall is down to the end of the hall here and turn right. You cain't miss it."

"I betcha Dino can miss it."

"Fuck you, Hiebert."

Tappendorf stands stiff as a natural history exhibit, eyes on Sergeant Howell. "At ease there, Hiebert," the sergeant says. "Okay, men, Mr Tappendorf wants to say a few words."

Tappendorf has his master pouch with him, stuffed with the marches. Pouch man. He unsnaps the cover and slips out four of the cards. "The parade begins at twelve hundred hours tomorrow," he says. "Everybody fall out here at eleven-thirty hours in the parking lot. Now get your pouches."

Sergeant Howell hangs by the door with the bandleader, hands at his sides, and watches us come back with our pouches. Tappendorf, holding his pouch in both paws, his mama must have been a kangaroo.

Tappendorf keeps his eyes on the cards in his hand. "These are what we're going to play," he says. "Put them in the front of your pouch. Okay. You have your 'Men of Ohio,' Number Seven. You have your 'Washington Post,' Number Twenty. You have your 'Colonel Bogie,' Number Seventy-three. You have your 'Hands Across the Sea,' Number Twenty-nine. Okay now, get ready for chow."

When my eyes come up, I'm looking right in Hiebert's eyes on the other side of the group from me. Eyes glittering and full of water and lips pressed tight and forehead rimpled like he's going to piss his pants if he can't bust out laughing. Me and the Texas Bastard having the same fit.

The bandleader's oversized chin lifts. His eyes move over the walls, the bunks. His voice comes from a dreamy cave. "This is a pretty good place, men. You have your building. You have your bunks." Hiebert's face, now red, heads toward cyanosis. The cords in his neck tug. I study the floor. Mr T gives a short-armed wave with the pouch in his hand and walks out of the room, Sergeant Howell behind him.

Hiebert jumps to the door and closes it, falls back against it and yells, "You have your fucking building! You have your walls! You have your ceiling! You have your God damn Sherman tank out there!" Indeed, there is a tank in the parking lot. Hiebert slides down the door till his butt touches his heels. "You have your fucking floor!" He falls over onto the shiny black tiles, hugs his ribs and howls.

I yell, "You have your paper clips!"

"You have your hands in your pockets tickling your balls!" Swink shouts.

"You have your shoes!"

"You have your socks!"

"You have your hands in your pockets playing with your cocks." More Swink.

"You have your birds!"

"You have your dust motes!"

"You have your chow!"

"You have your trees!"

Guys thrash on their bunks and roll on the floor. I roll back and forth on my bunk and do a coyote howl.

"You have your shit on a shingle!"

"You have your fork!"

"You have your goddamn knife."

"You have your fucking Men of Ohio."

"You have your women of Juarez."

"You have your miserable fucking life."

Everybody flops in spasms on their bunks. Then everybody is laughed out. A big deep breath comes up through me, through the room, and I sink face down against the scratchy wool.

The pinging of the mess hall triangle invades the close, dark somewhere-else like an approaching light until I discover myself flattened on an army bunk in New Mexico. Silver City. I rise, hungry.

Swink borrowed a book of duets from one of the sergeants and proposed to let his dinner settle while we play through the book. We play and talk. He talks about his plan to go AWOL, sooner rather than later. Zaza, his waiter-friend, will soon be in Los Angeles, getting set up to go to art school, and helped Swink hatch that direction for his desertion. Nothing to do with sex, Swink says. Actually, he says, one of his high school buddies, a guitar player, goes to UCLA, and that is his main reason for heading to LA. My boy is serious, I can see that. He's looking at having a good time, though, working to get booted out of the army. "Yeah, I think I'll go out to Los Angeles and visit Lennie Zimmerman and see Zaza too."

It gets dark, we put our trumpets away, find Gilson, who has been practicing with Turner, and get out on the street. Of which there aren't a lot in Silver City, where Billy the Kid once walked with his bad self, we learned. *The Outlaw,* the first *sex* movie I ever saw, back in Kayakaw, had Jane Russell in it, who walked toward the cot where old Billy was shivering. She said, "I'll keep you warm," started taking off her blouse, and then the screen went black. That scene stayed in our talk for days.

We come to a corner where a long low wooden sign on the grass says "Western New Mexico State College." The street is a quiet shady one, running east and west of us, half the damned world on either side of us. Nobody in sight. Swink sticks his fingers in the pocket over his heart and takes out a joint. "Let's go to college," he says. "We can sit here on the grass."

"I've been to college, man."

Swink pokes me in the shoulder with his bony fist. "So are you bragging or complaining?"

"Okay, I'll admit I don't know very much, but you ought to try it."

Gilson stops a few yards ahead of us, looks around, scouting. He says, "Let's move down by those trees where it's darker."

We move to the middle of the block where two elm trees grow out of the bank which is lined with stones the size of my head. The stones, firm in the bank and weathered, feel like they've been there a long time when I run my hand over them. We hop up on the bank and dangle our feet a toe-tap above the sidewalk. Swink lights the joint. The red-orange tip flares into an instant of chiaroscuro that's like time passing, gone before you know it. I shut my eyes and breathe. Swink bumps my arm, breath held, passes the joint to me. "Here."

I take it and offer it to Gilson. He's looking up into the trees and at the sky. "No, you go ahead," he says.

After sucking in a lungful, I hand him the joint.

My eyes go between the trees to the huge velvety cliché of the sky over me, over Daddy's grave, over my mother in Kayakaw, over my brother in some Piedmont League town, over my son and Stacy in Portland, Portland, my city of limited possibilities, over everything. The nothing that is the something over the dimly-understood everything. There really is no place like home. Not like in the old song—what I see is home is not a place, not a plot of land with a house on it. Not for me. A bunch of habits we get into with our stuff, that's what people call home. Man, out here in the warm night under my stars with the busted up ventricities and auricities of my cardial engine is as much like home as any place I've been, with grand, witty friends, brothers like I never had before, cats that we can talk say any words to each other, tell stories, and everybody is cool. I roll my spine one vertebra at a time down onto the grass. No Heavy Brother or army madness up here. In El Paso I don't see stars close like this. I say

"Let us go then, you and I,
When the evening is spread out against the sky
Like a patient etherized upon a table."

Gilson says, "Wait a minute, Schoolmaster. What did you just say?"
I say the lines again.

"Heavy," he says. He sucks in some smoke with a whoosh and gives the joint to Swink.

Swink takes it, sucks in some smoke, holds it, and coughs out, "It's from *The Love Song of J. Alfred Prufrock,* by T.S. Eliot."

"That's right, boy. Just look at them there stars. Either one of you cats ever been under ether? Been etherized?"

"No." Swink coughs and laughs. Gilson wags his head No.

"Well, I have. And you go into blackness, like blackness completely overwhelms you like a black silent night with no stars. Your body is dead."

At the word *dead,* Gilson and Swink freeze into scarecrows with no breeze blowing. Swink with his mouth open and the joint reached halfway toward Gilson, Gilson with his hand in mid-air reaching for the godly spark. Their eyes round on me in the dark and their breath is caught in their mouths. "Dead" arcs and arcs and arcs in the silence like a basketball bouncing across an empty gym floor. Dead, dead, dead.

"Shit, man," Gilson says, "that's heavy."

"*Etherized upon a table,* I was. And then after I came out from under the ether, I threw up a whole mess of blackish red jelly right there on the floor of the doctor's office,

> *"Jelly, jelly, jelly, all night long*
> *Hope ol' doc ain't done nothin' wrong*
> *Cause that mess that I done spit up*
> *Sure don't make me want to git up*
> *I say, jelly, jelly, jelly all na na*
> *Na na na na na—"*

"Hey, Schoolmaster, what the heck is that?"

"Oh that? I call it 'Post-tonsillectomy Ramble.'" A long inward whistle on the joint fills my lungs, flares and reddens the side of Swink's face. Some of the hot smoke goes into my nose.

"Swink says, "Things are starting to become allegorical."

The streetlight at the corner slices into the dark like a wedge of yellow cheese. "Yeah, I say, "you ain't just whistlin' 'Dixie,' boy."

We don't make the connection when I sit up to hand the dwindled joint to Gilson, and it hits the sidewalk with a splash of sparks. Gilson picks it up and takes a drag, holds it and passes the remainder to Swink. A laugh tunnels under his breath, gets hold of him, and rocks him like nothing usually does to Gilson.

"Spill it, boy, What's so funny?"

"Yeah," Swink says.

Gilson sits back and takes a couple deep breaths, his legs against the stones, hands under his thighs. "Well, you know," he says, "one time in Boston I was standing in back of some colored guys at a dance, and they were passing this joint around between them. One guy drops the joint, you know, and the other cats start in on him—'Man, what you doing, the thing's done fell on the floor. Why don't you be careful, fool,' and a bunch of stuff like that. The guy that dropped the joint—kind of a tall dark cat—bends over and picks it up and says real cool and slow, 'It ain't fell, it just stumbled.'"

"*done fell on the floah*" is more than Swink and I can stand even before Gilson gets to the lisping climax. We grab our sides and roll and bump our heads on the grass. Tears leak from under my clamped eyelids. We laugh till we have the dry heaves. "It ain't fell, it just stumbled! Man, you are just full of shit! That is so goddamn funny."

Gilson's whitish features show up pretty well in the dark. In daylight he would be smiling. We'd see a spread of pink come into his face too because Gilson, though hip, is a modest cat. Now, in the night shadow of the elms, he sits there under his peaked cap like he hasn't just imported some of the funniest shit in New Mexico. He's lamping me like it isn't dark, his look a change of subject. Sizing me up for a garment of some kind. "You know, Birdie," he says, "you're pretty great, man. But you'd be greater if you were from Boston."

Now what kind of off-the-wall jive that is, I don't know. The cat could be signifying about the way I handled the Heavy Brothers business, going to the CID.

"Now what the fuck is that supposed to mean?" I say.

Then: "Massachusetts Bastard."

Gilson's laugh gushes up then drains away. "I'm just telling you, Birdie."

"And don't call me no fucking 'Birdie,' man."

"That's what Howell calls you."

"Well, he's the fucking first sergeant."

Swink slides off the bank, stands in front of us with his arms spread. "Wait. Wait," he says. "I challenge that statement."

"What statement," I say.

"'You'd be greater if you were from Boston.'"

"Well, he would," Gilson pipes up.

Swink pumps his knees like a preacher, hands helping him talk. "What do you mean 'be greater?' Joe's pretty great right now."

"Yeah, he's great, but you know what I mean."

Cat says I'm great, but...

"Your statement isn't logical, Jerry," Swink says. "You have no way of knowing if Joe would be greater if he were from Boston. What do you mean by 'greater?'"

"Yeah, man, what do you mean by greater?" *You'd be greater if you were from Boston.* I see what Gilson means. He sees through to my countrified, square origins. I'm deficient because I ain't from some big-ass city with a jillion members. Maybe some of them peoples needs to get the fuck out of Chicago. Or Boston.

"Think of all the cool things to do in Boston," Gilson says. "And to see."

Swink is moving his feet, bobbing and weaving. He puffs to life a fresh joint. "What do you mean by 'cool things to do'?"

"Stuff Joe likes to do. You know. Music? He reads a lot?"

"You think he can't play the trumpet in Portland, Oregon?" Swink says. "I'll bet they've got books in Portland."

These New England Bastards, shadowy in the dark, are starting to crack me up. I know what Gilson is trying to say, but I love the cat anyway. He's trying to be helpful. And, hell, he might have a point. But Swink is on him like white on rice with questions, waving his hands in his face, and I'm helpless on my back, in another laughing fit, starting to get a sideache.

Swink passes me the joint. I sit up and pull in some smoke. "They've got books in Portland," he says. "Right, Joe?"

"*Si, si*, man, *beaucoup libros* in Portland." My sides ache.

Swink brings his finger down in Gilson's face. "It doesn't matter where you are," he says. "You've just got to *be* wherever you are. The only thing you can say for certain is 'If Joe were from Boston, he would be from Boston.'"

Help me, Jesus, but I beez from Portland. Floating above all this jive and bringing me close to expiration is the schoolbook fact that Portland escaped being named Boston back in 18-something only because a Boston cat lost a coin flip to a Portland, Maine cat.

A dog barks, coming our way. We rotate in the direction of the barking. Across the street on the sidewalk, a terrier-sized dog follows a woman who carries a shopping bag. The woman doesn't look back at the dog, keeps marching, bag at her side, going someplace she knows where with longlegged steps, that rattly little tattletale behind her.

Swink butts against the stones edging the bank, the joint beside his face between his thumb and forefinger. I stretch across Gilson into Swink's face. Swink puts up his hand like for me to cool it. The cat is fixing to pronounce.

I hold myself in place, eyes on his mouth. Swink's lips round, spread out, come together. "The woman is in her period," he says. "The dog can smell the blood. That's the reason he's barking."

I let out my breath. All around us, quiet. Trees unchanged. Same darkness. "Oh shit, man, that's heavy."

Blood dog and the woman disappear.

"Yeah," Gilson says. "Heavy."

We fall back on the grass under the etherizing night with the stars right on top of us.

3)

He's barely back from San Antonio, and I'm just back from Silver City, and we're here in our undershirts, blowing in unison through a long book of exercises he knows by heart without stopping except to sip some water, he actually sipping water. Fowler is listening close to how I match his sound. Says he wants to see if I'm staying in the woodshed.

Two days back from San Antonio and he's laughing and jiving and tickling himself to death here, like he must have remembered the hell out of some Alamo while he was up there with his girlfriend. He stretches out his arm, brings his hand back and scratches the top of his head. "How was y'all's trip to New Mexico?"

"It was all right. We just stayed in Silver City one night, did the parade next day, and came on back."

"Is they anything up there, man. In Silver City?"

What I understand him to mean is Are there any members up there, and what's happening with them.

"I didn't see anything, man. It's a very small place, you know. *You're pretty great, Birdie, but you'd be greater if you were from Boston.*

***

Nikki drove her car, lucky for me, because after the gig Freddy wants to go have a drink, he says, with a fine Mexican woman who has been tipping in regularly and eyeballing him. Since he's getting so short, he says, he's got to move fast. In a couple weeks Freddy will be gone. Home to Chicago. "Nikki will give you a ride back to Showalter," he says.

Nikki says, "Don't worry, baby, I'll take care of you."

We finish the last set with "There Will Never Be Another You." Nikki scats for a couple choruses, about as good as anything I've heard like that, scattering notes just like a horn. I throw some of her phrases into my solo. She laughs, shimmies her hips at me, claps. Nikki at the mike, singing, swinging, snapping her fingers, wading in song. Her great timing affects everybody on the stand. We're all in Nikki's pocket, swinging on her hips. Hipness.

Freddy has already cut out with his fine Mexican woman. Cooling it outside the entrance, I wait while Nikki collects her check. The mirthful gap in her front teeth lights her way coming out of The Box. She takes my arm. "All right then," she says. "You ready to go, baby?"

"Sure."

She presses my arm against her side in the crook of her elbow. "Boy, you sure can blow some trumpet," she says.

"Thanks, Nikki. It means a lot to me if you think so."

"Well, baby, I'm serious as a heart attack. You can play."

Then: "You in a hurry?"

"In a hurry for what?"

"To get back out to the fort." She keeps hold of my arm, leans around to scope my mug. Never noticed before how long Nikki's eyelashes are. "You want to stop by my place before I take you back out to Showalter? I'll make you some hot chocolate."

"Gee, Nikki, thanks. That could really show me something."

She laughs and puts her head on my shoulder. "You're not working tomorrow, are you?" she says. "Tomorrow is Sunday."

"No. Not working." The woman's voice and words set up some serious vibrations, but I'm not shaking or sweating.

We get in the car. "Let's stop by the house then," she says. "Maybe you'd prefer something stronger than hot chocolate."

"Whatever you say, m'am. Who am I to refuse such hospitality?"

She pats my thigh and lowers her voice. "Would you want to refuse it?"

"Oh, never."

Nikki hits all the green lights on Montana Avenue until we turn off into her neighborhood. I sit close to her, the way she sat next to me when we took her home in Freddy's car. My arm rests on the seatback behind her head, and every now and then her hair touches my arm. The music we've been in the middle of all night still percolates in our nerves. Nikki smokes during our drive.

"I didn't know you could scat like that, Nikki."

"Well, you've heard me sing only two or three times."

"True."

"You expect to know everything about a girl after hearing her only twice?" She pats my thigh and laughs like she thought this was really funny.

I say, "Some girls, yeah."

"Am I one of those girls, Joe?"

"Oh no. Far from it. You can really blow, Nikki. You're deep."

"Oooowee, talk to me, honey, 'cause you sho know what to say." She slows the Chevy and swings into her street.

My hand slips from the back of the seat to her shoulder. "I'm not jiving, Nikki."

"It's all right if you is, baby. I love it. And thank you." In front of her house, she pulls close to the curb. No lights on, except the porch light.

"No babysitter tonight?"

"No babysitter necessary," she says.

"Oh. With his daddy?"

"That's right. Come on in, baby."

We get out of the car. Third time at Nikki's house. Last time, it was a hug on the porch and then back to the fort, the hug I took to Silver City with me. She digs in her bag and takes out a key, unlocks the door, and reaches inside to flip on a light. I follow her into the room where the large old photograph in the oval frame draws my eyes from Nikki's flanks. She sets her bag on the coffee table.

"Who's the woman there," I ask her.

"Oh that? That's my grandmother."

"You look a lot like her."

Nikki rests her cheek against her hands beddy-bye style and says, "Lovely isn't she?"

"That's what I'm trying to tell you."

"She had some *Mexicano* and Indian blood in her."

"Some *Africano* too," I say. "Trumps them all, don't it?"

"Listen to you," she says. She stretches her arms out to me. I match her embrace with my own arms around her torso. We stay embraced, quiet, let the drumming of the evening subside until the right beat hits, and we ease apart. She pulls me to the kitchen where she turns on the light and takes milk out of the refrigerator, a saucepan from beneath the counter and a box of cocoa out of a cupboard. Looks like hot chocolate for real. She also comes up with a bottle of something I think is sherry and pours herself a small glass. "Care for some?" she says.

"Thanks, I'll wait for the chocolate."

In stocking feet, stirring, sipping her sherry, she measures in a couple drops of vanilla. "And the marshmallows," I say.

"Sure thing, baby. Sit down. Relax."

I sit at the table and watch Nikki whip the spoon around the pan. "Smells good," I say.

"Uh huh."

Pretty much like on the bandstand, with her stirring, tasting and wiping, Nikki steps from place to place in time to the music inside her. She raises the spoon like a conductor. "Okay. You're going to like this."

She gets two white teacups out of the cupboard and an eggbeater from a drawer. The chocolate froths from a minute of her beating, and then she pours the cups full. "Let's go in the living room," she says.

She picks up both cups and swings into the living room, me in her wake. Before she lowers our drinks to the coffee table, she waits for me to sit. Scent of her perfume gathers about the table.

"Ah yes," she says, "let's do have a marshmallow."

Nikki reaches behind the TV set, brings out a small wooden box and sits down beside me. She slides back the lid. A row of neatly twisted joints covers the bottom of the box which she sets on my knee. I remove one.

"By all means," I say. After my recent practice, I fire up the joint in a manner that lets the woman's ripe and smiling attention understand she ain't observing no amateur here. We slouch on the couch, close, and float the smoke back and forth, listening to her stereo, to Sarah Vaughn singing "Corner to Corner" that Nikki says she's studying. The chocolate begins to taste allegorically deep, as Swink would say, taste like the idea of chocolate, suffusing spiritual taste buds. If there is somewhere to go from this perfection of chocolate, my hostess will perhaps lead me there.

Nikki moves her shoulders and hands, singing along with Sara Vaughn through the smoke. Her voice has a lot of Sarah's stretchiness and that big ball of sweet hum that's always there, even in her talk. Nikki is still up from the gig. She takes a hit, hands me the joint, and gets onto her feet, moving to the tune. One thing I dug about Nikki on the bandstand from the first was the way she moved. Whatever she was hearing, it made her move just right. Like she's listening to Sarah sing this ballad and moving her shoulders and hips and feet here in front of me, lighter than the smoky air in the room. I'm digging her grandmother in the photo with its misty edges, not much older than Nikki in that picture, and I can see Nikki's humor behind the high cheekbones, behind the rouge the photographer rubbed on her sepia face. Woman that laughed a lot. Maybe danced. Dancing Negroes. Remaining sane, perhaps. Shit. Grandma Nanette might even have a gap like Nikki's if she busted out laughing. Open up them chops, Grandma. Leave me check that diastema.

Saw a portrait like that in Grandma's house in Kayakaw, in the back bedroom, of Grandpa Freeman, when he was maybe in his twenties, black and white, black oval frame like this one. Wearing a tie. Back in Indiana before 1900. Negroes must have shucked a whole lot of corn to pay for those pictures. Nice-looking chap, Grandpa. Get him together with Nikki's granny. Whoopee. Nikki's playing the record over and over

I go from corner to corner, aimless and blue

and doing all kinds of twisting, bending down damn near to the floor and corkscrewing back up. Grandpa Freeman and Nikki's granny on the wall start to move, brief boogie moves, and I fall over laughing.

Nikki swirls over to me. "What's going on, baby?" Over me, not Grandma, lips puckered into a word, hand extended like a word wing, bird wing. "Dance with me," she says.

She flutters her fingers before her chest, conducting me to my feet, into her arms, into the music with her, glued to her rolling, rhythmic belly. Nikki-ass Nanette. Man, oh bumpity man. The music ends. We must be danced out, up here on this asteroid where we're at. The full plum lips of my hostess cook my ear. "Let's take a shower, baby, and go to bed."

Nikki in her powder blue robe that's got dimples to match the brown ones in her face, making French toast and coffee, is a picture so far from the months of mess in mess halls that, for a flash, my muscles panic. My austerity violated!—in a kitchen with a woman fixing my breakfast. Let me the fuck out of here, find my horn, and get to stepping.

Her hand on my shoulder drains the panic, and she sets a cup of coffee in front of me. It's all right. I'm in the army, a soldier. We're not about to get hitched, or anything like that, don't care how far beyond chocolate the woman is. Shoot, Nikki must know all that. She says, "You want the paper, baby?"

"You got the paper?"

"Let me look out here." She gets up and dances out to the front, comes back and hands me the *El Paso Times.*

"Thanks, Nikki." I remove the rubber band and drop it into the palm she extends. She slips it over her wrist. I say, "Will I make a bad impression if I look at the ball scores a minute?"

"You've already made the best of impressions, Private Birdsong."

I'd be lying if I said after last night that Nikki's words didn't twist my wig. She makes a dance out of dishing French toast onto my plate. I scan the National and American League scores and set the *Times* aside.

"Don't want to spoil the impression," I say.

"You won't."

"Wish I could be sure of that. You're great, Nikki."

"Maybe you just bring out the best in a girl."

"Oh you were singing great a long time before you met me, honey."

"Singing, huh?"

"Yes indeed, and I can see you are a most scocious cook."

Nikki freezes and bugs her eyes at me. "Negro, you sure can talk some jive when you want to."

"No, no. I'm serious, woman."

She plops the French toast in front of me, grabs me in something between a headlock and choking hug. The rubber band on her wrist pulls my skin and stings. She lets go. "There," she says. "Eat your damn French toast."

"Seriously, Miss Lady, if I told you how you tore up my mind last night, you might make me your slave."

As if the syllable were a plum in her mouth, she says, "Oh?"

"Then I'd be terrified of you."

"Listen to you, boy."

"Swear to God."

"Better not do that." I feel the slap of her superstition. She brings her plate to the table and sits down. She closes her eyes, bows her head, and falls into a silent blessing. Opens her eyes. "Listen, sweetheart," she says, "you don't know just how safe you are with me."

The Angel Weems

1)

"The Lord giveth and the Lord taketh away." Daddy said that a few times. And that's the Army for me these days: There go the Fort Ord buddies, here come Levinski and Vogel. There goes Levinski, here come Washington and Polk and all that woe that will never go away, but here comes Swink with *Howl* that sticks to my ribs, Turner and Gilson with musical support. And wham, there goes Herb Vogel, sad sergeant, to Kingdom Come. But here comes Mercer James Fowler through Cedric Weems, another peculiar sergeant. There dims Stacy, but yes, up jumps Nikki, beyond chocolate, manna from Heaven. Woman can sing, so much music in her body. Yes, I am one thankful *soldado.*

Giveth more: Somebody, somewhere up in the Chain of Command finally dug the wise economy of moving the band up to Bolden Heights, combining the 224th and the 72nd under one name, The Seventy-Second Army Band, under the direction of Chief Warrant Officer Gordon O. Tappendorf.

Up here in our own buildings, we're a step away from the area roamed by the Heavy Brothers, though they do have that old Chrysler New Yorker. Nothing new from the CID investigation but I do breathe easier in Bolden Heights.

Here I am, bunking next to Swink, Gilson and Turner across the aisle. Tell me about cool. Muccigrosso and the Southerners are way down the barracks with their shit. Our own crib out here on the dry slopes of Bolden Heights without a whole lot of other troop noise around. The music is expanding, my soldierhood is starting to look short and feel like a balloon that doesn't want to deflate.

***

Giveth and taketh away: We're walking down Jeb Stuart Road, Swink and I, off the post, to catch a bus downtown. Swink has been talking about AWOL, now he's doing it. Going and coming—you get attached to cats and then watch them leave. Swink's not leaving for good, though. He just ain't studying war no more.

In the barracks, nobody there Sunday afternoon but him and me. He's throwing socks, shorts, his shaving kit into a canvas gym bag. Getting ready to take off. I'm at the foot of his bunk with my trumpet case in my hand, watching him. After I put him on the road, I'm going over to Merce Fowler's pad. Swink stops putting articles in the bag and opens his locker. He pulls out his personal trumpet, the Benge, in its black leather case, holds it out to me and says, "Here, man, have a horn."

At first, I don't get it.

He shakes the case at me. "You want it? Take it. It'll refine your voice."

"What are you talking about, man?"

"Do you want the horn?"

"Jesus, man, I don't have any money."

"Did I mention money? I'm giving up property, man. Take it," he says. "Give me a few bucks when you can, if it'll make your squeamish heart feel better."

Receiving the horn is a haymaker way bigger than my embarrassment. Swink has been through with serious horn playing for a long time, but Jesus, just like that, giving me one of the best horns made— he goes back to pushing stuff into his gym bag.

So now we're walking down Jeb Stuart Road, him in his sunglasses, looking like he ought to be in dungarees, climbing onto a sailboat. But he doesn't want to go home. He just wants to go and go. "You don't need to tell anybody," he says.

"Man, how unhip do you think I be? Gilson knows, huh?"

He runs the habitual tongue over his molars and says, "Yeah," with his mouth half open.

Then: "I'm sorry. I know you're cool, man."

We get off the bus at Alligator Park and walk west, him carrying his gym bag, me carrying the black trumpet case with my new horn in it. We're not in a big hurry, but he's got a lot of motion in him, short steps, head, arms, shoulders, going every which way. On the morning report I'll have to enter him Away Without Leave, AWOL.

A few years ago we were boys hot to learn the trumpet, trumpet hotshots, aiming to be virtuosos. We're fucked-up soldiers now. He's a fucked-up soldier, through with playing the horn, looking for a way out of the army. I'm a fucked-up virtuoso, a disintegrated burgher, cooling it in the army, looking to reintegrate, looking to achieve sanity if possible. "How long do you think you'll be gone?"

"I'll probably be back in a month or so. That ought to raise enough hell."

It's a dry, bright ninety-something degrees when our steps bring us to the road west to Las Cruces. Down the highway, the asphalt shines like water. Swink's got the right idea, wearing sunglasses. He sticks out his hand, and we shake. "A month, huh?"

"Yup. Then I'm going to tell them I'm a homo and see if they kick me out."

"Yeah, well, we'll see." We've been all through this. His mind is already way down the highway that splits the terrain between Los Angeles and here where we're kicking dust. I would walk a few miles down the road with Swink and listen to him talk about Zen Buddhism and Alan Watts he's been raving about lately, or anything else, but he'll probably get a ride quicker if I'm not beside him. I give his hand another good shake, drop it, and slap him on the shoulder. "Take it easy, man. We'll be looking for you."

He laughs and backs off, waving. "See you, Joe."

"So long, Merlin. And thanks again, man." I pat the trumpet case.

His head bobs from another laugh. One last wave and he spins his skinny frame and starts hoofing it west. Standing there with the trumpet he just gave me, I watch him stick his thumb out for two passing cars that don't stop. He waves again. He's still in sight when a car stops for him. He runs to the car, looks back, waves. I hold up the trumpet and wave it back and forth. He climbs into the car. A low billow of dust, and it's hi yo Silver. Away!

***

Corazon stands at the front door, looking out. I hit Fowler's gate and she comes out of the house, head down, trucking past me. I touch her arm to slow her.

"Hi, Cory, how are you?"

"Fine. MJ is waiting for you." She moves right through my touch, out the gate, but stops and looks back like in a story. Her chest rises as if she's going to say something, something sweet. She exhales and says nothing. And moves on.

Inside, just me and Fowler. I take out the silver Benge and blow a few long tones and lip slurs, let Corazon moderate in a long slow ascending arpeggio. My army-issue Conn isn't bad, but the Benge lets my breath in with less resistance. Easier to get the feel of a filled-up, juicy tone with Swink's horn. My horn, now. My teacher in Portland used Benges. One of my studio mates at The Horn Studio worked a summer in the Los Angeles shop and helped build his own horn. His own Benge. Never thought about having even an old Benge, cramped like I was back in Portland. And Swink, he just said, "Here, man, have a horn."

Fowler elbows himself up straight in his chair, takes a drag from his cigarette. "Say, man, you got you a new horn."

I take the Benge away from my lips. "You can hear that, huh?"

He coughs into the back of his hand, swallows. "Damn straight I can hear that. So what you got there?"

"It's a Benge."

"Oh yeah? Hand it here a minute."

Yeah, let him see it. I put the horn in his hand. He fiddles with the valves, wipes the mouthpiece with the heel of his hand, runs up and down some scales, goes up to a G above high C. A few bars of "Baubles, Bangles, and Beads," and he hands it back to me. "Where you get that axe, man?"

"One of my buddies gave it to me."

"Ain't you bitchin'? What you mean, gave it to you?"

"I mean he gave the horn to me. He's not interested in playing anymore."

"Man, I don't know what y'all got goin' on, but that's a nice horn."

"Yeah, I know. Swink is one of my aces, nothing going on."

"Just jivin', Cuz. You know how I am." He snorts. "He ain't no splib is he?"

Fowler's question wasn't intense, had the sound of a statement. Good time for something like a lie. When I think about it, Swink is not exactly not a splib. The cat is way hipper than the average white person. He's an *American,* not a *norteamericano.*

"No, he's a white cat. He just now cut out, went AWOL, trying to get himself kicked out of the army." My boy Swink, heading to Los Angeles, to chase around with his quick mad steps through Negro streets "looking for an angry fix" and a crazy time, seeing Zaza, talking shit nonstop.

"Why he want to get kicked out of the army?"

"I don't know."

Then: "He's one of these people that's mad at the system."

"Well, shoot, man, you got you a damn good friend there, anyhow, givin' you something like that. Come on, let's see if you can blow that thing."

We play blues in all the keys, repeating myself quite a bit, but I don't wear out. Think about Corazon and get some long lines going, think about Stacy and wander into off-key surprises, think about the blue-black weight of the Heavy Brothers, and story lines without words. Think about Nikki, swinging, with some snappy grace notes and gruppettos to the solid time Fowler keeps with his hands, feet, grunts, and humming. Me, working hard, trying to say colors, weight, contours, eyes, trying hard to be exquisite by implication, trying to sneak up on the ineffable.

He comes in with some bad gospel-sounding moves in his left hand in four and plays two whole choruses against it in three-four with his right hand. I say, "Whoa, man."

Fowler leans back till I can see his gold fillings, laughs crazy some more, dark glasses to the ceiling. I listen like a good third-grader.

"Go get yourself a beer or somethin' out the frigidaire, Cuz, and bring me one too."

Fowler roots in his chair till the frame squeaks, turns up his beer, takes a pull, and lets out a loud, "A-a-a-ah."

We soak in the afternoon heat and quiet with our beers, ears open, digging the inaudible spectrum of sound. He says, "Man, back in Chicago, day like today cats would be in somebody's backyard, playing music. Didn't have no jobs. Play B-flat blues all afternoon and drink. Be drinking that cheap wine and bootleg whiskey. Yeah, man, that was back during the Depression."

Chicago again. And the Depression. People still say The Depression the way they say The War, as if it were something unbelievable, except they went through it. My folks talked about The Depression the way Fowler does. We lost fifty thousand troops in Korea only a few years ago, but *The War* means World War Two. The Depression sounds bigger than Korea, almost as big as The War.

Fowler takes up his cigarettes and lighter from where Corazon placed them.

> *Place me, place me, baby.*
> *Place me all night long.*

He pulls a cigarette from the pack with his thumb and forefinger and lights up. Only way you could tell he was blind, watching him do that, is the way his head stays looking straight in front of him with those dark glasses on. Corazon has got him coordinated.

Old Merce can look menacing if he works at it, smoking, cigarette up to his mouth under those glasses, smoke coming through his fingers with their silver and turquoise rings in front of his face, healthy head of curly black hair going grey around the ears. A bad-ass boss of something. Music boss. "Yeah, Cuz, people didn't have shit back then," he says. "Lots of Negroes comin' up from Down South. Escapin', lookin' to butcher hogs to make some money. Sittin' in somebody's backyard full of all kinds of junk and shit, playin' old horns, banjos, guitars, might even be a fiddle. You could always find somethin' to sit on. Old car seat, icebox, broken-down davenport. Be a dozen cats back there, half of 'em in bib overalls, blowin'. Listenin', talkin' all kind of sugar dick jive, lyin' and goin' on about how many women they been had. Some cats too old to stand up long. Be takin' naps, wake up and play some more.

Sittin' there drinkin', talkin' shit all afternoon and playin' them B-flat blues till everybody was too drunk or too wore out to keep on."

Out of his words comes a sunny backyard watercolor of black figures in overalls, wielding funky golden horns, blue sky, uneven bricks, patches of green trying to sprout among the junk. The dark red moan of a bent cornet.

"Man, I was fifteen years old back then. Loved playin' that stuff with those cats and slippin' me a swallow now and then. Thought I was really doin' somethin'."

"You were doing something, Merce."

"Yeah, Cuz," he says. "Didn't know what it was then. Went to trade school, learned how to make keys and fix locks, but right there in that old backyard is where I got my real schoolin'."

"Shoot, man, that's what I call some real education."

"Yeah, it was," Fowler says. "It really was. Schoolin' in the blues."

2)

Every chance Nikki and I get, with her son at his father's place for the weekend, we spend Saturday night together. After her gig, we eat, smoke, screw, talk, sleep. We talk about learning more tunes, listening harder, swinging harder, working on our low ranges, getting deeper into chords. Talking about where our kids fit into the picture behind our ravenous chase after that something we're chasing. We feel it but we don't have the whole idea about it yet, but where it's at, we decide, is we simply want to complete ourselves. Do that, everything else will fall into place. I'm beating on the davenport arm, preaching, "And music is the siren call to completion."

Nikki says, "If you say so, Baby."

Nikki's got some self. She's not the clinging type. She likes me but told me right out she wouldn't get tied up with somebody like me, young, "unfocused," she says, with a whole lot to learn yet, no matter how crazy about my ass she might be. She said she noticed that girl, Merce Fowler's girl, looking at me that night in The Box. "And don't be trying to tell me you ain't been noticing back, baby." Cold sweat popped onto my skin.

No telling where somebody like me might end up. "I can't be bothered with raising another kid," she said, during one of her post-coital rambles. We had been smoking some of the good stuff, but digging the look on my face, she said real fast, "Oh, I'm sorry, baby, I didn't mean to hurt your feelings, but you understand what I'm saying."

What she meant jumps out of her words like a right cross to the jaw—that I'm not up to taking care of any kind of serious business, a reminder that leaves me shaky in the gut and disorganized in the head. Not great. The only thing that recommends me is that I have a certain amount of musical ability and can play the trumpet. They might be telling the truth, but they don't know what I've been through, Nikki and Gilson, both of them telling me they don't think I'm a very complete article.

I recover from the punch because Nikki has fine resuscitation skills, and, listening to her, I get hold of things, like the idea and the feeling that a single beat or a single note can be a lifetime to do all kinds of swinging in—this patch of sound, right here, now. A lifetime. A pinpoint of power. I'm telling myself this is serious business.

3)

Weems puts down his tray, looks left and right like somebody might be tailing him. One paranoid Negro, Weems. A hot summer noon, and I worked late in the orderly room, so I found this table to myself in the half-empty mess hall, where I can soak up some quiet, let the frosty glow of my new horn continue to sink in, and reflect on my lies to the military police as to knowledge of Swink's possible whereabouts, where I can ponder Fowler's lessons, the bliss of this time at Bolden Heights, specter of the Heavy Brothers notwithstanding, and my honorable discharge, approaching like the sound of the trumpet in Stravinsky's soldier's tale, when I shall be another body who once served in the 72nd, nobody missing me. But then here comes Weems, dark little crackling pile in combat boots. He jerks out a chair, sits his brusque butt in it, and pulls up to the table. He gives his shoulders a quick, pugilistic flip. "Pass me the salt, man."

I push the salt shaker over to him. He lifts the top of his bun and jabs the shaker toward the bare meat. No lettuce, no tomato. A couple small grunts accompany his jabbings, like when he's playing the piano and it starts to get good to him. He says, "How you doin' today, man?"

"I'm doing all right, how're you doing?"

"Goddamn diabetes is actin' up." He pronounces it like "die beat us," my mother's pronunciation. Weems ducks his head with each chew. A patina of sweat covers his puffy, leathery mug, and his bulgy forty-three-year-old eyes are yellowed in the whites and red-rimmed.

"Out all night, huh?" I say.

"Yeah. Went to the house with this chick I knew when I was here before."

I take a bite of my hamburger, where cardboardy texture kayoes taste in the meat. "So you got an old lady now?"

"Naw, man, it wasn't nothin'. I ain't tryin' to win no home."

Whoa. *Ain't tryin' to win no home.* That's what Weems said. Words dragged out of his morning-after, St James Infirmary mood, House of the Rising Sun mood. Post-cottonfield slavery mood. Ain't got nothing mood. Homeless in the army, aching, worn-out mood: *Ain't trying to win no home.* And crowding in with him, a jiggly band of raggedy ghosts, messed-up cats with nothing but trouble since Emancipation, red-eyed and lint-headed inheritors of no estate, homeless, running from slavery after slavery, nothing to pass on but woe, whose vision is their dicks might can win them some temporary warmth in a woman's nest. Man, oh man. Just trying to eat lunch.

Weems halts his chewing and ducking, runs his tongue over his front teeth, bulgy eyes on me as if just now seeing me. "Say, man, you know what?"

"No. What?"

"I played with whatsname last night, and he said you a bad little sombitch."

"What?"

"Yeah, Merce. Merce Fowler, at The Frying Pan last night. He said, 'That little sombitch can blow his ass off.'"

Weems picks up a frenchfry and sticks it in his mouth. Fowler does say I have a nice tone, but that's all he ever allows, except for groaning and saying, "Got damn, man!" when he doesn't like the way I'm playing. Fowler has got one eight-letter word for me: *practice.*

"He said that about me?"

"That's what I'm telling you, boy."

"Shit, man, I'm really glad to hear that. The cat never says anything about my playing, you know. Just says, 'Practice.' You sure he said that?"

Weems stops chewing, bugs his eyes at me. "Why I want to lie about it, motherfucker? I'm tellin' you what the cat said."

"Sorry, man. Sorry. Thanks. I'm just so glad to hear it. The cat has never said anything like that to me."

"What the fuck he need to say? Anyhow, Merce knows what he's talkin' about, man. Listen to him. The cat is heavy."

"Oh yeah, he's heavy. You don't have to tell me. And I really want to thank you, Cedric. You know, it was you that introduced me to Merce."

"Yeah."

We finish eating, the Angel Weems and I, and he heads off to sick bay to get something for his condition.

Coming through Slaughter

Fowler's ears know I just walked in the house. He keeps playing, slow-moving chords in both hands, and humming to himself, humming his big hum and grunting. First in line on the small table between him and his chair, among Corazon's arrangement of cigarettes, lighter, and ashtray, is a highball glass half full of whiskey. Fowler's hand reaches back, his head in profile. His fingers curve around the glass, carry it to his mouth. He places it back on the table and comes down heavy on a bass chord with some funky trilling. He sways like somebody praying down by the riverside. That's Fowler. Could be praying.

Daddy would dig some of Fowler's music if he could forget about sin for a minute. Sound that's got traces of Daddy's whistling in it.

"Come on, Cuz, get out that axe. You warmed up?"

Swink's trumpet, my trumpet, is still a surprise whenever I open the case, the pearly silver Benge lying there on dark red velvet. "Yeah, sort of," I say. "We played a gig this morning."

He stops rocking and plunking, relaxes his shoulders and goes into a smooth intro, shuffling his huaraches in a slow four. "Awright now, let's get some of this."

He starts into "I'm Old-Fashioned." I slur and purr through the chords once and then try the melody. I've been wearing out the record since Swink laid it on me, writing out Lee Morgan's solo so I can look at it. Fowler's knuckles charge back and forth across the keys like a herd of horses when he plays runs of notes, brown rumps bouncing up and down. I try to play it as baroque and juicy as I can with a light swing, but Fowler is way down the tunnel ahead of me. Way inside the music.

"Lookee here, Cuz. Let me show you somethin'." That's what Fowler says every time he's about to unveil something he thinks I'm ready for. The cat really understands the concept of readiness. "Here's somethin' you can do to make some of this jive sound more hip."

He shows me how I can substitute certain chord tones for the original ones in a tune. Substitute tones that really work, sound right, with a little surprise to them, an extension of possibilities. Something my ears pick up sometimes, but I didn't know what was actually going on until Fowler showed me. "Substitutions" he calls them.

He tiptoes his fingers up to the end of the keyboard and finishes the tune like he's brushing breadcrumbs off a tablecloth. That done, he whirls a quarter turn on the stool, towers up and moves to his chair, puts his hand on the arm, turns his rear, and eases onto the cushion.

"Yeah, Cuz, when you soloin', don't be afraid to take some chances. Messin' up can teach you a whole lot, if you're listenin'. Just chomp on into them things. You got the music in you." By far, Fowler's loudest notes of the day.

Then: "Boy, you need a drink."

"What? Am I playing pitiful, man?"

"No, no, Cuz, it ain't all that bad. We played enough for today, that's all."

Ain't all that bad.

"Oh."

"Fix me another drink, too, will you, Cuz? You can use this glass here for mine." He holds up the highball glass with its two almost melted ice cubes in the bottom. Damp glass in one hand, horn in the other, having absorbed the mixed music of the three modes in Fowler's talk, I set the horn in its case. Leave the case open so I can dig the cool silver body of the Benge if Fowler and I are going to sit and schmooze, me not able to see his eyes.

On the kitchen counter, a fresh bottle of Jim Beam stands at the end of the line of glasses, minus the drink or two Fowler tapped from it. I toss the remains of his ice cubes into the sink, rinse his glass and get myself a glass from Corazon's line of sparkling clean ones. One of Fowler's ice trays doesn't have the divider in it, just a frosty jumble of cubes from the original dozen. Corazon probably took the divider out to make it easier for

Fowler to fix his own drinks. There it is, in the sink, cool grey enforcer of form. *Aluminium* the British say. She might come back over before I leave.

I drop a couple fresh ice cubes in each glass and pour the whiskey, Fowler's about two-thirds full, mine just under half, then raise my voice. "You want water with your whiskey, Merce?"

"Yeah, that'll be good."

"A little water it is."

For my own drink, I take out the ginger ale and pour until it reaches the rim. Cool bubbles jump into my nostrils when I take a sip. I set Fowler's drink beside the cigarettes and ashtray on his table. He takes a long drag on his cigarette, fingers and palm covering the lower third of his face. Head of the syndicate look. His hand swings away from his face and there's his mouth with its curving corners, a motif one digs in Corazon's face. His hand lowers to the ashtray in time to shed a long ash. He exhales a narrow sheet of smoke. "Thanks, Cuz," he says.

I would say "Okay, Boss," but I don't want to disturb the groove we're in. My knees touch the coffee table when I sit on the sofa. I say, "You're welcome."

Fowler picks up the drink with his cigarette hand, fire and firewater at his lips. Smoke curls around his head. He sticks the forefinger of his free hand into the drink and stirs the ice cubes. Takes the finger out and sticks it in his mouth. Don't want to waste no whiskey. He rubs his finger along the front of his shirt and takes another sip. "Yeah, thank you," he says. "It's good, Cuz."

As much as I love heat, my throat welcomes the cold bubbles and sweetness of the ginger ale with whiskey after an hour of playing. "Good. I aim to please."

Fowler rocks back, and a yawn stretches his words. "Listen at you," he says. "You doin' all right."

Could be an echo of Weems's report. Fowler's merry mode. He puts the glass to his mouth and floods the edge of his mustache again. Whiskey drains until he brings the glass down.

I set my glass beside the case and lift out my trumpet, open the spit valve and shake the horn. Nothing much. I take out the six-inch square of chamois skin Swink left in the case and rub the silvery tubing.

"You think you got the idea of them substitutions, Cuz?"

"Yeah."

"And just remember, if you got a third and a seventh, you got two other notes you can use to make a dominant. You got that?"

The chamois slides smooth as French against the curving silver of my trumpet. We should say *shahm-wah*. "Yeah, I think so. Just need to practice."

"That's right. Practice."

"Yeah, practice." *Chamois Davis Junior*. Some bad jive.

Fowler holds his glass up and jerks it around in the air when he speaks. "Look here, Cuz, you goin' to have to come down to my gig and sit in one of these nights."

Whoa. The cat is actually inviting me onto the stand with him.

Like I said, Fowler's gig is basically rhythm and blues at the Frying Pan, not exactly what I'm interested in. But still, he thinks I'm ready to be up there with him. "What will I play, Merce?"

"Play what I tell you to play. I know you been goin' over to that other place." "That Other Place," only integrated place in town, where jazz happens, where Nikki and I got in the groove.

Fowler isn't slurring his words but he's pretty well lubed. In around the valves I rub the chamois. I say, "You mean The Box?"

"I mean the goddamn Box. College boy and all that, I hope you don't think you too goddamn good to come over and play a little gut bucket sometime."

"Oh no, Merce. Nothing like that."

He rumbles right over my protestation. "I played all that shit you cats at The Box be trying to play."

Be trying to play.

"I know, man."

"You come on over next weekend. All you got to do is be ready to play some blues in a few keys. I know you can do that. And people goin' to like that sound you got."

I take a large swallow of whiskey. "Yeah, I can do that."

That sound. Part of my voice, that I'm trying to get into the horn, something full and dark with some Heraclitean fire at the bottom of it, something smoldering and red. Something between Clifford Brown and soot and me and the night. Solid, hoarse, rough and juicy. Maybe should try a flugelhorn, get a contralto sound. "Ever try a flugelhorn, Merce?"

Fowler turns up his glass and empties it, sucks one of the icecubes into his mouth and pops it back into the glass. "Yeah. Why?"

"Oh, I was just wondering. You like the sound?"

"Course I do. It's the only thing, sometime. But then sometime I hear a whole lotta echo around the tone, like you blowin' inside a barrel or somethin'."

Yes, I can hear the spongy dark echo Fowler means, but that's what I want sometimes. Be down in a lower, darker place. Notes from underground.

"Flugelhorn is all right," he says, "but it ain't got the fire a trumpet has got." Fowler's words land so heavy they damn near blow the flugelhorn out of my head. "How about another drink, Cuz?"

"Sure. Let me get it for you."

"You through with yours?"

Mine is half gone and starting to get watery. Inside of my head starts to get watery too, trying to imagine sitting in on Fowler's gig. Corazon hasn't shown up. "Almost through," I say.

Fowler rolls his shoulders back, moves his head left, then right, working his neck muscles. "Go ahead and finish your drink. I can wait. Gettin' hot around here, ain't it?"

"Yeah it is, but I sort of like it. I'll get your drink. I'm drinking pretty slow."

I'm in the kitchen getting drinks. Fowler out there singing:

> *Here's my definition of a cigarette, dear brother.*
> *It's a fire on one end and a fool on t'other.*
> *O, cigareets and whiskey...*

Whoa. Through the heat waves outside the window, at the fence, Daddy, in his wide-brimmed cavalry hat, standing beside the horse, studying me and shaking his head, giving me a bad grade. He steps away from the fence and walks toward town, shaking his head, leading his horse by the reins.

My glass needs more whiskey. I fill it and take a swallow. I refill and taste. The booze burns my throat just right. Two fresh icecubes and more whiskey perk up Fowler's glass. Might as well be smoking, too, the way the room has thickened up with his puffing.

Cigareets and whiskey and wine and wild women

Fowler's ashtray, starting to get full, has migrated to the spot where I want to set his drink, so I put the glass in his hand. "Here's your drink, Merce."

"Thanks, Cuz."

"Hey, Merce, I didn't know you was one of them country music cats."

Fowler's head goes side to side once with a big snicker. "It ain't country when I sing it, boy. It's all music, like I'm tellin' you. You bring your ass down to the Fryin' Pan next weekend. Hear?

"Okay, Merce."

"Look, boy, I ain't jivin'."

"I didn't think you were jiving, Merce."

"What I'm tryin' to tell you is, you're there."

"There?"

"That's what I said, Cuz. You ready to get out and do somethin'. Else I wouldn't want your ass up on the stand with me. You just keep practicin', though, and don't think you know it all because you don't know shit."

First time, even if he's drunk, we're drunk. I'm *there. Bad little sombitch* Weems said Fowler said. It's a quiet graduation. Bad as I wannabe. Should have me some robes here.

"Thanks, Merce, I owe you a lot."

"Don't owe me nothin'—you owe music a lot. So you bring your ass down to the goddamn Fryin' Pan and play some music."

At Alligator Park, I'm body-heavy to sinking down and melting on the sidewalk, trumpet case weighty at the end of my arm, but Fowler said, *"You're there."* Got my free arm around the streetlamp post right where I stood when Stacy looked back at me that time and patted herself over the heart and got on the bus. Last time I saw her. Arm ain't so free. I free it and give my heart three light pats. Bus, busted hearts. Dusted soot. She's gone.

Bus needs to get here. The hot sidewalk steams my feet through my shoes. Century plants on the other side of the park twist upward into green flames. Buildings over there wavery. Diesel fumes wash in around the bus when it stops, and I hold my breath till I'm on and dropping coins in the fare box. Three big Negroes my age move to the back and spread out on the rear seat. Some big-ass triplets. Don't know them but they feel familiar, GIs. Tough-looking brothers, lolling in sunglasses. Never been able to get used to sunglasses. I ooze back to a window seat opposite the rear door and slide in with my trumpet beside me. Heat from the sidewalk still radiates out of my soles. Somebody might write, "Birdsong has a radiant soul." Not weighed down with a whole lot of goods. Got rid of property. In toverty and patters he...losing moi moind.

My eyelids are too heavy to open. Able was I ere I elbowed Fowler's booze. Try to roll the git up lids.

"Bolden Heights."

Busdriver's voice. Blasted me awake, but where the hell am I. Breathing all this hot air. *The River Styx must be nearby.*

"Bolden Heights." Next stop for the 72nd Army Band. I move my hand to the seat next to me.

What the fuck? I look on the floor. Under the seat. No horn. My Benge is gone. I jump up and face the back seat. Empty. I grab onto seats, pull my way to the front of the bus. "Excuse me, driver, did you see those guys who were sitting on the back seat leave the bus?"

The grey-haired driver keeps his eyes on the road. "Yeah, I saw 'em," he says.

"Were they carrying anything?"

His eyes hold to the road, statue driving the bus. "I never noticed."

The pole behind the driver's seat is hard and slippery in my grip. I bang my head against the stainless steel. "Shit."

"This your stop coming up here?" The driver knows a chump-ass GI when he sees one.

Everything inside my hull sinks into a sick pile, heart, lungs, stomach, liver, pulled down, yanking on my windpipe. All I can do is one little croak, "Yeh," and get off the bus.

I kick the ground and yell, "Fuck," into the weeds that don't care and the air that sucks up my cry like nothing, go to my knees and gouge the ground with my fingers, fit to eat dust.

Morning is long after losing the Benge, typing Swink AWOL on the morning report again, listening to the First Sergeant crack corn, sitting through another lame rehearsal. After work, I duck out on Gilson and Turner, can't think about going to the mess hall. Can't think about practicing. Only thing I can think of doing is to go to Fowler's house. Sit on his front step if he isn't in.

I get to Fowler's gate, and here comes Corazon out the door. Eyes on me, she stops. I say, "Hi, Cory."

She's close enough I feel body heat. "Hello, Joe."

My eyes go to the ground, study her feet, painted toenails. Fowler can't see her red toenails. It's so sad.

"What's the matter, Joe?"

"I've got to see Merce."

She studies me until I look up at her, and then raises her arm toward the house. "He's in the living room."

Fowler is in his armchair, smoking, listening to *LeGrand Jazz* that I loaned him, a glass of ice water on his table that Corazon must have put there. "You back mighty soon, Cuz."

"Yes. Sorry to interrupt your listening, Merce."

"Ain't no big thing," he says. "Here, let me cut this music off." His fingers find the switch and he shuts off the hi-fi.

I say, "You know what happened yesterday after I was over here?"

Fowler puckers, deliberate, as if he might be trying to guess, and takes a drag that burns the Viceroy down close to the filter. "No, Cuz. What?"

"Somebody stole my horn."

He mashes out the cigarette. "That new horn?"

"Yes."

"Goddamn, Cuz. Out to the barracks?"

"No. it was on the bus."

"On the bus?"

"Yes, on the bus. Three fucking guys from Showalter, I'm sure it was."

Fowler puts his hands on his knees, bunches forward. "What happened, Cuz, they take it away from you?"

"No." Too goddamn much booze at your house, I could have said, but that was lame. Poor stewardship, I could have said. I could have said weakness. Could have said it resulted from being a natural-born fool. "Man, I was tired when I left here yesterday and I fell asleep on the bus."

Fowler's big face and dark glasses point toward me as if he can see. "And you woke up and your axe was gone."

"Yeah, and there were these three cats in sunglasses that got on the bus with me downtown. And they were gone when I woke up and so was my trumpet." Now it hits me how intoxicated I had been by Fowler's imprimatur and his booze, to not register the size of the suspects and that they could have been really dangerous, could have been some of Washington's and Polk's people.

"Of course they was gone," Fowler says.

"And I'm telling you I am one sick army private."

"Imagine so, Cuz. That was a real nice instrument."

I pound myself in the chest with my fist. "I feel like jumping off a goddamn bridge or something, Merce."

"Hold up, Cuz. Ain't no need to get radical."

My throat is sore, tight and dry. Swink might not get excited about it, I imagine, but I'd look like some new kind of a fool, losing a Benge trumpet on a bus in broad daylight. And then some possible mess with the Heavy Brothers that I was just starting to feel free of. I get up and walk to the kitchen door and back to the sofa and back to the kitchen door again.

"Be cool, Cuz," Fowler says.

"Be cool?"

"Yeah, be cool. What did these jokers look like? Splibs? Mexicans? White? What they look like?"

"Colored, man, looked like cats from the post."

Fowler turns up his glass of ice water. Colorless liquid flooding around his mustache is a surprising sight. I say, "Man, I could use a drink of water."

"Get yourself one."

In the kitchen I throw two ice cubes in a glass and fill it with water. I drink half of it and fill the glass again and go back in the front room. Fowler is sitting up straight, hands on his thighs. One hand moves over the chair arm to the table and finds his cigarettes. He fishes out one and lights it, blows out some smoke. "Lookee here," he says. "Tell you what you do."

"Do?"

"Yeah. You know them pawn shops and secondhand stores down towards the bridge?"

"Yes."

"Well, you go down there and scout them places out. Take a good look in all of them."

Damn. Fowler. An idea. Something to do.

"If you happen to see your axe, don't get all excited and start askin' questions," he says. "The joker that got it is dealin' in stolen property and he ain't goin' to be no nice person. You just browsin' around. Understand?"

"Yeah, man, I understand. Don't raise suspicions."

"Right, that's what I'm talkin' about—if you see it, call me right away or come by. We'll talk about it some more."

"Man, I'm ready to go right now."

"You best be, Cuz. That horn could be on sale right now."

The first pawnshop I come to looks like the biggest one on the street, cleanest one too. In the window, a shiny stainless steel toaster, rifles, hunting knives, cameras, a wedding veil. No musical instruments. A sign stencilled in block letters on a piece of cardboard says, "We buy gold."

The two baldheaded white men behind the glass counter and show-case pin on me the minute they hear the bell ring from my opening the door. Short men, cueball heads wearing specs, the cats look like brothers. The one with the thicker glasses studies my empty hands and probes between his incisors with a toothpick. "Looking for anything in particular, boy?"

The other one stands with his belly against the counter, hands flat on the glass top, looking straight ahead, studying something in the air nobody but he can see. These cats have been practicing their game for a long time.

"Sort of thinking about a trumpet," I say.

The one with the thicker specs, without turning, points a thumb over his shoulder to a couple tinny trumpets and a cornet hanging on the wall. I squint at the nowhere horns, but we're triple hip behind our faces that I'm not buying anything. "Not quite what I had in mind."

The second place I go into, same thing, and it's five o'clock and I can't do any more looking until tomorrow. Tomorrow, after working in the orderly room, after rehearsal, and after a review the 72nd has to play.

Downtown, walking around, shops closed, time is the bundle of jive I've got to get through before I can start looking for the Benge again. Bullshit in the barracks. Mess hall in the morning. The morning report. Band rehearsal and the gig. At the YMCA I call Nikki on the pay phone and tell her I'm downtown, walking around. "You want to stop by, don't you," she says.

"Yes, I guess so."

"Come on by, baby."

So I walk up to Alligator Park and catch the bus to her place. Nikki meets me at the door, gets the feel of me with her hug. "What's wrong, baby?"

I sit on her piano bench, her old upright behind me, she on the edge of the sofa in front of me. "I really have messed up, Nikki."

"Messed up?"

"Yes."

"Tell me about it."

Perspiration wets my forehead, but I give her a quick rundown.

"Let me get this straight," she says. "You were riding the bus in the middle of the day and you fell asleep and somebody took your highly prized horn?"

"Yes."

"What in the hell were you doing falling asleep, baby?"

Without a hanky, I swipe my brow with the back of my hand and study the floor. She shakes a cigarette from the pack on the coffee table. "Falling asleep on the bus in the middle of the day in El Paso, Texas, while carrying something valuable," she says. "Mmm, mmmh."

"Well, I was over at Merce Fowler's house, and I had a few drinks before I left."

Nikki stands up, the cigarette and her lighter poised apart. "So you were drunk."

"Well, I don't know."

"Joe, you don't have a problem with alcohol, do you?"

"Me? No. I don't drink that much. You know that."

She lights the cigarette, takes a long drag, and blows out some north wind. "Listen, sweetheart, I don't know anything but what I see."

Over me with her arms crossed, lips tight and exaggerated, she looks like she wouldn't need an excuse to crack me over the head. "I don't want to be talking about your people or nothing, baby," she says. "He's a great musician. But you keep hanging around that cat and try to keep up with him drinking, you're going to be losing more than a horn."

She says that and steps away from me, around the coffee table, into the kitchen, taking sympathy and warmth with her, leaving me to remember I do drink weekly with Merce Fowler and he's way bigger than I am. And then some with the boys. Nikki starts a clash of private percussion in the kitchen, cupboard doors, dishes, pans, knives and forks. I move over to her old upright and fiddle with some scales, both hands. My left hand is getting used to shell voicings. I play the melody of "I'm Old-Fashioned" with my right hand and comp like Fowler showed me with my left. Nikki's voice rides the scent of coffee from the kitchen. "Play that again."

She sings along this time. The pulse of her sound, even from the kitchen, touches me, and I stay as careful as I can be with my primitive accompaniment. Only a few bars, but my head lightens. Nikki says, "We should do that one again sometime."

"As long as I don't have to play the piano."

"How many sugars do you want in your coffee?"

She's giving me coffee. "Just stick your finger in it, Nikki."

"Hey, baby, I don't put my fingers where I'm going to get burned," she says. "No, no, not no mo'."

Whoa. Like you want to see the body that said that, I get up from the piano and peek in the kitchen. Nikki is at the table, all that rhythm inside her, pouring coffee into two mugs. I walk up beside her. "Two sugars, thank you."

"So what about your horn," she says.

We stand at the kitchen table, side by side, arms touching, drinking coffee, and I tell her what Fowler advised me to do. She lays her hand on my cheek, pats, a pat firm enough the woman could be cuffing me on the sly, but then applies her moist lips to the cuff site.

"Good luck, baby," she says.

2)

The stolen trumpet cramps my fingers when I type in "Pfc E3 Swink, Merlin, AWOL." AWOL to LA, to SD (smoke dope) and SA (screw around), come back and claim to be queer, looking to get kicked out of the US Army, which I don't write in for the fifteenth day. Could write that in and maybe get some interesting results for myself.

But no, I ain't that far gone yet.

***

The Benge isn't sitting in the window. It rests in its case on a ledge back of a grimy counter. Somebody has probably been inspecting it. So the third time is charmed at this junk store with some of everything piled to the ceiling. All kinds of old chairs and tables and lamps. A big wooden Spartan radio, dusty and mute, like the one Daddy bought before the war that my brother and I were lying in front of when a voice said, "Japanese warplanes have attacked Pearl Harbor." Junk hangs from the ceiling too, stuffed birds, chairs, lampshades, a silver-painted balsawood model of a B-29.

A wiry old white cat, wearing dirty glasses, maybe in his sixties, prowls behind the counter, touching things, moving things in the display case. Wristwatches, a couple gold pocket watches, two or three pistols. The greasy felt hat on his head has a brim wavy as a potato chip. Looks like he lives in the musty place and never washes the grime out of the wrinkles in his mug. "Looking for something particular," he says.

"Sort of," I say. "I just moved into a new place and I need a few things."

The man doesn't get around too fast, but I make out sharp ballbearing eyes behind his flimsy rimless spectacles. So much dust on the lenses, could he see through them. I make no move toward the Benge, study the pile of old chairs. His feelers are out toward me whether he can see through his dirty glasses or not. Keeping me in sight, he reaches back and closes the trumpet case and sets it on the floor below the cash register.

I push on the back of an oak library chair and find it solid, a good chair to sit in and read or sit in and practice. "How much for this library chair?"

The old man stretches his chin up and looks down through his dusty glasses. A high nasal drawl comes out of him. "That one there is twelve dollars."

"Got some cheaper ones there." He points a grimy finger in the direction of the heap of chairs.

"Yeah, but I don't see anything that appeals to me."

"Appeals to you? Hah. You got to go with what appeals to your money, boy."

Old cat, standing there in his pitiful-ass potato chip brim all crusty, specs look like they got cardboard lenses, teeth looking like stumps after a forest fire, and I'm thinking Man how much would you charge to haunt a fucking house, and the motherfucker has my horn, the horn Swink gave me, down there on the floor by his fucking feet, a goddamn rogue right out of Dickens, squeaking like he could give me some advice. What appeals to my money, boy—wish I *would* buy some of this beat-up shit.

My reading and my upbringing restrain me.

My eyes careen half out of focus around the shop and back to the chairs jammed and stacked in the middle of the floor. I take in a deep breath, way into my diaphragm, but keep it quiet. Dirty Man lifts his arm to scratch his opposite shoulder blade, and I see something behind him that gives me another nice long breath: an old tin lunch pail, shape of a barn, smudged dark red paint half gone, and lying beside it on waxed paper, part of a sandwich. Dirty Man brings his lunch to work. Not much chance somebody delivers it to him every day. He must not live in the shop. "Well," I say, "looks like I'm out of the market here."

"Suit yourself, boy."

God damn right, suit myself. Checking out the cameras, guns, and jewelry under the thick scratched glass, where the thieves probably laid my horn for Dirty Man's inspection, I count steps along the showcase to the door. "Do you buy gold?" I ask.

He opens his snaggle-toothed mouth in what I guess is supposed to be a grin and says, "I buy anything."

Yeah, like stolen horns. And from anybody. I dig that his look and words are an overture. I open the door and set the bell ringing its three rings, and raise my voice, "Then you've got to let me sell you a bridge sometime."

The old man's dusty lenses jerk my way, and his mouth gaps open like an outrageous kabuki face after a bop on the head. Before he gets anything out of that twisted gap, I'm out of there.

At the corner, I cross the street and start running, broken field, weaving in and out of people who haven't lost their horns. Ought to run all the way to Fowler's house, but by the time I got there I'd be dead. The bus to Missouri Street and I hit Alligator Park at the same time, and I run right onto it.

Bust through Fowler's gate and bang on the screen door which is locked. He's in there. I call him. "Merce."

Nothing. In there sleeping. Sleeping it off, probably. Nikki ain't lying. I go around to the side of the house, between the fence and the cactus and century plants and yuccas, and pick my way to the bedroom window, trying not to mash any plants. The window's got a screen on it, and an old conical trumpet mute props it up. The shade is down. I slap a couple loud eighth notes on the window frame. "Merce!"

This time there's a big grunty animal sound from the bottom of a river or a dream. "Whawnh."

"Merce, it's me, Joe. Get up. I found it."

"Found what?"

Man, oh man. "My horn, Merce, my horn."

"You got it?"

"No, man, but I know where it is. You said come tell you. Let me in the house." Talking to the pulled-down shade through the window I'm the blind one, not Merce. In there coughing, getting his feet into his huaraches, probably scratching his head and his belly and feeling around for his blind man glasses.

His voice comes through the window. "Go on round to the front. Be out in a few minutes."

Backing off from Fowler's window without mashing any plants or getting scratched takes balance and twistability, and I do it. At the front door, I hear Fowler sandpaper out of his bedroom and go into the bathroom. He's in the bathroom with the door open, pissing like Yosemite Falls, and then there's the toilet flush and the faucet running.

Shake the screen again, on a chance. It's locked. Here he comes, one hand out in front of him, a step at a time in his huaraches. *Lento.* I put my face up against the screen. He's not staggering, but his face is puffy. "Hey, Merce."

His hand slaps the door jamb and he unlocks the screen, says, "'ey, *Jose.*"

He turns his back and for a moment it's like I'm behind a hill blocking my view of the room. "You okay, Merce?"

"Hell yes, I'm okay. What you expect?" he says. "But I was sleepin' deep and dreamin' some sombitch was beatin' on my window, callin' me, tryin' to get me to look at somethin' I couldn't see."

"That was no dream. That was me, man, banging on your window. Me. I located the horn."

Fowler swings his butt into the armchair and laughs his thick smoky laugh until he's on the verge of a coughing fit, and I see I've been suckered. He slaps his thigh. "I'm sorry, man," he says."You know how I am. You found it, huh?"

"Yeah. And you said let you know if I located it. Well, I located it."

Fowler rubs his chest inside his shirt and scoots himself more comfortable. "Good, good," he says.

Fist in front of his yawned-open mouth, he slides his other hand over the arm of the chair onto the table till his fingers contact his cigarette pack. I'm watching a slow motion movie short, "Post Nap Behavior of the American Jazz Performer, Mercer James Fowler," who shakes a smoke halfway out of the pack, pulls it the rest of the way out with his thumb and forefinger. He tamps the tobacco end of it on the table and raises the filter end to his mouth. The cigarette lighter disappears into his big fingers, but flame jumps into the end of his cigarette. He caps the flame and lets smoke drift out of his mouth. His meaty forearms fall outward across the sides of the easychair. "Now what did you say, Cuz?"

At the end of the sofa close to him, I keep my voice from coming out full crazy. "Merce, what it is is I found the horn. Where it is."

"Oh yeah? Yeah. Good. Where is it at?"

"Little funky place, couple blocks from the river, a block off El Paso Avenue."

Fowler brings his hand up, fingers across his lower face, cigarette between them. "Mmmmm." The low grating sound in his throat has some note in it but doesn't quite turn into a hum. "What we gonna do now?" he says.

"That's what I want to know."

Fowler moves his shoulders up toward his ears and shrugs them down and sits forward. "Lookee here, Cuz, this place got an alley in back of it, don't it?"

"I think so."

"What you mean, you think so? You got to know so now. Ain't got time to be fuckin' around thinkin'."

I open my mouth to say something, but Fowler's voice all woke up now flattens me. In his teaching groove all of a sudden, voice from the mountain. "Well, I know," he says. "Hell yes, them streets down there got alleys."

"Okay, man, okay."

Fowler sits back and gathers his elbows against his sides. "Just one cat in the store?"

"Yeah. Just one old guy, looks about sixty years old. White cat."

"Course. If you fuckin' with money around this town, you got to be white." He coughs, hawks up some phlegm, swallows it, asks, "Look like the cat is living in the store?"

"Didn't look like it. He brings his lunch to work."

"Probably got a back room."

"Oh yeah, there was a cubby hole in back. I remember I could see a safe, a big old black thing with gold writing on it. Sitting in there."

"Wasn't no dog, was they?"

"No."

He drags on his cigarette, points the two cigarette fingers at me. "Listen. You got to go back down there today."

"Yeah?"

"Yeah."

He swats the smoke in front of him. " Tell you what you do, Cuz. You walk through that alley and see what kind of back door he got. If he got a lock in the door, a padlock or what. It's a one-story place?"

"Right."

"Good. Then you watch the place, see how the cat closes it up and when he leaves."

"Yeah."

Fowler makes a short, snorty sound, taps ash into the ashtray. "You been to college," he says. "I know I don't have to tell a smart young cat like you not to make your ass too obvious down there."

"No."

"Lucky it's early in the week," he says. "Won't be a whole lot of traffic. Just hope he ain't sold the thing before we can lay hold to it."

Oh shit.

"What are we going to do?"

"Get the goddamn horn back, Cuz. What you think we goin' to do? It's your horn, ain't it?"

My horn. That Swink gave me. My head rattles.

"Now get on down there, and then come on back here," he says. "I hope you ain't got nothin' else to do tonight." He stops for a minute as if to blot up any reaction I might have. My lips don't move.

"Good," he says.

I cool it under the canvas awning that shades a fabric store window across the street from Dirty Man's place. Up against the store window and out of the way, I watch Dirty Man through the parade of border humanity passing in front of me. He wouldn't recognize me if he could see me in those thick glasses of his. He probably can't even see across the street. All that dust on them too. He's back on his elbows, against the ledge where I saw the Benge behind the counter. Lounges that way a long time in his funky old hat.

Closing time, he locks the front door from inside. He moves around, touching things, stops at the cash register. Don't see how the cat made any money, never saw anybody go in there. He's not leaving very fast. Terrible if I was wrong, he lives in the place, and somebody delivers him his lunch. Fowler never thought of that. The old guy has got to be tricky. There's a burst of light at the rear of the shop and then dark. I hold my ground, keep watching.

Nothing inside the store moves, so I walk to the end of the block. Quite a few five o'clock pedestrians. I don't hurry, stay mixed in with them. At the corner, I cross the street and walk toward the head of the alley.

Dirty Man crosses right in front of me, lunchbox under his arm, just as I'm about to turn into the alley, and goes on past, leaving me in his smelly wake of tobacco, sweat, onion, machine oil. He was so long coming out of the alley he could have been snooping in garbage cans. Damn. But he didn't notice me, didn't even see me with those glasses of his. People never notice me much anyway, white people, all my life, except at school, confusing me with some other Negro. Like the time I was waiting table at the country club and this old lawyer at the table looks up at me and busts out, "Hey, look at this boy. He looks just like that fellah uh, uh, Johnny Davis Junior."

Dirty Man didn't notice me. I go down the alley to the back of the shop. Nobody around. A quick look in my man's garbage can, I don't see any cans, bottles, cereal boxes, nothing in it says somebody lives in the place. Don't know what he uses for a bathroom, maybe goes nextdoor. A solid plywood panel covers the space where the backdoor once had a window. A combination lock holds the hasp shut, the kind we used in high school gym class to lock up our stuff.

Burglary. That's what Fowler has in mind. I put my problem in his lap, and he's got a solution all right. He's going to get somebody to steal it back, my horn.

Whoa.

It's me he's expecting to break into the place and steal it back. So fucking slow, I am.

Got to get it back. Won't even have a horn when I get out if I don't have the Benge.

I put my forehead against the screen and holler into the house. "Anybody home?"

Corazon's smooth strong chin, prow of a caravel, floats out of the kitchen above her dignified drill across the living room. Girl could look haughty if she worked on her technique. I keep my eyes away from her legs in the white shorts. Her chest rises from a deep breath, and she pops the hook out of the screw eye. Fowler's chair is empty when I look in the living room. "Hey, where's Merce?"

She says, "Aren't you even going to say hello?"

Before I can open my mouth, Merce's voice booms from the kitchen, "I'm in here, Cuz—let the boy alone, baby. You can go on home now. Come on in here, Joe."

Corazon swings her hips toward the voice. Lips pressed tight, windy breath in and out through her nose, she studies the floor, then my face. The deep shiny umber of her eyes is heavier than I am. I'm breathless. She says, "M.J. said you were coming and I fixed you something to eat."

And then gone.

Too fucking soft, me. Or losing my mind. She said those words and everything in the world collapses to a table where a girl fixes food for me to eat. And me, grateful as a stray, hungry, homeless dog, the breath I take has a shudder in it. Shit just sneaks up on me.

"Man, you want some this food you better get in here pretty soon." Fowler is not jiving. He's got a taco up to his mouth that will be gone in a couple bites. A half-gone glass of beer touches the edge of his plate.

"Sit down, Cuz." Beside him on the floor is a bulky green toolbox.

"What's going on, Merce?"

"Nothin' shakin' but the leaves. What you got to say, Cuz?" Fowler's eating stirs up a toasted corn and bean smell that makes my stomach growl. Red and green of tomato slices and shreds of lettuce bulge out of the taco shells. I sit down and put one on my plate.

"Well, I took a good look at the place and watched the old guy leave," I tell him. "He's not living in the store."

"Yeah?"

"Yeah, looks for sure like he brings his lunch to work. I checked his garbage can and I watched him leave with his lunchbox. And the back door has a combination lock on it."

Fowler raises his chewing face. "In the door?"

"No, the hanging kind, you know, that holds a hasp shut."

"That all?"

"Might be a lock in the door too. Plain old house door with a key-hole. Place is actually an old house."

Fowler takes a swig from his beer, runs his tongue along in front of his bottom teeth, puffing out his lower lip. "Unh huh," he says.

He reaches for another taco, and I take the last. He slides his foot over and kicks the toolbox. "You see this," he says.

"Yeah."

"Open it up."

I unsnap the two catches on the lid and open it. It has two levels, a tray on top with several screwdrivers of different sizes and a pair of heavy metal cutters, a set of allen wrenches, and a lot of pieces of wire and metal, twisted, bent, or fabricated so you figure they're some kind of tools, homemade. "Man, oh man."

"Yeah, Cuz," Fowler says. "You got the idea?"

"Oh I don't know, man."

"What? You scared?"

"Well, no, man, but..."

Fowler whacks the table with the base of his beer glass. "Negro, you think the Mexicans and the Indians wouldn't take back they land if they had the firepower? I guarantee you, they would."

"No. Yeah. Man, you're right." Now if I had a posse of Heavy Brothers I might just bust in there and take my horn back.

"Well, if you're scared," he says, "maybe I understand." He lifts his glass and takes a slow sip, sets it down.

"Man, I'm not scared."

Fowler acts as if he didn't hear me, weight of his elbows and forearms against the wood, blind man glasses swinging side to side. "What you could do, I suppose, is go in there with some of your boys and distract the cat and run out with it."

An idea with some flash at first, maybe not as ugly as my idea, but my main boy is missing from the picture with his AWOL self. With Swink and Gilson, for starters, I could imagine it. Maybe get Muccigrosso. Maybe Cedric. Too many people, hard to get together. Too easy to fuck up. "Man, I said I wasn't scared. Tell me what you want to do."

"No. You tell me what you want to do. It ain't my horn. We could cut that combination lock off or probably find the combination. And that one in the door ain't nothin'—we can use a skeleton key on that."

"Oh, man, I don't know. What I would like to do is to get in and out without leaving any signs."

"You ever pick a lock before?"

"I've tried."

"Well, you don't exactly have to pick one now since we ain't got no padlock on that door." He reaches for the toolbox. "Lift up that tray for me."

I lift the tray. He scoops around under a collection of locks and pulls out a ring of old-fashioned house keys, lead-colored, that all look pretty much the same. "One these sombitches will get that door lock."

The way he says it leaves me with no doubts.

"Now I got to show you how to open that other one," he says.

"I didn't know you were a burglar in your youth, Merce."

Fowler runs his hand across his cheek and mouth like wiping a smirk off his face. "Naw, Cuz. Didn't I tell you I went to trade school when I was young? Locksmithin' is what I took up."

Fowler could be jiving, but he did say he went to trade school in Chicago. I know how he is. His fingers find several combination locks he brings up and sets on the table between us. "Okay now. You see any-thing here looks like the lock on that door?"

One of the locks on the table is indeed the same brand of lock as the one on Dirty Man's back door. I put my finger on it and push it across the table against Fowler's hand. He rubs his fingers over it. "You say that door got a lock like this on it?"

"Right. Like that one."

Fowler pushes the lock back to me. "Here. Let me hip you how you open one these things." He goes to lecturing and demonstrating how to open an unfamiliar combination lock. "This one here is simple," he says. By holding the shackle just right and listening, he could manipu-late the dial and find the numbers, but I have to be his eyes. So he finds numbers, and I work the combinations. "Some these things got they own personalities," he says, "but good chance what I'm showin' you will work because that ain't no heavy duty lock. Course if it was me, I'd just take my cutters and cut the sombitch off."

I ape Fowler's movements with the shackle and dial, and his listen-ing for sounds inside the lock, over and over, until I start to get hun-gry again. Hunger is beginning to twist my attitude by the time I get the lock open.

Fowler's head jerks toward the opening click as if he's connected to the sound. "You got it, Cuz."

Hot damn. Hunger gone, I slide off the bench and stand up, open lock hanging off my fingers, pump my knees a couple times. The empty, sunny yard outside the window looks like a grin. "Wow, Merce, this is really hip. Turn me loose, man."

Fowler pushes the rest of the locks across the table toward me. His hand goes in the box again and puts two more on the table. "Sit down, boy," he says. "You ain't through with nothin' yet. You got to practice. And I think you better take them cutters, case you can't open the combination. Don't want you runnin' back here wakin' my ass up at three in the mornin'."

***

All I need Gilson to do for this gig is patrol the end of the alley while I'm trying to get in the store and get my horn. At noon chow I ask

Freddy if we can use his car to go pick up Fowler's cutters and recon Dirty Man's place and if we can use it later for the job too. He's down with it. "One thing, though, man," he says, "when y'all come back to the club, you got to come up and play something."

Freddy holds the car keys up in front of me and pulls them back when I reach.

"Y'all gonna play?" he says.

"Yeah, man, if I get the horn."

"All right, then." He drops the keys in my palm. "Be looking for you."

The 72nd finishes its business for the day by four o'clock, and I drive downtown with Gilson to show him the alley, and where we want to park the car. Like Fowler told me, I also have Gilson go in the store and try to spot the Benge. On the floor back of the counter where I last saw it, perhaps, assuming it's still in the place and not, for God's sake, sold. Cool that Gilson is white. Another colored cat coming in there after my visit, just looking around, Dirty Man might figure he's being cased.

Gilson's pasty face looks blank coming out of the shop toward the car. I stretch across the front seat and open the door for him. He gets in, eyes straight ahead, out the windshield. "It's in there," he says. *In theah*, sweet New Bedford accent.

"Oh man, thank you, Jesus. Give me five, Jerry."

Gilson drives. We don't say anything. Just before midnight, I'm sitting on Turner's plastic seatcovers fighting down visions of myself running like hell with the Benge under my arm, alarms going off behind me, jumping into a waiting car, smashing into a roadblock, jumping out and taking off down an alley, vaulting into a garbage box, hiding under garbage. Shoot, man, I'm not going to fuck around with nobody's combination, I'm going to use Fowler's cutters on that lock. No, I'm not.

We drive south of Alligator Park and pull up a block from the mouth of the alley. I've got Fowler's ring of skeleton keys, a penlight, and my bare hands.

Gilson hugs the steering wheel with his forearms and looks over at me. My dark face must appear sooty to him because I can barely make out his pasty features. "You ready?" he says.

"Yeah. Bring the cutters."

We get out on the sidewalk. The keys tinkle against each other when I slip the ring off my arm and try to push it in my pocket. Gilson watches me, holding the cutters against his hip. I contemplate his pockets, say, "You got a bigger pocket?"

"Don't think so," he says. The ring goes about a third of the way in his back pocket and slips out when he moves. He keeps a hand on it so it doesn't hit the ground.

The knock of a car engine sounds in a close-by street, getting closer, banging on the warm night and my ears. Headlights. Jesus Christ!—an old Chevy that could be green with black fenders comes around the corner, only the driver in it, hat pulled low. It disappears past us.

"Hey, man, we've got to move," I say. "Give me your cap and those keys."

Gilson hands me the ring and rests his hand on his cap.

"The cap, man," I say.

He takes off the cap and gives it to me. I set the ring on my head with the keys spread out around it. "Hey, come crown my brow with keys of myrtle. I know the tortoise is a turtle."

Gilson's hand claps down on my shoulder. "Keep a lid on it, Schoolmaster."

Cool metal touches my scalp in places, makes it itch. "Never done anything quite like this."

"Really?"

"Never. Have you?"

"Yeah," he says. Once in high school."

Gilson, Jerry, the coolest, best-behaved soldier I know. "No shit? I'm consorting with a criminal."

"Juvenile delinquent. The record has been expunged."

We're at the alley, which is dark except for light that falls into it from the streets at either end. Nobody in sight. We're stepping light in our tennis shoes. It's dark and one lane, old concrete, no light on in any of the places, but we can read the backs of the buildings. Careful not to kick anything. We come to the rear of Dirty Man's shop, halt, and let darkness and time pool around us. Nothing happening to the left, up the alley, nothing to the right, down the alley, so we tiptoe the last few steps to Dirty Man's door.

We stand shoulder to shoulder to hold in the shine from the penlight that Gilson holds on the lock, and I start searching for the combination. My fingers aren't shaking. They do Fowler's drills with no luck the first couple times, and my stomach starts to get butterflies and sweat pops out at my hairline. Gilson moves in with Fowler's heavy cutters and with one forceful cut severs the shackle. I slip the lock loose and put it in my pocket. Gilson steps back to the alley and looks up and down. I dislodge my wreath of skeleton keys from under Gilson's cap and stick one in the keyhole. Doesn't work. The night tenses up again when the first half-dozen keys don't work. But the seventh one does, and the door opens with only a small squeak. I take off Gilson's cap, put the keys in it and wave him over to me.

"What?" he says.

"Here." He takes the cap and keys. "Thanks, Jerry. Give me the light. See you in a few minutes." He hands me the penlight, puts the ring of keys under his cap, and steps off, carrying the cutters, to cover the end of the alley.

The cubbyhole back of the shop is crowded with the safe and all kinds of musty junk I can't see in the dark. I get down on my hands and knees and crawl to the front.

Headlights from a car oozing past throw too much light into Dirty Man's shop, and I hit the dust again. Weak, pissy smell of mouse turds in my nose next to the floor. Back up on my hands and knees, my hands get further education in grit and splintery wood, and probably mouse turds too. I breathe way in and let it all the way out. Night and silence and darkness come down on the place again, and I start moving my hands and knees along the floor.

The first instrument case I run my hand over is an alto sax, then a clarinet case. Two trumpet cases, both about the same size. My hand is on the right one, I think, and I pull it under me. I take out the penlight to be sure. Yes, the right case.

I hug it to my chest and hustle out past Dirty Man's cubbyhole back-room into fresh night air. The door closes with a woody squeak, and I feel for the metal of the hasp and bring it over the hook without any clashing. I take the lock out of my pocket and slip the severed shackle through the hook. Everything back in place. Everything like it was except Gilson's got the skeleton keys, and I can't lock the door lock. Shit. Got me an imperfect non-crime. Best laid plans of mice and men, yeah. But I've got the Benge.

I step out into the middle of the alley with my trumpet at my side. Just a cat walking home from a gig. Good old Gilson is down there at the end of the alley, smoking. Waves at me, like Get a move on, with his cigarette hand. But what's the hurry? Things couldn't be cooler if I were from Boston, lad.

Turner, on the bandstand, sees us when we walk in The Box, pins his eyes on the trumpet case in my hand. I wave to him and head for the john to knock dust off my clothes, wash up, and fondle the Benge. In there, I open the case.

When I see what's in the case I have to sit down on the floor, and I stay hammered there, chin into my chest, for I don't know how long. It's not my silvery Benge in the case, for God's sake. It's an old brassy Selmer like Tappendorf's. Switched cases. Some of Dirty Man's dirty dealing. Switched cases.

I'm still on the floor, trying to hold my head together when somebody bangs on the door. Gilson's voice. "What's going on, Schoolmaster—you coming out? Freddy wants us on the stand."

His words reach my ears but don't shake loose any motive to respond.

More knocking. "Joe, you're in there, aren't you?"

In theah. Strain in Gilson's voice. Concern.

"Yeah."

"Well, what in the hell is taking you so long? You got a problem?"

"Yeah." Words are still failing me and the spot under my butt has become comfortable. My clogged head weighs a ton.

"What is it, man? Why don't you open up?"

I don't say anything.

"Listen, Schoolmaster, people are going to be needing to use this toilet any time. In fact, I need to piss right now."

I pull myself up and unlock the door. Gilson pushes in wide-eyed at me. I point to the open trumpet case on the sink.

"Holy shit," he says. "That's not your horn."

"No."

"What are you going to do?"

Voice comes back. "I think I'll go jump in the fucking Rio Grande."

"No, seriously, man."

"Ask me after I get through having this nervous breakdown—I thought you had to piss."

"You're not going to have anybody's breakdown, Schoolmaster." He touches the horn. "It looks like a pretty good horn."

"Yeah, it's a good horn."

"Well, that's something."

"Yeah, but it's not the Benge. That Swink laid on me. It ain't mine." I shove him back from the sink and snap the trumpet case shut. "I'm taking this thing back over there where I got it, right now. Tell Freddy and Nikki I'm sick. Don't worry, I can walk over there."

"You're not going back in that place, are you?"

"No, man, I'm not that far gone. I'm going to set it at the backdoor."

"You coming back here? You want me to go with you?"

"No, man, thanks. Stay here and play."

"How are you going to get back to Bolden Heights?"

"Man, I need to walk. Maybe I'll walk back."

Out of the john, out the back door with a wave to Gilson, the false trumpet in my hand, weighing a ton. Outside, the sidewalk and street are empty. Then I see him, standing on the other side of the street, light around him in his dark suit, white shirt, tie. The Book in his right hand against his chest, ready to step up to the pulpit. Not looking my way. I start walking, he starts singing as he often did before he got into his message.

> *Paul and Silas went to jail,*
> *Had no one to pay their bail*

Pacing me, other side of the street, looking straight ahead,

"You inhale the opiate air in the empty room of self-love and think you found heaven.You found nothing but trouble. You found trouble and rumors of trouble. You stagger to your knees from the weight of the choices through which you arrived at the you of this moment. Oh yes you do.

"I'm here to tell you, saints, the way in is the way out. You got to step back from vanity, from the pride that you walked in with. You got to step back and back. Back to the sweet peace of humility and the hope of redemption."

I come to the head of the alley behind Dirty Man's shop, carrying the false horn. I should keep the case at least, take the horn out and keep the case which belongs to me, leave the horn at the back door. Daddy walks behind me now, carrying on:

"You got to get your mind right. You got to stand up for the Word. You got to walk in Jerusalem just like John. We have all got to face the music on That Great Gettin' up Day."

It is a pretty good horn, like Gilson said, and the thought of leaving it naked at Dirty Man's backdoor isn't right. It needs the case, and I set it against the door and head out of the alley. No Daddy behind me.

3)

The front door is open, and fresh coffee smell in the air says Corazon is on the premises. I get my face ready and tap on the screen. She appears.

"Is Merce up?"

"He just got up."

"Well, let me in, please."

"You could say 'Hello'."

"Oh, sorry, Corazon. Hello. *Buenas tardes.*"

She unlocks the screen and holds it open for me. Inside, I pass through a fruity whiff of her shampoo to the sofa and would flop down and stretch out if it wouldn't be so gauche.

"What's the matter, Joe?"

"The matter?"

"Yes, the matter."

Then: "You want a cup of coffee?"

"Cup of coffee?"

"That's what I said."

"Cup of coffee, sure. Thanks."

"Come on in the kitchen," she says.

I slide into the breakfast nook, cross my arms on the table and rest my head. Corazon pours a cup of coffee and brings it over. I don't raise my head. It would feel so good if she would lay her hand on my head or rub her hand across my back.

"You don't feel good," she says.

After a deep breath, I sit up and take a sip of the coffee. "Thank you for the coffee—no, I don't feel so good."

Water stops running in the bathroom. Fowler's huaraches slap along the floor till he crowds the door frame in his black glasses, inhaling the coffee-laden vapors.

"Hey, Merce," I say.

"A-a-ah, my man *Jose*. How you doin', Cuz?" With a touch from Corazon he fits himself in opposite me at the table.

"I've seen better days, Merce."

Corazon's eyes rest on me like warm towels before she sets a cup of coffee in front of Fowler. Coffee-colored eyes not blinking, she studies him.

Fowler says, "You didn't have no trouble with the job, did you?"

"Yeah, Merce, I did." I tell him what happened.

"Ain't that a bitch?" he says after I get through the story. "No tellin' where that horn is by now. Nobody with any sense would be showin' it around here."

"Yeah." The shock of that horn in the Benge case in the lavatory still takes me down. I rest my head on my forearms again.

Fowler finishes his coffee. "'ey, Cuz, wake up," he says. "Did you bring your other horn today?"

"My other horn?"

"Yeah. The Army give you a horn and you still got that one, ain't you?"

"Yes."

"Ain't nothin' wrong with it, is they?"

"No."

Corazon moves from the sink counter to Fowler's side and bends to kiss him on the forehead. "I'm going now, MJ," she says. "I'll be back at six."

She slides a warm palm across the back of my hand on her way out.

"Tell you what we gonna do," Fowler says. "You play my horn today." And that's what we do. His French Besson plays nicely, but it's not my mouthpiece and it's not the Benge. Fowler doesn't say another word about the Benge.

After we get through blowing, he says, "Look here, boy, I got somethin' for you, somethin' you ought to have. Cat come through here with it last week."

"Yeah?"

He pulls open the drawer in the end table beside his chair. "Yeah, Cuz. Look in here and see if they ain't a piece of paper with some writin' on it."

The piece of paper I take out of the drawer contains several typed, mimeographed lists of tunes in groups like "blues," "bebop," "standards." At the top of the page in capitals are the words "Top Forty."

I say, "It says 'Top Forty.'"

"That's what I'm talkin' about," Fowler says. "What you need to start doin' right now is learnin' all them songs on that piece of paper."

"Okay." He can't see me but maybe he can hear how weak my voice sounds.

Names of half the tunes on the sheet are familiar to me, although I couldn't stretch out on more than a couple of them right now. The titles of the bebop tunes and some of the blues have just lately been seeping into my awareness since I hooked up with Turner and Gilson. It's a bunch of heavy lifting.

Fowler's voice gets louder. "If you goin' to be gettin' out and playin', you need to know at the least them tunes on that piece of paper. Get you a fakebook and start workin' on them. Should know 'em in all keys. You understand what I'm sayin'?"

"Yeah, Merce, I do." The titles are like Fourth of July fireworks in some distance before me, and I feel the heat and pressure of Fowler's possession of all this music and more in his body and mind, kindling the air between us.

"You take somebody like Sonny Stitt," he says. "That cat knows every goddamn tune that was ever written."

"No shit?" This knowledge does not lift my spirits.

"Swear to God, Cuz. But you don't got to try to do that, you just got to be studyin' and learnin' tunes all the time."

I return Fowler's horn to the case and set it on the piano. "Thanks for letting me use your horn, Merce."

"Anytime, Cuz, you know that."

His words splash me with the blues. The cat is not interested in helping me mourn my loss. No Benge, but I've got Fowler's charge with this list that I fold to quarter size and slip into my pocket.

Turner

1)

"How you doin', brother? We ain't talked in a long time, have we?"

Caught. Up in here. Shouldn't have been here in the Copa drinking by myself, anyway, but my concentration has gotten ragged, reading or practicing the horn, and I have episodes of pinpricks and sweating. *The way in is the way out.* Haven't been able to really dig into the list of tunes Fowler gave me. Washington, standing over me and my drink, thick brown hand stuck out. I shake it and say, "I guess not."

Polk dips his head and grunts.

"We ain't got no hard feelings here, have we?" Washington says.

"To tell you the truth, man, I do have some feelings that aren't so comfortable."

His eyebrows shoot up. "About what, bro?"

"That kid from the band that you guys beat up the other week was the wrong guy. He was exactly the wrong guy." *Doing evil for evil,* Daddy would preach.

"I don't know what you talkin' about, man."

"Yeah, I'll bet."

Polk bodies up next to Washington, says, "Maybe the boy was keepin' him some bad company."

"Shut up, man," Washington tells him. Polk looks like he just received a backhand upside the head.

I say, "He's nothing like those other guys."

Washington studies the floor with his hands on his hips, shaking his head, then, "Man, what the fuck you talkin' about? They all paddies. What he doin' with them motherfuckers if he so different?"

His vehemence and reason flatten me, though it doesn't change my feelings about Dino. I see it, and my gut tells me of it, the sick, incurable distance between us. "I'm just saying you hurt the wrong guy," I tell him. "You hurt him bad."

Polk looks at Washington as if he'd like permission to slap the fool out of me.

"Okay, man, look," Washington says, "you never know when you gonna want our help. You help us, we help you."

Then: "You let me know when you want to show us to the right motherfucker. Hear?"

They don't offer me a ride.

***

I close the orderly room door and then ask Sergeant Howell, "Okay if I close the door a minute?"

"Go 'head, close it," he says. What's on your mind?"

"Can you get me in to see those CID guys, Sarge? I think I might have something that'll help them with the investigation."

Howell's brown eyes clamp a moment of evaluation on me. "Sure, Birdie, I'll work on that."

Later in the day, he tells me I have an appointment at the CID office the afternoon after tomorrow.

It's Washington that gave me the idea with his *Let me know when you want to show us...* I tell the CID people they can catch the perpetrators in the act by following a simple scheme I lay out for them. The Heavy Brothers have targeted Jarboe. Jarboe goes to a dance night at the USO on Thursdays. I'll lead the brothers to the scene and point out Jarboe for them. When the brothers jump Jarboe the CID can move in and make arrests. They tell me they'll think about it and get back to me.

In the rehearsal hall, buzzing into my mouthpiece, pissed off at the CID's slow take on my idea, I'm getting hotter and hotter at the idea of Washington's crew of vigilante bullies or anything like them, running loose. Intimidating people. Hurting people. Trying to lean on me. I take full breaths and blow quiet long tones.

Daddy stands in the corner in a listening attitude. I take the horn away from my lips. He holds up his hand, doesn't want to hear from me. "Don't forget that you are a soldier," he says, "part of an army that you lightly joined in your darkness. Understand now that any power you have in the interest of justice lies in the institution."

Whoa. Listen to Mr Daddy.

* * *

In Juarez, at the Copa, they have never failed to approach upon discovering me at the bar, drinking. They don't suspect, but I'm here to see them, letting nature take its course. They don't flank me this time. Washington takes the stool next to me, Polk to his side.

"How you doing this evenin', bro?" Washington says. He lights a cigarette.

I let the words out lazy but my radar is on. "I'm doing okay."

"Is that so?"

"Yeah. Everything is fairly cool." Some sketchy thing is happening behind our words.

Washington takes a drag, blows out smoke. "*Fairly* cool, huh," he says. "Things be *real* cool when you decide to cooperate."

"Cooperate?"

"Yeah. You know what I'm talkin' about. Serious business."

"Well, you cats sure fucked up some business the last time I noticed."

Polk is off his stool and behind me. "Nigger, I ought to kick your paddy-lovin' ass right here."

My elbows remain on the bar, my eyes watching him in the mirror. Washington discourages him with a heavy arm behind me. He says, "Sit down, fool. You know bro ain't all that wrong."

Polk smolders back to his perch. I take a long sip from my tequila and Pepsi under Washington's interested eyes.

"Okay, man, look," and I tell him the same thing I told the CID after they finally got back to me with their approval.

***

"He's the one in the middle," I say. Hiebert, Jarboe, and Helzer come onto the street half a block away. The street is a narrow one of low brick buildings housing nondescript businesses and the USO. Darker now just after sunset than on that first hot day in El Paso when I came looking for a Coke. *We don't serve colored.* I could run out there and kick that fucking door again. Hearing Daddy, the thought raises a laugh that I suppress. Pitiful-ass place. Really different business today. There should be a dozen MPs behind that door.

Not much foot traffic yet. I'm sitting between two Heavy Brothers in the backseat of the Chrysler, watching Jarboe, running his mouth between Hiebert and Helzer, headed toward the USO entrance at our end of the block. Washington, another heavyweight, and Polk are in the front seat, Washington under the wheel. Polk and the other cat up front slip black hoods over heads as do the guys on either side of me. My stomach begins to dance as the trio nears the entrance where Jarboe baptized me with that water and ice.

"Okay, go," Washington says.

The speed these big cats jump out with, they've had practice. Two of them snatch Jarboe, punch him hard in the gut and in the face and throw him to the ground while Polk and the other guy menace Hiebert, Helzer and a couple interested bystanders. The cats are kicking Jarboe with combat boots, overdoing it I'm thinking, when the MPs swarm out and start to mix it up with the brothers. Jarboe is sprawled underfoot, and I'm breathing hard. The MPs are all good-size, two of them Negroes. They've got nightsticks and .45s. The brothers dig the imbalance pretty fast and put up their hands.

One of the MPs points toward the Chrysler.

"What the fuck is this here?" Washington says. He guns the engine, pulls away from the curb, and presses the old boat down the street. Out the back window, before we lumber around a corner, I see MPs jump into a black Dodge that starts to follow us. Washington's eyes get big when he checks the rearview mirror. It's a pathetic getaway car, this old New Yorker with its worn-out fluid transmission. What makes him think he can run away from anything in this tub, only he knows. The cat would have been smart to surrender. I'm sweating, throat-stopped, and on the verge of praying to anything that might be out there. One pitiful fool. The music could end right here.

Dust and heat fill the air inside the car, and the smell of oil. Washington, squeezed around the wheel like a ball turret gunner, is speeding, swerving, and braking, throwing me all over the backseat. He lays on the horn and busts through an intersection where pedestrians jump for their lives. Jesus, there could be shooting. I lie across the seat and brace myself. These guys don't have any guns I've ever seen. No real firepower beyond their musclebound anger. Shooting isn't likely. Surely, the chasers know they'll catch up with this wreck. If Washington wasn't crazy, he'd stop and give himself up.

I close my eyes, try to calm myself with breathing. Daddy's voice: "Now you're soldiering."

Shaky as I am, his voice and his words about the power of the institution give me a little juice. "Hey, Washington," I say. "What's going on?"

It's a good minute of careening and bouncing before he shouts above the engine noise, "I hope you don't know nothin' about this, man, because if you do you are one dead nigger."

Cat is out of his mind. I don't say anything, stay flattened against the seat until I raise my head to see he's reached the main road west toward Las Cruces. He's giving the twelve-year-old Chrysler all it can take in this losing run, and I figure my chances for survival are better than his if the CID does its part. The black Dodge is staying with us, a few lengths back, in no hurry to close. The backseat has grown hotter. The engine sounds too loud and I smell oil. The way he's pushing this thing could have slung all the oil out. He's got to run out of gas, maybe soon. Could be some kind of footrace then. Let us have no identity mistakes, Lord. Washington squints way down with his mouth drawn up like an angry, mean kid, his anger huge, black and unrealistic. The existential wound I've felt in Washington's stunted humanity looks as lethal as Herb Vogel's depression. The cat is driving like a movie madman. For nothing. My stomach feels sick for both of us. And then I hear the explosion. Not a gunshot but the explosion of a tire. Washington's eyes pop wide and he fights the wheel like in an old-time movie but can't control the careening heap that shudders off the road and begins to roll.

I'm nowhere, weightless. Nothing here but awareness of nothing. Until Daddy's voice, singing:

Let us drink wine together on our knees

Somehow, I'm filling: Bah bah do bah-bop.

Let us drink wine together o-on our knees

Wee-ee do bah

When ah fall on mah knees

Sah bop'm dwee bop

Wid mah face to da risin' sun
Oh Lord have mercy o-o-on me

Slah doobie tah dwee

No sun, but there begins to be sky, bright, clear, and warm. No idea where it is, this powdery bed I'm waking on.

"Here's the other one over here, Sarge." Hands under my armpits, heisting me to glory from terra formerly cognito. Somebody moves my legs, and one of them hurts. My clothes are full of dust, dust all over me like I've been rolled in flour. Is this a stretcher I see before me, the handles toward my head? And it's true on the battlefield bandsmen become stretcher-bearers, but these aren't band members. Borne again! past swirling faces to an ambulance with a big red cross on the side. Inside the ambulance already, Washington's a big pile of dusty brown meat on a stretcher, asleep or unconscious. His chest quivers. Two medics check his eyeballs. In the ambulance after Daddy's stroke, I watched the medics do that, through which I could see what they were looking for, and it was a chilling thing. They slide me in beside what's left of Washington. Sla doobie tah dwee.

Washington did die in the ambulance. Skull fracture, crushed chest. Corpse in the ambulance beside me named Washington, like the name of my home soil named after the Father of Our Country who owned a slew of slaves who took his name. Some of bro's forebears could have originated on Cherry Tree George's farm...enough to mess up bro's mind. Messes up mine.

At some point in the roll of the Chrysler, I flew out the back door and ended up with abrasions, ground-in dirt, cuts and bruises, and a shattered kneecap. The CID concocted an auto accident story for me, told me I'd do well to keep my mouth shut about the operation, and, through Sergeant Howell, that the Heavy Brothers were no longer a presence at Fort Showalter.

It's true, in the mess hall at chow time, I'm aware of a few missing heavyweights.

Sitting in the near dark at my desk, crutches lying across it, blue light from the courtyard coming through the windows, I'm still sorting, trying to sort my way up to this moment. Whoa.

"Something you ought not to forget," he says.

He sits across from me, at home behind the first sergeant's desk in cavalry khakis. But we're the same rank now since I just got promoted to specialist 4th class, same as a corporal.

"Not forget what?"

"What you just went through—the saving power of the institution."

I hear *saving,* I brace myself—I ain't *saved,* I ain't gonna be *saved!* Truth is, though, Daddy is sounding a little different lately. I don't feel the church groove coming on. Never heard him use the word *institution* like that before.

"Saving power?" I say. "I just barely missed getting my ass killed."

"Relax, boy. You remain among the quick."

True, stark difference. Washington is not here. A threat to everybody turned back. My knee is injured and I lost the Benge, but I feel unfazed and I have my voice and some measure of justice got done because I used my voice. The biggest thing, I see now.

The CID probably told Jarboe no such shit would be happening around Showalter again. His usual shifty-eyed bopping around the area lets me know he has no idea of my part in his wounds and in his safety. I'm not sure he learned anything from the pounding he took. He talks up what happened to him like a victory for him and the Confederacy and the army.

Where Jarboe is concerned, my heart is far from pure.

"No, you soldiered but you ain't nobody's hero," Daddy says. "Maybe you learned a little something."

Nobody except the first sergeant and the CID knows my story, but Daddy's words put me at peace with that. "Hope so," I say.

"Yep," he says. "Nobody's hero, but you soldiered."

2)

Not long after I'm off crutches, I'm halfway out of Freddy Turner's car, ready to see Nikki to her door, but she holds onto my arm, not ready to get out. I slide back behind the wheel, still bubbling from the gig. Convalescence has been a period of *mucho* musical progress.

She says, "Let's sit here a minute, baby. I want to talk to you about something."

Whoa. Conversations with women that start like that have always been prologue to some kind of jolt to my nervous system. A teacher. A principal. A girlfriend. A wife. Conversations with Daddy too. "I want to talk to you about something." Nikki saying it.

"What is it, Nikki?"

"Joe, you know I care a lot about you, don't you?"

Some species of alteration, man. Can't run, my knee. "Well, yes, you sort of give me that idea."

She gives a short laugh, takes her hand from my arm and goes in her purse for a cigarette. "You ought to have the idea by now, boy," she says. "And the caring's not going to change."

Nikki's voice is warm as ever, but, facing it, the way she says "boy" gives the word a categorical force flavored with impersonality that with the speed of light creates a new kind of space between us. Yeah. My gut clenches. She flicks her lighter, and the smooth ripe fruit forms of her face live in brown, cherry, orange, and black until she caps the flame. She blows a cloud at the windshield, puts the lighter back in her purse, and brings her body closer to me, against me, to administer the *coup de grace* or whatever the hell is coming. Her body touching me, I let out the breath I've been holding. Her voice is soft enough I could be imagining her words, woman here breathing me a spirit ditty. "Baby," she says, "I want you to understand that I really do care about you. But I don't think I have to tell you that the long-term thing isn't in the picture for us. Do I?"

Wasn't trying to win no home, anyway, but my skin goes tight and cold. "No, you've kept me pretty hip to that."

"We're not kids," she says. "We've both been married. Fact is, I'm still getting my divorce."

"Yes, Nikki, I know that."

She slides out of contact but pats my hand. "What I want to tell you, though, is that I've met somebody, an older fellow I intend to have a long term thing with, and you and I we're not going to be able to continue our little orgies here. That's not how I do business." She gives it a one-beat rest, scoping my state, and then slides her arm around my shoulders like a teammate, smoky hair against my face. "But Joe, it will break my heart if we can't stay friends. I admire you so much. You know how close we are, going to bed or not."

Man, oh man. TKOed. Cut, sent down to triple-A for the rest of the season. For the fucking duration. But she's right, nothing for me to say, her arm around me here, plush as ever, cheek against mine, explaining how I ain't going to get no more. We've still got gigs to do, and it is true that musically we're blood kin. And Fowler just gave me a boatload of work to do. What I've got to do is act as if I'm taking this hit like a man.

And like I didn't just lose the great horn Swink gave me and damn nearly my life in that raggedy piece-of-ass Chrysler with Washington.

The older fellow is a warrant officer at the airbase, Nikki says, a divorced guy in his late thirties that she's known for quite a while, who plans to retire in a couple years and return to Houston. He's an electronics specialist of some kind who will have a good job. Nikki says he gets along with her son, and he digs the idea of her singing career. She didn't say when he had time to develop a groove with her son, but that's none of my business. Maybe she struck oil for herself. Mae should have some luck like that. As for me, Nikki's tidings just pile on more blues. I'm beginning to get it that the blues is about losing things—your baby done left you, somebody died, you got no home, no job, some sombitch or your old lady trampled your dignity, you lost faith, your trust was violated, you made a costly wrong choice. You might sing 'em because you feel good about getting away from somebody, but that's not my case. You might sing them because you just love to make sounds. The blues is pretty damn comprehensive.

***

The letter Mae sent along with the photo that she returned, photo of myself in uniform with horn for my son, started right in, *"You certainly have your nerve sending this picture without saying anything to anybody. I don't know what you were thinking. Who do you think you are anyway? You haven't been anything to your son since you left us. If you want to send anything to Raleigh you should ask me about it first. You haven't tried to communicate with him since you've been in the army. You don't know what the situation is here and all of a sudden here comes this picture. Which I did not show to him and which I am sending back to you. That is all I have to say for now."*

I lie on my bunk, the photo on my chest, studying the perforated tiles overhead. A clashing of thoughts raises hell behind my eyes. The place is deserted and my loud breathing makes a spraying sound in the air. Sweat running off my brow. Got all squared away in khakis, tie, and visor hat, just wanted the kid to have a memento of his father in uniform. Didn't even let him see the picture.

She did say I don't know the situation there. And that's right. I got carried away, didn't think. Thinking of myself first. I have no idea about her old man. He might be an all right guy. I roll off the bunk, toss the picture into my locker, and walk over to the rehearsal hall. I buzz into my mouthpiece for a while, blow long tones, run through scales and chords. I pour myself into the horn.

"Man, you got to hear this," Freddy says. He pulls out a record and hands me the album jacket.

He sets the record on the turntable and moves the needle to one of the inner tracks. "Check this out, man, 'I Remember Clifford.'"

It's a ballad, not blues or hard bop, a musical elegy, written by a saxophonist friend of Clifford Brown. Very much in my *sans* Nikki groove. Dizzy Gillespie's trumpet solo flushes my doldrums, and we listen to the tune until we've got it memorized. Freddy says, "I heard this thing at The Melody Shop, I said, 'Joe has got to hear this.'"

"It's righteous, man. Thanks." We slap hands.

"I knew it," he says. "I knew it."

"Yeah, you really did. Man, you can't imagine."

The tune settles in like something I've always known. Like loss. Like mourning. I'm mourning the loss of the Benge. What to say to Swink when he comes back and I no longer have it. Mouthpiece against my lips, air from my lungs, support from my gut, filling my army horn with sound, I practice "I Remember Clifford" until I can hear words coming out of it and write some of them down. When I get a set of lyrics together that seem like what I'm looking for, I take them with me to Fowler's house and sing them for him. He digs it and shows me a couple small things.

Freddy thinks my lyrics are cool too when I lay them on him. I say, "Do me a favor, man."

"What?"

"Show these lyrics to Nikki and ask her if she'll learn them so you can do the tune with her. But don't tell her I wrote them. Okay?"

Not telling Nikki I wrote the lyrics has nothing to do with the fact that she fired me. I just want Freddy to get her unbiased reaction. Might want to keep writing song lyrics. "Sure, man," he says, "if that's what you want. I bet she likes them."

3)

What really kills Gilson and me when he walks into the rehearsal hall isn't Swink's long hair and scraggly beard. It's the guitar case slung over his shoulder. The three of us stand there slapping palms and laughing like fools.

Turner steps up and takes Swink's hand, inspects him up and down. "Look at you, boy. Just look at you," he says. "I see you still one crazy young melon farmer. What is this jive here supposed to be?" He raps the guitar case with his knuckles.

Swink's face is a bony lightbulb. He shakes Turner's hand and gives him a couple jabs on the shoulder. "It's just what it appears to be, Freddy. Jesus, am I ever glad to see you guys."

"Yeah, man."

"Are you hungry? You had something to eat?"

"Yes. I mean no. I mean I could use something to eat."

In the café in Juarez, where we munch burritos, Swink tells us, "Zaza digs the Los Angeles scene, and he's met some guy in his thirties who thinks the sun rises and sets on him and is really interested in Zaza's work. He's studying painting and printmaking."

"Sounds cool," I say.

Gilson says, "So, Merlin, you brought back that guitar with you."

"Yeah," I say, "what about that?"

Swink's eyelids close halfway down like I've never seen before. We're only inches apart, but he scans our faces as if we were landscape. "What about it? I'm studying the guitar and I'm going to play it, write songs."

"Really?" Saying "me too" about writing songs seems lame since I only now have stuck my toe in the water. The subject belongs to Swink.

"Yes, really. While I was out on the coast, I saw Brownie McGee and Sonny Terry. And I heard Woody Guthrie on some records. You know about them?"

"Nope." Gilson and I shake our heads.

"They're fantastic, man. Those old guys are what it's all about. Anyhow, listening to them, I started in getting ideas."

"Oh yeah?" Gilson says.

"Yes. I've had a few guitar lessons in my time, and the urge to write some songs is bringing it all back home, man."

"Don't tell me you're going to try to sing," I say.

Swink draws back and folds his hands together. "And why not?"

"I don't know. Can you sing?"

"Of course I can," he says. "Anybody can sing."

"No, man. I mean can you really sing?"

"Listen, singing is about making music. I know how to make music. I don't have to do it like Mario Lanza or Harry Belafonte or Elvis Presley."

"Nobody said you have to, man."

Gilson says, "Please, not like Presley."

Swink takes a swift sip from his glass, sets it down. He says, "My message has been in urgent need of expression for a hell of a long time now. You understand what I'm saying, Joe—blowing on a brass horn just couldn't support what I want to say. I want to put my breath into words. In Los Angeles, the answer hit me when I heard the stuff coming out of those old guys." His words provide a touch of balm for my sore feelings from losing the horn he gave me.

And having just written my first lyrics lessens the slap from his crack about "blowing on a brass horn," and, anyhow, I dig that what Swink is saying is true for him.

"Shoot, man, sounds like you've been touched," I say.

Gilson says, "I agree, Schoolmaster."

Swink says, "I'll show you guys some stuff later on."

***

Nikki Nanette walks into The Box just before eight with a dark brown cat about my size behind her who has got to be her warrant officer. He seems cool, like a man with a good understanding, doesn't get fidgety when she stretches her arms around me. "You guys haven't met," she says. "Miles, this is Joe Birdsong that I told you about. Joe, this is Miles Weatherspoon."

We shake hands and say, "Nice to meet you." He looks about thirty-five like Nikki said, and in good shape, as if he might do a lot of exercising. His eyes aren't jumpy, and his handshake has some muscle in it.

"Miles," I say. "I'm jealous of the name."

"Yes, but I can't play a thing," he says. "Nikki tells me you play up a storm."

"Well, Nikki's pretty generous. I know she sings up a storm."

"Give me a little credit for having some judgment, baby," Nikki says. "And by the way, I like your song very much."

Oh man. "You do?"

"Freddy didn't tell me you wrote those lyrics till after I sang them."

"Cool. He followed my directions. All the words were easy to sing?"

"Oh yes. You'll see."

"Good."

Turner rattles his car keys in my face. "Here," he says. "Get your axe, man. It's out in front."

I take the keys and motion Swink to come with me. This feels like the time to hip him about my bad luck with the Benge even though a hot tide of mortification boils across my epidermis. Swink watches me open Freddy's car trunk and take out the horn. He says, "New trumpet case, huh? How's that horn working out?"

"There's something I've got to tell you, man. The horn was working out great until it got stolen."

Swink falls back a step, as if from a shove in the chest. "Jesus. How'd that happen?"

I tell him how it happened on the bus that day. "And, man, I have been just sick about it and I'm sweating from embarrassment now."

Swink stands quiet for a minute and then slaps me on the shoulder. "What the hell, Joe, shake it off. You only lost a horn. You didn't lose music."

Oh man. We've been standing with the trunk lid open. I bring it down and press it closed, glad for the simple job, because of the sweetness and relief created by Swink's words. I doubt that he could imagine the relief and inspiration I feel. We start toward the door without talking.

At the door, I say, "You know, we're going to play 'I Remember Clifford' tonight. I wrote some lyrics for it, and Nikki's going to sing them."

"Really?" Swink says. "How cool."

"And I'm going to dedicate them to you, Merlin. You don't know what a help you've been." I breathe easier, but my words feel much smaller than his generosity and understanding.

"Well, gee, thanks, I want to hear this."

"Yeah you do. So sit down and dig it." He slides into one of the bench seats along the wall close to the front, and I go up on the stand and whisper to Nikki about the dedication. Freddy introduces the band,

and we start out loud and long with an up-tempo blues in B-flat. Then Nikki steps up, snaps her fingers in an easy ballad tempo, and we ease into "I Remember Clifford," Nikki singing the tune to my words:

> *Days of the broken heart*
> *When time held all our youthful dreams apart*
> *I heard his horn, a sound like home*
> *the hills, the streams, the moon and stars*
> *Mem'ries from lost Edens...*

Oh man, so lush, so true, so melodic, Nikki. Shoot, it didn't need to be Sarah Vaughn up here singing my words. I get in some decent licks and play a chorus of melody before Nikki takes it again, Freddy and I behind her, Gilson brushing the drums like a pro. She sells it, and the people clap long. Her warrant officer claps. Swink sits there clapping and nodding his head like *Pretty hip, pretty hip.* Nikki reaches for my free hand and pulls me up to the microphone beside her, a wounded co-champion, into the sweet field of her bouquet. She lets go of my hand and claps. "A hand for Joe Birdsong," she says, "who wrote those very fine lyrics. Dedicated to his friend and fellow trumpeter, Mr Merlin Swink." She points to Swink. I bow and salute with my horn.

Before she cuts out with her man after the gig, Nikki tells me to be at her house on Saturday afternoon to look at some charts with her. Just like that, an order. The New Order. "Bring your horn by the house, baby."

* * *

Nikki doesn't play much piano, and her old upright has a few out of tune keys, but she plays enough to accompany herself and me. I try using a couple different mutes. On a few tunes I can play in her keys, I take a turn on the piano, and it's a gas, Merce Fowler's example pushing me. Women singing. Eats me up. Nikki is nowhere near as deep harmonically as Fowler, but she's deep enough, rhythmically powerful, and she's got an ear like a dog, got perfect pitch, can hear all kinds of stuff and scat more ideas than I can manage at this time. We mess around, trading fours, me on the horn, her singing, until she wears me out. She says, "Can I get you something to drink, baby? A coke or something?"

"Sure, Nikki. Thank you."

She gets up and gives me a short hug around the shoulders. "Nice work, Joe, you really are gaining command," she says. "Let's go in the kitchen."

Gaining command. Captain Birdsong. I put away my horn and follow her, sit at the table. "Yeah, that was a gas. Thank you, Nikki."

"It was fun, wasn't it."

"I'm trying to tell you."

Barking starts in the back yard, one of the dogs. Nikki straightens, thumps the table with the side of her fist. "Damn," she says. "Where is that boy?"

The barking gets louder, and at the backdoor window the head of the boxer, Buddy, comes into view with each sooty-faced leap and bark for attention from the kitchen. Nikki says, "Excuse me, baby. The monsters are hungry, and Marques is supposed to be here to feed them."

She gets up from the table and goes to the backdoor where the boxer is making like a dolphin, leaping his slobbery jowls into view. Her knuckles tattoo the window. "Buddy! Shut up!"

Buddy doesn't rise again. Nikki dances out to the front door, and I hear the screen open and the call, "Ma-a-r-r-ques!"

The gate's creak reaches the kitchen. "Boy, you better get in here and take care of these animals. They know you should've been here fifteen minutes ago. How come you don't know?"

"I'm sorry, Mama."

"Get in there and tell it to those dogs. I know you could hear Buddy down there at Ferguson's. You know how he is."

"Yes, m'am."

"Then why didn't you bring your little behind on home?"

"I don't know."

"Well, you better be trying to find out."

The boy pops into the kitchen, waves to me, and scrambles under the sink for a bag of dog food that he takes out the back door. Nikki comes back to the table with two Cokes from the refrigerator. "That boy," she says. "You need a glass?"

"No, thank you."

Nikki's exasperation has weight behind it, but I dig that mostly it's a controlled performance, a heavy song, that gets movement out of the boy. She knows what she's doing. Hard to say it, but when I hear the authority in her singing and in her dealing with Marques, I see that Nikki's got something I haven't got. My head feels full of cotton and there's a hint of a throb in my wounded knee. A squall of pinpricks and sweat threatens, but I manage a deep breath and it passes. Nikki puts the drink in front of me and sits down at the table. Same eyes, lips, same zaftig composition, but no longer mine the way she was. Looking closer at her eyes now, I see her seriousness, *somewhere I have never traveled*, a place from which she moves to be with me.

She takes a cigarette from the pack on the table and lights up, exhales, studies her hands. "Young man, you've got a lot going for you," she says.

Young man. "You really think so?"

Nikki sits back in her chair and crosses her arms so her cigarette hand is at her shoulder. Her eyes level on me, no smile on her lips, aren't going to be derailed. "I'm serious, Joe."

"Sorry, just trying to be funny."

"I know. You do that a lot, to escape."

"Escape?"

"That's what I said. To escape from talking about things."

I take a full breath and let it out. "You're probably right."

"No *probably* about it." She taps ash into the ashtray.

Then: "I said you've got a lot going for you, Joe, and I meant it. I wasn't jiving."

"Thank you. I didn't think you were jiving, Nikki."

"The reason I said it is because I see how easy it is for young guys like yourself to let things go to their heads and mess up. In all kinds of ways."

Turner told me the woman could get serious. She takes a long drag on her cigarette and blows smoke to the side.

"Well, I sure have done my share of messing up," I say.

"I don't know much about that, but I sure can imagine it, you getting married young as you said you were. That poor girl didn't know what she was letting herself in for."

Her words thump like on a bass fiddle string, and I hear my fumbling with Mae, vagueness with Stacy in the overtones. All I can say is, "Oh?"

"That's right. I know you weren't one of these mean, stupid fools, baby. It's just that you were never really there. Just like you're hardly really here."

"What are—"

"Let me finish, baby. It's all right you're where you're at because I understand it. I understand that ninety-nine percent of young guys are interested in one thing above all else."

"Oh yeah?"

"Oh yes, baby. Themselves—they're interested in themselves above all else. That's all they can see. Claim they love their mamas so much, but themselves and what they want is all they can see. And you're no different. Look at what you've been doing, the things you've told me about yourself, and tell me it's not the truth."

Leaflets stamped with my relations with ex-wife, son, Stacy, my parents, brother, the suffering world, shower down on me in support of Nikki's declaration. Corazon thinks of Merce Fowler first, her father, considers his well-being before anything else. Corazon, toward whom my impulses have always been first of all carnal. First impulse was to covet, steal her fine flesh from the blind man. If my face were wax at this moment, it would drip right off my skull.

She says, "It's what keeps young guys from seeing some things you ought to be paying attention to, baby. Like your kid."

"You're telling the truth," I say.

"Another thing, you've been to school and you seem—I say *seem*—like you've got pretty good sense, but you need to realize you're going to be exposed to some serious temptations if you stay in this business." She taps the sheet of music lying beside her coffee cup.

"I'm staying in it. You don't think I can handle temptation?"

"You may be able to handle some of the temptations, but I know one you definitely need to look out for."

"What's that?"

"The pussy business, Mr Birdsong—you need to think about it."

Her smooth dark cheeks, plum-colored lips, are right in my face, locked cold. Watery beads ooze onto my brow, damn near about to run. "What do you mean? You don't see me zipping over to Juarez all the time."

She stubs out her cigarette and sits back. "Baby, don't waste my time. You know I'm not talking about no Juarez, although I'll bet you've been over there for more than tequila and weed. Remember, this is me you're talking to. With whom you have spent long nights in bed?"

After that salvo, I avoid her eyes. "Okay," I say. "I can see the pitfalls, some of them, at least."

"You ain't seen half of them yet, baby, and you better pay attention because you are not a hard cat. In fact, as immature and delicate as you are, I don't know how you got as far as you have in this world."

Immature and delicate. That one kayoes me, and as I come whimpering back to consciousness, I can see what the woman sees as if she created a picture without needing to have actually seen my numerous escapes from pedestrian disaster.

She says, "Get that wounded look off your face—I'm sure you know what I mean, Joe."

Then: "Seriously, it's a good idea to think about some of these things hard before you find yourself in a situation. Use your head. Use your damn head. I wish somebody would've talked to me about fifteen years ago. But I survived, sort of."

She has survived, but I haven't yet. Two Jay didn't survive, stuck in Kayakaw in a shotgun marriage mess. Maybe I should just stay in the fucking army. She wishes somebody would have talked to her. "You seem to be doing all right, Nikki."

"*Seems* is right. I've paid some dues, baby, and not necessarily because I wanted to. I'm thankful for my son, but it ain't been nobody's picnic. I hate to think of you wallowing in a whole lot of unnecessary mess, though, with all the good stuff you've got to offer, the kind of mess you make for yourself."

Elbows on the table, forearms crossed, she studies me. "Listen, baby," she says, "the thing to keep in mind is if you know something is wrong for you, don't do it."

She says that, and it's like the first time I ever heard the words. My bad choices line up like wasted POWs whose sickly outlines, the older ones, I barely discern in memory. My face must look bad to her. She puts her hand on mine, massages. "And listen, baby, when I said you're delicate, I didn't mean that you're weak. You're not weak."

"Yes, I am. I've been weak in a whole lot of ways."

"I guess I haven't seen all that much," she says. "I feel so much strength in your music."

"Yeah, I've made too many weak choices." My throat is so tight I have to force out the words.

"It takes a lot of strength to admit that, Joe."

She said that, but I know she doesn't dig the way I split from Mae and the boy. Another Negro Running Off and Leaving Babies Behind, she said like a newspaper headline one night in bed. Until she stabbed that label onto my ass, no such category ever occurred to me. Membership in a category of members. Weak men.

"Just take care of business, baby," she says, "and you'll get by. I know you will."

"Thanks, Nikki. I'm really a lucky fool, knowing you."

"Well, I think I've been lucky too. You've made me think about a few things—I have a young son, you know."

"Yes, I know. So do I."

She answers my words with closed lips and a moment of studying the backs of her hands and her nails. Then she says, "And I want to tell you again, Joe, those lyrics you wrote were terrific. I knew you could talk terrible, but I didn't know you could compose words like that."

"Thanks, Nikki."

She claps her hand against my cheek. "I hope you understand that what you've got is pure gold. And what else you better understand is that a fool and his gold are subject to separation from each other."

At the door we're standing close, getting a good look into each other's eyes. Nikki's eyes are as dark as Corazon's, set in darker ground. There's body heat, but it's not threatening. Her inner and outer weight, so close, is bracing. I breathe her in and kiss the side of her face. "Thank you, Nikki. Looks like I hit the jackpot today—the music was great, and I got a disquisition on character development."

"I don't know about no disquisition, baby," she says. "I just hope you heard me."

What I heard, I could have told her, flattened me even as I dug the truth in her words. Nobody since Daddy had hit me this hard without all the fire and brimstone, with such fleshly force, dousing me with awareness of my foolishness.

Like my latest fuck-up, sending that picture for the kid. She didn't have to be so pissy about it, but Mae was right. I should have inquired before sending the thing. I have got to start thinking, stop stepping into do-do.

***

Dear Mae,

My sincere apologies for sending the picture of myself intended for Raleigh. You are absolutely right, I should check with you before sending anything to him. Again, I'm sorry. It was a dumb, self-centered thing to do.

If I haven't already mentioned it, I'm planning to settle in Chicago when I leave this place. I will stay in touch with you regarding support payments for Raleigh after I get out of the army. Please understand that I intend to be as much help to him as I am able. I will listen to any suggestions you have in the future, concerning our son.

Sincerely,
Joe

How High the Moon

1)

Turner has his arm out, holding up my progress away from the table where I sat with Swink and Gilson to hear the end of the first set. "Wait a minute, Joe. Ain't you going to play?"

"Can't, man. I'm carrying this horn because I was over at Nikki's messing with some of her charts all afternoon. These cats here, and I, have got plans to walk back to the post."

With the charge I'm carrying from the afternoon with Nikki, I'm long-legged ready to walk. We've been talking about doing this walk for weeks, as soon as my knee was ready: drop some pills, walk and talk all night in the desert before any of us leave Fort Showalter. My knee is sometimes stiff in the mornings, but I'm no longer feeling pain in it. And I'm starting to get short, and Swink could be gone any time. He's not long back from his stint in the stockade and appointments with a psychologist who asked him if he gives blowjobs. Swink didn't say what he told the psychologist, but he's sure his plan to get a Section Eight discharge is working. It's time to walk. Swink has the fistful of pink pellets in a plastic bag.

"No, no. Wait a minute," Freddy says. "Jerry ain't going noplace. He's got to play drums this last set. Ain't that right, Jerry? Calvin had to leave, and he's done gone."

Gilson holds his hands up like What can I do, man, and I know he hasn't played yet today and would rather sit in with these guys and cruise back to the base later in Freddy's short. I can dig it. If I hadn't spent the afternoon with Nikki, I'd be for staying, too. Freddy needs him. I say, "Okay, we'll see you guys in the morning."

Gilson takes my hand and shakes it and then goes up on the bandstand. He shakes hands with the bass player and sits down at the drums. Freddy smiles on this activity.

"Hey, Freddy," I say, "do me a favor?"

"What you need, man—let me guess. You want me to take your axe back to the post."

"Right. You understand how much I trust you, man. Let me put it in your trunk, and you be a good elephant and take it back to Showalter."

"This has got to be some of Merlin's crazy shit," Turner says, "walking back to the post."

"Swear to God, Freddy, we all three got the idea together," I say. "I did it before, you know."

He walks out to the car with Swink and me, opens the trunk, and I set my horn inside. "Thank you, Frederick," I say. "Now don't get rear-ended on the way home."

Turner laughs and gives Swink a short punch on the shoulder. "Y'all some crazy melon farmers."

Swink says, "Freddy, you are a man of wheels. Josephus and I are natural men."

Turner pushes him in the chest with a flat hand and says, "Man, get the hell out of my face before I put my foot in your ass."

Swink and I face west where the Franklin Mountains lie slammed on the bolson, looming like relief sculpture of giant beasts under the bright moon and the endless dark behind it. We each throw down half a dozen pills and step out, talking about great.

Freddy Turner is great. Herb Vogel was great. Tanya Mendel is great. Clifford Brown is great. Kerouac is great. Great blooms in puffs before us out of which emerge the names of great ones. Max Roach is great. Barr is great. Benito Juarez was great. The waitress in Silver City is great. The preacher from Montgomery is great. Senator Kennedy is great. Senator Kennedy's mother is great. Bob Cousy is great. Trotsky was great. DeGaulle is great. Anna Magnani is great. Marlon Brando is great. Did you see how great the bass player back there at The Box is? The bass player is great. Mingus is great. Chou en-lai is great. Patrice Lumumba is great. Alan Watts is great. Allen

Ginsberg is great. Stanley Kunitz is great. Cassius Clay is great. Jomo Kenyatta is great. Thomas Hardy is great. e.e. cummings is great. The Dalai Lama is great. Pope John is great. Eleanor Roosevelt is great.

Walking. Walking like we know where we're going. We know where we're going. Into the night. *Oh dark, dark, dark...* We're walking nowhere, man. Into the night with the whole human race. The same undivided night that has covered every human that was ever born. Night, an enormous room with black velvet walls you never reach. Air is great. Our bright little moon is great. Radiance from reflection, man. We're lean walking machines. Walking in the night air is great. To be free of the Heavy Brothers is great.

It's a warm night, growing warmer, and I'm beginning to sweat.

Whoa, ho.

Soundless hooves beside me, pacing me, and a shiny black shoe of all things in the stirrup, bumping against the rifle box. Don't have to look up. I look up. He's wearing his Sunday suit and got the book against his chest. Same get-up as last time on the road. Today would be Sunday... Swink doesn't know we're walking at a horse pace.

J.S. Bach is great. Nikki Nanette is great. Corazon is great. Gilson is the greatest, our pink-faced brother.

Daddy slides out of the saddle and falls in behind me, horse gone. He walks close in my footprints, wordless. Swink and I continue spewing candidates for *great*.

The sky begins to lighten behind us. We've walked far enough west so that we're huffing up a slope that in the moonlight was the black lower leg of a giant sleeping beast. Walked down to the bones, past the bones, we stop. Daddy, though, he keeps going with no look back in the grow-ing light toward the rocky heights until he disappears. On to glory or someplace. Demilitarized. Dematerialized.

He'd started singing:

Precious Lord, take my hand
Lead me on, let me stand
I am tired, I am weak, I am worn

Deep slow swing of the music, of Music under the music, beyond hip, drifts over us.

Walked out and talked out, we sit on big rocks above Bolden Heights, watching the light expand over El Paso, over Fort Showalter. Barracks and rehearsal hall of the 72nd down there, asleep under their green tile roofs. Light grey doves roost on power lines between poles stuck in the ground all the way down the hill. Damn near the only birds you see around here, same color as the ground where they spend a lot of time, during the day, and you don't notice them.

Swink's face under the black fuzz of his cut hair is chalky in the no-glow. We could do some more numb walking, but my knee has had enough, and this is a good spot to watch the sun come up.

Here it comes, new day.

Swink rubs his palm against the ground and picks up a handful of pebbles. Dirt sifts between his fingers. He opens his hand in front of his face and blows dust away. Spikes of light from the sun start to shoot from behind the hills east of the city. The birds on the power-lines look black with the sun behind them. Swink's face takes on color from the light. He shifts the pebbles to his left hand, opens his hand and studies them. He selects one and gives it a toss about ten feet in front of us. He tosses another one. And another. Sitting shoulder to shoulder, him tossing, me watching. Swink pitches another one and speaks as if he's delivering a ho-hum afterthought. "The thing to do now," he says, "would be to have sex with me."

Whatever the hell these pills were that we took, they were efficient in installing me within layers of talk about poetry, Zen, about Los Angeles, about his sessions with psychologists, about his vision of writing unpatriotic songs and playing the guitar, about my vision of a sane, literate jazz future—a winding distance from his present suggestion. Ordinarily, the idea of sexual contact with another male feels like an embarrassing, unengageable proposition. Now, Swink's proposition gives me the giggles. The cat's words crepitate like a phone call over a bad line from the moon. Too unreal—just like Swink with his too creative and spoiled ass, call from the moon with some shit like he thinks I'm Zaza or somebody, like he thinks his reality is the only one. What I should say is "Merlin, you may be the cat I would, for some reason, most dig crossing the desert with, but you are one loco young *pinchimadre* if you dream your bony, hairy-legged ass holds any sexual magnetism for me. Now, if you were Zaza." But that's too rough, and I don't say it. I don't know what to say.

Swink watches one of his tosses hit the sandy ground. He flicks his wrist again. I see his game. He's trying to hit the last pebble he threw. I bump his shoulder with my shoulder. I say, "Sorry, dear, but I have a headache."

Swink stays dodged away next to me, his face starting to take on more color from light coming between peaks in the hills east of the city. So-called mountains I don't know the names of. Swink never laughs much because he's always wired-up amused, busy telling everybody else what to laugh at. He snorts now and tosses another pebble. "Pretty funny," he says.

I stand up, put my palm out in front of him. "Give me *cinco*, man."

Swink ignores my palm but takes my wrist and hoists himself up. He claps his palm against mine and gives my hand a shake. Studying the clear blue stones in his eye holes, I don't find anybody home. Bands of sunlight shoot between the hills like enfilading fire across the city. Day has arrived. Swink and I make our way downhill to the barracks.

2)

Corazon, behind the screen, fills Fowler's doorway and watches me step onto the short porch. Girl's wearing white shorts and a white sleeveless blouse that set off her flesh in the manner that unhinges my eyeballs. She unhooks the screen and pushes it open. "Hi, Joe," she says. "Come on in. MJ is still taking his nap."

There was a time she would have said *Pajaro*.

"Hi, Corazon. How are you?" She doesn't give ground as I slide past her and set my trumpet beside the coffee table. We haven't been in a space like this together for weeks. Now the force of Merce Fowler's proximity, snoring down the hall, surprises me. And Nikki's words bloom in my ears. Corazon's legs and arms shine. The magnetism of her lips generates flames around me, in me.

"I'm doing okay," she says. "Are you all right?"

"Yes, I am."

"Can I get you something to drink, Joe?" She steps toward me, close enough that I could touch her if I chose.

"Oh thanks, Cory. I'd love a glass of water."

"Water?"

"Yes, I think I'd better stick to water today."

"Come on in the kitchen," she says.

In the kitchen, she joins me in a glass of ice water. Side by side, we lean against the sink counter and sip. Water and movement modify the flames. We stand looking across the kitchen at Fowler's electric range.

Corazon gives me a gentle bump with her hip, "You seem different today," she says.

"Different?"

"*Si.*"

"How?"

"Not so happy and gay."

She must see a trace of blue from my ramble in the desert. I say, "You want me to do a little dance?"

She bumps me again. "No, *Pajaro,* it's okay."

Pajaro. My arm slides around her waist and she turns into the embrace. Fowler coughs in the hall, and we roll back to our previous postures.

"In case I didn't say it, Cory, I am happy to see you."

"I'm glad of that. You know, there's one thing I wanted to ask you about."

"What?"

"You're not going to be in El Paso much longer," she says, "and I want to hear you play at that place where you play sometimes."

"You heard me play at The Box once."

"Well, that was just for a minute. We were on our way home from a meeting."

"Come on down any time."

She bumps me with her hip again. "I don't know nobody to go there with."

"How about the girl I saw you with?"

"No, not her. She just stopped with me because I begged her."

"Well, okay. Can you get to the place and meet me there? I can get you a ride home."

She grabs my hand in both of hers like an excited high school girl. "Oh thank you, *Pajaro*. I could do that."

I finish my ice water and set the glass beside hers on the counter. "*De nada*. And thank you for the water."

Fowler is splashing in the bathroom, flushing, faucet on, faucet off, and Corazon pours a glass of water timed for his appearance.

He looms in the doorway. "'ey *Jose*, what's going on?"

"Nothing shaking but the leaves."

"I wondered who she was in here talking to."

"Who else would she be up in here talking to on a Wednesday?"

"Search me, man, you can't tell nothin' about these women nowadays."

Corazon puts the glass of water in his hand. "Here, take this water, MJ. And stop trying to be smart."

Fowler drains half the water and sets down the glass. "I ain't tellin' nothin' but the truth, baby."

"That's what you always say."

"'cause I always know what I'm talkin' about."

"Hah," she says, the first time I've heard an explosive sound like that from Corazon. She puts a light hand on my shoulder to say, "I'll see you at six, MJ. Good-bye, Joe."

On the bandstand, Turner gives me five along with his knockout smile. It's his last gig at The Box. In a couple days he'll drive home to Chicago. He looks over my shoulder, stretching his neck to see Corazon, her bare arms shining next to Gilson at a table. Swink has got CQ duty. "That that girl you been going to see over at whatsname's house," Turner says, "sitting over there next to Jerry?"

"Man, I go over to whatsname's house to play music, in case you haven't been able to tell."

"Now who you think going to believe that?" Freddy falls back and looks at me with his chin between his thumb and forefinger. I told him a girl was meeting me at the club and asked to use his car to take her home before The Box closes. So I can drive off with Corazon anytime, get her home before midnight. Corazon is such a sweet and solid number that if there had never been any Mae or Stacy, and if I hadn't run up against Nikki, I might not be going noplace, Chester, can almost imagine it. She's a smart girl and she likes to touch, but I can see now I'd better watch how I touch her, and she needs to touch up her English and go on and become an eye doctor. I've looked at some of her grades, and she does way above average in science and geometry and algebra. She was into calculus her last semester. Her grades in English look good because I'm sure she'd be one to take care of her assignments. I can see that she reads quite a bit. She writes correct standard English, not like the usual kid who writes the same mistakes he speaks. I can hear that she hangs around with kids who sound like her, not to mention Fowler, not to mention myself, hashing up the language around her, and she didn't get much speech instruction. I don't feel much from her mother except Corazon is as neat as a fresh Johnson & Johnson band aid. Mae was like that too, but she smoked. Turner's eyeballs remain busy. "O-o-wee, man. She sho is fine. I got to give you mo credit."

"More credit for what, Negro?"

Having got the rise he was looking for, Freddy bends into a short laughing fit, puts his hand on my shoulder. "I'm sorry, man, I thought you was just interested in books and music."

I hold my trumpet close to his nose. "This is not my weenie I'm holding in my hand, Frederick. It's a musical instrument. Let's play something."

Turner draws in his elbows and straightens up, as if remembering he's in church. "What you want to play, man?"

"Let's do 'There Will Never Be Another You'."

Corazon listens and watches with her mouth half open. I don't dig words like rapture, rapturous, and all that, but when I start in on my solo, her eyes get shiny and she's breathing in some special kind of air with the music and she's going to float away. And I can't put on the brakes. I'm playing to her, playing hopscotch, playing Red Rover, playing the smell of cut grass on the thigh of an August night, man, looking for some of the hip dissonances I learned from her father, and drawing it out as sweet and groovy as I can, watching the weather on her brow, cheeks, lips, in her eyes. Hard to imagine an audience soaking up music the way Corazon takes it in.

Turner's car has a quiet-idling engine, and half a block early, I cut the headlights and kick in the clutch so we can coast to the front of the house, where I brake and turn off the key. Across the street, her mother's windows are dark. Corazon rests her head on my shoulder, and I let my arm fall around her.

"How did you like The Box tonight," I say.

She reaches her hand across to my cheek. I put my lips against her palm. "Neat," she says. "I thought it was neat."

Fowler's house is dark except for a small bulb over the front door that lights up the house number over his mailbox.

"How did I sound?"

She raises her head from my shoulder and twists around to face me. "Oh, Joe, you sounded so good."

"Really?"

"Really. And I don't like jazz music that much, most of the time."

"You just liked it because it was me playing."

Corazon's shoulders move as she talks. "Of course, silly, but I can tell when somebody is playing good too. And you were playing real good."

"Merce has helped me a whole lot."

Her hand warms my cheek again. The girl has been listening to Merce all her life and could have a better ear than mine. "I know he's helped you," she says. "MJ likes you so much."

She brings her face nose to nose with mine, tilts her head and pushes her parted lips against mine, her hand still on my cheek. Corazon's lips are soft and gingery, and she kisses better now, but she's still green, and I'm working to stand firm against enjoying too much sugar here. The curve of her ribs presses against my palm. "So, Cory," I say, "are you starting to get ready for school next year?"

Her ribs twist away from my hand, and she squares herself up against the seatback, eyes out the windshield, arms stiff at her sides. I say, "Hey, what's the matter, baby?"

"Nothing."

I slap the steering wheel. "Nothing? Cory, that was the quickest change in the weather I've seen since Truman was president. What's going on?"

Her profile in the dark front seat is all I'm getting.

"What's going on, Cory? Tell me."

Her head doesn't move when she speaks. "I'm not going to school."

"What do you mean?"

"I'm not going to school next year."

"But I thought you wanted to go to college."

"What for?" Up, down go her shoulders.

"What for? So you'll have an education. I thought you wanted to be an eye doctor."

"I was just dreaming, you know? I can't be nobody's eye doctor."

Her grammar slaps me, but I don't stop. "That's ridiculous, Corazon. You know you can do it if you really, seriously want to."

She puts her hand on my knee. Her face stays fixed on the dark in front of her that takes the edges off the forms in her face. Her voice shrinks, loses air, when she swings her head halfway toward me. "I want to get married," she says, "and have a family."

Here, in Freddy Turner's dark car, it's like when you're sitting in a classroom and your mind has been having a sweet ramble in the fields behind the blackboard, and the teacher has asked a question, and you realize Oh shit she's asking me, the last apple-knocking clown in the place she should be asking.

I take hold of Corazon's hand. "Cory, you're eighteen years old."

She draws back her hand. "So?"

No, she wouldn't listen if I told her the last eighteen-year-old girl I married suffered a disaster called Birdsong that's got overtones forever. Begging me to marry her. I say, "What do you want to get married for?"

"I just told you. I want to have some kids." She whips her face all the way around, eyes wide. Could have said "wild" too because wild is in the air inside the car. "Rosie and Alma are getting married in October."

"Rosie and Alma?"

"Two of my best friends I graduated with."

She wants to have some kids. Some. I've already got one, which is way too many. Oh man, she and her girlfriends, playing house with babies all over the floor and hanging on their hips. Walking around El Paso, I have dug that scene. And there's probably even some racial shit she hasn't thought about. The picture makes me gag: me, kissing Mae after the vows, everybody so with it, believing my numbskulled, fraudulent front. I slide close to Corazon and put my arm around her and try to come up with the best words I can find that don't tie the subject to me. "Marriage is a really serious step to take, Cory."

"I know it is." She isn't lying. She believes. She is serious enough for it. Mae was serious enough for it. That's all she wanted, have some babies, cook, keep a tidy little house, and wait for John Henry to come home with the bacon.

She stares into the dark beyond the windshield, swelled up, as if she can't understand why her golden arms and legs, her glossy, flowing black hair and rosy, gingery lips haven't done the job on me. Maybe I could tell her what an exquisite piece of humanity I think she is and how hard it is not to think of lying between her legs, face into her breasts, but I've been there and messed up, and it scares me to think of messing around with Merce Fowler's girl without serious intention.

Her voice comes just above a whisper. "I love you."

"I think the world of you too, Cory, but look at us. Look at me, just divorced, got a kid, got to figure out how to take care of my kid and my music too." She doesn't even know about Stacy.

Her eyes remain trained into the dark. She says, "I'll help you."

Corazon knows how to help.

"Listen, sweetheart, I need to help myself first. And you need to help yourself. I want you to have something for yourself."

"What are you talking about?"

"You need to get yourself an education, Cory. That's what I'm talking about. You're a smart girl, but you haven't really studied yet."

Sniffling, shoulders jerking, she starts to cry.

"I'm telling you, Cory, people don't know shit, and they'll think you're stupid as long as you use the kind of English you do. Basic stuff, like all those double negatives you use, and you always say 'you wasn't' when you should say 'you weren't—things like that."

"I talk the way my friends talk."

"Yeah, well how many of your friends have thought about becoming eye doctors? That's a great thing. But you're not going to get very far if your friends' English is all you know. You've got to talk to some other people. Rosie and Alma are getting married, you say. So they're going to have babies and babies and babies until they're spilling out in the street. What, you want to be a fat mother of five at twenty-five? No thank you, honey."

She puts her hands to her face and starts bawling as if she just lost a child. And I'm seeing this picture, all this fucking crying and feeling sorry for yourself because you don't understand shit and don't want to take a few hard steps to understand. And then because you didn't take a few hard steps your ass is buried in misery. Me and half the high school kids I taught, going in that direction, maybe more. She's bawling, and I'm breathing hard and getting louder.

"Really, baby, forget about getting married. It's too early. It's a trap." The whole cramped, crawling meat image of multiplying misery floods my eyes all the way to India. "Yes, it's a trap. You're too damn sweet and beautiful for your own good, Cory, and I love you, but am not thinking about getting married and messing up your life. I am not going to do that again. You need to go to school and study. And listen, honey, you know I'm only saying this because I care about you. You know that, don't you?"

Her forehead bobs against the dashboard in time with her snuffling. I pull her against me. Corazon's body is hot and fragrant, and her face and her hair alongside are soppy with tears. I soften my voice just above a whisper. "Listen," I say, "you know that, don't you?"

"Oh, Joe, Joe." She throws her arms around me and starts smearing my mouth with her lips and tongue. My mind is not changing, but she kisses all the rhetoric out of me, and that other thing floods in, jamming my cool air vents. Fowler is not home from his gig yet. I say, "Let's go in the house, and you wash your face and get yourself together before you go home."

We get out, press the car doors shut, and go in the house without turning on the lights. We can see our way around in the murk. Corazon goes to the bathroom and runs water while I stand by the sofa, concentrating on my breathing. I pull back the windowshade, peek at the street and the dark bulk of Turner's car until I hear Corazon come back in the room. My eyes have adjusted to the dark, and I see she's naked, carrying a bundle that she drops on the coffee table. She pushes the coffee table away from the sofa and sits, finds my hand and moves it to her breast. I get jelly knees. My mouth waters at the same time I'm about to choke, and the air feels like a hot rope yanked in and out my nostrils. "Joe," she says, and falls back full length, pulling me down on top of her. Her body is thick, smooth and alive against the barrier of my rags, but without savoir-faire, and I'm able to think about Fowler's possible arrival at any time while she whimpers and grabs and kisses my face and mouth, replica of a scene or two with Mae when our interests in bed didn't coincide. I wrestle my way off the sofa onto my knees beside her. "Baby, this is no way to go about things. Merce could show up any minute."

I gulp some air and get to my feet. She rolls off the sofa and pulls herself up, clamps her arms around my waist and grinds against me, aggravating my hardness and dividing my mind, but I make like a statue. I'm trying to detach myself from her without being rough when she growls, and her whole hand catches me smack across the jaw, and I see red and at least one bright star. Her knuckles come back across my mouth, and I know I ain't gonna to blow no serious horn for a week. She beats me in the chest with one fist and she's got the other cocked for a haymaker. Man, oh man. The girl is too big and strong for me to stay passive, so I clinch with her, lock my chin against her neck, and lift her off the floor. She kicks air and beats on my back, and I'm staggering, knee trying to buckle. When her kicking stops, I set her down but stay in the clinch. Her bare stomach jerks against me. I lick her salty water from my lips, feel my upper lip fattening over one of my canines. Both of us are hugging and puffing. We keep our arms tight around each other till we settle into one heavy, slow-breathing body, half of it clothed and zipped over my stiff, aching penis. I keep my teeth clamped tight so I don't come unzipped. I unglue myself from her and shake her shoulders. "Baby, you've got to get your clothes on. Please. Please do it now. Now."

She sweeps her clothes from the coffee table and goes through the charcoal dark into the bathroom. I go in the kitchen and get an icecube from the refrigerator, wrap it in a paper napkin and hold it against my fattened lip.

A car engine hums out front, and a car door slams. The too sweet knife of panic shoots up through the top of my stomach into my throat, until cowardly comfort in Fowler's blindness dawns on me. His daughter is still a virgin. He won't see my lip. We didn't raise any serious odors.

I raise my voice to say, "Merce is home."

Corazon comes out of the bathroom clothed, stands in front of me, then hangs against me like a loose garment. She speaks as if from her sleep, *"Encenda la luz."*

I lead her into the front room and switch on the light. The salty taste in my mouth is blood, I see, when I touch my tongue to a fingertip. Corazon slips her hand out of mine, takes a couple steps to the sofa, sidesteps behind the coffee table and sits at Fowler's end. She keeps her eyes away from me. Their clear black and white is blurred with red and wet. Ruddy in her cheeks too, black hair stuck alongside. She scoots to the end of the sofa and does something I've never seen her do before.

She stretches across the chair to the end table where an open pack of Fowler's cigarettes lies and picks up the pack and shakes it once, twice. A cigarette falls halfway out. She opens a drawer in the table, reaches in without looking and brings out a replica of Fowler's lighter that she uncaps and thumbs into flame.

Fowler is at the screen, opening it. I go to the unlocked front door, but before I open it, I holler, "Hey, Merce."

Key in one hand, trumpet in the other, Fowler stands there. The car that delivered him swings out from in back of Turner's Plymouth and rolls away.

"'ey, *Jose,* what you doin' here, Cuz?"

"Sorry, Merce, Cory and I just came in from The Box. Didn't want to surprise you too much, just wanted to say good night. How are you doing?"

Fowler's lubricated voice is low in his throat. "Mmm," he says. "That you smokin', baby?"

"*Buenas noches, Papa.*" Another new note from her.

I say, "Are we messing up an assignation or something, Merce?"

"Listen at you," he says. "Maybe I ought to be askin' you that." He angles his nose toward the ceiling and sniffs. "I know that ain't you smokin', Cuz."

"Nope." If his nose is as good as his ear, Fowler's house is for sure no place to be messing around.

"What you doin' smokin', baby?"

Corazon's lips don't move, and her arm stays tight across her waist. I take the trumpet case from Fowler's hand and set it on top of the piano. He goes to his chair, and I move back to the sofa through his boozy, smoky wake.

"Thank you, Cuz." Still not putting out any warmth, he pushes his elbows into the thick chair arms until he gets his bones adjusted. His hand finds the cigarette pack. "You smokin', huh, baby?"

The softness of his low voice registers a concern I hear for the first time.

"*Si.*"

Corazon hasn't looked at me since we came into the room from the kitchen and turned on the light. To test the temperature of things, I touch her elbow. She twists away. We sit without saying anything, Corazon's smoke the loudest thing in the room.

I say, "Well, Merce, only a few more weeks and I'll be out of here. Sure going to miss you, man." The bulge in my lip is a rubbery surprise.

"Yeah, miss you too, Cuz," he says. "You don't just got to stay away, you know." He thumbs his lighter in the way Corazon imitated and lights his cigarette. "Hell, Cuz, for that matter you don't just got to leave."

Fowler's voice is smoky and just this side of sounding piqued, but the hint of a proposal leaks from his words. I don't say anything.

I can feel him listening hard to Corazon's silence. Her, sitting there on the sofa, smoking, wet red eyes narrowed.

"Somebody else here is goin' to miss you too, Cuz."

"Yes. I'm going to miss the two of you. A lot."

Corazon lets a blue curl of smoke drift out of her mouth. A tear leaks down her cheek. She sweeps it away with the back of her hand

and checks out my face for the first time since we came in the room. Her eyes get big, like Washington's last look in the rearview mirror, and her mouth is scary-movie wide. She jumps up, blubbering, hand over her face, and breaks past me out the front door. Fowler's shoulders twitch at the bang of the screen.

I go to the door and watch her, walking fast out the gate into the dark street. The red ash of her cigarette sails to the right, throws up a bracelet of sparks when it hits the ground. She goes straight to her door where there's a momentary rectangle of light when she opens it and goes in. I close Fowler's door and sit on the warm spot where Corazon sat before. A few inches closer to Fowler the cushion is cooler, and I take in a good breath of the smoky air.

"She jumped up and left, man."

"Yeah, Cuz, she's upset. That's why she come on speakin' that *Espanol*. Been doin' that ever since she was a little girl."

"First time I've seen her upset like that."

Fowler puffs his cigarette. "First time you ever got ready to leave town, Cuz."

Got some fat in the fire here. What to say, I don't know. Fowler knows what to say, though. He says, "That's enough of that shit for tonight."

Then: "And listen here. You bring your ass down to The Frying Pan, night after tomorrow. You hear?"

Don't know what my lip is going to say in two days, but there's only one answer.

"I hear you, Merce. And look, you still want me to go to the barbershop with you tomorrow?

"Yeah, man, if you can do that."

3)

"Here, Cuz, put this sombitch back. I got you with me, I don't need nobody's white stick."

Mid-afternoon might be a bit early in the day for Fowler, but I think I hear a continuation of the gruffness from last night. He's all business, ready to go, in a blue yachting cap a la Count Basie and a light sportcoat.

I take the cane from him. "Put it here by the door?"

"Yeah, that's cool."

Since he walked in on us last night, the cat has taken on this reserve that's not like him. We're still friends, it feels like, but there's some uncertainty dogging our peace. Just when I get in the groove musically, here comes some jive from outer space. Inner space. Somewhere. If she hadn't been smoking—it probably put two or three things on Fowler's mind besides whatever else was there. And speaking that Spanish. He's been good about not cracking wise or acting funny. He ought to understand by now that I wouldn't be sneaking into his house to screw his daughter. My ass is innocent. Tantalizing, but I have never liked the idea.

Out the gate on the path that would be a sidewalk if the city laid some concrete, a short, elderly Negro woman moves toward us. Stops. She's carrying a net shopping bag. Her hard eyes, softened no doubt by biblical concern for the blind man, go up to Fowler's face, the site of his affliction. "How you today, Brother Fowler?" she says.

"Oh I'm tolerable, Sister Beauchamp, tolerable."

Sister Beauchamp's sanctified eyes bead on me like I ain't no beautiful field. Sharp old blackberry eyes, brown-stained whites. I know her type. A condemner of sparing the rod, disciplinarian of sons, grandsons, nephews, looking at me like "Boy, I wonder is you got any sense." Sister Beauchamp finishes studying me. The tightened lines around the righteous woman's mouth tell me she's not so sure I'm approvable. However, her slight head dip could be a signal of positive acknowledgement before she takes her wiry frame on down the path to glory or wherever she's headed.

"You ever walk down here by yourself, Merce?" I'm cupping Fowler's elbow in my left hand and we're stepping along without a hitch.

"Oh yeah. Every once in a while I take that damn stick and get out here."

He takes direction from me, but I can feel his body knowing the way to the barbershop, and for the last block I'm thinking I'm a tail on a kite. Beside the door of the adobe building that houses the hair cutter, a painted wooden pole marks the shop. Red, white, and blue.

On the other side of the window, a barber works over the lathered-up customer stretched like a corpse in front of him. The barber looks up and spots Fowler and me approaching the door, dodges away from his customer, and opens for us just as I'm about to take the handle. "Hey now, Mr Merce," he says, "come on in here and have yourself a seat. Be with y'all in a minute."

An overhead fan stirs the air. We move into hair oil smell, pomade smell, soap smell, and a faint dry odor that has to be the ghost of cut hair. A set of posters that illustrate different haircut choices lines the wall above the seats for waiting customers, and you can study them in the long mirror on the opposite wall. "Duke." "Brushback." "Flat top." "Quo Vadis." On the end wall, above the empty shoeshine stand, hangs a calendar with a photo of a church above the tear-off months. There's nobody in the shop but Fowler and me and the barber and the corpse, but I can hear weekend talk bouncing off the walls. Cats in here flailing between fact and fiction. A good place to sit in the corner and buzz into my mouthpiece.

The barber holds the razor away from us and backs up beside the stretched-out, lathered man. He looks at me, checks out my hair, showing his big yellow front teeth that spread like a capital letter A. "How you, young man?" he says.

"Fine," I say.

Fowler feels for the back of one of the chairs along the wall and lets himself down onto the plastic upholstery. "How you feelin', Lawson," he says.

The barber keeps his eyes on the coffee brown path his razor is clearing through the lather under his customer's chin. "Standin' firm in the Lawd."

Standing firm. Tall bony member in a white shirt, the barber, about Daddy's age. Thick glasses and lips. Given his fair complexion and straight hair, the man had a boatload of white forebears. I beat down a miasma of obscene musings. The man stands firm in the Lord, finishing his millionth shave.

"Aw right then," Fowler says.

The barber fans his man's face with a white towel, then cranks the chair into a sitting position and puts a mirror in his hand. "Think that'll get it, Rev?" he says.

Rev is wearing overalls, but his steady look and the firmness around his mouth, preaching could be his weekend gig, sort of like Daddy. He tilts his head forward at the mirror and rolls his eyes upward, checks the top of his head, pats it. He checks the back of his head, reflected from the wall mirror. Airy grunts escape his nostrils when he moves. He hands the mirror back to the barber. "It look fine," he says, just fine, Brother Jones."

The barber unpins the cloth from around Rev's neck, takes a whisk with long white bristles and goes to whisking away snippings from the man's collar and shoulders. "Well, praise the Lawd," he says. "Praise the Lawd."

Rev gets out of the chair and digs in the pocket of his overalls. He hands the barber a couple bills. The barber goes in his cash drawer for change. Rev puts his hand on the barber's forearm. "That's all right," he says.

"Praise the *Lawd*," the barber says.

Pushing my shoulder against his, I stretch toward Fowler's ear and with my teeth together mumble on one note, "ManIdintknowyouwuz-takinmetonochurch."

He snickers, bumps me off him. "It's cool, Cuz."

Merce Fowler, filling the chair now, the barber swings a fresh cloth around his neck and pins it at the back. He dips his head my way. "This some yo' kin, Mr Merce?"

Fowler draws his lower lip in under his teeth, just like Corazon does sometimes, takes his time, then drawls, "No connection that I know of."

Fowler has been good, until recently, about signifying concerning Corazon and me. A dab of barbershop bullshit, this little crack that he lets lie like a dead mouse in the middle of the floor, hearing my deep silence.

Then: "This here's my friend Joe, Lawson. He's a musician."

It's me, Joseph, the soldier.

The barber straightens and steps over to me, hand extended. "Lawson Jones," he says. "It's nice to meet you."

Close to chamois, the feel of his hand. "Joe Birdsong," I say. "Nice to meet you too, Mr Jones."

He steps back over to Fowler in the barber chair and starts picking at Fowler's hair with a coarse black comb. "He ain't from round here, is he," he says to Fowler.

"Naw, he's from up in Seattle. Naw," he says, "'scuse me, he's from Portland. Portland, Oregon."

The barber stops combing Fowler's hair and goes to studying me, making certain I'm not an Eskimo or something. "Is that right," he says. "How you get down here, young man? Must be in the Air Fo'ce."

"Army. I've been out at Fort Showalter."

"In the Army, huh?"

"That's right."

"He's in the band out there," Fowler says. "Pretty good little trumpet player too."

The barber keeps on combing and picking at Fowler's hair, fluffing it up for the clippers. "Say, tell me one thing," he says. "Is they many colored folks up there in Seattle? Seattle?"

"Portland."

"'scuse me, brother. Portland?"

"Well, yes, seems like plenty of them to me," I tell him.

"Just don't hear about nobody from Portland," he says. "You goin' back up there when you gets out the army?"

"No, I don't think so."

"No?"

"No."

"You ain't stayin' in El Paso, is you?"

"No, I'm going to Chicago."

> *Goin' to Chicago,*
> *sorry but I can't take you*

"Goin' to Chicago?"

"Yes." Damn straight. I've got nothing to say to Portland right now. Or Kayakaw. All the questions. Going to Chicago. Freddie Turner up there, still fresh out of the Army, fixin' to fix me up, if he does what he says he's going to do. Go up there and blow.

"What you goin' do in Chicago? You got peoples in Chicago?"

"No, but I've got a friend or two there."

"You got much time left?"

"No, not much time left, getting down to my last days."

He takes Fowler's black glasses off and sets them on the counter below the long mirror. Fowler's blind eyes are half rolled up into his head, pitted, ridged scars around the sockets. Hard to look at. The barber picks up his clippers, takes out the head and clicks in a different one. "Me, I'm from Mississippi," he says. "Been out here fifteen years now." He says "Missippi," same way Jarboe says it. If Jarboe and the barber said it, the word would sound the same, but I could hear one of them was white and the other one colored, like with jazz trumpet players. Jarboe might sound a little different since the brothers cracked his skull. Something in the throat. The barber switches on the clippers and starts buzzing over the top of Fowler's head. Trimmings fall to the yellow linoleum.

"Mississippi," Fowler says. "I keep axin' you, man, what took you so damn long to escape?"

Corazon doesn't say *axe*.

The barber cruises the clippers along the side of Fowler's head where his hair is beginning to whiten around the ears. After each stroke he takes a short look and then makes his next move. He's got a groove going that he doesn't get out of while he talks. Talk is part of his groove. "Everything in its time, Mr Merce. The Lawd works in mysterious ways."

Fowler's curvy upper lip stretches wide. "He sure as hell do. If that woman over there in Montgomery had not of got stubborn, you still be ridin' the back of the bus here in El Paso. Waitin' on the Lord."

"Bible say, 'They that wait upon the Lawd shall renew their strength, they shall mount up with wings as eagles; they shall run, and not be weary; they shall walk, and not faint'."

By the time he reaches the end of his utterance, the barber is just about chanting.

"Listen at you, Lawson," Fowler says, "I been tellin' you for ten years, waitin' on the Lord don't do nothin' but get your head beat longer."

They fall into something like a musical silence, a rest broken only by the buzz of the barber's clippers.

Some operatic shit for sure.

The barber says, "Well, if you cain't see it, I guess you cain't see it till you see it."

The outburst of scripture swung me back to the simple wooden benches, the potbellied stove and the hard-pressed Bible believers in Daddy's church. I let out a long quiet breath.

Through with their sparring match and back in his groove, clipping Fowler's hair, the barber raises his voice in my direction, "Young, man," he says, "tell me one more thing."

One mo' thing.

"Yes, sir?"

"Up there where you from, is they many colored churches?"

"Oh yes. Quite a few."

Fowler makes a humph sound.

"What kind of churches they got," the barber asks.

"Well, you know, the usual ones, I guess, Mr Jones—Bethel A.M.E., a bunch of Baptist ones, Church of God in Christ, quite a few storefronts, Pentecostals."

"Which one you go to?" He says.

Two hours of church on Sunday with Mae and the family, suit and tie, heavy dinner, afternoon round of visits, everybody in front of the Ed Sullivan Show in the evening. Long gone, busted out. "Well, sir, I can't say I go to any of them, really."

A sound between the bleating of a sheep and the whinnying of a horse escapes from Merce Fowler, shaking his body. The cat's behavior indicates an interest in all this that surprises me. Mr Jones takes a practiced step back until Fowler settles.

The barber sets down his clippers and takes up a comb and pair of scissors. "You mean you don't go to church, young man?"

"I'm afraid I don't. I did go one time in El Paso when I first arrived here."

Comb and scissors move over Fowler's head. "I can see you been spendin' too much time 'round Mr Merce here," he says.

"You mean he might be a bad influence on me?"

The barber draws his lips together in a pucker. "Naw, the Lawd love Mr Merce no matter what he do. I just say I can see you been spendin' too much time 'round him."

Fowler gets the chuckles, then laughs himself into a coughing fit. The barber puts a paper cup of water in his hand that he turns up. I'm seeing that this is like a visit to the gym for my man. He holds the empty cup out to the barber.

"Hold off talkin' that stuff, Lawson," he says. "You can't take advantage of the blind man today. My boy here can tell me if I ought to pay for this messed up haircut you givin' me. Keep talkin', you liable to end up with nothin'."

The barber goes to work on Merce with rhythmic swipes of his whisk. "Oh he don't look like he want to get mixed up in nothin' like that, Mr Merce. I can tell you myself you got you a fine-lookin' haircut."

The barber puts Fowler's black glasses back on for him, unpins the cloth from his neck, whisks him a few strokes more, and looks at me. "You wasn't wantin' a haircut, was you, young man?"

"On no, sir. I just came in with Brother Fowler."

Tripping back to the house, Fowler says, "Lawson is all right. He believes in his Bible, and the cat can quote you chapter and verse all day long. But that's him. That ain't me. People want to stay down on they knees waitin' on the Lord, that's they business. Me, music is carryin' me over Jordan. That's where I stand." He's like a field of electricity is crackling around his body. If it were night, the cat might glow.

" I hear you, Merce."

"The thing is, Cuz, when the thing comes to you and you know it, you got to surrender to it. Forget cars, pussy, barbecue, fast cash. Forget all that shit. You stay true to yourself, you'll get what you need, and the sounds will keep growin'."

We arrive at his gate. He says, "I'm all right from here, Cuz." It's nearing his afternoon nap time.

"I'll see you to the door, man. I want to say something."

"Oh yeah? What you got to say?" He opens the gate and moves to his front door, me behind him. Before he opens the screen, I maneuver him around so that I've got his ear.

"Look, Merce, what I wanted to say is I hope you don't think there's been any funny stuff going on between Corazon and me. I can see how you might suspect something, coming in on us like you did last night. Things were actually a little tense when you walked in, but I want you to know I've stayed away from getting involved with Corazon. Corazon is a real sweet girl, but I can't do anything for her, and she's not the reason I come over to your house. I mean I care about the girl but I don't want anything coming between you and me, our business—you know what I mean?"

Fowler's big hand finds my shoulder, pats it. His voice drops to its heavy core. "I do, Cuz. I know what you mean. And I appreciate you spellin' it out. That's somethin' special. I could hear all along that you wasn't just another jive cat."

"Thanks, Merce."

"And you got some serious work to do. And you making me think you can do it—boy, let me get in here and get this nap."

He gives my shoulder a squeeze, unlocks the door, and goes in the house.

3)

The Negroes in The Frying Pan dig the horn at my side, say "All right, now," as I make my way to the bandstand in the middle of the music and position myself behind Fowler, next to the drummer and the bass player. The tenor man, a dark, heavyset cat Fowler's age, is putting all kinds of body English into his solo. I see people Fowler's age in the crowd, some with gray hair. Negroes all mashed up against each other in The Frying Pan. Lots of young guys must be GIs here. My first time in a place, except for the Baptist church in Portland, and once at a dance during Sea-Fair in Seattle, this dense with Negro-icity. There are a few white-looking faces in the crowd that I can see are members.

Many shades of brown flesh, red lipstick, shiny dresses stretched tight as baloney skin over women's behinds, the whole thing undulating in half-light and the heavy, humid breath of smoke and booze, the reek of sin and iniquity Daddy preached about so much I thought they were one word: *sinaniniquity*. Thought I knew me a long word. And bluesy music. Them old blues. Every Sunday, one sister at the Pentecostal church squealed during her testimony, "O-o-oh, jazz, I just hate that stuff." After church, my brother and I had laughing spasms, remembering her manner.

Fowler at the piano is laying into "Please Send Me Someone to Love," people dancing slow and nasty, a shame before God.

Cats on barstools face the dance floor, elbows back up on the bar, crocodiles on the riverbank, only their eyeballs moving, watching couples on the floor move their muscles and bones and heat together. A woman in a blue dress with trembling frills arcs away from her partner, elbows going like pelican wings, snapping her fingers hard and slow, hollers, "Yes, Daddy." Fowler isn't jiving, singing the song, if he does throw his face up toward the ceiling with a wild-ass grin on it. He hears me set my trumpet case behind the piano. "Sing the song, man," I say.

He throws an "All right" into the middle of the lyrics, sings to the end and then goes into a solo with a lot of gospel licks in it that the people slow rock to, throwing their shoulders back and forth. The Frying Pan is a place for getting physical.

I say into Fowler's ear, "Can I get some of this, man?"

"Oh yeah, Cuz. After the turn-around."

He finishes his solo and brings his lips to the microphone.

> *I lie awake nights and ponder world problems*
> *And my answer is always the same*
> *That unless man puts an end*
> *to each damnable sin*
> *Hate will have the world in a flame*

People smoking, drinking, grinding on the dance floor, and I'm listening to Fowler sing this righteous tune here at some kind of juncture with sin and iniquity, back among the believers, back in the meaty, steaming church.

Through the melody once, my damaged lip feels like it'll hold up. I try to give the music some of the subterranean juice I hear in Fowler's singing. Underground water. A deep spring. A joy spring. Not-by-bread-alone spring. Get in as many low notes as I can, a lot of stuff about sitting out on the earth, digging, feeling, being, seeing the shit for what it is, past all the fucked up contradictions piled onto the garbage dump of life. Man oh man. Into another chorus, circling and circling through passages of weathered bronze, purple, blue, into the navel of things. "Yes, Lord, baby," a high female voice hollers, in a red dress, she is, trying to screw her hips off or screw them on, the way she's twisting.

Daddy, Mama, too, wouldn't be caught dead up in all this old cigarette smoke and whiskey and beer, people out there dancing nasty, but they would love the sounds I'm putting together right here.

"I hear ya, Cuz." Fowler rattles the keyboard with both hands. They'd love that too. Done. People clap. I shake hands with the drummer and the bass player, bow to the tenor man. Fowler leans into the microphone. "Thank you ladies and gentlemens."

Standing behind him, in the heat of the people, my hand on his shoulder, I dig the faces I can barely make out, warm eyes embracing us through no barriers. Deep in the flank of Texas, women of all kinds of shapes, loose hips, peachy cheeks, shiny mouths. It's a too rich cobbler. Lead us not. *You don't have to be looking for trouble, it be sitting right there in front of you, fool.* I flinch at the thought of Nikki seeing into my head. I flinch too at a flash on the Heavy Brothers, so joyless, so fucked up in their heads about race, looking at this crowd of people enjoying themselves.

"Let's give the young man on the trumpet one them nice El Paso welcomes," Fowler says. He starts to clap. A few hands follow him. "Mr Joe Birdsong from Seattle, Washington."

"Awright now!"

I give half a bow and hold up my horn to the crowd.

Fowler squares up to the keyboard and rocks back and forth a couple times. "All right y'all," he says.

He plunks into an introduction to "One Mint Julep", a novelty Fowler and I have kicked around at his house that I remember hearing in high school. Colored quartet, singing it then, swinging it. In no time, Fowler's got a floor full of people swinging and sweating. He and the bass man do some heavy thumping and pausing that makes everybody laugh and holler. It's a song of many verses, and Fowler makes a marathon out of it. The sax and I play through the head once in more or less unison. Fowler solos for a while, followed by some wild stuff from the saxophone. The action on the floor looks like a basketball game with forty players working for scoring position. I jump crazy for a couple choruses, with nervous, exaggerated syncopations and staccatos. People whoop. I throw in a lick from the Second Brandenburg Concerto, blowing for the people, or selling out to them with cheap effects—anyhow, sweating with the crowd, keeping things stirred up, carried on whatever this wave is. Somebody hollers when I blow some high funny stuff, I do it again.

Somebody hollers, "Act up, man." And I let loose again, screeching, preaching, carrying on like some kind of fool that just took all his clothes off. And I'm Daddy now, preaching, "Let the church say, 'Amen,' and the people shout, 'Amen.'" And he says it again, and the people holler louder, and he gets higher, gets to chanting, "And Moses went up on Sinai, yes he did, saints, and God spoke to Moses and He said to Moses, You got to go down and count the people, oh yes He did, saints, said You got to organize the people. Hear me now!"

The tenor takes another loud chorus, full of honks and squeaks and body English. The cat is strong and this is saxophone territory, yes Lord, Fowler rocking back and forth with his mouth open, hands all over the keys in this funky groove with the bass and drums. He throws his head side to side, black glasses turned to the crowd, sings out,

A mint julep

He's got the people trained.

A mint julep

Fowler again, *A mint julep.*
The congregation comes back, *A mint julep.*
Let me hear ya one more time. *A mint julep.*

A mint julep

Then everybody's mouths, mine too, open wide together:

One mint julep
Was the cause of it all.

Fowler draws out some shakes on the keyboard while the people holler and clap and squeeze and pat. The tenor and I run up and down scales and chords, and the bass and drums boil along with Fowler until he rips his arms into the air and we cut.

Just people clapping now, glassy-eyed, relieved, sweating, feet sanding the floor, pleasured sounds from throats, redeemed. Smoky as hell place, pungent with sin and iniquity. Behind my eyes, in my chest, in my throat, it's after forty days and nights of rainstorm, sky washed clean. Island, green and shining, yonder in the sun. Man, I'm a piece of sky. I'm a piece of land. I'm a bucket of water. Standing here next to Fowler, horn hot in my hands, people looking at us, drinking us up.

He lifts his third drink since we got back to the house. I've had only one with some Beam in it. "Yeah, boy," Fowler says, "it does my old heart good to hear a young cat do like you did down yonder tonight. You got to go down in the swamp and disturb the alligators, man, get loose like that—you a college boy and all that, and no tellin' what you might do, but you got to be able to play it greasy sometime. Everything you play can help you."

"I believe it, Merce."

"It's all music."

"Yeah."

"Life is music."

"Yes, man." I feel it as his truth.

"Ain't jivin', Cuz. Every last goddamn thing be tryin' to swing."

4)

Dear Stacy,

You haven't written for a while. What does it mean, baby, if anything? I hope you're not sick or in a bad way otherwise. You know you can tell it all at this office. My time is getting short around here, bless Jesus, and I think I've made a big decision. You are the first one I'm telling about it because I still feel closer to you than anyone in Portland.

I've decided that when I get out of the army I'm going to Chicago ("Hog butcher of the world!") to live and work and study until times get better. One of my buddies here was a trombone player that I played with all the time and he's from Chicago. A really good guy. He's going to fix me up with the basics in Chicago, and we're going to start ourselves a quintet or sextet. (It's all your fault, baby, for telling me I seemed to have jazz in me. Remember? I and others have found that to be true. And it be leadin' me to Chi-town.)

I've got to do it. What I'm talking about is what I've seen, and what I've seen is that I'm no good for anything but music, can't put my whole soul into anything but music. Life comes to me through music. And I've got to keep learning about it, keep listening, keep studying, keep play-ing, or I'm lost. Teaching school isn't a bad job, but I couldn't ever get my whole soul into the act. I don't have the kind of belief and care and hope it needs. And it was the same when I was living with my wife. Leaving the kid behind doesn't feel so good when I think about it, but it was like I wasn't there most of the time and I wasn't going to be there because there was no me to be there, thinking about sounds, and Mae got to wanting to kill me because she never understood where I was at.

You and I. Sitting here thinking about you, I can get all worked up, start to salivating, but from this distance I can also see that our future isn't in set-tling down together someplace in a box with a roof over it. You need to keep writing. Write poems. You also need to get yourself to college. It will really help you do what your gut is urging you toward. You hear me? You've got a whole lot of weird talent, but you need to bring all that jive under some mental governance, honey. Seriously. Study the history of the language. Study some Shakespeare. I'm telling you the truth, baby. It will do you some good, help you see in this dark-ass experience called life.

    Being down here and meeting some of the people I've run into, I can see how I was lucky to grow up in Kayakaw thinking I was a person just like everybody else and could do any fucking thing anybody else could do. Me, J.B. I get down here and I see a lot of people that look like me with attitudes about being some kind of disabled variation apart from general humanity. It makes me sick. It makes me crazy.

    My hip white buddies from the East Coast have seen more black action than I have. One of them, I know, thinks I'm some kind of diluted specimen of negro-icity. It's like there's a whole lot about being colored in this country that I'm just starting to become hip to, but that stuff seems remote in the newspaper, sitting out there in Kayakaw or little white Portland, playing Hayden and Purcell and trying to get into the symphony. Playing jazz has opened up some new alleys. Got to go down 'em. I get to listening to Clifford Brown, Charlie Parker, Dizzy Gillespie, Miles Davis, Mingus, Coltrane, Thelonius Monk, Bud Powell, and it's like "Yeah, yeah, oh yeah, that's right, godDAMN, that's it." You know what I'm saying, Stacy? It gets into the dark part that I've been missing without knowing I was missing it, like I didn't know I was HONGRY till I connected up with some of this here food. That's what working this music is doing for me. If I were a bell, baby, I'm telling ya I'd be ringing like a motherfucker.

    And you're a part of it, don't forget that. I can't forget it. No matter where we end up, that's how it is.

Love,
John the Baptist

5)

Corazon's second note came in a small white envelope with "Pajaro" written on it, that was on Fowler's coffee table when we came in from The Frying Pan, begging me to forgive her for losing her head and hitting me in the face and eye and making my lip bleed. I didn't think she realized her finger caught me in the eye so it turned red and, along with my lip, made me have to listen to a certain amount of speculation in the barracks. But she can smack me again if it makes her write more sentences like she wrote: "I couldn't stand it if you were to think I'm one of those wild girls that only knows how to strike out at people when she's unhappy. I'm so embarrassed with the way I lost control of myself, Joe. Please don't think I'm that awful. Please forgive me. And I really was horrified to see that I had injured you and I feel so terrible, *Pajaro*."

Recalling her hot tears and bare flesh in the dark at Fowler's house makes my teeth float. Plugging my ears to the wail of Corazon's nubile charms might be the biggest victory of my military career. She tells me I have to come to dinner at Fowler's on the Sunday before I leave El Paso.

***

Call me simple, but all other considerations diminish their diameters at Fowler's pad when Corazon knocks three times and walks in, wearing a silky red sleeveless blouse with a lacy fringe that hangs loose at the waist. Small gold cross on a delicate gold chain around her neck.

Her hips fill a fine black skirt with moving muscular music. Her black wavy tresses stream extra glossy across her shoulders and the white gardenia over her ear carries a magic I might not be able to answer. The rose in her cheeks, overtone to the red of her lips signals the unmatchable speed of her winged feet. Her strong shoulders and yellow-brown arms muscle into perfect hands that can catch and shoot. Her eyes burn black and white as if she's been praying all morning. Oh, man. I go to her, put my lips to her cheek and inhale a chord of scents that keep me against her skin longer than a peck, keep me soaking in her muscles and heat.

Then she's gone. Over to Fowler. She puts her hand on his shoulder, bends and kisses him just above his blind man glasses. Her voice has never sounded so full, and I don't know how to say it, except *reverential*.

"*Com'estas*," she says.

Fowler's bass rumble falls into the same groove way down where they sing together. *I do not think they will sing to me.* No *com'estas* in the English of my time. "How you, baby," he says.

Me, outside the groove. Outside the family. Corazon and Fowler inside the warm bubble of blood relationship.

Going to Chicago alone, I am. *Cold, impossible, ahead.* I remain by the coffee table. Corazon, beside Fowler in his chair, shifts her eyes my way. I say, "Cory, you look great."

Her cheeks dimple up for the first time since she walked in, and that puts us warmer than we were before. She says, *Gracias, Pajaro.*"

Dinner is a suite of Mexican dishes upon which Corazon poured her full attention, which keeps Fowler and me dishing up compliments. Fowler turns up his glass and lets the last of the whiskey and water drain into his mouth. He takes in what's left of the ice cube too and crunches it. Corazon and I still have half our ginger ales left when he excuses himself for his afternoon nap. Sitting on the couch, the dog inside me at ease, fingers of her left hand between the fingers of my right, a hint of moisture gathers where each finger touches.

"I have something to talk to you about" she says.

Again, the worrisome prelude. But before I can think or say anything, she says, "I *am* going to go to school. I just got weak and sorry for myself the other night, thinking about you leaving."

In her eyes I see innocence and belief. "Oh, Cory, I'm so happy to hear that."

"I know I can do it," she says. "I always wanted to go to college but I never knew nobody who went except my teachers."

"*Any*body," I say.

She claps her hand over her mouth and widens her eyes. She takes her hand away and says, "I'm sorry. I know I've got to get out of that habit."

"You will if you want to," I say.

"I want to. I thought about what you said in the car about people thinking you're dumb because of how you talk."

"Really?"

"Yes, and that's the truth. Nobody ever said that to me before."

"Well, that's because people who know you know that you're very

smart, Cory." I kiss her hand and then put my arms around her, surprised by the surge of sweet feeling above my belt that only wants to
hold her close and make her feel supported. She relaxes against me.

I put my lips against her ear, under her gardenia, hair on my teeth,
strings of it across my tongue. She moves her hand over my back, massaging, then laces her fingers with mine and pulls me to the front door.
"Come on," she says. "You've never seen my room."

"What?"

"Nobody's home," she says. "I want you to see my room before
you leave."

Corazon's room has white walls and a blue ceiling, one window. At
the foot of her bed is a dressing table with an oval mirror on a stand.
A glamorous photo of Merce Fowler in dark glasses sits on the table, a
three-quarter view, a trumpet not the Besson he now plays in his hand.
"For my baby, my heart, Corazon," is my guess at the scrawl in blue ink.
Beside her bed is a combination nightstand bookcase with two shelves
full of books. No sign of beads or crosses other than the small gold one
she's wearing. I say, "Aren't you a Catholic, Cory?"

"No," she says, "my mother belongs to the Baptist church."

On the wall above the dressing table, facing her bed, where I might
have guessed I would find a picture of Jesus pointing to the big red
valentine in his chest, hangs a large framed diagram of the eye, drawn
with much detail on good paper with various colored inks. There's a
side view, sectioned, and a front view. Parts of the eyeball are labeled,
and short printed explanations in neat black capital letters spaced over
the surface create a design that catches my attention before I realize I'm
digging an illustration of the human eyeball. The detail and intensity of
the work draw me to closer study and a quick review of the parts of the
eye. In the lower righthand corner I find "by Corazon Trujillo" in more
neat, printed letters like the ones I learned when I studied mechanical
drawing in junior high.

"Cory, you did this?"

"It was part of a science project I did last year. I made a clay model
of an eye too."

"I didn't know you could draw like that."

"I had to do it for the project. I'm not a very good artist."

"I wouldn't say that, baby. You must have got an A on this. It could almost be in a medical book." She squeezes my hand, studies me studying the drawing. Corazon, deep into seeing. "Cory, how could you not think about going on in school? Jesus, you had me worried with that talk about getting married and having babies."

"I told you I was feeling desperate that you're going away, *Pajaro*. But I know you don't want somebody like me."

Pinpricks of panic and embarrassment spread over my body at the dishonesty of so much of my behavior with her, now exposed by her simple, liberating statement.

"I'm not leaving the world, Cory," I say, "and you need to go to school before you do anything else."

"That's what I'm going to do."

In Corazon's room I see that I've missed knowing a lot about her. What did the cat say—"Lust and light are enemies..." The volumes with the black spines in her bookcase are a couple works about the eye and conditions of the eye. "Are you going to be an optometrist, or a medical doctor that works on eyes?"

"I don't know yet, *Pajaro*."

"Well, if you don't do that, maybe you ought to major in art. Anyhow, you've got plenty of time to decide. Excuse me if I say it's great that you've got things in focus, Corazon."

She brings my hand up and gives it a light slap, kisses it, and looks at my wristwatch. "I do know one thing," she says. "It's time for me to wake MJ. Come on."

Then: "Oh, excuse me. I almost forgot."

She pulls open a drawer in the vanity and brings out a small cream-colored folder, a graduation photo. She says, "I wanted you to have this."

"Thank you, Cory. Just look at that—Girl, you are so fine." Her writing opposite the photo reads, "For Joe, who has made a lot of difference. Love always, Corazon." I put my arms around her, hug her again. Dog stays down. Corazon, a part of the world's potential comfort.

Fowler feels his way out of the bedroom, into the kitchen, and Corazon puts the glass in his hand. "Here's some water."

"Thank you, baby." A big sand man, Fowler is, quaffing the water. Corazon takes the empty glass, he burps, facing me like a seeing person. "Look here, Cuz," he says, "I'm going to give you a cat's name and address in Chicago. You go see him."

"Thanks a lot, Merce. I appreciate it."

"Another thing—you not gonna have a horn when you get up to Chicago, are you?"

"No, but I'll find one pretty fast."

"Don't worry 'bout it. I got a old Selmer back there you can take with you. Use it long as you want."

"Oh man, Merce, I don't know what to say."

"Just say, 'I ain't gonna let nobody steal this sombitch.'" My face gets hot. He goes into a short laughing fit. Then: "Baby, take the boy back there in my closet and let him get it." He moves off into the bathroom.

Choked up, hard to tell what I'm hearing for a moment. Corazon's got me by the hand, leading me into Fowler's bedroom. His closet at the foot of the bed runs the width of the room. Corazon pulls back the sliding door, and I see more of her order in suits, shirts, sportcoats, hanging there, and the shoes lined up beneath them. She points to the black trumpet case in the corner at our feet. I pick it up and open it on the well-used Selmer that I can see will do just fine. It's the horn Fowler holds in the picture that Corazon gave me.

My chest is full. I hug the horn and kiss Corazon on the cheek.

She turns me toward the door. "Would you like a drink of water?"

"Yes, I would, thank you." She gives me a glass of water like the one she gave to Fowler. Gifts.

Water running in the shower, Fowler squeezed into the small space like he's wearing it, I can see it. Warming up his pipes, humming and singing.

Hold out, baby, I'll be back one day
Hold out, baby, I'll be comin' yo way

Could be some of Fowler's signifying—I know how he is. Could be my imagination working overtime too. Anyhow, I could sure use some pipes like Fowler's.

"Joaquin, we goin' to drop Joe at the bus stop," Merce hollers from the front door. His driver has just pulled up in a venerable grey Studebaker whose paint job looks like undercoating. Fowler is ready in a double-breasted lavendar suit with black pinstripes, a light olive green shirt with a roll collar and a blue silk tie with gold stars. He's wearing new black alligator slippers whose shine matches the shine of his brilliantined hair. Corazon inspects him.

Ready for The Frying Pan. A saddening tug from my insides.

She comes over to me and we hang onto each other. I say, "Now you've got to write to me, girl. I want to hear how school is going. Okay?"

"Of course. Just make sure you write back."

Fowler stands with his horn at his side. "Y'all better not make me late, carryin' on this jive."

Corazon's arms press around my neck and I allow my hands one last sinful slide across her buttocks, raising a whimper from the dog inside. We put our faces together again and then let go. *"Adios, Cory."*

"Adios, Pajaro."

I take Fowler's elbow. "Let's go, man."

Out the gate. Fowler into the front seat, me in back with his old trumpet in my lap. We pull away from the curb. Corazon doesn't do the bye-bye—she waves her hand from side to side, clearing a window in the air.

The Studebaker has a muffler that doesn't muffle much. The spicy, woody, herbal scents of Fowler's hair and body applications compete with the car's noise.

Fowler says, "Listen here, Cuz, I want you to keep practicin'. And you go see that cat I told you about and give him that note my girl wrote for me."

"Oh yeah, I want to meet him. And thanks again for letting me use the horn till I can get one."

"Don't worry 'bout it. You got some good shit goin', boy."

"Thanks, Merce. If I do, I owe it all to you."

Fowler gurgles out a laugh. "Listen at him, Joaquin. How many times I got to tell you, boy? Don't be tryin' to jive the jiver."

"No, man, no jive. I'm serious. You've been a hell of a lot of help to me. You know it. You're just talkin' shit. And I thank you."

"Well, I appreciate it, Cuz, and I enjoyed havin' you around."

Then: "I think my girl did too."

"Cory is one great girl, man." The soft, smeary truth of my statement threatens to burst like a water balloon. I say, "She needs to continue her education, though."

"Yeah, I think you sort of brought that out in the girl, and I'm goin' stay behind her," he says. "A while there, boy, I thought I was goin' lose her."

"Lose her?"

"I thought y'all might get together and go on off."

"Aw, Merce, I told you my situation."

"Situation, smituation, boy, I know how you young sombitches are. A hard dick ain't got no sense."

Sweat beads on my brow. "Well, man, I can't argue with that. But after what I've been through, I hope I've learned a little bit of something. I've got to work on my music, learn a few things about the world, and make sure my kid is taken care of."

"Yeah, I know how that is. Take care of your kids, boy."

"Kid," I say.

Fowler overfills the front seat, big enough to be the voice of authority. "Oh, you goin' to have some more," he says.

"You didn't have any more."

"Now how you know that, Cuz?" Shut my trap—Fowler could have been married five times and have ten kids for all I know. I don't know about his life much beyond what I've seen in El Paso. Corazon and I have no history, either, only what smoldered between us for a few months. Stacy and I have more and deeper, still shallow. The weight of my ignorance about everything crushes all the air out of me.

Joaquin pulls the Studebaker over opposite the bus stop at Alligator Park and pushes the gearshift into neutral. I reach over the seat and shake his hand. "Thanks for the ride, Joaquin, and good luck."

"Yeah, man, good luck to you too."

I get out on Fowler's side, stick my hand in the window and take his big paw. My fingertip around his hand touches the turquoise of one of his rings. "Well, so long, Merce, and thanks again, man."

"You come see me anytime, Cuz. I got that extra room, you know."

"Yeah, man, I hope to."

"And write," he says. "My girl will read it to me."

Corazon, her hands holding my letter, her eyes on my handwriting, her lips forming my words that she reads to Fowler... Write a letter for her voice to read to Fowler. Make her lips and tongue go where I direct them, so she'll feel the words all through herself, reading them out loud to Merce, yeah.

The Studebaker pulls away, grey smoke out of the exhaust pipe, on down the street. The dry scent of Fowler's cologne remains on my hand. No use waving to a blind man, so I hold my hand in front of my nose and listen to Fowler's cologne fade.

6)

Gilson looks up from his bacon and eggs, swallows. "The schoolmaster advances to Chicago."

"That's right. Going to join old Freddy. Going to miss you New England Bastards, but it's time to quit this gig. You guys are coming up to see me when you get out, right?"

Mouths full, they nod yes. Swink is chewing like he's only half present, but he's close when I look in his eyes. "You'll hear some great stuff in Chicago," he says.

"I'm hoping so."

"You will.

"So, Merlin?"

"Yes?"

"You've got another appointment with the head shrinker today?"

"This morning, yeah."

Going away, the 72nd going on like a stream that'll never miss me. "And there's a job this morning too?"

"Yeah," Gilson says, "we've got a review."

After breakfast, Swink and Gilson slap me on the back, shake hands, and walk off to rehearsal. The army rules. I turn in my bedding and combination locks. At Finance, I get my separation pay and my plane ticket. I come back to the barracks, put on my dress greens because it will be chilly in Chicago, and call a cab.

***

The plane is a Lockheed Constellation, that has always made me think of water, its fuselage shaped like a long dolphin. The triple rudders give it an even more out-of-place look among American airliners. Till now, I've only dug it in pictures. I check my duffel bag and get on the plane, in dress greens, and settle into my window seat. The seat beside me is empty. I hug the trumpet in my lap and watch El Paso and its outskirts, its so-called mountains become a brown blur below and disappear. The Constellation reaches altitude, gets in a nice groove toward Chicago, I trust, through the ocean of air. Hard for somebody to steal a trumpet up here. I slide the horn under the seat in front of me, between my feet. A blue-eyed stewardess who resembles my idea of Desdemona stops with her fingers on the headrest of the seat beside me.

"May I have a pillow, please," I ask.

"You sure can," she says. She goes away and comes back with a square blue pillow. "Here you be, sir."

"Thank you."

Here I be, indeed. I stuff the pillow in the angle by the window and lay my head against it. It was a late night, talking in the barracks, and in no time I'm gone.

In front of a class, working like hell to get them to understand the idea of subordinate clauses when the pep squad bounces in, in their red and black sweaters with a chenille megaphone across the chest under the word *Colonials,* carrying pies they are, that they start selling to my class.

"No, no, no!" But the pep girls jump and squeal and pass out pies, and the kids are buying them as if I'm not even there... .

Walt Whitman comes walking through a field of amber waves of grain. He's got on that old hat with the potato chip brim you see in pictures,

and his beard blows in the breeze just like the grain. He swings along
with his walking stick. Oh man, Walt. He halts and points his stick at me.

He says, "Get yourself together and sing the song, man. Sing the song."

The song? Jesus, Walt. Wait!

He's gone, way down the road out of sight in an old Studebaker... .

Nikki, dressed in a cowgirl outfit, red kerchief around her neck under
her round, dark-chocolate face. Big Tom mix cowboy hat. She's pounding across the desert on a mustang—Mustang Nikki!—and she's tow-
ing me like a glider. Me, way up here, hanging onto a cable, watching
the wake of dust froth behind her horse. She lets go of the cable, and I
float down to the ground, down, down, down until my cheek touches
cinders that press into it from my settling weight.

I stand up and beat and brush dust and cinders off my clothes and
skin, raising a cloud in front of me. It dissipates. Shoot, I'm wearing
a morning coat and grey striped pants and a white tie and high hat.
Hidee hidee ho! I'm walking. Walking on the cinder path. Try strut-
ting. Do some cake walking, walk off these blues. A one, a two. The
path gives out and I'm in the undifferentiated desert. Ain't no cool
midnight walk under the moon, though. Sun is starting to broil my ass
in this morning coat.

Ahead, in the middle of the nowhere flat, I see two figures, one dark,
one light. Could be a mirage. It's hot, but I'm stepping.

The first figure turns out a woman in a long white dress with a train
I walk along beside before I catch up and dig she's wearing a veil and
stands holding a bouquet of bleeding hearts in front of a low altar. On
the other side of the altar he stands in a long black robe, his Sunday
suit under it, white shirt collar and knot of his tie peeping. He's looking down at a pocket-sized book in his hands. It's *Howl.* Yonder behind
him, in shiny showroom condition sits an old Chevy, green body, black
fenders, tin cans tied to the rear bumper.

I come up beside the woman at the altar. He works his lips without
looking up. "Dearly beloved," he says.

My throat grabs, I have to pee, I can't get my mouth open to yell the
Everlasting Nay.

He looks up from his book, triumphant, coffee-colored face going in all directions, grinning, teeth bright like never in his life.

Whoa.

My head toward the woman. She raises a hand to her veil and tosses it back over her black wavy hair. Wide curving rose red lips, strong golden chin, her eyes a brown so...her fingers light on my shoulder.

"Sir?"

Fingers light on my shoulder. You don't call a private "Sir."

The eyes I open to are blue. The stewardess's pink lips are moving: "Sir, please fasten your seatbelt and prepare for descent."

About the Author:

Harold Johnson is a lifelong resident of the Pacific Northwest. His childhood years were coeval with World War II, which he remembers as a time of great focus in the nation and tranquility in the Yakima Valley where he was born. After graduation from Yakima Senior High School, he took himself to Portland, Oregon, for college and work. Between the Korean and Vietnam wars, he spent two years in the United States Army as a bandsman, ultimately stationed at Fort Bliss, Texas. After the army, he returned to Portland where during the turbulence of the 60s he married, taught English, studied music, studied and taught visual art. During his teaching years, his creative writing efforts were devoted to poetry. Retirement from teaching offered the time needed to pursue the project of his first novel, *The Fort Showalter Blues*. He has also published two chapbooks and *Citizenship, poems by Harold Johnson* (Many Voices Press). He currently resides in Portland with his wife, the painter Anne Johnson.

CPSIA information can be obtained
at www.ICGtesting.com
Printed in the USA
FSOW02n0612290515
7440FS